Flight of the Kroughs

By

D. Raymond Anderson

This book is a work of fiction. Places, events, and situations in this story are purely fictional. Any resemblance to actual persons, living or dead, is coincidental.

© 2003 by D. Raymond Anderson. All rights reserved.

No part of this book may be reproduced, stored in a retrieval system, or transmitted by any means, electronic, mechanical, photocopying, recording, or otherwise, without written permission from the author.

ISBN: 1-4033-7164-4 (e-book)
ISBN: 1-4033-7165-2 (Paperback)
ISBN: 1-4107-3914-7 (Dust Jacket)

Library of Congress Control Number: 2002094251

This book is printed on acid free paper.

Printed in the United States of America
Bloomington, IN

1stBooks - rev. 04/18/03

Flight of the Kroughs

As he descended the eastern slope of the mountain that impounded Virtue Valley, Utah, USA, the signs planted along the way announced places and names he recalled being aware of as a boy then young man. One read "Entering Big Blue country, home of Bear River State University". Another one read "Virtue Valley USA, Home to the Worlds largest Swiss Cheese Factory". Lastly, the most impressive billboard boasted "Entering Bridgerland, Visit Bear Lake". That last sign revealed the valley's most important claim to fame. Due to over trapping, Jim Bridger was notorious back in the 1830's and 1840's for helping to destroy one of the valley's most important resources, beaver.

It was also rumored that Jim Bridger, aided by his friends, helped inspire among the local native tribes the belief that there existed no such creature as a white woman. Supposedly, that belief was inspired by the fact that Bridger and his friends took native women as wives, rather than dragging frail eastern women into their mountain wonderland. Therefore, the local native tribesmen reasoned that white women didn't exist. Most enlightened people didn't take that belief seriously.

The passage of time, however, and the need for a gimmick to draw tourists, had dignified Jim Bridger's reputation. This, in turn, insured creditability of dozens of sites scattered throughout the valley that were dedicated to his memory that were both real and concocted.

As he rounded a long simple curve, the valley floor burst into his view.

Small towns, their names written in Glen's memory beneath each one, lay splashed on the tartan landscape. As the red Ford settled with the highway onto the bottom of Virtue Valley, Glen, as never before, became aware of the fact that when becoming intimately engulfed by the landscape, it loses its patchwork definition, the view of which he had enjoyed from the foothills.

Now he could see how the acres were divided into random sized areas by fences of barbed wire that clung to overmatched cedar posts that leaned in all manner of degree; posts and wire that had long since been defeated by tumbleweeds being chased by the relentless east canyon winds. Then visible evidence appeared around him of man's imperfect creations that are in competition with the wishes of nature.

Shoulder deep and house wide furrows snaking through the valley floor that once carried liquid disbursements from mountain banks of snow now lay dormant...waiting only for the odd flash flood to justify their existence. Because, great man made, Corps of Engineers designed, government financed sub-banks, known as reservoirs, now impound the precious moisture, which, In turn, is doled out through arteries of canals. Those canals feed capillaries of ditches that distributes the water throughout Virtue Valley's rich bottom soil.

The time had come for him to turn east.

Glen continued his journey of rediscovery, his car riding smooth on the grass framed narrow road. He passed-by vaguely familiar, now remodeled or further neglected farms and homes. Having traveled roughly one and a half miles, he automatically glanced obliquely to his right; he had reached the place where he could see the piece of land that was once his brother Chad's farm. The thoughts that had passed through Glen's mind for the past twenty minutes were merely vague mental commentaries concerning the environment that had surrounded him. Now, however, his re-discoveries were increasingly more personal. He decided to stop and have a look, if only from a distance.

The farm lacked the pre-world war appearance that Glen remembered it having in nineteen-forty-seven. He could see no rusted to decay horse drawn equipment drowning in seat-high weeds scattered about. And there were no pigpen remnants cluttering the place. It looked as if some gigantic machine had leveled the farm fence to fence. Such must have been a considerable chore, Glen thought. Because, as he remembered it, the lay of the land had been haphazard. Some parts suddenly too high, making some parts just as suddenly too low. Some parts of the farm were too wet, and because water can't run uphill, other parts were bone dry. Also, parts of the farm were no more than islands of useless scrub maple brush. But, as the farm was another story, Glen returned his attention to the road, resuming his journey.

Within the short period of five minutes, He once more changed directions, steering his Ford to a southerly direction.

The vehicle, creeping along at but a crawl while the driver swept the evermore familiar scene with his eyes and mind, moved past a couple defunct enterprises. Skirted with weeds, they were of gray concrete block construction, post WW 11GI Bill financed failures. Victims of big ideas, small management skills, and lack of demand for their services.

Suddenly, Glen braked his car to a stop, in front of old Bear River City High School. Old, because ten years previously, a new larger county school had been built in a more central location in Virtue Valley. Consequently, the old high school had suffered that most devastating of embarrassments: it had been demoted to a Junior High School

Fatter and taller now, Glen yet remembered individually the trees scattered around the grassy knoll on which the school building sat.

The sight of the building quaked Glen's memory to an even greater degree than had the farm his brother had briefly owned.

Because it was July, he was unable to enter the place and satisfy his urge to have a good look around. Therefore he did the next best thing: he strolled leisurely every fractured walkway of the deserted campus. As he proceeded, memories poured from his mind like a movie projector gone crazy. Specific happenings, some pleasant, others not so pleasant, danced from his subconscious with great speed. Some will be told of later. As, Glen decided, it was time to move on.

He guided the rested Ford around a gentle curve, where, the road became Main Street.

After following the roadway across a swampy pasture area that protected the school from the distractions of the downtown area, he passed the City Limits sign. "Bear River City, population 2000, please drive carefully". Three hundred more than when he left he figured.

When he was a growing boy, and as it yet was, River City was a two story town. It could be described as such in many ways. The buildings in the business district didn't rise beyond two floors above the sidewalk. Nor did the extent of that business district – which was an obvious exaggeration – travel more than two blocks.

There had once been two dry goods stores: Jensen's at the west end and Allen's at the east end of the downtown area. The city had boasted the existence of two pool halls, separated by only four doors. A gas station sat at the east end of the center of commerce, and one sat at the west end. The only real difference that Glen noticed, then was, that Jensen's market had been swallowed –up by its pool hall neighbor, and the other pool hall had gone out of business. Also, the gas station at the west end of town had been closed, but was still standing.

While creeping along main, the first place of real significance he saw was the building sitting on the corner of Main Street and First West, next to the converted market. It was the largest building in Bear River City…the dance hall. It was appropriately called "The Dancing Springs". Glen remembered it as being the gathering place for The fun loving folks, most of whom didn't worry too much about rising from their beds Sunday morning to attend church.

The varnished and shoe leather buffed floor was about one hundred feet in length, and eighty feet in width. But the feature that made the ballroom famous was the middle oval section of the floor that measured about eighty by fifty feet, and rose three inches above the rest of the floor. It was mounted on huge springs. When the music was cheek-to-cheek, the floor would gently rise and fall like a feather riding the current of a soft breeze.

But alas, much like the store next door, the place now lays dormant. The fact was, according to the town know-it-alls, the declining popularity of the dance hall coincided with the rise in popularity of "rock and roll music". According to them, that style of music was responsible for polarizing the different age groups; the older members of the crowd could not adjust to the new rhythms and sounds and the younger couples would no longer tolerate traditional dance music. Therefore, rather than try to cater to both tastes in music, the owners of the building, Bear River City, decided to close its doors.

To protect their young people from the corrupting influences of such "wild, valueless and obscene" goings-on was the real reason admitted some of the former city officials after the passage of a year or two.

Also, in the minds of some good citizens of River City, another outpost of the Devil was the movie house. Now, in nineteen-eighty-four, it was no more than a hole in the ground surrounded by piles of rubble.

Regardless of the fact that that rubble was all that remained of the theater, it caused many memories to come front and center in Glen's thoughts.

He recalled that in his early teenage years, his real reason for going to the movies, with money earned working in the hay or milking some farmers cows, was to stare at and fantasize about certain situations with the girls his age. The number one object of his dreams was Ellie Thurston. Ellie's father, Dr. Thurston, was the town veterinarian. To have-nots, such as Glen, Ellie was an untouchable. In fact, in his mind all girls in Bear River City were off limits to him. He made up for that mean deprivation by using every opportunity to look and imagine.

His next, and final stop in the downtown area was nearby Allen's Market. It was located across the street from the only service station remaining in town.

The yellow brick store had faired better than Jensen's market, the pool hall, the theater and the dance hall, it had prospered.

During the war years, 1941-1945, Glen's three older brothers were involved up to their elbows in different parts of the world. James Lawrence, the oldest of the three, Chad, second oldest and Roland, a mere child of fifteen and a half when he had lied about his age – with Iver, his father, giving his blessing, in order to enlist, each sent part of their meager pay home to help support the family.

When there was nothing in the house suitable from which to create brown bag lunches, and to save having her children walk the mile home for lunch, their mother, Irene, opened a charge account at Allen's. There, the children were allowed to charge enough snacks to tide them until supper. But they were to treat the account with utmost frugality. Irene would long consider that to be a great mistake. Soon, whether or not, they carried a sack lunch, the children abused the privilege almost daily. In no time at all, the children had managed to run up a bill of one-hundred dollars...plus. Mostly on cupcakes, twinkes, pepsi and ice cream.

Glen left the rest of his memories stored, for then, coaxed his Ford to life, then continued his trip east up Main Street. He soon topped the hill

Flight of the Kroughs

leading to the bench that overlooked Bear River City. He drove by the cemetery slowly. Iver, his father, Irene his mother, Viola, his older sister and David, his baby brother were all buried there. Glen's father, sister and brother had all died in the short space of one year. A very bad year,

Glen continued on his way for another block, stopping at 661 East Main Street, Bear River City, Utah, Zip 84255. The three rooms of shelter looked, as it indeed was, deserted. In fact, the feeble Krough home had been silent since 1969. So it was well on the way through its declining years. Now it was, to a disinterested passerby maybe, no more than a gray, swaybacked, falling-down shack. The old homestead stood impounded by patches of tangled weeds and trees of every description. And beyond the lazy barbed wire barrier, new multi-level giants with pretty lawns watched with impatient arrogant conceit the little house fall into merciless decay, while hoping that some uncaring bulldozer would soon see to its demise. Cupped shingle covered eves that cast shadows over windows boarded shut with third-hand scraps of wood, which, as it appeared to Glen, locked up ghosts of life sounds that, for him, used to be. Images crowded Glen's mind. Irene, his mother, Iver, his father, and twelve brothers and sisters, ten of whom survived to occupy those three rooms. And, that too, is another story.

As he sat on a battered five-gallon bucket in the shade of the fun scarred box elder tree, Glen began to reconstruct the past. He asked himself, "Where did Dad come from, where did Mother come from, and what became of the thirteen offspring. And what kind of life did Iver make for Irene?"

Glen began his mental journey by wondering why Iver's first attempt at marriage fell by the wayside. The answer to that question had remained a mystery to Irene and her Krough kids as well. However, as is the custom, rumor filled in the blanks left by the absence of fact. Of the numerous accounts of the affair, several seemed logical to Glen. One was that Iver's first wife ran or had him run out of Bear River City because of his meanness, which was caused by a sharp temper. Another possible reason was Iver's inability to accomplish anything of lasting value. Not because he was lazy, far from it. Nor was he short on imagination. For, he could dream, figure and scheme with the best. In fact, while leaning against the pig pen fence, sharing his spit squeezed through a wad of days work chewing tobacco with a couple of scrounge hogs, Iver could dream up gold mines, a mysterious Inheritance, plantations and mansions. But when it came time to put shovel or hammer to work making just one of his dreams a reality. . .nothing happened, no matter how hard he wished.

However, the reason that seemed most likely to Glen was that his father was a great starter, but a poor finisher. Relationships included. So whatever his problem, Iver had good reason to depart Bear River City. But why the long trip to such an out-of-the-way place as Brookside, Alabama?

Beside the fact that he was, in all probability, running from something, Glen believed his father was, at the same time, searching for something. But for what? That was a mystery that, with some study, might be solved. But Glen, or no one else, ever took the trouble to learn the real, unvarnished truth, because that was buried with Iver in the cemetery a block away, under ranks of Colorado blue spruce.

Alabama, in 1984, may not be a considerable trip from Virtue Valley, Utah, U.S.A. But when compared to that trip in the year 1918, it was the difference between traveling by a mule with three legs, or traveling by Cadillac. And as far as Glen could discover, his dad had never been much at saving money. So having ready cash with which to finance the trip was very unlikely. That left him but one option…he must have worked his way across the country.

Glen imagined his dad settling for rides in the back of hard rubber-tired Model "T" pickups, or hopping a smoke-spewing freight train. And at times, plain old fashioned walking. If the dead could talk, Iver would have rose-up from his grave and complained about just how much of the trip he did make on foot.

Sadly, when the traveler finally reached the vicinity of Brookside, Alabama, he found country as hard and demanding as the journey he had just completed.

Not knowing exactly where he was, he crawled from the wagon he had bummed a ride on, and stood at the side of the road and dusted himself off at the sign pointing east that said "Armstrong Coal Company, Brookside, Alabama, 4 miles". As he was flat broke and the sign offered hope of employment, Iver figured he had reached the end of his trip. He picked his blue denim sack, filled with his few earthly goods, from the ground and headed in the direction pointed out for him by the friendly sign.

Rolling hills, thickly wooded with elm, oak, and yellow pine mingled with heavy low brush that the Utahn could not identify seemed to go on forever.

Because all that Iver could see was the hill before him that he was trying to conquer, it always looked like the last one. But when he reached its top, there was always another one blocking his way. From its summit, just like the last one, the stranger would issue the next hill a loud blast of profanity.

When he did, finally, top the last knoll and looked down on Brookside, Iver realized straight away that if it weren't for some barking dogs and smoke from chimneys rising from the jungle-like valley floor, he could have just as easily hiked right on past the place.

Along the trail, whatever precious earth space was available was occupied by a combination of discarded trash and miscellaneous chunks of used up mining paraphernalia, all knitted together by the thick brush.

Flight of the Kroughs

Generally speaking, in Iver's eye anyway, the men of Brookside were a sorry looking lot. Which was a hypocritical opinion. Because he couldn't have looked worse after surviving the trip he'd just finished. Iver's first impression of the men was that they all looked the same. To him, they looked as if they had gone on a crash diet and some looked as if they had failed to survive the crash. Most of them seemed to be small men, very slender, short on teeth, with long faces and tired eyes. Their gaunt faces were permanently traced with deep lines, just as permanently dyed with the black dust from the black underground arteries in which it was their misfortune to have to work.

The buildings scattered around the hillsides were sway-backed and seemed to lean against the steep slopes for support. Most were coming apart due to the lack of nails and too much rain. Iver wondered how the folks in "Nigger Town," as it was called by the local regular whites, could live in what he imagined must be even worse conditions.

Some of what he saw made the converted chicken coop he'd lived in with his parents and six sisters soon after immigrating from Denmark seem quite comfortable. Every building, including churches, mansions, or shacks, was surrounded by at least a dozen varieties of untended flowers, bushes, and weeds. It stretched the powers of the stranger's imagination to distinguish the difference. And the dogs; There were hundreds of dogs, all of them underfed. More than once, Iver was sure he might need to donate a leg to one of the starved mongrels in order to salvage the rest of his body. Sometimes the people he met were just as hostile as the dogs. They, the men, that is, always drank when they weren't down in the mine, so Iver laid the blame for their orneriness on the bottles of home brew they consumed. Like any man, able bodied or not, Iver took a job in one of the Armstrong Coal Mines. In the Jefferson County mining area, there was no welfare system. So those out of work could only depend on the generosity of family or neighbors or, in Iver's situation, total strangers. Luckily, he had an honest face. Those who were employed at the mine, it seemed anyway, had few worries. If they needed clothing, groceries or supplies, it was easy for them to go down to the company store and charge whatever they needed against their next paycheck. But when payday came around, it wasn't unusual for some to discover that they were in debt to Armstrong Company store beyond the limits of their paycheck. This, it turned out, was the main worry of those few worries. After a day of eating wild berries, not poison he hoped, and green apples from the worn out yet usable Methodist church yard, Iver pilfered a night of sleep in the belly of a wrecked coal car. Then he endured another day of berries and apples.

So, half rested, the young man from out west took up his pick and shovel signed for at the company store and disappeared beneath the ground with the grey herd of the graveyard shift.

Iver was quiet but made his presence known by the amount of coal his body moved during a shift. He threw his shovel and flung his pick as if there was something to prove. But in truth, Iver had already acquired some training in the use of a pick and shovel. Back in Virtue Valley, Utah, as a young immigrant laborer, he had helped construct some of the many irrigation systems strung out across the valley. So the only differences in the two jobs was the degree of physical labor involved, and the environment in which the labor was performed. After nearly a week on the job, the foreman approached Iver and began to inquire as to where he had come from and compliment him on his work. The answer Iver gave to that first question ignited a slightly one-sided conversation.

"So yalls from Utah, huh?" As he was the boss, and a good deal older than himself, if not in age, then surely in mileage, Iver let the question pass as not requiring an answer. Knowing that at least he had made Iver feel uncomfortable, the foreman let go with a burst of laughter such as the greenhorn miner from Utah had never heard in all his life. To him it sounded like a sack of tin cans being dragged from a swamp through a gravel pit, or maybe a man trying to die from pneumonia. Iver stared at the convulsing black-skinned white man in stunned disbelief. "What's the matter, kid?" yelled the shift foreman. "Haven't yall ever heard a real man laugh atcha before? I've been in this God-damned hole for twenty years now. And after about ten of them it gets in yer chest. Nothing a man can do about it, only keep on workin' till it kills him. Then the devil rips out yer pitch black lungs and guts to keep the fiery furnaces of Hell burnin. And do the big-assed bosses in their fancy wood paneled offices in Birmingham care?" He answered his own question. "Shit no. When one of these poor suckers from the mine dies, they just throws the body in a hole and put his shack up for rent."

"Anyway, where's yer horns?" the boss continued.

"Who told you that bullshit?" Iver replied.

"Why, it's common knowledge that every Mormon man has got to have at least fifteen wives, forty-five kids ... and horns."

"Well, look at me," Iver pleaded. "I haven't got even one wife. And I haven't got any kids. And even you can see that I don't have horns poking out of my head."

The foreman thought for a moment ... "Then you must be some God-damned misfit and the Mormons must not want you ... Get back to work."

The conversation had been short but to the point, and two important facts had emerged from it. First, Iver had become acutely aware of the effect a lifetime of labor in the coal mines could have on a healthy body. And, although he had never considered mining as a lifetime career, the personal contact he experienced with the foreman planted in Iver's mind the seeds of discontent. And second, he had told his first lie in Brookside. It was a lie Iver would repeat time and again to those he became involved with.

For a time, the people he met while tramping the hills to and from the mine and the encounter with his foreman soured Iver's impressions of the local folks. But, before long, he had the good fortune to become acquainted with the Coburn family. Even more important than making new friends was the fact that Iver could move out of the coal mining company's tool shack and move into a sleeping area located in the attic of Rosanna Coburn's home. And from Mother Coburn's position, it was a break also.

Because Mr. Coburn had deserted his family for relatives in Tennessee, the family had little to exist on; the dollar a day earned from the new boarder wouldn't, on its own, amount to much, but, when added to the money taken in doing the wash for single miners, it gave the household, that included Mrs. Coburn and two daughters named Viola and Irene, some financial independence.

So Iver collected his sixty dollars from the paymaster. With his denim bag, now a little bulkier, slung over his left shoulder and his pick and shovel over the right one, he headed up the path along the river looking for his new lodgings.

After an appropriate period of introduction and small talk that Mrs. Coburn used to size up the handsome young man from Utah, she led him directly to his sleeping area. As they made their way up the seldom used mildewy smelling stairs, he in front, she three steps behind and below, a oneway uphill conversation concerning rules and regulations bounced off Iver's back.

When they reached the top, Iver discovered a small room, oblong in shape, with open rafters, and planks lying loose on the ceiling joists as a floor.

Then Rosanna announced her next to last rule; "As you can see, young man," (Iver took that description of him as a compliment) "the only light you will have is that small window above your bunk. So, if you can read, and if you have any reading to do, or if you can write, and if you have any writing to do, you have my permission to sit in the front room or sit on the front porch until seven p.m., at which time the front door will be locked, and you will be expected to retire to your room."

Then she arrived at her last rule. Rosanna's eyelids gathered around her eyes and her lips became thin and rigid. Seeing her face take on such a firm look, Iver felt sure something serious was about to be laid on him. She looked Iver square in the eye, and with a hint of suspicion, said, "stay away from my daughters."

Straight away Iver knew that part of his reputation had proceeded him on his move to new quarters. But the real message Rosanna issued, as he interpreted it anyway, was that Iver was one of those heathen Mormons and she didn't want any of her daughters carried off to join some secret harem out west somewhere. With a flushed face, he nodded his surrender to the rules to the back of Rosanna's head as she disappeared down the now darkened stair-case. About halfway down, she stopped, and turned back to face Iver. And in a slightly softer tone informed him that supper would be on the table at six o'clock ... sharp. "Be on time," she said. "Because at six-thirty the girls will clear the table." Again Iver nodded his understanding and Rosanna disappeared into the late afternoon gloom of her unlit front room.

Iver moved from the top of the stairs into his assigned space and sat on the edge of his cot which, he noticed, constituted half the furniture available to him. The other half was a four drawer dresser with half the drawers missing.

Through the shadows, he watched the hands of his beat-up alarm clock crawl toward the hour of six. Not wanting to appear anxious, or starved for a good home-cooked meal, Iver waited until eight minutes after the established starting time for the evening meal before ambling unsurely down the stairs to the large kitchen/dining room combination.

As he reached its entrance, he paused for a few seconds and glanced at each of the people sitting at the long, sagging table. Rosanna occupied the chair at the head of the table. On her right sat Viola and on her left sat Irene, age seventeen. The chair at the foot of the table was empty, but was set with utensils. Iver arrived at the obvious conclusion that the empty chair at the foot of the table was assigned to him, so he sat down and offered a shy, yet polite, greeting to the others.

From the start of the meal, the new boarder began pilfering looks at the family that had taken him in. Rosanna was aware from the start what was going on and she understood, for the time being anyway. In a short time, looks began to go in circles; Irene would steal a look at Iver, he would return the glance, then Mother Coburn would shoot an icy glance in Iver's direction. After which, she would see to Irene with a sharp rap on the ankle, under cover of the table, of course.

Navy bean soup, whole wheat bread, uncured pork side meat, and for dessert, some kind of fruit juice, stiffened into a pudding with corn starch, was passed around the table with no conversation and consumed with no complaint. Secretly, Iver felt as if he could have easily devoured what was left of the food himself. But as that would be less than gentlemanly, he politely accepted seconds on everything. Then at the silent urging of their mother, and after the new boarder had finished his second go at the food, Irene and Viola rose to their feet and began clearing off the table, and prepared to do the dishes. Iver, feeling nourished, leaned back on his chair until it was on its back legs. Then with a put-on stretch and yawn, he directed a request at his newly acquired landlady, and a split second following that request, fire danced in Rosanna's eyes.

"May I smoke?" he had asked in a routine way. "Absolutely not" she shot back in a sharp raised voice. But when five minutes worth of self-consciousness, on Iver's part, and the same five minutes worth of reconsideration on her part had elapsed, she looked back at her new boarder, and in a more pleasant style, told him that he would be permitted to smoke on the back porch. "Unless, of course, the girls are present, or nearby."

Feeling a bit preached at, Iver, in haste, not because of embarrassment but because he had only fifteen minutes until curfew, headed for the back porch.

The screen door slapped behind him, bounced back, then slapped at the back of the house again. Iver sat down and dangled his legs over the side of the porch. He pulled a bag of cheap tobacco from his shirt pocket, rolled a nearly round smoke, using brown paper from a wornout lunch bag, then lit up. To the accompaniment of the strange sound of numerous bugs, he wondered much about his newly-found situation. He also wondered as much about the three people who were willing, or forced by circumstances, to share their home with a stranger such as he. More or less, when he thought about those people, it was more about Irene, and less about Viola, not because one was more attractive than the other, but because one was older than the other. That qualification served only as a basis on which other positive judgements concerning other desirable attributes could be made in the near future. And those judgements would influence concrete decisions that Iver would make, likewise, in the near future.

Right from day one, Iver observed his new family closely, but with particular attention paid to Irene. She stood five feet five, and weighed in at a compact one hundred and fifteen pounds.

To Iver, Irene seemed, and was, nearly as quiet as mother. She had dark, nearly black, hair. Her face was slender and featured high cheek bones. It was said by those who should know that there was Cherokee in her Coburn blood.

But what attracted Iver the most about the young lady's face was its expression. He wasn't quite sure whether the wide-eyed look and her slight smile said innocence or mischief. All in all, quite a woman, he thought, as he moved from the back porch.

As he marched - Iver had always held his body straight to enhance his slight frame - through the front room, he gestured a good night to the three women with a wave of his hand and tilt of his head, but no words. When his goodnight glance fell on Irene, Iver again thought, quite a woman.

When conversation between the Coburns and the Mormon from Utah became somewhat more relaxed, Iver's age, as it naturally would, became a topic of interest around the supper table. Rosanna sensed that when the subject of age, his in particular, was raised, Iver seemed uncomfortable. So she decided to confront him with the question: "Just what is your age anyway, Iver?" He shuffled his feet under the table, then pushed away, and leaned his body on the chair's back until it was on its back legs. He heaved a false yawn, and sighed, then in an unconcerned way replied, "Twenty-eight." Rosanna's face showed surprise, because, that was just about what she had guessed, give or take a year or two. Viola's face also showed surprise. And Irene's face showed wide-eyed interest, maybe even esteem.

But Irene did not know that Iver had, In response to her mother's question, expressed his second lie in Brookside, that time about his age. For, had he told the truth, his answer would have been thirty-eight. Therefore, her look, along with her sister and her mother's, would have been one of shock. Regardless of its validity, his just learned age fast reassured Rosanna that any relationship, either accidental or manipulated between Iver and her daughter would be impossible. Because an older gentleman just didn't encourage a lasting relationship with an inexperienced woman. If he regardless, it wasn't many weeks before he found it difficult, if not impossible, to ignore the oldest of the two daughters. He took advantage of every chance presented to him to show his interest in her without, of course, revealing his strategy.

Because it was Rosanna's custom to retire to her bedroom following the evening meal and leave the clean-up to the girls, Iver was presented with a perfect opportunity to demonstrate his attraction to Irene. She did nothing obvious to welcome his attention, but she did nothing to discourage the attention either.

At first, he just lingered at the table after Mother Coburn had departed and talked to the Coburn girls. After three days using those tactics, he shifted to the next phase of his plan which, in fact, was less of a plan than an instinctive reaction to opportunity. Such as, volunteering to help with the after supper cleaning-up. Irene and Viola eagerly accepted his help and didn't suspect strings being attached.

Having achieved success with that move, it was time, Iver thought, to make the boldest maneuver yet. So he schemed up his next move as he lay stretched out on his bed staring into the near total darkness of his room.

Flight of the Kroughs

He would intimate to Viola that, after the evening meal had been dealt with, and after her mother had retired to her room, that she should also entertain herself elsewhere, and he would help Irene with clean-up and dishes.

That following evening, the idea dreamed up the night before by Iver worked to perfection.

Viola agreed to leave the kitchen, Irene agreed to accept Iver's help, and she was beyond herself with excitement. She felt just a little bit childlike standing beside the ruggedly handsome near stranger. But she also felt something else. She experienced a sensation somewhere between the need for the companionship of a father and a more primitive urge she could neither explain nor recall feeling before.

In any case, there they were, side by side, feeling a bond tighten around them.

That rung cleared, Iver considered the next step on the ladder of complete acceptance of him by the Coburn family. That phase of his plan struck much fear and unsureness in his thoughts. Winning over Rosanna, no doubt, would be a difficult assignment for him. But Iver had already devised a scheme to accomplish that difficult task also: He would set himself to that job the day following the one on which he and Irene had shared the doing of the supper dishes. By that time, Iver had earned a place on the day shift at the mine, so it was no problem for him to arrive at his rooming house early on that next day. Irene and Viola were on the front porch swing engaged in half-hearted small talk. They stopped their flimsy conversation when Iver mounted the steps. He greeted Irene in a warm and polite fashion ignored Viola, then walked on into the front room, looked around, then, moved straight to the kitchen where Rosanna was engaged in preparing the evening meal.

She looked up from putting biscuits into the oven and wondered silently what he was doing there. Mother Coburn waited for him to stop and explain his presence. But, to her surprise, he whistled his way past her and out the back door. She figured her boarder to be going for a smoke.

Fifteen minutes later, the door re-opened and Iver marched in carrying a substantial load of oak for the stove in one arm, and a bucket of coal at the end of his other arm. It seemed to Rosanna that for the past several days Iver had been acting differently. She settled for an explanation that told her Iver, after six weeks, had finally come to think of himself as part of the family.

Feeling himself that he had cracked the shell of withdrawn quietness surrounding Rosanna, Iver began to engage her in conversation while he tended the kitchen stove, and while she cooked.

Rosanna wondered why it was so easy to enjoy their discussions. If she had known Iver's true age, most of the mystery would have evaporated. Because, in fact, compared to Irene, Rosanna was closer in age to Iver by twenty-one to seven years. Although she was older than he, Rosanna was near enough to Iver's secret age to easily speak about many subjects with him. The most logical topic was, and with no surprise to Iver, religion.

Much had been written and said in Alabama concerning Mormons, or Latter Day Saints, as they preferred to be called. Most local preachers considered Joseph Smith's church an abomination. Their dislike was primarily due to two Mormon beliefs: first, the practice of polygamy; which Iver thought, in a comical way, might be from envy. He based his assumption on the eager way in which the males at the mine questioned him about the practice. The females, of course, considered the practice of polygamy a ritual of the devil. But it seemed the news of the practice being outlawed by the Church in 1890 didn't spread much beyond the limits of Utah. So it was with great surprise to Rosanna that Iver refuted the principal. The other piece of doctrine that grated on other religious organizations was the Mormon belief that their leader was a living prophet of God, and, that he received revelation from God, even in those modern times. No matter her contempt for it, Iver would stick by his acceptance of that principal, and would valiantly defend it against Rosanna's Methodist ridicule of "such nonsense", as she labeled it.

Not only did the two argue religion and occasionally politics, but several times the subject of children as well. Again, Mrs. Coburn was amazed at the insight Iver showed on the subject, "in spite of having none of his own," she thought. But unknown to the Coburn family, was the fact that Iver did have children. . .two young daughters, ages fourteen and fifteen. So it was no wonder he showed such a keen knowledge concerning family life.

Regardless of Rosanna's wondering, Iver had accomplished his objective. And now it was time to make his most daring move.

Iver spent several nights staring into the dark space of his room considering the immediate future.

"Now," he mumbled to himself, "If everything goes as well on this phase of my plan, by this time next month, which would be March 26, 1919, Irene could be mine. God, I hope so" he whispered with desire.

Iver believed that a person had to make his own luck, but he also knew that desire, on its own, would not be enough. Opportunity must be available and taken advantage of.

For the next two days, Friday and Saturday, Irene's lurking suitor waited for his chance, and it was handed to him on Sunday. The two girls were in their rooms preparing themselves for morning worship services. As was the new custom, Iver and Rosanna sat at the kitchen table talking over cups of coffee.

"What would you say, Rose, if I accompanied your young ladies to church?' Looking shocked, but not wanting to miss the opportunity to convert the heathen Mormon, as she sometimes thought of him, Rose stuttered, "Well now, I think that would be nice. Just a minute, I will tell them to wait on you."

The three of them, Iver in the center strutting, Irene to his right, and on his left Viola, moved down the lane toward the decaying chapel.

At first the trio walked in silence, but it wasn't long before Irene commented on what a lovely day it was. Viola agreed, and nearly in the same breath, asked her older sister if she might run on ahead and go to church with one of her friends. Irene gave her permission, and Iver offered a silent prayer of thanksgiving. He also slowed the pace at which they walked.

Not much was said except for short commentaries on the unusual warmth of that first day of March.

Irene felt warm and secure walking beside her escort, maybe even proud.

Although Iver's clothes were not top notch for Sunday best, he did have the top button of his tieless shirt secured to its hole and was unusually clean shaven. Again their pace slowed.

By the time the pair arrived at the chapel, the services had long since commenced.

Realizing this, but showing no disappointment, Irene took her escort by the hand and led him, in a state of surprise, around to the back churchyard. She quickly continued her side trip for another hundred feet beyond the back of the church, dragging an excited yet stumbling Iver behind her.

She finally stopped at the lip of a grassy area, with a southern exposure, that sloped gently down into a little valley,

There they sat down side by side, and let the warm sun drench their awakening bodies. Irene felt splendidly attired in her Sunday best dress for what was happening to her.

They talked much about many things when they resumed their quiet conversation. Irene told of her family history, but naturally she left out the shabby part. Iver, likewise, told of his family history ... for the most part, because they concerned him, he left incriminating facts in their closets.

As they discussed the edited versions of their respective family's annals, the sun continued its relentless journey, as did the clock.

Too soon, Viola's soft tug on Irene's shoulder signaled that it was time to start the return trip home.

As they started up the trail toward the Coburn house, Irene gave Viola an inquiring look. Viola gave Irene a reassuring smile in return, and Irene knew her secret was secure.

After about one hundred steps, Iver suggested to the younger sister that she again go on ahead, and as before, she agreed.

When Viola was out of sight, he took Irene's hand and led her to a large oak a safe distance off the pathway. Then, taking both her hands, he leaned her against the large tree trunk. He looked directly at Irene. Through a flushed face, he confessed his feelings for her. He waited long enough for an emotional response from her before taking the next step. He received her signal in the form of a squeeze from the small hand that had circled his fingers. So he felt obliged to place a quick but clumsy kiss on Irene's forehead.

She said nothing in return, but through wet eyes, let her identical feelings be known. She wanted to shout, even scream.

She wanted to laugh, but it was easier to cry. She wanted to grab her man, as she now thought of him, and disappear through the curtain of bliss that now surrounded them. But the thought of her mother, and how she would react upon learning of her feelings for Iver, brought Irene back to earth. At that moment she knew that, regardless of Rosanna's approval or disapproval, her future course was set, and Iver would be the captain of her ship.

During the month of March, the two of them found the times and the places in which to show their regards for each other. It was then March 25th. And Iver, puffed up after several minutes of self-reassuring, marched into Rosanna's kitchen, just as he had done for the past month and a half. However, instead of going out the back door to do his assumed chores, he stopped. After a moment, he offered Rosanna a chair. She was suspicious, but accepted his gallant gesture. Iver wasted no time. He drew a deep breath and announced,

"Irene and I want to marry."

Mrs. Coburn's head slowly dropped to her chest, then she turned it away from him. On her face was a look that said, "Oh, shit, I knew this would happen."

After an eternity of silence, which was really only one minute, Iver persisted "Well, how about it?"

"What gall this pushy bastard has," moaned mother Coburn. She stared Iver in his eyes, and with a weak voice said, "I'm going to be honest with you, Mr. Krough. I don't like you and I don't think I ever will. But Irene is nearly eighteen and she don't need my official permission. And what chance, or say, in the matter do I have anyway? There is no husband or father here to throw your ass out of the house." She continued ... "But don't

Flight of the Kroughs

expect me to attend any ceremony, or for that matter, give my blessing. And, another thing, I hope she don't come crying back here to me holding her belly, because I won't know her."

Know her or not, Iver knew he had won, and he was about to come apart with excitement. He could hardly contain his glee until he reached his sleeping area. Iver bounced up the stairs three at a time. And in the safety of his space, he silently shouted and punched at the stale air with his fist. His fist and mind finally under control, Iver whispered, "God, can it be true? She is so young and beautiful. How can I be so lucky?"

Then it was the morning of March 28, 1919, and Rosanna was making good on her vow by remaining in her room. But for Irene and Viola, the morning sparkled with excitement. Iver had sprung from his bed early and made himself respectable with a bath and an unusual mid-week shave. Irene had dropped a note through the mail to her older brothers, Berdie and Claud, who lived and worked in another town called Cardif. They agreed to bring their Model "T" to Brookside and carry the wedding party to the Jefferson County Court House in Birmingham. There, like before, Iver was less than honest, because he gave his full name as Iver Henery Krough, when, in fact, his full name was Iver Hans Krough. Of course, Irene would not question him about the discrepancy because the subject of full names had never been a matter of discussion between them. After satisfying the paperwork requirements, the party continued on to a small town on the edge of Birmingham called Ensley where, in a small Methodist chapel, Irene gave herself to Iver in marriage. The ceremony was conducted by an official minister of God, the Reverend A. J. Springfield. After being delivered the required solemn words that united the couple and an eloquent sermon directed at the newlyweds by the preacher, Iver and Irene, along with her two brothers and younger sister, went to a medium fancy restaurant in Birmingham where they celebrated the wedding with a medium fancy meal.

While there, the subject of Rosanna became the topic of conversation. Berdie was the first to show courage enough to speak the obvious. He looked at the pair and reminded them that Rosanna was irreversibly opposed to Iver's being part of the family. It would be impossible for Irene to invite her husband back to the Coburn home. Iver said nothing in return ••. just stared into his after-dinner cup of coffee. Irene quietly confessed that she was aware of the fact. Claude, understanding the helplessness of their situation, and regardless of his own mild dislike of his new brother-in-law, suggested that the pair return to Cardif with him and brother Berdie. Nods of approval went around the table. After the post dinner coffee and smoke was finished, they all headed back to Brookside, there to collect Iver and Irene's meager belongings.

D. Raymond Anderson

It seemed Rosanna had anticipated the young couple's plans, for when the marriage party arrived at the Coburn house, they found Iver's clothes and Irene's clothes piled on the front porch. Irene had planned to take some of the personal treasures she had accumulated over the years with her. And some pictures too. But to her sorrow, there were none of those things in her pile. She looked up at her window and felt like crying, but decided to accept what was doled out to her and offer no argument.

Viola reappeared from inside the house, meeting Irene face to face. She was pale and obviously sad. Viola told Irene that their mother had gone to visit one of her friends .. she didn't know who. Irene concluded, and correctly, that her mother did not want to suffer the embarassment of parting with her under such strained circumstances.

Irene took Viola by the hand and said a quiet good-bye to her. Viola then broke into tears. Irene turned her back on her younger sister and headed toward the car carrying both piles of belongings. Viola followed her sister down the path with her eyes. And the feeling that she would never again see her sister and friend overwhelmed her. She ran to her room and collapsed on her bed in a fetal position and sobbed. Irene dried her wet eyes as she, her new husband, and her two brothers headed northwest to Cardif.

Because the town of Cardif was a mining town just like Brookside, it wasn't difficult for Iver to find work. With the change of his domestic situation came a change in Iver's mood and plans, because, without being conscious of it, a scheme had begun to grow in his mind, a scheme to continue their trip northwest, to Utah.

After working the mines of Cardif and saving every cent he could lay his hands on, he was able to put out $35.00 to buy his own Model "T". With what funds he had left from his savings in his pocket, he loaded his pregnant wife, and what of their belongings the little car would carry, and headed northwest towards Kansas, and ultimately, Utah.

As they went along their way, Iver interrupted the trip to work as often as it was necessary. When they did stop for work, he had devised a special way of finding it. He didn't simply pull into a town and walk the streets looking for temporary employment, oh no, not Iver. He used his special technique. And one, if not the most important, criterion of his plan was the size of the town. It had to be large enough to guarantee the existence of some kind of work and small enough to insure that he and his pregnant wife would be noticed. So when the lucky city had been chosen, his initial task was to find a very conspicious place to park. That accomplished, Mr. Krough then unloaded their eating equipment, bedding, and what few tools he owned. Next, he would, for no reason except for appearance sake, put the jack under one corner of the Model "T" and raise it off the ground and remove a tire and wheel, which he would toss to one side of their campsite.

Flight of the Kroughs

Then his final act was to lift the hood of the car. After all of those careful preparations, Iver would sit down and lean against a handy object, such as a tree, or even his car, and wait. It worked every time; because sooner or later, usually sooner, some caring, or just inquisitive, soul would come along and investigate their mechanical problem and their welfare. And it wasn't long before Iver was provided some kind of work, and his beautiful wife had a more comfortable place to sleep.

When December arrived, they began to watch the calendar and the road more closely because Irene was about to climax her first and very difficult pregnancy.

At last, after five long, grief filled months, they crossed the Missouri-Kansas State Line, and the pair congratulated themselves for making it to their first planned stop, at Pittsburg, Kansas.

As his plan called for them to stay for several months, Iver decided to forego his tried and tested plan for finding work and do it the old fashioned way. Luckily, after only five discouraging days used-up walking the dusty streets of Pittsburg, Iver found work at a mill that turned grain into animal feed. His was the job of carrying or wheeling bags of wheat, oats, or barley to and from waiting wagons or trucks.

Everyday Irene thanked God, after her husband had gone to work, of course, for the cooperative weather during that December. The good weather was important to her, because Iver and Irene had been sleeping at the car the first two weeks in Pittsburg, he under the car and she on the seat of the car.

"But now it is payday for Iver" Irene dreamed, and they could finally move into a house, or at least, a room in a house. Because Iver had put his considerable bullshit talent to work, Irene was pleasantly surprised to discover her husband coming up the lane from his work early. So, money in hand and jabbering with joy, the pair set out to find suitable lodging - suitable meaning, of course, whatever was available. They walked every street in town twice, it seemed, with no success. So they decided that, since it was Friday, they would give up for then and start out early the next morning. "In any case, Irene is in no condition to walk anymore anyway" thought Iver. As he and Irene had given up looking for a home anymore that evening, they decided on a shorter, more direct, route to their campsite.

As they walked, Iver wanted to kick himself for not using his tried and true method of finding lodging. But just as they reached the very edge of town, they spied an empty home. Tacked to the front gate was a note saying "Please call next door for information". Iver said not a word, and before Irene could say anything, she found herself standing in the street alone while Iver was at the specified door knocking. Mrs. Krough waited self-conciously in the middle of the street while a conversation between her husband and the landlord took place. In ten minutes Iver returned to his wife who had, by then, moved to the edge of the street and told her to return with him to the house of the landlord.

"Why?" she asked, feeling embarrassed and out of place.

"Because they want you to wait there while I go get the car and our stuff."

"You mean -?"

"Yes Irene, the place is ours" Iver said, cutting his wife's question short.

It wasn't much - three wee rooms and a shed over a well - but by the fourteenth of December Irene had turned the shack into a home, and none too soon either. Just two days later, on the sixteenth of December, the first of their thirteen children would arrive.

To most young couples a birth was a blessed event, but not so for Iver and Irene.

The country doctor's face showed extra lines of concern as he pulled the door shut behind him as he emerged from the bedroom. He stood for a second just beyond the threshold with his left hand resting on the white ceramic door knob; then he moved grudgingly across the warped planks of the front room floor toward the kitchen. Iver was sitting, nearly hiding, in a dark corner at the kitchen table. He had already guessed that something had gone seriously wrong, but he was afraid to ask what or to whom. He nervously waited for the doctor to speak his piece. Looking him right in the eyes, the sad-faced doctor took hold of Iver's trembling hand and said "There is nothing more I can do." Mr. Krough's eyes went wet and opened wide, then he shouted "Oh my God, Doc, not Irene." "No, Iver, not Irene. Go to her now, she needs you so."

Although he would never admit it to a living soul, Iver felt a measure of relief upon finding that it was his infant daughter who hadn't made it and not Irene.

Though the loss of their first child was tragic for Iver, in truth he viewed it as more of a temporary setback than a failure. But, contrary to her husbands pragmatic approach to life and its obstacles, Irene's view was more romantic. She couldn't write off such an event as "just part of life" as easily as her husband did. In any case, had she recognized it as such, Irene would have known that the death of her first child was a stern warning. A warning of a life with more than her share of hardships and disappointment.

Regardless of Irene's extended period of mourning, Mr. And Mrs. Krough finally put their sorrow behind them and the next year passed by quickly, and when the fifth month of that year had arrived, so did Irene's second pregnancy. And when the sixth month of that year had arrived, Iver was loading their belongings in the Model "T". "There are better jobs in Kansas City" he told his wife.

Flight of the Kroughs

At first Irene resisted the move using as her reason the fact that their first born had died shortly after one of their "ingenious" moves. Finally her will to resist caved in. Not because she thought Iver was right, but because she tired of arguing about it.

Packing their goods into, and on, the old Ford lacked the excitement of the first time because some of the romance had been brushed away by Irene's first encounter with the harsh realities of married life.

Iver lavished his wife with attentive care, trying desperately to transmit some of his blind confidence and superficial strength to her. Finally, swaying and creaking under the load, and regardless of Irene's feelings, the little car bounced across the deep ruts that its skinny tires had worn into the yard, then onto the highway.

As they headed North, Irene gazed expressionlessly out of her window at the passing landscape. The trees were full of rich June green, and their leaves were gently stirred by an affectionate southeasterly breeze. As she surveyed the new vistas unfolding around her, she thought to herself "maybe Kansas City will be better for us." She then turned toward Iver, and he caught just a glimpse of her acquiescent smile.

Then Irene began to consider the near future. "More and better jobs Iver says. I hope he's right. I want my next baby to come into the world having a thing or two, and I will be so thankful when this trip is over."

Two months later the battered Model "T" squealed to a stop in front of a dilapidated frame house on the southern edge of Kansas City, Missouri. Iver lost no time looking for, and finding, work; he went to the KC Stockyards and told them of his vast experience in the cattle feeding business, and they were so impressed that they hired him on the spot.

From that day on it was his job to feed and look after the welfare of the doomed animals.

Although Irene considered the new place to be a temporary home, she quickly, somewhat contented, went about the task of converting the just rented, sorrowful looking structure, into a warm comfortable abode. Because the furniture was in better condition than the house, and because Irene had more time to prepare, and thanks to some generous neighbors, she made good on her determination to bring her next baby into more dignified and comfortable conditions. So, in spite of it being February, and very cold, Irene seemed confident and at peace, waiting for the important event to occur.

On Sunday, the eleventh of February at eight o'clock in the morning, nature began to prepare Irene's body. The ladies in the neighborhood had already organized themselves to help the doctor deliver the coming child. So, it was only a matter of notifying one of them.

Soon the Krough kitchen was full of clean white sheets, clean white diapers, and clean women dressed in white. The kitchen table was loaded down with food too boot.

Iver sat nervously fondling a lukewarm cup of coffee in an out-of-the-way corner of the kitchen wondering aloud just how much longer it would be. Once in a while he would strain his hearing and detect a soft groan escaping from the bedroom.

After what seemed like several hours - when in fact it had been but an hour and a half since his wife had dispatched him to fetch the neighbor ladies, and the neighborhood doctor - a shrill cry split the silence of the kitchen and brought Iver to his feet, his nerves to attention. A few minutes later the doctor came out of the make-shift delivery room. His sleeves rolled up to his elbows and his rumpled clothes made the doctor look aged beyond his years when matched with his tired face. This time there was better news.

"Well Iver" drawled the doctor, "your wife has given you a fine healthy son." Iver sunk to the chair in relief. "How soon can I see her, I mean them?" he stuttered.

"Well let's see now, give Mrs. Jackson a little time to tidy up."

The doctor then proceeded to caution Mr. Krough about the fact that the new mother must have plenty of rest. The new father knew that the neighbor ladies would see to that, but little did he, or the doctor, know that in a scant three days Irene would be on her knees scrubbing the bedroom floor.

Mr. Krough acknowledged his understanding of the doctor's orders as he showed him the door. He waited in the kitchen in the throws of impatience holding onto his cup of cold coffee for another fifteen minutes.

He could hear the movement of objects, and the shuffle of feet coming from the bedroom, and he began telling himself that making him wait so long was a pile of bullshit.

Before he had a chance to mumble anymore discouraging remarks to himself, the door between the two rooms swung open. Two small neighbor ladies trotted out and only smiled at Iver as they passed him by on their way to the front door. But Mrs. Jackson, a formidable person to say the least, wedged her substantial frame in the gap between the kitchen and bedroom. She looked at Iver in a suspicious way, then read her list of orders to the anxious father.

"Now, Irene needs lots of rest Mr. Krough, so for a week or so you will have to wait on her instead of the other way around. She has already been through one terrible ordeal, we don't want her to go through another, do we?"

Flight of the Kroughs

Iver's stomach came to a boil then settled down as his memory took him back to the time of their first child's birth - and death. Then he silently told Mrs. Jackson to "Kiss his you know what, and take her bluntness and leave." As he thought those words, she did ••• leave that is.

Iver entered the bedroom and discovered what the scraping and sliding noise was all about; the women from the neighborhood had arranged all of the bedroom furniture into different locations. Ordinarily he would have expressed wonderment at such a useless exercise, but as soon as he viewed the setting, he understood.

The one large and two small ladies had moved the full sized bed, with Irene and the baby in it, over to the window with the southern exposure.

Iver moved across the floor and dropped to one knee beside the bed. He studied the new prize; then he studied his wife.

"What a beautiful child" he said proudly. "So strong looking and long. I'm sure he will grow to be a strapping young man in a few years." Then as a shaft of sunlight danced through the tattered shade, he softly cupped Irene's face in the palms of his hands then placed a whisper of a kiss on her full, naturally blushed lips. The mid-morning sun poured generous energy through the southern window, providing a warm glow to the scene.

Suddenly, after a silent pause, Iver posed the question concerning a name for the young man. In the process of managing their lives leading up to the successful birth of their child, little thought had been given to creating a list of suitable names from which to choose.

Irene took her husband's hand, gave it a squeeze, and told him that he had first choice.

After thinking for a moment, he commented, "He is a strong looking lad, so he ought to have a good strong name. You know, Irene, that I lost two brothers to influenza back in eighteen, how do you feel about using one of their names, or better, part of each?" They chose the latter, and would call him James Lawrence Krough.

Having chosen a name, Irene's face relaxed into a warm smile. Then in deep concentration, she stared at the ceiling. "James Lawrence, what a fine strong name" she whispered.

The new parents conversed long into the afternoon with Irene doing most of the talking. Iver did little except nod and agree, which illustrated, though his wife hadn't yet realized it, the difference between her age and his secret age. For she was young and could still dream, and he was on the verge of passing into the age of cynicism. So, had the innocent young mother known all there was to know about him, it would have been no surprise to her that when she too was thinking aloud about how much stronger and how much taller James would become, Iver became detached from the scene. His mind was traveling on a different train of thought. Because, an itch was growing inside him that was too deep to scratch.

Baby James squealed for food, and his father was quickly snatched from the fence he had been straddling between the real world with his wife and son in it, and his dream world carpeted with green pastures.

Irene took baby James Lawrence to her warm loving breast and lightly fingered his dark silky hair while he satisfied his need for nourishment. Iver watched and became so emotionally involved in the scene that it alternately sent hot flashes of joy throughout his chest and face, and cold chills of he knew not what down his spine.

James received his fill, a change into clean clothes, then fell into a contented sleep beside his mother's warm protecting body. Within five minutes Irene joined him. Mr. Krough walked softly from the bedroom and pulled the door shut behind him.

He went to the well, from which, he pulled up a bucket of water, then returned to the kitchen range and made a fresh pot of coffee. When it had brewed, he poured a cup, then sat at the table and thought. He asked himself what he was afraid of. Right away he got no answer from himself. After forty-five minutes of intense self analysis, and four cups of coffee, part of the answer finally occurred to him. Irene was young and could dream about what could be and had the will, if not the means, to make the dream real. He, on the other hand, was past forty now, and all that he knew he could provide was the means to barely survive. Oh, Iver yet had his dreams, but his problem was that the dreams were never carried to a successful conclusion.

By the time James had reached his six month milestone, Iver acted on the nagging impulse that had tormented him for those same six months.

It was payday Friday. He signed for his final check, then headed for the south side of town. But before going home, his scheme called for him to make stops at a couple of stores on the edge of town, not very far from where they lived. An hour later Irene watched through the window as he jumped out of his Ford and fished three packages from the rumble seat.

It required no great power of deductive reasoning to describe the contents in one of the bundles. It was roundish measuring in the area of three inches thick by eight inches long. "It is definitely from the butcher shop, and it is no doubt liver" Irene guessed.

Then she dared to guess again, and hoped for hamburger, but the two remaining packages were a mystery to her.

Iver kicked his cow dung caked boots off at the porch; then he entered the kitchen.

He chucked the soft round package on the kitchen cabinet, then he tossed the other two mysterious packages at his wife. Before she could begin ripping the string and tearing the paper from the largest of the packages, Iver planted an extra special kiss on her cheek. His suprising gesture if not making her suspicious, it definitely raised her curiosity. Irene tolerated Iver's patronizing advances, put her feelings of uneasiness aside, then resumed her assault on the larger of the two bundles. When she at last arrived at its contents, she discovered six yards of fine cotton print material. As Irene held it up to examine the pattern and quality of the goods, he informed her that the lady at the dry goods told him that there was enough for a dress and enough left over for an apron, which would make one of her old dresses look new ... "useless information" mumbled Irene silently.

She draped the cotton cloth around her neck and over her shoulders. As she stroked its texture, she thanked her husband and complimented him on his excellent taste in material, then wished she had returned his kiss. She then turned her attention to the third bundle. When she opened that one, a pair of baby shoes emerged. They were little James' first high laced, hard soled, shoes. The young mother turned the shoes over and over in her hands. As she did so, she told her husband that it was a little early for such footwear, but they would keep for three or four months.

Irene was happy for her young son, and happy for herself also, but at the same time she could tell that some sort of scheme was brewing inside her husbands head. She decided against any attempt to satisfy her curiosity right then by challenging him to tell her what he had in mind. But, as it turned out, she didn't have long to wait before finding out anyway, only about three hours in fact.

It was then nine thirty p.m. and the couple was lying in bed, back to back, and both were fully awake. Iver was first to break the thin silence as he rolled toward his wife and raised his head, propping it on his left arm and hand.

He began to speak to the back of Irene's head. "They're opening a new meat packing plant in north Kansas City, and they need a lot of help."

Irene pilfered a secret smile of relief in the moonlit dark-ness.

Iver continued, saying "more money and no work on Saturdays."

Irene heaved a carefully disguised sigh of relief.

Although she knew they would need to move, she also knew that it would only be across town. Her silence pleased Iver.

Knowing that his pending adventure was sanctioned by his junior partner, he rolled lightly out of bed the following morning at six thirty. He lit a fire and made a pot of coffee.

He enjoyed the first cup by himself in contemplative silence. In a sort of mental practice run, he moved his view around the kitchen. In his mind, he packed everything they owned into the little Ford. When he had finished his exercise, he was a bit apprehensive about whether or not the little coupe would carry everything. He decided that they would take with them what was important, and throw on the trash heap what wasn't. That worry dispensed with, it was time for another cup of coffee, only the next pouring was for two. One of them he delivered, as he whistled through disappearing teeth, to his not so overjoyed wife. She was up and nearly dressed, and her mood not withstanding, Irene accepted the hot drink with a gracious smile of average intensity.

Irene then sat on the edge of their steel-framed bed and took two sips. She then straightened to her feet, walked quickstep into the kitchen, told Iver that there was much to do, then fixed them each a hearty breakfast, to, as she put it, move on.

A scant two hours later the rumble seat of the Ford was loaded with pots, pans, dishes, silverware, clothes and food.

Tied to the roof of the car was James' sea trunk bed, which was also filled with miscellaneous personal property.

Iver made one last tour around the house and yard but saw nothing that they had overlooked. They then mounted the car's running boards and stepped in, Irene mildly reluctant and he full of excitement. In the rearview mirror the chief wanderer viewed only a slightly larger pile on the scrap heap than he had anticipated, and at that he was pleased. "Not bad" he complimented himself - silently, of course.

"A new job, more money, by God I think this time, no ... I know, my ship has finally docked."

Had Irene been able to read his thoughts, she might have thought back at him "Pretty lofty thinking for a person on his way to slaughter innocent cows, worn out from too many births and too little grass, and bulls worn to barely a flabby nub; not to mention the fact that you haven't been hired yet."

Iver, however, kept his straight and narrow mental course while weaving the over-loaded car on its merry trip, and dreamed his way north across Kansas City. Although the move took less than a day, to Irene the move was still a traumatic event.

"As one cow looks and acts like another, and their home is merely a chunk of earth with boards around it, it will be easy for Iver to re-adjust, but not so for me" thought Irene. "I have to take another rundown shack and turn it into a home, and I have to get acquainted with new neighbors."

Before looking for a place to live, Iver asked for, and received, directions to his place of potential employment. Just as he had seen in his vision, there was a sea of cattle, but unlike Irene's description of them, they were young six hundred to a thousand pound prime beef cattle and each one of them had a date with that "one-way" iron-gated stall.

Iver's body quivered with excitement. To display his confidence, he informed his wife that they wouldn't sleep in the car while he waited to be hired ...they would look for a place to live straight way. Luck seemed to favor them; they found a place not far from the smelly meat packing plant where Iver was positive he would find work.

The next morning was Sunday, so Iver had to lie in bed late, since he had nothing else to do. For the rest of that day he just walked the floor with his hands in his pockets waiting for it to end.

He welcomed Monday morning like a politician welcomes money. He reported to the front office of the Meat Packing Plant where he proceeded to exaggerate his qualifications, and was hired; all in the space of one hour. His job was head gate keeper, and from the point of view of the cattle, their grim reaper.

Good money not withstanding, Iver soon grew weary of dealing the fatal blow that provided an ample supply of choice steak to the many fancy eating places and elegant homes of Kansas City, not to mention of course, guaranteeing a plentiful supply of liver, heart, kidney, tail, and that special delicacy - ground up scraps known as "hamburger" for the employees and other less fortunate folks. So, he again employed his considerable boasting talent in a successful bid to be transferred back to a job for which he was better qualified, tending to the needs and the feeding of the animals.

For nearly two years he cared for his transient herd, and during that two years Irene created from almost nothing, a comfortable, it not elegant, home. It was also enough time for her husband to help her achieve her third pregnancy, and for Calvin Coolidge to inherit the White House.

"Just another tight-fisted, God damned Republican" Iver would curse. He distrusted Republicans nearly as much as he disliked doctors, except, of course, when his wife needed a doctor to help her bring the new Krough kid into the world.

And that time, it was a picture perfect girl. She was dark like her mother, and she looked a lot like her Aunt whom Irene had sadly left broken hearted back in Brookside.

Iver and Irene decided to call her Viola. Two in a row, the happy mother bragged gratefully, and silently. Without her knowing it, the pain of losing her first one was blurred from her conscious memory.

Viola reached her six month milestone quickly as far as Irene was concerned. Because her husband was making good money, when her children needed something she could supply it.

Before another two weeks had passed, however, Iver began to act uneasy. It was clear to Irene that he had, once more, come down with his mysterious itch.

Besides the fact that it was time to celebrate Viola's half year anniversary, it was also Christmas time, and, as before Iver marched up the path to the house carrying an arm load of packages. When he entered the kitchen, leaving his cow-dung caked boots on the porch, of course, he marched stocking footed across the kitchen floor, and placed his offerings on the table. Iver had expected his wife to attack the parcels immediately, when she didn't, he urged her on with a generous gesture with his arm. Finally responding, more-so to please him than to please herself, Irene studied the three parcels for a teasingly long time, perhaps a full two minutes. Then she passed her husband a cool, suspicious look. Next, and only half interested, Irene shuffled the colorful boxes around on her kitchen table. Iver ached for his wife to be overcome with joyous curiosity, but rather, she slowly and carefully took each box apart and placed its contents on the table. She then examined the goods expressionlessly and speechlessly. Secretly, the young mother was glad for herself and Viola for the new dresses, and also for James for his pair of stripped bib overalls.

As before, Iver had done an outstanding job of shopping. To his disappointment, Irene displayed only mild satisfaction. By then she had become wise to the ways of her partner, and knew that there was more wrapped up in those boxes than early Christmas presents and that her growing family's circumstances were about to go through a drastic change. But, on that occasion, Irene, out of genuine concern for her babies, voiced worries she dared only mumble in the security offered by silence before: that Iver must, this time, consider his family's welfare and not just his own.

"Another fact you must take into account, is, that we are finally on our feet. We have a nice home, plenty of food in the cupboard, adequate clothing, and two hundred dollars saved-up", she bravely preached.

So, on that pre-Christmas evening Iver nodded his understanding of Irene's apprehension as they had sat in bed talking it over. He maintained his insistence that the urge he felt to return to Utah was more than he could overcome, and that, in the long run, the move would benefit them all. Irene stood her ground stubbornly to the extent that she coaxed a promise from her impulsive husband that they would, at least, delay the start of their new adventure until the coming of spring, which was no puny concession for Iver to make.

She felt, after the conversation had ended, that she had been allowed to win the battle, but had been manipulated into surrendering the war.

He, on the other hand, felt good about the compromise he had achieved. However, it did create a slight problem for him: he had quit his job.

The next morning Irene packed his lunch as usual, and off he went to eat crow for dessert.

The people at the Packing Plant were glad to hire him back. Afterall, the foreman reasoned, he had been a good worker, and it beat breaking in another man.

Flight of the Kroughs

From that evening forward, the thought of that impossible trip haunted Irene. "But after all," she thought, "the Preacher said 'for better or for worse', but how come there is so much more worse than there is better?"

Iver thought much about the bold move as well, but in a more positive, even aggressive fashion. He wasn't filled with doubt and dread like his wife. His vision of the future traveled down an exceedingly narrow path paved with euphoric certainty and was littered with a good share of fool heartiness to boot.

No one could have labelled Iver a fool though. If he were, some of his wild adventures would never have been accomplished.

So the common sense worrying was left to Irene by default, and, as if the worrying was not enough for her, the major share of sacrifice was expected of her as well.

After some of the tension generated by Iver's shocking decision had subsided, he informed his wife that she would need to get by with half the house money she was accustomed to so she could put the rest in the bottom dresser drawer to save for the trip.

As an expression of spite, and as a practical solution, Irene merely inserted more potato and bean dishes into her husband's diet. Iver failed to notice the difference, but he never failed to notice the travel fund. Before retiring each night he counted it to satisfy himself that all rules concering the money were being observed. In fact and, much to his delight, he was ahead of schedule - dollarwise, thanks to his wife's management skills.

The weeks passed quickly for her, but slowly for him. Turning winter to spring and spring to late spring.

The funds were accumulated, and Irene's nerves came closer to the surface. To her, from Missouri to Alabama was half a world travel, but Utah was on another planet, and the more she fretted about the move, the wider the distance between the two states became, and in her mind, there was no happy thought of the journey ending - only the dread of having it start.

With little fanfare, but to a silent chorus of left to right head-shakes performed by her neighbor lady friends -which were aimed deliberately at Iver, Irene gathered up her two babies and placed them in the car. Then in a puff of blue smoke, they began their journey west.

By the time her husband had shoved the shifting lever confidently into its highest gear, Irene's mind was already filled to overflowing with negative thoughts. True, she had at last put her foot down, demanded, and received her way in the selection of the season during which they would make the trip. But, as the first mile of that trip registered on the odometer, a disturbing fact occurred to her; had she given the subject more consideration, she would have realized that when making such an extended trip, so much time would be consumed that more than one season would be used.

Right beside that disturbing fact lay the reality that that time of the year held its own unpredictable peril. Autumn had its rain and early frost - winter had its blizzards, freezing rain, and bitter cold - and early spring had its late snow, frost, and normal rain. But worse, in the flat lands of Kansas, nature's season with a mean streak - late spring and summer – provided wild weather as well, which came in the form of torrential rains and sometimes with a tornado twin.

So, in deference to the fact that it was early summer – the first of July of 24 - nine p.m. was, in any man's language, late in the day for travel. But Iver boldly steered the valiant Model "T" carrying himself, his family, and all their earthly possessions without complaints over the highway. At the same time Irene was reliving, in thought, the fifteen minutes that had just passed, when, after much building of nerve, she had suggested to her husband that, since they were passing through a small town, and since the car had already done more than an honest day's work, they should stop for the night. Maybe find a friendly church and park beneath one of its trees if it had any. But all that she received for her logical request was a look from her companion hat sarcastically asked "What the hell do you know about things?"

So, she offered no more counsel on the subject. From past experience Irene had learned that her point of view made little impact on her husband's bullheaded self-confidence. As, for Iver, it was always just one more mile of an empty gas gauge before stopping to refuel, or just five more miles before stopping for the night. So the young mother kept the remainder of her concerns a secret and returned her concentration to the narrow dark road and what she feared the night might hold for her babies. Mr. Krough, the supreme commander of the vehicle, boldly urged the fatigued automobile onward for a few more miles, then started on a new batch of miles. How far they had travelled so far that day Irene could only guess.

Gently, and without their knowing it, due to the blackness, the lay of the land had begun to rise and fall and the road faithfully followed.

Very soon after that, Iver awakened to the realization that they were moving through a wide series of gulleys that seemed to be spaced about one quarter of a mile apart.

Not long after discovering the ripples that corrugated the surface of that part of Kansas, Iver noticed another, even more unsettling fact; the moon and stars had been curtained behind thick black clouds. Due to that discovery, Iver, at last, experienced a quiver of uneasiness. Soon his uneasiness changed to out-right concern when wet specks began to appear on the dusty wiper-less windshield like pock marks. As the tiny solitary

Flight of the Kroughs

vehicle curved downward over the brim of the deepest wash yet encountered, the suddenly organized storm's first wave of attack, consisting of pea sized drops, began ricocheting from the car's tar impregnated canvas roof. In Irene's private opinion, the sound was like a warning beat from a million distant drums. A warning that would, most likely, go unheeded by her husband, of that she was sure. But on that occasion, Mrs. Krough had made a rare mistake in judgment concerning her husband. Because, in truth, Iver only pretended not to pay heed to those ominous signs. If honesty had been his forte, he would have needed to admit that it was too late to analyze their circumstances. All they could do was hope for the best.

After about thirty seconds of the storm's softening-up barrage, the threat from above became promise, and the clouds broadcast their full, unrestrained fury upon and all around the pitiful little group crowded into the Model "T". Through the slimy darkness, Irene's eyes emitted the terror she felt, first for her children then for herself. She wanted to scream, but was afraid to do so because she feared angering the force that was consuming them even more. The only alternative left for her was to offer a silent prayer to her God, and beg that God to overrule those forces, or, better still, allow her to waken and find that the trip was nothing but a bad dream. But her God must have had a bad connection because the raging storm answered her pleading by pounding the struggling Ford with fistful drops of rain.

Iver could only guess the direction of the road. As, seconds apart, jagged spears of lightening split the boiling sky, succeeded by exploding clusters of thunder that shook to life and rattled loose areas of the Model "T" that were, until then, unknown.

Yet the car and its precious cargo continued to fall, feeling longingly for the bottom of the gulley.

Due to water saturated brake shoe linings, the speed at which they drove to the bottom was dictated by the degree of slope of the hill. When they did finally reach the bottom, Iver would learn that brakes would not be necessary anyway, because, after sloshing to a quick stop, he discovered yet more disturbing facts. First, due to the racket produced by the storm, he hadn't noticed that the car's engine had quit, thanks to a swamped electrical system, and second, but more frightening, the heavy downpour of rain had turned the once dry floor of the gulley into a surging river two feet deep.

To some unconcerned bystander it might have been a comic scene reminiscent of many silent movies of the day, to see the old Ford plop to an abrupt stop in the temporary muddy river. But to Irene, and maybe even to Iver, it was far from a comedy.

For just an instant they only sat there in stunned silence. Then Irene felt the water moving past her feet and up her ankles.

She was sure that the water was about to swallow them up, car and all, and James and Viola would surely die.

For an instant she was ready to let what would happen, happen. Then Iver looked at her. for the first time he confessed his stupidity ... if not by word of mouth then at least through facial expression. She turned her tear streaked face away from his view so she could hide an "I told you so" look.

The water soon reached the top of Iver's shoes and poured inside to swamp his feet, then he too became panic stricken. As always, when he found himself in an uncomfortable situation, the first words that came from his mouth were linked together with profanity; "This God-damned son-of-a-bitchen piece of junk" - referring to his defenseless car of course.

"You take Viola, and I'll take James .. then you get the hell out of here."

By the time the last of his words ordering his crew to abandon ship had been drowned out by the rain and surging water, Iver had turned toward his door and was jerking its handle to the unlatched position, as, he was hell bent on escaping their death trap. But, it seemed as if the young mother had, to some extent, anticipated the order, thereby, reacting to the danger quicker than her husband. So by the time her husband circled to the rear of the quickly foundering car, she was already lunging and stumbling through the stream of hip high putrid water. Water that carried all sorts of foreign objects in its swift current.

She was headed for the safety offered by high ground. As he, with a terrified look on his face, and with an even more terrified and screaming child slung over his shoulder gained on his wife through the agitating water.

Irene suddenly stopped. She was hit with the disturbing realization that, even if they should survive the flood, they had nothing that would be dry to change into. Or, not one blanket to keep the family warm, so they might die of exposure.

She turned back toward the car and began shouting to Iver, hoping to gain his attention in the noisy darkness. By the time the pair was nearly face to face, she finally achieved success. Continuing to scream so to be sure her husband heard her correctly, Irene told him that she had stacked the bedding on the shelf between the back of the seat and the rear window, and that he should give her James, then return to the car and rescue the covers before the water went higher and carried them down stream.

"While you're at it", she added, "bring the box of clean clothes that rested on the same shelf".

Iver willingly obeyed her order, though unsure of its wisdom.

By the time he had retrieved the blankets and the box of clothes, and had led his family up the eastern slope of the gully to the protection afforded by the limbs and leaves of a large oak tree, the rain had finally stopped, which for the Krough family, was some, but little comfort.

Flight of the Kroughs

Irene carefully rolled each of her bewildered, but quiet, children in a blanket, then tossed a blanket to her husband, the last one she kept for herself. Then she joined Iver in changing into dry clothes.

After that difficult exercise, the young mother collapsed to the ground, she spread her blanket across her shoulders and down between her back and the trunk of the benevolent tree, to the damp Kansas earth. She then tucked a child under each arm and pulled the ends of the blanket around the three of them.

As she sat supported by the strong tree, staring south-east, which was the general direction of her beloved Alabama -Iver sat, likewise, supported by the same tree, but, facing in the guessed direction of Virtue Valley, Utah. "What the hell am I doing here?" he asked himself, over and over, again and again ...silently, of course. He folded his arms and rested them on his upbended knees. In a minute or two he dropped his forehead onto his arms and pinned his stare on the invisible earth. His mind was blank, which was just what his imagination wanted to hear.

He suddenly found himself wandering along a wet, two-rut farm lane. Soon, he came upon a once sound farm house, but, even by Iver's lose standards, it had been let go.

Shading his eyes from the low morning sun, the distressed visitor searched the ragged scene for signs of life; the sound of animals, or better still ... people. He spied nothing surrounding the homestead to suggest any life.

As he turned his study back to the house, he was pleased to discover a silent silvery whisk of smoke climbing to the sky out of the crumbling red brick chimney. Iver leaned over and folded a neat cuff in his trousers, tucked his shirt in properly, removed his hat and pushed ten fingers, counting thumbs, through his hair. He flexed his shoulders, then headed up the seldom used pathway to the front entrance.

First he tapped shyly on the door, but nothing happened.

Next he gave the door a good confident knock, but, still no response.

Having nothing to lose, he then pounded boldly until the door rattled on its oxidized hinges. Iver waited a few seconds ... nothing ... so he started to turn away, but halfway through his turn he was frozen in place by the sound of a husky, yet feminine voice.

"What do you want mister?"

Iver realized that the voice was coming from the safety of an upstairs window.

"Had car trouble two, maybe three miles back, and I need help."

"You alone" the voice asked suspiciously.

"No, my wife and two kids stayed with the car."

"Got anything on you that's worth a damn?" the woman asked.

"My wallet" offered Iver hopefully while wondering why he had taken the trouble to answer such a seemingly irrelevant question. "But there's only a couple of dollars in it."

"That'll do" she said. "Put it on the porch, then you can go to the shed and harness up the mules and go get your outfit and family."

Iver was so relieved that he thanked the, so far, invisible woman until he ran it into the ground. He did as he was told, and within an hour he returned driving his Model "T" slowly with the two mules in tow, and his family piled in the front seat.

Seeing her mules returned safely, the woman moved down the stairs and opened her front door. She noticed the two babies clinging to Irene, and her mood mellowed. "Well, just don't sit there with your face hanging out" she shouted to Iver, "get yer wife and kids out of that sorry piece of junk you call a car and bring them in the house."

He left her animals stay tied to the bumper of his car and, again, did as the woman told him.

As the barely elderly woman led the Krough family through her front room to the kitchen, Iver and Irene experienced parallel feelings of uneasiness. The front room was dark and he was sure he saw dust rising from the floor and draped furniture as they trooped through. When they arrived at the kitchen it was straight away obvious to the visitors that this was where she lived. He made his assumption based on the fact that there was a cot, rocking chair, and night table crammed in one corner of the cluttered room, and Irene most likely used the same evidence.

They finally introduced one another, and her name turned out to be Anna.

She gave her permission to the Kroughs to stay the day and night to rest. From her cupboard and cellar, Anna rustled up a good meal for her company, then suggested to Iver that he take his family to the back porch where he would find a couple of steel cots, there they could get some real rest. He willingly obeyed.

How long he slept, he wasn't sure. But, when he quietly got off the cot and started through the kitchen door, he noticed Anna sleeping soundly on her own cot.

Instead of bothering his hostess, he decided to explore her place. As Iver walked every foot of Anna's homestead, he saw evidence of a once productive farm. Equipment of every conceivable purpose was scattered about the place, but was buried in several years of unharvested and uncontrolled grass and weeds. On the northeast corner of the front piece of ground was a magnificent red barn with a round roof. Such a building was rare and lit up Iver's interest.

Flight of the Kroughs

He decided to explore that also, but when he got close enough to touch and feel the barn's siding, he realized that every opening was locked tightly shut. Iver wouldn't tell Anna of his trip to the barn, but what mysteries were locked inside haunted him constantly.

That evening, after everyone had enjoyed their rest, another good meal was put on the table, this time, with Irene's help.

After eating, Iver decided it to be only fair for him to go outside and find some chores to do. He chopped wood for an hour, then cleaned up around and set fire to the garbage pit. When he re-entered the house Anna was obviously pleased. After an hour of discussion, the hostess and her guests returned to their beds, and Anna slept with a placid smile on her face, as she had been reminded of the joy derived from conversation and company.

The first day stretched into two days, and those two days into a week, and the week into a month. By then Anna and the Kroughs had come to love each other deeply. Also Anna had come to appreciate Iver a great deal. During the month he spent at Anna's home, he had fixed the roof, glazed a couple windows and washed the rest, chopped the grass and weeds to ankle height, and was digging a new trash pit. When he had just tossed the last shovel of dirt out of the hole in the ground, he looked up, and standing over him on the edge was Anna. In a tender, motherly way, she coaxed Iver from the pit. When out, she led him to a bench that was situated under a willow tree that had branches and slender limbs that cascaded limply to the ground, making it necessary for Iver to separate the growth for the pair, like it was heavy green drapery. Then they sat on the bench.

She took his hand in hers. "Mr. Krough" Anna began, "I have come to have great regard for you and your family. So now I think that it's time that I tell you a little about myself."

"There was a time, a long time ago, when I had a wonderful husband,- in fact he was a lot like you - he was a handyman of sorts. I'm sure you have heard the worn out phrase 'Jack of all trades' repeated many times. Well, my husband was. But, unlike the saying, he was master of them all."

"He made money on cars, on farming, in lumber, and even junk, which he collected, traded and sold. And his territory stretched from Denver to Kansas City - east and west, and from Omaha to St.Louis - north and south."

"In his travels my husband collected many treasures. I couldn't bear to dispose of them and, certainly, I would never sell them."

"To be quite honest with you Mr. Krough, I don't really know what he had stored up in that old barn, only that he always kept the most valuable of his treasures locked up there."

"Now though, I know what to do, and it's like being released from a kind of a prison."

"Iver" Anna said, looking him deep in his eyes, "here are the keys to that barn; everything in there is yours."

He could hardly believe what he was hearing.

Anna squeezed the keys into Mr. Krough's perspiring hands. Then she smiled, now, he knew that she was serious.

"Now tomorrow morning, early, you go to your barn and take stock. After you have removed from it what you wish, I would like for you to put a match to it for me."

Iver could only shake his head ... yes, it said.

"I'm glad we have had this talk, now, put yourself and your family to bed early tonight."

Faithfully, at six thirty the next morning, he went to the barn and opened wide its main door. Before him stood a shiny new, large truck - about a two tonner Iver guessed. He ran the palms of his rough hands lovingly over it's slick green and black finish. But impressive as the truck was, he knew there was more.

Box after box was stacked in every corner and every square foot of floor space. By noon, after Iver had rifled each of them, he stood knee deep in treasure.

There were complete coin collections, stamp collections, solid silver service sets, rare art objects, and boxes of gold and silver coins. Iver frantically dumped boxes of important, but unwanted, items and used those boxes to hold what he had selected. Then he quickly loaded his boxes onto his truck, then he ran to its front, twisted the crank, and wonder of wonders, it started. Filled with excitement, he started back to the cab to stop the engine but was surprised to see Irene and the children standing in the barn doorway ready to leave.

On the back porch of the house Anna stood smiling ... and Iver knew then himself that it was time to go.

Mr. Krough, his wife, and their two babies piled in the truck, then he backed it out of the barn. When he had cleared the building by ten feet, Iver lit a match and pitched it into a barn full of paper and empty boxes.

He turned the truck around and headed onto the road waving to Anna as they left. As they headed onto the road, Iver looked into his rearview mirror and was surprised to see that the house, as well as the barn, was a blazing inferno.

Suddenly his brand new truck started to pitch and roll, and something was tearing at his shoulder. Soon he could hear Irene faintly calling his name, and the violent motion stopped.

Mrs. Krough looked down at her confused husband, who had gone from a sitting position against the oak tree to a fetal position on the damp Kansas ground, and told him that he had been going through a rough sleep. She

Flight of the Kroughs

asked if he was alright. Mr. Krough shook his head clear of the disappointment he felt upon waking from his half day dream and reassured his wife that he was fine.

As Irene had sat with her back against the cool tree, there was no pleasant dream for her.

While she was looking southeast, the first thought she experienced surprised her. She remembered, that, while standing in the waist deep water fearing for her babies' lives, she, for the first time ever since their lives merged, had ordered her husband to do something, and he did it with no hesitation.

Although it was a satisfying recollection, Irene decided that it would be safer to gloat privately. Other thoughts would cross her mind as well as the seemingly endless night crawled by. Of those thoughts, most concerned her current situation. The realization that, in fact, her journey had started long before she met Iver ... indeed before she was born, occurred to her.

She had been told by her mother that her Grandfather had once owned a four hundred acre farm in Carter County, Kentucky back in the second half of the eighteen hundreds. The principal crop produced was legal whiskey. However, one season - his last one - Grandfather was overtaken with greed, so neglected to secure the necessary legal permission. Considering the money the whiskey manufacturer turned moonshiner was about to earn that season, one of his brothers became acutely jealous. So he hiked up into the hills, barged into his brothers brand new secret stil site, and demanded a share of the profits ... in exchange, of course, for his silence.

Naturally Grandfather Coburn became instantly enraged and promptly threw the "freeloading, blackmailing, son-of- a-bitch" off his property. The brother, scorned, stomped down the mountain, but after stomping about fifty yards down the slope, he stopped and turned back toward the summit. From that safe distance he shouted his warning. He told his brother that first he was going to report the location of the illegal business to the sheriff, then he was coming straight back to the camp with his shotgun and blow his head off.

Although Irene's Grandfather could have stayed and put up a fight, he decided against it for the sake of his wife and children, not to mention his fear of landing in jail. So he hightailed it to his farmhouse at the foot of the mountain and quickly hitched his pair of mules to the wagon; then he ran to the house and told his wife of his plans ... she said he could go to hell, she wasn't leaving. "Well you have a choice then, you can stay here all alone, or get on the wagon with the three kids." She climbed onto the wagon with her children - their dog - their clothes, and their kitchen range. And away the pair of shakey mules went pulling the fully loaded, iron tired, wagon.

They traveled southeast and took up residence on the Kentucky side of the Ohio River. There, their grandson Jackson Coburn, met Rosanna Mitchell.

By the time Irene had been born, and had grown to a young lady, the Coburns had traveled south through Kentucky, then south through Tennessee, and finally into Alabama, stopping at last at Brookside.

And all the way the men folk mined coal. It occurred to Irene as she leaned against the trunk of the protective oak tree that her current trip was only another leg of a journey, its ultimate destination a mystery to her.

All of those thoughts came to her while she faced southeast. She then turned her head in the direction of her husband.

How strong Iver's features looked, especially when the flames from a respectable fire he had created from damp grass and twigs danced on his face. It was then, for the first time, that she noticed something physically different about him.

Because the wind had piled her husband's abundant, rain-soaked, black hair on top of his head, it revealed silver grey roots. The young woman wasn't surprised by her discovery, only unsure of its extent due to the unreliable light given off by the fire. After all, he was thirty-two by that time, as far as she knew anyway. In any case, Irene had been conditioned to believe that graying at the edges made a man look dignified. It was supposed to give a girl a feeling of security.

But, in truth, what little security Iver could offer his young wife at that moment wouldn't fill a bull durham sack. Not even the one he was about to throw away after dumping its contents into a chunk of brown paper bag.

With each of her arms circled around a dozing child, other thoughts continued to grow in Irene's mind as she sat watching her husband. She recalled how diligently Iver had worked at convincing her that the trip would be a snap. He told her of the many pioneer women who had crossed the plains to California, Oregon and Utah, just a little to the north. "And more remarkable" he told his wife "they made the trek with nothing more than oxen, mules, or horses pulling iron-tired canvas-covered wagons, and they were the luckier ones because others even walked the dusty, and sometimes, muddy trails, pulling hand carts.

Upon hearing those sobering tales of hardship and heroism told to her by her husband, Irene began to wonder. She speculated more about the women who had made those trips, and less about the men. She wondered if they, the women, had been given the choice of making or not making such trips. Had it been worth it in terms of health and safety of the very young and, even more so, the very old. Irene had heard or read somewhere about the many graves along the trails that contained the bodies of babies and grandparents.

Flight of the Kroughs

Then she re-focused her thoughts upon her own situation. She wondered if she herself had been given a choice or, more honestly, had she allowed herself a choice. Was she just like those pioneer women who were so conditioned by their acceptance of domination by men that she fortified her right to make a choice. Then another sobering thought occurred to her: "Suppose I had put my foot down in Kansas City and Iver had decided to go on without me or the children - then what? And just suppose all those pioneer women had done the same. The result would surely have been the same - thousands of fatherless children."

"Because", her thoughts continued, when religion calls, or the dream of riches or even the dream of a better life takes hold in a man's head, the best and only thing a smart woman can do is hold on to her man and let him have his dream because, it seems, destiny comes first, family second. But, Irene went on "those earlier travelers did have one ... no, three advantages: number one, they had safety in numbers. Number two, they didn't have to depend on a mechanical rattle trap of a Model "T". They used horses that only ate grass and made fertilizer. And, finally, if the pioneers got hungry enough, they could, as a last resort anyway, eat their transportation. I would like to see Iver try doing that with his precious Ford."

After all of that staring and thinking, mother and father Krough joined their children in a shallow sleep.

While in their trauma induced daze, they failed to hear the squeak of wet leather on wet leather, and the clink of bare metal hanging loosely from the sides of a pair of mules pulling a wagon down that long, steep hill. When the skinner in charge had first observed the lost-looking family huddled under the leaves and limbs of the oak tree, he must have rearranged, but used the same sentence Iver had when he asked, "What the hell are they doing up there?"

Seeing the Model "T" axle deep in mud at the bottom of the gulley answered his question.

The lower middle-aged skinner could only fashion half a whistle through a set of teeth that were only half there, but he would do his best. He told himself that it made more sense to whistle than to climb up the steep hillside because he wasn't too sure about whose shoulder he might be shaking. So he sucked in all the air his lungs would hold, then released it with a shove through his teeth several times until, at last, the largest body moved.

Actually, Iver had gone through just a bit of play acting. He had come out of his sleep when the sound of loose tack slapping the sides of the mules first split the early morning air. It was the fact that he didn't know what was making the sound that made him remain motionless.

His worry laid to rest, Iver pitched forward, rose downhill to his feet, and ambled in an elevated state of embarrassment to meet the curious stranger.

After the handshake ritual and the exchanging of first names, the pair turned and walked toward the silt-impounded Ford. As they restrained their gate down the hill, Arnold, Ivor's new friend, preached to him that they were all very lucky, and he hoped that he had learned something about the weather on the plains of Kansas, "And other thing," Arnold piped, "I lost twelve good hogs down this same damnable rut last night. By tomorrow they will be picked-apart by the crows and the other pigs that were better swimmers - God knows where they're at."

Seeing that the stranger was intent on continuing his journey, Arnold suggested that they hook the mules to the stuck vehicle and pull it to his farm back up the road. Then, while the morning sun dried it out, the family could rest at his farm house, where the wife would be honored to fix breakfast for them.

Iver agreed without hesitation. So he turned toward the tree and motioned to Irene to come to the road and join them - and bring the kids. She yelled ok, but he would need to come help. Iver gave a quick look at Arnold then moved swiftly to the oak tree and helped gather up blankets and children.

Arnold's wife must have seen the party coming because when the mules had deposited them at the kitchen porch, breakfast was on the table.

Iver and his host consumed their meal in a hurry. From the kitchen they went to the front porch where they decided that, in recognition of the trauma suffered by the little Ford, it would be wiser for the Krough Family to spend not just the day, but the coming night, as Arnold's and his wife's guests.

"Now that is a sensible decision that Irene will appreciate", Iver boasted silently.

After arriving at that decision, the men strolled to the barn yard where the recuperating car was parked. Rummaging through the trunk they found, much to Iver's disappointment, that most the food stored for the trip was ruined. So they just heaved it over the fence and let the surviving pigs fight over the junk.

From the barn Arnold led Iver to the root cellar. On the cross beams hung bag after bag of dry beans, dried corn, and dried green peas. And in one corner, piled on dunnage, were ten sacks of flour.

The next stop on the tour was the smoke house. There Iver gazed jealously at ranks of dark brown delicious smelling hams and slabs of side pork.

Iver and Arnold then returned to the house where all of the kitchen chores had been accomplished by the women folk.

Flight of the Kroughs

The four of them went back to the table, and, over several pots of coffee, they spent the majority of the day getting better acquainted.

Late in the afternoon Iver went to the barn with his new friend and gave him a hand doing the chores. That finished, the two men again returned to the house where more talking was enjoyed, supper was consumed, the children prepared for bed, and yet more conversation took place among adults. Then the two couples occupied their beds.

Although Arnold and his wife wished their guests a good nights sleep, Iver and Irene would not be so lucky.

Iver, while tossing and turning could think only of getting back on the road.

Irene stared into the darkness most of the night wishing they were heading east rather than west.

It seemed to the pair that sleep and the sun arrived together, as a soft tap on the door brought them from their beds as tired as when they climbed into them the night before.

After a quick wash-up Iver and Irene found breakfast on the table. Arnold beckoned to them, so Irene urged the children to the table. A special prayer was offered by Arnold to insure a safer trip for the Krough Family. He blessed the ford as well.

When the morning feast had been climaxed with a cup of coffee, Iver slipped his hand into Arnold's and gave it a good sincere pump. Irene then embraced her hostess and friend, and with her husband and children, headed toward the freshly washed Ford.

When they reached the side of their automobile, Iver pulled the trunk lid up to return the clothing that had also been washed, a pleasant surprise greeted him. For, placed neatly in the trunk, Iver found a fresh store of food, which included ham, bacon, beans, corn, peas, flour, salt, sugar and coffee. Iver gave a confident look back at Arnold and his wife, who were standing on their porch, and he offered the good people an appreciative wave. Irene also looked back, but into the face of her just recent hostess, and it would have been difficult for a disinterested judge to determine which of the women was pleading for rescue the most. Feelings not withstanding, off they went via the farm lane then onto the highway where they retraced their tracks through the damp earth that lay in the bottom of the wash.

As day after day passed, and as miles by the hundred were traveled, as if it were making a gesture of apology to the travelers, the surface of Kansas became increasingly flat. That fact boosted Irene's spirits considerably with every day that had passed. With every every mile covered, the lay of the land continued to flatten even more. Likewise Iver's spirits rose higher with each trouble free day and mile.

However, since her initial feeling of relief, Irene had begun to experience an uneasiness building inside her. After all, she had never seen that much earth in one piece before, and after getting her first unobstructed view of the plains of Western Kansas, her uneasiness turned to downright fright. Because, she had been raised in the seclusion provided by the thickly wooded hills that had surrounded her. Now, though, there was nothing to absorb her gaze or echo her voice. So she worried much about her strange environment. Then a terrifying possibility occurred to her; "what if the people of the dark ages were correct. What if the world is flat. It would be just our luck to plunge over the edge of Kansas into a bottomless pit filled with all manner of monsters in a place called Colorado." But, to her pleasant surprise, Iver drove across the invisible barrier between the two states without even a bump.

Irene, her two children, and her husband, now in Colorado, continued their uneventful adventure, but now their course was northwest, and again she had to adjust to a change in geography.

A chain of mountains such as she had never seen before seemed suddenly to loom out of the prairie to the west of them. "Maybe" half kidding herself "that snow capped rock fence is the end of the world. And maybe God, in his supreme wisdom, put it there so people like me can't fall over the edge."

In spite of Irene's worried looks, the further northwest they traveled, the more imposing the Colorado Rockies became. And just when it seemed to her that Iver was going to crash the Model "T" into the first rank of foothills, he brought it to a stop. The young mother then wondered aloud as to their whereabouts. Iver casually answered… "Denver".

Before she could ask her next question, her husband gave her the answer.

He informed her that they would stop there for two days and see to the needs of themselves and the car. So they camped that night on the edge of Denver, behind an abandoned filling station.

After Irene had bedded James and Viola down in the trunk of the car, she and her husband sat near their campfire and took inventory.

Iver figured out that they could get by with a couple used tires, a new fan belt, a large tin of tube-patching material, and a case of oil. The rest of their trip would use thirty five gallons of gas, and to replenish their food supply would cost ten dollars.

As the elevation was already over five thousand feet and would rise to nearly seven thousand feet in Wyoming, they would need to buy a couple blankets to augment their current supply. All of that added together, and subtracted from their money supply left a thirty dollar surplus in their travel fund. "Not bad" Iver boasted - trying, without being evident, to reassure his wife.

When Irene compared the thirty dollars with the mountains, high wild deserts and the passes that yet traversed the land between there and some place in Utah, the money wilted in importance.

Everything they had planned to accomplish in Denver was, and on time.

Bright and early Mr. Krough, full of confidence and clean shaven, cranked the tin lizzy to life and off in a northwesterly direction they chugged.

Grudgingly the little Ford, though overloaded, snaked its way up the tiers of hills and through the pass into Wyoming. Everything went according to plan without mechanical or human incident. . .for the first half of the state anyway.

The tires required no patching, the water hoses held up, and the four-cylinder engine didn't burn too much oil. Iver was higher than the mountains he had just dragged his family through. However, Irene felt not so good. In thought she half accused her husband of taking her through a place that didn't exist; some alien land outside the United States. She reassured herself by consulting their beat up, coffee-stained, road map. And, sure enough, Wyoming and Highway Thirty really did exist. "However, she thought "the makers of the map were smart enough to leave the details about the terrain a secret."

As good as the travelers luck was on their trip through the first half of Wyoming, it turned on them as they embarked on the second half.

It was at a place called Rawlins that the nearly impossible journey began to systematically take the over-matched automobile apart.

Although it was but middle September, the Krough family had just spent a cold windy night on the west outskirts of Rawlins. After pouring what was left of the coffee on the quickly dying embers of their breakfast fire, Iver hearded his family into the car, intent on resuming their trip. On a signal from her husband, who was standing at the front of the vehicle, Irene turned the ignition switch to the on position. Iver spun the crank and cussed until the cold four cylinder exploded in proper sequence to a start. Before the thing quit he ran to his door, jumped in, threw the crank under his seat, pulled the lever into first, popped the clutch. . .and all he received for his trouble was insane metallic clattering. Having considerable experience with wornout old cars, it wasn't necessary for Mr. Krough to Investigate the area from which the racket came to determine the actual malfunction. But to dramatize the true seriousness of the problem, he grasped the stearing wheel with both hands so hard that his knuckles turned white. Then, when he had rested his forehead on the north pole of the steering wheel, Irene's worry increased. She wondered if, at last, the Model "T" had whipped her man.

But a few minutes later, during which time his spirit was reborn, Irene could be seen through her car window shaking her head as her husband stood at the south edge of the road, with his thumb pointed east.

Little time passed before the disabled Model "T" was being towed back to the downtown part of Rawlins behind a smoke-spewing two-ton truck that sounded bad. "Worse than their own vehicle" Irene thought as she sat in their car enduring, along with her husband and children, burning eyes from the truck's polluted exhaust.

When their rescuer unhooked their car from his truck in front of the first garage they came to, Iver wasted no time in opening negotiations with its owner. Mrs. Krough sat watching their debate over the cost, and became very embarrassed. She had been taught that to haggle over price was less than dignified. She couldn't understand why, if he didn't like the price, why he didn't just shut up and go someplace else. Without, unfortunately, realizing just how they were going to get to that someplace else

Eventually, a fair price was agreed upon by Iver and the garage owner. And within the short space of ten minutes Mr. Krough reappeared from the rear of the shop carrying a like new, but well broken in, rear axle. And also included in the deal was the mechanic's permission for him to use what tools that were necessary to effect the exchange of axles on the Ford.

Obviously having felt more than just satisfied over the deal he had negotiated, he gave his wife a real shock.

"Dear" he said "why don't you take the kids to the store and buy them some ice cream or a soda pop. While you're at it, get yourself something. While you are gone, I'll pretend to be a mechanic and fix this klunker good as new."

"Bull" Irene thought. She grabbed her purse and the opportunity offered her, and dragged James while carrying Viola up the sidewalk before her husband had realized what this temporary attack of generosity would cost him. Under more normal conditions a goodie to him was something out of an orchard, or an unguarded garden that they happened to be passing.

Later, after the frail automobile had been wrenched back together and they were well down the highway headed west again, the leader of the group figured what the stop had cost him. "Ten dollars for the axle, two dollars for grease, the cheap bastard could have thrown that in ... one dollar for bull durham, and fifty cents for treats ... let's see now, what's left" he whispered. "We spent a total of thirteen fifty in Rawlins so that leaves ... sixteen fifty, plus gas money." After the sixty second audit of their resources, Iver experienced a slight sinking feeling inside, because, although he had budgeted for forseen circumstances, sixteen fifty isn't a hell of a lot to cover any more surprise emergencies such as the one we encountered this morning, he warned himself.

Flight of the Kroughs

Iver's warning to himself not-withstanding, and to prove the law that said "whatever can go wrong, will" the Model "T" did, in fact, give Iver and his family more problems.

After traveling only the hundred or so miles between Rawlins and Rock Springs Wyoming, six and a half hours apart, two tires gave up on the journey and blew their guts out. Iver felt as if good luck had abandoned them all-together. He searched the town of Rock Springs high and low and back to front for the best deal he could find on a pair of used tires and tubes. The best price he could coerce out of anyone was five bucks a set at a shifty-looking service station on the wrong side of town.

Regardless of where he bought them or what he paid for them, Irene was relieved to see her husband coming up the hill toward her rolling two tires and carrying two inner tubes over his shoulders and criss-crossed across his chest like bandoleers.

On the road again the following morning, Mr. Krough again audited their funds; "two tires and tubes ... ten dollars, one extra inner tube ... two dollars, and a new can of patching ... fifty cents. Let's see now, that adds up to twelve fifty, and we left Rawlins with sixteen fifty ... that leaves four dollars plus gas money." Again his stomach bubbled with uneasiness.

Lucky for them, they did make an uneventful trip through the rest of Wyoming and, finally, into Utah.

Iver was nearly out of his head with excitement when the Model "T" carried him and his family into Ogden. He knew that just on the other side of the Wasatch Mountains, at a distance of about forty five miles, stood the finish line of their miserable trip.

As usual, Irene experienced a totally different sensation than did her husband. She knew that on the next day she would meet the Krough clan which, as all difficult pending situations did, caused her to spend a sleepless night. As she studied the stars hanging over the snowcapped peaks, Irene told herself once and again that she would gladly turn tail and endure the same hardships as before if she could only return to Alabama and not have to go through the traumatic ordeal of meeting and getting aquainted with all her husbands relatives.

Iver rolled his crew, including his wife, out of their beds in the early morning pre-dawn. Mrs. Krough fixed the children a breakfast of flapjacks and side pork, and she did away with a pot of coffee, with some help from Iver. Then they resumed their trip.

However, before a mile had accumulated on the odometer, the car blew a water hose. As it turned out, the split hose was only a symptom. The real disease was a bad water pump. To fix that problem cost Iver what was left of his emergency fund and two of the four dollars remaining in the gas fund.

By the time the water pump incident had been concluded, it was noon.

Mr. and Mrs. Krough sat on the driver's side running board, and with James and Viola at their feet, they ate a dozen apples. Though it was an exceedingly plain meal, it was cheap; in fact, it was free. Iver didn't get caught taking them from the man's orchard ..,

Hunger pains dulled, they were on the road headed north again.

When they reached Brigham City they turned east toward Virtue Valley, USA, but just as Iver had guided his Ford and family around the corner and headed up the road that weaved its way through the mountains that separated them from their final destination, a sharp explosion rattled their subdued concentration.

By that time Irene had become wise to the ways of old Fords, so she knew straight away that they had just lost their left rear tire. It was the sounds that came from her husband that more so stirred the miniature environment inside the car. "and no spare -God Dammit" he shouted.

He pulled the wobbling vehicle to the right and stopped it free of any possible traffic. He then jumped out of his side of the car and quickly circled to its rear. Without so much as a split second pause, or the aid of a jack, Iver set about ripping the twisted mass of mangled rubber and severed cord from the left rear wheel, and without offering a word of explanation to his wife, he jumped back into the car and off they went on a bare wheel and three cord-bare tires. They were fresh out of spare tires.

Thirty minutes later they reached the summit of Granite Pass, and their luck was, though bad, consistent.

That time, Irene reckoned the explosion to be the right rear tire. She was thoroughly correct.

Iver leaped from the car and repeated his "ripping off a tire without jacking up the car" routine.

As they sat atop Granite Pass, it wasn't difficult for Mr. Krough to audit the travel fund. "Two dollars" he mumbled hatefully. But, in their present situation, all the money in Utah couldn't have helped them. Because, although they needed two tires and two inner tubes, there was no place to buy them, and the same for gas. They were extremely fortunate to have a fifteen-mile down-grade facing them.

After skinning the useless rubber from the wheel, Iver climbed back into the captain's seat of the ear. However, on this occasion he hadn't bothered to crank the thing, he merely moved the shifting lever to neutral and let 'er go ... As the Model "T" gathered momentum, Iver looked at his wife and told her to hang on. "No kidding" she said to herself!

To the sound of bare steel grinding on course gravel, the alien-looking craft carrying at least three terrified passengers, charged down the slope of the mountains that encircled Virtue Valley. Along the way, the few signs planted at the edge of US 79 became more familiar to the driver. One read

Flight of the Kroughs

"Welcome to Virtue Valley, Jim Bridger's Wonderland." Another read "Visit Bear River Lake - a Fishing, Swimming and Boating Paradise." Iver remembered the Dam as being the site at which Mr. Bridger hid his beaver skins from the Indians until rendezvous time. Then after they rounded a long simple curve, the valley floor burst into view.

After settling with, and at the will of, the roadway to the bottom of the valley, their route that had changed from east to north turned east again, and the sign blasted the news to Irene that Bear River City lay only a half dozen miles away, and her agony mounted.

She knew that, thanks to the miserable journey, she and her children looked like tramps, but she hoped Iver's people would understand.

Regardless of her hopes, Irene quickly put some spit curls in Viola's hair and adjusted James' clothes as best she could.

Iver seemed to be immune to the spectacle they portrayed, and the commotion that they created as he rammed the tireless contraption past the cemetery, then past the church he had avoided in his younger days. Hanna had been intrigued by the noise, and walked to her front gate to investigate.

As she arrived at the gate, Iver emergency braked the steam spewing and half tireless Model "T" to a sliding stop in a puff of blue smoke and dust. Irene was weak with embarrassment. She wanted to hide, but didn't know where to go.

Iver stepped down from the valiant little car and received a firm, but cool, greeting from Hanna, his mother. Hanna then turned toward the car and motioned her daughter-in-law to come out so they could have a proper meeting. Irene obeyed, and removed herself and her children from what had been their home for the past three months.

Introductions suffered, it was a very short time - perhaps ten minutes - before Hanna had James and Viola on her back porch of her two room house and in a galvanized wash tub of lukewarm soapy water.

Just an hour later Iver and Irene were standing beside that same tub. However, then the water was warmer and the tub was located in the more dignified confines of the front room.

By the time the travel-crusted pair had finished scrubbing themselves, Hanna had put a magnificent dinner on her table.

Although Danish cooking tasted distinctly strange to Irene, she enjoyed it all the same.

Iver relished every mouthful before he allowed the tasty food to go through his throat to his stomach. When he had finished the meal and had taken the time to consider it, he was amazed at how quickly he had forgotten what a fine cook his mother was.

As Irene sat self-consciously at the table holding Viola on her lap and doing her best to restrain James, Hanna started a conversation with her son.

D. Raymond Anderson

She told Iver of a house she knew about that was located one block east of the cemetery. And, that if he was interested in renting it, he should go talk to the owner, Alfred Allen, and soon.

Soon, because people were still being converted to Mormonism in the old country in great numbers. And many of them were immigrating to Virtue Valley. So a house, regardless of its condition, didn't wait empty long.

After the family had finished the fine meal and Irene had helped with the clean-up, Hanna suggested to Iver that the children be put down for a nap, and that his wife should stretch out on her bed and get some decent rest…he agreed. True to her nature, Irene didn't relish the thought of lying on a strange bed without her husband beside her. She thought resisting the invitation might make her seem ungrateful.

Soon after Irene had retired, Hanna sat her son at the table behind a cup of strong coffee. Iver could easily tell that something was on her mind.

"Iver", she began quietly, using her native language, "I hope you realize the hell your disappearance caused your father and me. I searched all of northern Utah and southwest Wyoming for you; thank God your father works for the railroad, because without those free passes I would have just sat here and worried"

"To impress upon you just how desperate I was to find you, I even traveled To Ogden and Salt Lake City. There, I had my fortune told by Gypsies, I had my palms read and told of your disappearance to physics. All in the hope that I might find a clue to your location."

Hanna rested her right hand on her prodigal son's left hand. She looked compassionately into his eyes. "Iver, I know that when you left Carrie and the children, you were broken hearted. But that was no excuse for you doing what you did. Now, however, you are back, and as far as I'm concerned, all is forgiven. Now go rest beside your new wife."

After the best night's sleep the newly arrived Krough family had enjoyed in months, Iver did as he had been told. An hour later he returned, holding his right arm in the air dangling a key from between his thumb and finger in a symbolic gesture that said to his wife and mother, "I have rented the place."

Mr. Krough, his face full of smile, quickly loaded his family into the rested Ford and went, under a halo of racket and dust raised by its tireless wheels, to move them into their new home ... a home that was stationary.

However, before she had allowed her son and his family to leave her house, Hanna had informed her son of the fact that all of his sisters, along with their husbands and children, would be at her house for the next Sunday's dinner, and that he and his wife and children would be expected to

Flight of the Kroughs

also be there. He had reluctantly agreed, then headed for the rented, but not paid for yet, house.

It wasn't far, three blocks east and one block north, therefore, the trip took but an instant.

Two rooms, a screened-in porch and an outhouse was what Irene found when she explored the place. Iver was familiar with the old grey house already. So nothing about the home surprised him.

There was one pleasant surprise for Irene though. For, standing inside the screened-in porch was a Singer sewing machine, not unlike the one her own mother had used with which to teach her back when she lived in Alabama.

On the surface it looked in great shape. The wood hadn't lost its varnish, and the metal parts were yet shiny black. The only part of the machine to show real wear was the foot treadle.

Irene stepped sideways all around the Singer. She dragged the palms and fingers of her hands over its surface. She opened all of the drawers and fingered the bits and pieces of sewing notions that some charitable soul had left for her, and right away plans began germinating within her mind.

At that very moment she felt truly blessed. For the past three years she had guarded a brown paper bag. Inside that bag, neatly folded, was a six yard piece of fine cotton print material.

By her actions Irene showed right away that, although Iver was, or seemed, unconcerned about the coming Sunday, she was very concerned, maybe even excited.

So, as soon as they had unloaded the Ford, and thanks to a small loan extended to them by Hanna, the young housewife dispatched her husband to Allen's mercantile.

With him he carried two lists. On one of the lists was written the items of groceries they needed - Iver was to satisfy that list first - and on the other list were the words thread, bias tape, buttons (three-fourths inch across, and white) and ric-rac. Finally, he could stop at the service station for used tires. And he was to make a fast trip of it.

Later that same evening, having already settled their goods into their assigned places, and having already cleaned the place, and having all the necessary components, Irene set herself to the task of making the best looking maternity dress the Krough klan had ever laid their eyes on. In fact, it would be her first ever dress of that sort. In her three previous pregnancy episodes, she just hand stitched modifications to ordinary house dresses.

This time, though, for herself, and for Chad also, who would arrive on the 29th of November, things would be different she hoped with much determination.

D. Raymond Anderson

So, thanks to her husband's generosity three years back, and thanks also to Alfred Allen's sewing machine, Mrs. Krough was confident that she would present a respectable picture at the next Sunday's dinner. That she did.

The young southern lady stood out among her stout and loud in-laws like beauty in an ugly contest. She was the subject of much conversation. And she was very aware of it. But, for her, there was a highly discomforting problem ... language.

The forty-odd years that the Krough's had lived in America hadn't completely erased the use of their native language from their conversation. That day's gossiping was no exception. It bothered the young stranger considerably, making her feel quite uncomfortable.

Not a minute passed that one of the ladies didn't steal a look at Irene and speak something to another lady in the Danish tongue. Naturally, she didn't know whether the comment, in fact, concerned her or not. And, if it did, whether or not it was positive. She was and, by a wide margin, the most attractive female attending the dinner - that, in spite of her extreme pregnancy.

Irene did some staring and sizing-up of her own. And, as she did, two facts became clear. Except for the youngest one, Ivers sisters were chunky - except in a couple cases in which they were downright large.

Second, Iver appeared to be Hanna's Jens' only son present ... but if Irene remembered the introductions correctly, she was certain that she had been introduced to at least one unaccompanied lady inlaws. But Irene had guessed her husband to have had only the two brothers, the ones for whom James was named. So that was one item that she would discuss with Iver when they returned home.

When they did return to their own place, Irene was told by her husband that, although there were six boys including himself, only he had survived infancy or influenza ... which made Irene feel sad.

Having heard his explanation, she wondered if she ought not have asked her husband to explain.

"Funny thing," she explained to Iver, "although I am a fourth-generation American citizen - though admittedly from another part of the country - and in spite of the fact that your people are not long from Denmark, I felt more like the alien immigrant."

He took his wife by the hand and consoled her by telling her that many of the comments expressed concerning her were indeed complimentary. And those comments that weren't complimentary were expressed out of jealousy. He further reassured Irene by predicting that his sisters' coolness toward her would soon warm ... that prediction would remain unfulfilled.

Regardless of her intermittent sensations of insecurity, the young southern lady felt good about her first Sunday dinner with the Krough family. She was also pleased with the encouragement she had received from her husband - "A little bit out of character for him" she though. In fact, back in Kansas, she might have experienced a twinge of suspicion.

The next day, Monday, the expectant mother felt even better after Iver had returned from job hunting. Because he brought with him the exciting news that he would start work the very next day at Martin's Slaughter House.

His job was about the same as one he had held back in Kansas City ... tending to the needs of doomed animals.

Consequently, on the day Chad was to arrive, all was in readiness; there was food in the cupboard - there was coal in the bin - and there were clothes to put on the children's backs, including the new baby.

Irene was very happy. At last, she could show her stuff as a wife and mother. And not have to worry about being uprooted and dragged off somewhere on some incredible journey.

Over the next twelve years other important events took place. Not the least of which was the birth of six more Krough kids. Which, when added to the three already growing, made a grand total of nine.

Irene had changed in those twelve years from a young contented mother and wife into a worried young mother and wife. Although she would never apologize for the existence of any of her children, there were times when she felt like a two-legged brood sow.

The latest children, in order of age, oldest to the youngest were called Erma, Roland, Clara, Glen, Jackson, and Harvey.

By that time it was the year of thirty-six, and Iver had rediscovered his mysterious, but only dormant, itch. So he gave up the security he enjoyed at Martin's Slaughter House and embarked on a career that would satisfy him for the remainder of his working life.

A "Jack of all trades" handy man is how Iver labeled himself. Or, as he sometimes enjoyed putting it, "I'm handy at doing almost anything that needs doing ... and at a thing or two, very handy." Then, if Irene happened to be nearby - or any lady for that matter - he would issue an obvious wink.

He always joked to his wife, and others, that what he was looking for was the perfect job. "And what manner of job might that be?" his listener would nearly always ask.

"Well", Iver would answer with a put-on drawl, "The kind of job that pays a hundred dollars a day - every day is payday - and there is no work on payday." Knowing that such a situation was probably a myth, if not downright non-existent, Iver took on any job that fell into his lap.

As he was known around Virtue Valley as a hard worker, many farmers sought his assistance. So his summers were used up in the hay fields surrounding Bear River City.

Then, in the fall of the year, Iver left his family and traveled to Idaho to do the potato harvest.

In the winter time he pawed through the many rubbish dumps hiding around Virtue Valley looking for iron, copper, zinc, and aluminum scrap. When a worthwhile load had been accumulated, he hauled it to Smithville to sell to Hank the Jew.

Then, in the spring, Iver would leave his family again and travel to Wyoming to shear the sheep.

Through all of that financial uncertainty and lonesome abandonment, Irene remained at home in dreary circumstances.

Employing some kind of innate genius that surprised even herself, Mrs. Krough made a house fit for two people tolerate eleven people. Even more remarkable, she made money enough for a few days stretch and last nearly the whole month.

As Irene sat alone at night, she would sometimes take inventory of all those good and positive things that Iver had promised would happen to them after they arrived in the Promised Land of Utah.

But, try as she would, only one event of any importance would occur to her. In 1932, the year Glen was born, Iver purchased from their landlord, Alfred Allen, the lot directly across the road from the house that they were renting from Mr. Allen. Onto their lot, with the help of a team of bay horses borrowed from his boyhood friend, LeRoy Jensen, he dragged a one-room log cabin.

Onto that Iver, using one of his many adequate talents, attached another room that he made from new and used lumber.

Naturally, then, in his superior opinion anyway, he believed that he had created an adequate home for his wife and children - and at minimal cost.

By the middle of 1936 Alfred had begun to use his monthly visit to the modified cabin more as a religious crusade, than for its original purpose: to collect the fifteen-dollar payment on the property. During each visit, after pocketing the fifteen dollars, Mr. Allen would sit the Krough family down and preach them a protracted sermon.

Although to a great extend self appointed, Mr. Allen possessed a special calling in that Mormon community. In fact, he was so special - so chosen - so God fearing - that he didn't need to attend regular church services like his lesser co-members did.

He received his divine inspiration and direction in the safe sanctuary of his barn. Where he also hid his current and back issues of the Christian Science Monitor.

Flight of the Kroughs

In fact, Alfred had been interested in Iver's religion, or lack of it, for many years. Beginning long before Iver had skipped town and traveled to Alabama.

The story went something like this: it seems that when Iver was in his teens, he was somewhat of a religious dropout. And, it also seems, that, at the same time, it became church policy to make a concentrated effort to re-activate all inactive Mormon young people ... no matter what steps were required. So, as Alfred Allen was still a young man then - not much older than Iver actually - it might give him an edge in communicating with the young rascals, so he was chosen to spearhead the effort.

Alfred was the logical choice. He was a good and faithful member of the flock. And he had not, as yet, received his "special calling".

That difficulty notwithstanding, Mr. Allen seized the opportunistic challenge to re-instill religious fervor among "those young backsliders."

Hard as he tried, he managed scant success. So Alfred cooked up a scheme that, seemed to him anyway, little short of brilliant. In fact, his plan was simple and went this way:

The local church leadership would cease to insist on formal attendance by those who had succumbed to the devil's way. That concession pleased many of the more hard-nosed members. In their minds, the young backsliders weren't good enough to sit in the same building as they. But, at the same time, those same members agreed to admit that those who lacked worthiness, of whom Iver was a member in good standing, did possess some good, if undeveloped, qualities. And it would be good to round them up and have them meet somewhere, as long as they didn't meet in the church house.

Mr. Allen eagerly initiated his plan on the very next Sunday afternoon.

Having made most of the preparations on the previous day, he had all in readiness. So on that Sunday afternoon all that Alfred could do was wring his bony liver-spotted hands and wait to see if any of his young subjects would respond to his Saturday invitation to meet each Sunday afternoon on his back porch to receive their religious enlightenment.

Full of the missionary spirit, Alfred returned home from Church that Sunday and, with Mrs. Allen's assistance, set-up several folding chairs in a half circle on their back porch.

At about two o'clock in the afternoon young men began to show up from every direction. Mr. Allen was ecstatic. As each of them mounted the steps to the back porch, he was greeted with a skinny arm sticking out of a peeled-back shirt sleeve.

After Iver had been properly greeted with his handshake from Mr. Allen's frail, milky-skinned hand, he occupied the chair closest to the edge of the porch, which, he figured, would be furthest from the preacher and closer to escape.

Then, as he sat there in silence, he thought about the handshake

"Like shaking hands with a sweaty corpse" he mumbled. By two-thirty the special religious education class for the reactivation candidates were assembled on Brother Allen's porch.

A Gentile passerby might have wondered how come all those sitting on the porch were male. It might have caused that Gentile to wonder if there was no such person as an in-active female in the Mormon Church.

Had there been a good Mormon standing by, he would have explained to the passerby that all worthy men in the Mormon Church were Priesthood holders. And, that, when he took a woman in marriage, the task of getting or keeping her active was his responsibility.

Brother Allen's meeting was a triumphant success. After each of his subjects had left the makeshift meeting house and had lit up a cigarette, they too experienced a glow.

But alas, the news that such a group existed leaked out. Soon, through word of mouth, it became common knowledge throughout the town and among the nice young worthy members of the three church subdivisions, called wards, of Bear River City. It wasn't long before Mr. Allen's special group became known among those nice members as "The Smoking Deacons."

Alfred cared little for the gossip circulating throughout the community concerning his bunch and cared even less for the title attached to it. Not because it brought down mockery upon his students, because in truth they rejoiced in the notoriety. But at the very least, and out of the desire to preserve his own good name, Alfred had hoped to keep his association with the spiritually motley bunch as hushed as possible.

"But", Iver would laughingly state later in life, "that would be like stuffing a substantial fart into a double-breasted suit and smuggling it into church on a hot Sunday without it being noticed."

His early weeks of success with the group notwithstanding, Mr. Allen's bold experiment soon took him through weeks of frustration. As, graphically speaking, declining interest and declining attendance followed the same curve. And so, three months after its birth, the group's purpose, and Alfred's mandate expired and so was disbanded.

Regardless of his failure with the "Smoking Deacons", He wouldn't give-up trying to activate Iver and, hopefully, steer him into the realm of the faithful. So Alfred Allen must have sensed some unbloomed quality in Mr. Krough, or he enjoyed taking on a hopeless challenge. He never failed to cultivate every opportunity-gained by chance or contrivance - to attempt to influence Iver's religious attitudes.

Flight of the Kroughs

In those later years, when they were both a little older, and after the "still Smoking Deacon" awakened to his nemesis preacher's tactics, he began to consider ways of taking evasive action.

In truth, he had little trouble with the problem in the fall and spring seasons. For, then, he was off to either Idaho or Wyoming.

But in the summer and winter seasons it was a different situation. Those seasons Iver spent most of his time in Virtue Valley working the hay fields or refuse dumps. "What to do" he wondered. But, true to his nature, by the time for winter scrap collection had arrived, Brother Krough had devised a grand plan. That plan would guarantee, he prayed, that he wouldn't have to sit through a lengthy worn-out sermon when the devout pain-in-the-ass called by to collect his money - and of course, deliver that heavenly message.

As he was a creature of habit - self discipline he called it - and next on his list of those things important - right under spreading the word - was promptness, Iver knew that Alfred Allen would strut the two blocks to the Krough home and arrive precisely at seven p.m. on the first day of each month. Having access to such intelligence was like the general of one of opposing armies having knowledge of where his adversary general and his army were going to mount their attack, allowing him the opportunity to prepare a deceptive defense.

Being cognizant of Mr. Allen's rigid schedule, which he had learned of many years earlier on Alfred's back porch, Mr. Krough was sure that he had dreamed up an adequate deceptive defense; he would simply delay the start of his daily scrap collection rounds.

That meant that he would finish late. Which also meant that he would arrive home too late to be spiritually uplifted. In which case Iver would receive double satisfaction: because, he knew that Alfred would go home only half satisfied. He could then enjoy his last-of-the-day cigarette and his last-of-the-day cup of coffee in contentment while, at the same time, complimenting himself for outsmarting the preaching stringbean.

Later, as he sucked the last drip of black liquid into his mouth, he would softly chuckle to himself, "Oh shit, what a crying shame."

At last, spring had arrived. Therefore, Iver was off to Wyoming to shear the sheep. So he didn't need to worry about unwelcomed visitors.

But the cool season passed quickly. It was time for him to return to Bear River City.

It was a bright, mild, June afternoon when a man could roll his window all the way down and listen to the cool wind flap and balloon a brand new red flannel plaid shirt sleeve while spinning glorious dreams of suddenly becoming wealthy.

D. Raymond Anderson

By nine o'clock that evening he had traveled as far as the Wyoming/Utah border. Because he knew that it would take him until the middle of the night to reach Bear River City, Iver decided to stop and sleep overnight in his Model "A" pick-up.

He didn't catch the name of the town as he coasted in; he just found a satisfactory place to park. It turned out to be beside a closed for the night service station.

There was but a sliver of a moon that night, and the town was without benefit of street lights. So, consequently, Iver was parked, deep in though, in a sea of darkness when ten o'clock arrived.

Although it was unlikely, if people had been walking in the darkness and passed by Iver's truck, they might have been taken aback watching a glowing object traveling in an arc between nine and twelve o'clock, as he sat absorbed in the blackness relishing his last-of-the-day cigarette.

He had no knowledge or sensation of falling asleep; all he knew was that he was someplace else.

Iver first noticed her as he sat alongside the road in his truck feasting on free apples.

She was at her well pulling up a pail of water: hand over hand. Her back was bent to ninety degrees under the weight because the truss that had supported the pulley and the pulley were both in a state of critical disrepair.

Feeling exceptionally gentlemanly, he sauntered to her picket fence - a fence that had once been fully white, but had, through the years been shedding its enamel coat until, by then, it was only scabbed here and there with tiny islands of white clinging to an oblong sea of grey.

He leaned his weight on the barrier, supporting himself by placing the palm of his hands on the points of the pickets.

"Use some help?" Iver shouted.

"No thanks," the sweaty, but curious, woman shouted back at him.

Suddenly, just as the last syllable of the last word of response passed between her lips, the rotted rope that hauled the bucket up gave way, and the bucket did a tumble dive to the invisible bottom of the well. And before she could stop herself, she looked to the stranger with a discernable plea for help emitting from her face.

Iver did an awkward, yet youthful, scissor leap over the pickets and joined the upper middle aged woman wasting looks into the deep black hole in a weed corrupted garden.

His brain was spinning like a roulette wheel. And he hoped the marble would land on the concept which he could use to help her, and maybe get a cup of coffee to boot.

"I do so need the water" fretted the woman.

Flight of the Kroughs

"Well, I have plenty of rope in my truck if you have another bucket somewhere", offered Iver.

"Yes, I do have another bucket. And I would be happy to pay you for the rope."

"That won't be necessary, because it will be my pleasure," Iver responded politely.

When Mr. Krough returned from his truck, he carried in one hand a coil of rope, and in the other hand he carried several strands of hay bale wire. And his hip pocket sagged under the weight of pliers and a hammer. The woman seemed to be quite sure of what the stranger had in mind, so she went into her house to fetch the replacement bucket.

When she returned, Iver was standing proud, with a cocksure grin on his face, beside the well that, as if by magic, he had repaired ... truss, pulley and all. Resting his butt on the stone, belt-high wall that protected the deep hole, Iver waited with one end of the new rope which he would tie to the new bucket. He took charge of that chore as well.

Next, he tossed the pail over the side. Down the damp shaft it went.

She watched as the new rope slid between Iver's thumbs and palm, until a soft splash broke the pail's fall. Then her look of concern evolved into a look of relief.

He confidently pulled the loaded container to the surface, and volunteered to carry it into the vaguely familiar lady's house.

She quickly took him up on his offer. Inside, she invited her rescuer to sit with her and take some fresh coffee. After proper hesitation, he agreed to do so.

Her place wasn't messy, just dreary, neglected, and gray looking.

The place reeked with the decaying orders of twenty thousand or so greasy meals, and as many pots of coffee.

"A definite lack of proper ventilation" was what Iver laid the blame on, as he tagged behind the lady of the house.

Nor was she a mess ... not the kind of mess that is the by-product of poverty anyway.

But her greasy, and graying, chocolate colored hair, and terra cotta tinted skin, also greasy, was evidence of diminish personal concern and care.

Iver took a seat at her kitchen table which stood in the middle of the dingy kitchen environment and watched as the woman prepared their coffee. He wondered what she was all about. They consumed their hot drink and all the while carried o much conversation.

Soon they had used-up what was left of the day. So the woman offered, and Iver accepted, a bed for the night.

"Got any money?" she asked her surprised guest over coffee the next morning.

"A few dollars" was his reply.

"Damn few I'd bet ... well, I have a lot of fixing-up that wants doing around here, and you seem to know where the business end of a hammer is, so what do you say to hanging around for a few days, and earn a dollar or two."

"OK, why not?" Iver answered. And the deal was struck.

Mr. Krough wasted little time getting started. By the fourth day, he had the place shipshape and shining.

In the mean time, something had changed within the walls of the home as well. While watching her hired man restore the outside of her home and the area that surrounded it, a spark was kindled within her, which, led to a kind of rebirth of interest in her house and herself as well.

So, at the end of the fourth day, as was the drill after tying up all of his handy-man loose ends, Iver entered the back door.

When he arrived at what had once been a dining room but had, in his opinion, until then anyway, been let evolve into a junk room, he was overcome with astonishment.

For, standing stately at the head of an elegant table that was loaded to capacity with food, silver and crystal dining wear - such as he had only seen in pictures of royal banquets - stood the woman, in equally grand attire. For the first time, Iver recognized that those articles of furniture that had been covered with dust trapped in grease, which he had labeled as junk were, in reality, fine goods that had most likely been built in Europe.

"Go wash and bathe," she ordered. Without knowing why, Iver pivoted, then started on his way to comply with her order. After taking only two and one-half steps, the woman stopped him with the mere sound of her voice.

"Iver, you will find hanging in the dressing room, right next to the bathroom, a clean suit of clothing, please put it on, I'm sure it will fit you." Iver acknowledged his amended order with a bow of his head and disappeared from her presence.

When he returned to the dining room all spiffed up and feeling as if he were dressed to attend a state funeral, his hostess was much impressed.

They sat down at opposite ends of the table. Overwhelmed by the magnificence piled between them, they engaged each other in light conversation as they enjoyed the tasty fare.

Iver dared change the tone of the conversation when he finally summoned the courage to ask the woman her name.

"Rose," she answered. And her high cheeks reddened just a touch. But at the same time a chill traveled up Iver's spine, because as best he could

Flight of the Kroughs

remember, he had never told the lady his name, but she seemed to have known it all along.

Then she changed the course and the intensity of the conversation.

"You know, Iver, I was once a socially prominent lady. My husband was rich beyond your imagination ... he was into gold mining you know."

With those words just uttered by his dolled-up hostess, Iver's back straightened, and his ears widened just a bit more. She then told Iver of the gold mine fields and of the mansion she had once owned and the servants she had managed while living in San Francisco. Hearing of her history, he couldn't help but look around him and compare.

"I know," she said, "This place suffers by comparison, but when my husband disappeared in the hills, I just had to get out of that place. It didn't matter to me where I ended up or in what." Then the room fell silent, and they finished their meal.

Suddenly, the woman again broke the quietness. "Before you retire to your bed tonight, Iver, I want you to come to my bedroom."

The last of the food that Iver had just tossed into his mouth stopped in his throat. After a minute of near choking, he managed to get the stuff started again. And the feast concluded with no more talk.

He retreated to his assigned area of the house and agonized over what would take place later that evening.

At roughly nine-thirty p.m., he tip-toed to the main bedroom and tapped shyly on its door. A soft voice beckoned, and Iver's legs turned to mush, but he bucked up, and entered what had been, until that very second, forbidden territory.

The room was draped lavishly with cranberry red velvet, pink satin, and white silk lace.

The woman herself served as the crowning ornament to the decor of the room as she sat in her red velvet chair sumptuously robed in a white satin gown. Iver was overcome, with, he knew not what. She ordered him to sit.

He was obviously excited; that was impossible to hide, but, at the same time, he was intimidated, so he made no advances. Fearing, of course, that he might misunderstand the lady's intentions. She spoke first.

"Iver, I want you to move my bed aside. Then throw back the Persian rug. When you have done that, you will find that two of the floor planks are loose. Raise them and also throw them aside. There you will find something that I'm sure will interest you."

Mr. Krough cleared his throat, then jumped from his armless chair to do as he was told.

First he placed himself between her bed and the tapestried wall; he pushed with all his might. Finally he was able to slide the bed to the center of the room. Next, he flipped the pure white Persian rug back and pushed it beneath the lace trimmed four poster bed. In an instant he noticed the two un-nailed planks. He dropped to his knees and jammed his work-hardened fingernails into the cracks, pried the floorboards up until he could get a hand under them, then threw them carelessly aside.

What lay before him would have warmed the heart of Midas ... even in his grave. For looking up at Iver were the faces on bundles of currency. And, beside the bundles, making them pale by comparison, were piled sacks of gold dust. The strike was so rich that it frightened him. So he stood on his rubbery legs and gave the woman a puzzled look.

"Don't be afraid, Iver," she half whispered, nearly teasingly. "It's all yours... all of it." You can take it with you tonight when you leave."

Iver could only stare in disbelief at the fine lady.

"Go on," she insisted, "feel it, stroke it, learn what real wealth is."

Iver obeyed. He dropped to his knees while at the same time trying to solve the meaning of the smile on her face. A smile that seemed to be taking the edge off what he was feeling over his good fortune. Because, that smile seemed almost malicious. He again concentrated on what lay stashed between the floor joists.

He stirred the cache. And as he did, he felt something soft brush his cheek and a disturbance of the air around him. When he reacted, he found a large burlap sack ... one, that in Idaho, would hold a hundred pounds of potatoes, lying at his knees.

"Load it up," she again insisted.

Iver snatched up the coarse brown bag and began to stuff riches galore into it. But it didn't seem to him as if he was having any impact on the storehouse of riches.

Regardless of that impression, when his bag was half full, he stopped. He then looked up at his smiling benefactor and said, "I'm sorry, Ma'am, but I just can't bring myself to take anymore."

"Whatever makes you happy, Iver," she said.

The pair looked deeply at each other, and an unspoken message transcended the silence.

Iver picked up his heavy bag of riches, backed out of the bedroom, then bounded down the stairs in threes headed for his truck.

He heaved his burlap sack on the spring-bare seat; then he jumped in beside it. In a rush to make his getaway, he took off in a cloud of dust and engine smoke.

He drove for two miles with his foot pushing the accelerator to the floor of his pickup. Then, suddenly, he jammed the brake pedal to the floor of his pickup and liberated the accelerator.

When he had brought the truck to a screeching halt, he asked himself a serious question; "Why didn't you take it all, dumb shit, what were you

Flight of the Kroughs

afraid of ... so far as I know, taking what is offered to you would be no sin - or cause you no terminal disease either."

So he did a quick, neat, U-turn and headed back to her house ... the house with the treasure in the floor.

He arrived at the spot where he thought he had just previously parked, and in no time flat. He stopped, quaking with anticipation. He leaped from his outfit, and headed for the house, without breaking stride.

He took five quick steps, then his body - and nearly his heart - came to a sudden stop. The house was no longer there.

Iver began to run wildly around the deserted streets searching and screaming for his buried treasure.

He ran, stumbling, here and there, and up and down the same street over, and over again. He lost his truck, and he lost himself. Then Iver noticed a glow on the horizon. Instinctivly he ran toward it.

When he had found the glow, he found his truck and he found her house. Licking tongues of fire reflected in the truck's windshield.

Iver was convinced, though he didn't want to believe it, that he could see the woman named Rose, with that same malicious smile on her face, silhouetted, even beckoning to him, in those flames.

He tried to enter the house, but the heat repelled him. He yelled profanities at the fire, but it raged on. Finally he shook his fist at the woman, but her smile only intensified.

Then, screaming redundant words, he staggered to his truck and climbed in. He laid his sobbing head on the steering wheel. All he could hear was his ship falling to the sound of earth shaking racket as it collapsed into nothingness. The fire left nothing - not even ashes.

When Iver's head cleared, he realized that the pounding he had heard was caused by something beating on his truck ... It was the owner of the service station trying to wake Mr. Krough from what, it seemed to the owner, must have been a traumatic sleep. Without even so much as a good morning greeting, Iver started the pick-up's engine and sped south.

Chugging up the east side of Ephrim Pass, which sliced through the mountains that surrounded Virtue Valley, in his boiling Ford, Iver thought a great deal about home.

He knew his wife would be glad to see him. But if things went as they usually did when he returned after an absence, shortly after their greeting, Irene would sit him down at the table, slip a cup of coffee in front of him, then shortly after that, she would put a list just beside his steaming cup.

Of the several items on her penciled column, the first four or five items listed were food. Next, she had listed, by name and article of clothing needed, each of her nine children. At the bottom of the paper, she always noted what the total cost of the items might be.

D. Raymond Anderson

After he had studied the list and had envisioned his hard-earned money taking flight from his pocket and disappearing into bottomless Smithville cash registers, he would do as he always did in that situation; he would shove the piece of paper across the oil-clothed table to his wife while telling her that, in a day or two, they would drive to Smithville and see about it.

Iver knew that Irene knew better than to expect everything on her list. "That's why she always inflates it," he chuckled to himself.

Beside the fact that in his mind he had to watch his money take wings, he knew that his religious tormentor would be lying in wait for him.

"So," he thought, "I will need to make arrangements for work in a hurry."

At two-thirty p.m., Mr. Krough pulled into his yard at Bear River City and killed the pickup's engine. He studies his two-room house for a few seconds, then he thought about his dream.

Mr. and Mr. Krough got their greeting out of the way then moved into the house where they sat down to some hot liquid refreshment. As expected, things proceeded exactly as Iver had imagined they would.

However, and lucky for him, he was home not more than two days before he had lined-up work in the hay fields. To insure his late return home, he simply volunteered to see to the after-work needs of the horses and to service the haying equipment.

By the end of that summer, Alfred got the message. He discontinued his monthly missionary visits to the Krough house, but he became a little more hard nosed about collecting the monthly payment on the property on time.

To celebrate his victory over Mr. Allen, Iver secretly slipped into town and visited Gene's "Happy Tap" pool hall. There he gladly shelled out money for four quarts of locally produced beer ... beer that, in an eastern connoisseur's opinion, tasted like it was made from memory and not from a recipe. "But," as the barkeeper truthfully said to Iver, "the fact that it's three-point-two beer is irrelevant because it will still do the job ... it just takes more bottles to do the job."

From the pool hall by way of a circular route so he wouldn't need to pass his house, Iver headed his Model "A" pickup east, up the road cradled in the bottom of Left-hand canyon, his destination being brother-in-law Bug's Logging Camp.

People had called him Uncle Bug for so many years that some had forgotten why. So his real name didn't count for much around Virtue Valley.

When Bug had caught sight of his in-law dodging his way through the boulders and stumps toward him with two bottles of beer wedged between the paled knuckles of each hand, he tossed his axe aside and made a dash for his own truck. From under the seat, springs bare except for a flimsy cover made from burlap potatoe sacks, bug yanked a two-thirds full jug of rot-gut wine.

After a greeting fashioned from earthy words and adorned with light profanity, they sat down, side-by-side, on a freshly fallen aromatic log and got down to the business of getting fairly drunk.

Along the way the pair managed to argue, but not solve, most of the hot political and social issues of the day. Before, of course, their numbing tongues turned the words they spoke sideways.

Realizing that they were out of drink and arriving at the threshold of inebriation at approximately the same time, Iver and Bug spat their bleached wads of tobacco in opposite directions, one wad east, one wad west.

They then wrestled their rubbery bodies onto a grassy area nearby that was just large enough to hold the two men comfortably - regardless of the pinecones nestled under them. There, they both stretched their muscles and bones in the purified rocky mountain air while the very late September sun poured its velvet warmth against their faces and V-shaped bare chests.

As they languished in their chemically induced daze, Iver and Bug spun separate, but equally glorious, dreams of treasures yet to find, and pleasures still to be experienced.

But Irene was suffering visions of a different sort as she stood on her front porch searching the world around her. Pleading to anyone who would listen to please make Iver appear.

All she knew, was, that her husband had made a sudden trip into town. For what reason she hadn't been informed.

Then as she turned around to re-enter the house a shocking thought occurred to her. "What," she considered to herself as she bit her lower lip, "if Iver has taken off for Idaho and the potato harvest without saying, at least, goodbye. And worse, did he take all the money with him?"

She quickly cured her momentary lapse of trust in her husband by telling herself that deep down inside herself she knew he would not pull such a dirty trick.

"Even for him such a move wouldn't be logical. After all it is only the thirtieth of September, and the potato digging doesn't start until around the tenth of October," she further rationalized.

Although the foregoing series of thoughts had frightened, then reassured her concerning one set of circumstances, it ignited as much, or more, worry about another: "Where is he, and is he safe?"

Iver and his brother-in-law finally exited the mouth of Left-hand Canyon at about nine-thirty p.m. By then the residue of alcohol on their breath had died.

The pair waved goodbye where the graveled mountain road hooked up with the main road that divided Virtue Valley into approximately equal parts. Bug turned north and headed for his home in Smithville, the county seat, and Iver went west toward Bear River City.

When he entered his front door, the front room was without light. But in the darkness Irene was lurking. She was well rehearsed and ready to confront her husband with a hundred or so incriminating questions. To which, she was convinced, Iver would blurt out as many self-damning answers.

Upon seeing her husband and knowing he was safe and that he hadn't deserted her for the potato fields, instantly her anger was dulled, but not blunted.

She reached up into the blackness and pulled the greasy string that was hooked to the fly-speckled light hanging from the ceiling, suddenly, the room took on a yellowish gray shadowy tone. Which, might have caused some stranger insect traveling across the foot worn linoleum to stop and stare at the crack-corrupted ceiling through the gloom and wonder it life could really exist up there.

"Bottle ass, you could have, at the very least, told me you were leaving and where you were going and when you planned to return home" Irene scolded at him.

"Oh, I was just up Left-hand Canyon giving Uncle Bug a hand."
"Giving him a hand my hind end!" Irene shot back at him in a whisper forced through a tight-set jaw and rigid lips.

She then pointed in the direction of the oven in which waited boiled potatoes and hamburger gravy that she had kept warm for him reasonable period of time. But, since Iver had been absent for an unreasonable period of time, the food was cold.

After pointing out the food for her husband, Irene turned away and made a quick round of bed checks.

Viola, Erma and Clara slept in a bed in the corner of the front room opposite mother and dad. In the back room that also served as a kitchen Glen, Jackson, and Harvey slept on a mattress at the west end; that group slept in very uncomfortable conditions as Jackson was a bed wetter. For which he suffered much emotional abuse at home from his brothers and sisters, and at school from the other children.

At the east end of the back room/kitchen was a cot that folded out to make a full-size bed that contained Chad and Roland - and sometimes James, when he wasn't off wandering other parts of the country somewhere.

Mother Irene made sure that they all were nicely covered with either blankets or coats, then she let out a soft sigh and crawled onto her side of their bed, leaving her husband at the table forcing down a dish of dehydrated potatoes and thick-skinned gravy.

"Serves him right," she chuckled in secret.

Flight of the Kroughs

Having stared at, and stirring at, his unappetizing food for the better part of an hour, Iver stood up and softly moved to the pig swill bucket where he quietly got rid of it. Then he, too, rolled into bed.

As Irene was still fully awake, she turned from the wall she had been facing and a natural, but hushed, conversation took place between she and her husband. As always, the subjects were economics, politics and war. Also, as usual, Iver took charge of, and dominated the discussion.

Irene had difficulty in dealing with the fact that there existed such logical reasons for making war. To her, war had always meant that country A was greedy for what country B had, so it went to war to get it. Which, in turn, put country B into the position of having to defend itself, so, it was forced to make war as well.

Iver talked himself into a state of diminished self control arguing otherwise to his wife ... and others as well.

"Shit," he would moan despairingly, "war is the natural way for a country to carry out its relationships with its neighbor countries. Everybody knows that it's the most dependable way for a country to get what it wants or needs; it's been that way since time began."

"I heard Mr. Heater say on the radio this evening that there might be war in Europe soon. And regardless of your reasoning, Iver, I still believe war to be a senseless and brutal means of solving a problem," lamented Irene.

"Well," Iver said, "Germany is a good case in point to prove my theory. The lousy economic conditions in that country laid the way open wide for a person like Hitler to make impossible promises to the German people and to have those promises believed by enough of those people to make him a political force to be feared - or to be joined."

"Before long he will lead his country in lockstep to war ... and for what? To restore the German empire and make it the economic power that it once was, that's what for."

But try as Irene would, the most she could ever make of politics was that it was a hobby for the middle class. And that economics was an obsession of the rich. And that fighting a war was the duty of the poor. Not that she believed that such was a divine principle but that was just the way things worked out.

Knowing he wasn't about to influence the way his wife perceived world political protocol, that night anyway, Iver rolled toward her and planted a meaningless kiss on her cheek. Meaningless because Irene knew, that, to Iver, a kiss was merely a handshake with the lips.

And things went that way for another two and a half years. They were two and a half years made-up of weeks and months that Irene spent without the benifit of her husband's help in caring for their ragged gang of kids, which had increased by two. Now there were eleven. The two new ones were called Karia and LuAnn.

By that time it was nineteen-forty. And, just as suddenly as Iver had been infected back in thirty-six with the urge to wander to find work to do, in nineteen-forty he was just as suddenly blessed with a miraculous cure. And Irene secretly thanked God.

He went from one extreme to the other, seldom if ever, leaving the mountainous limits of Virtue Valley.

At about the same time, he discovered two brand new occupations - and expanded in an old one. In order to do that, he went into debt to buy a two-ton Chevy truck.

First, as Iver fancied himself a talented farmer, regardless of the fact that the extent of his experience was that of tending to the family garden, he rented several plots of ground around town and contracted with the Consolidated Canning Company - commonly called the "CCC" - to grow peas and beans. The major threat to his success as a farmer, though, was the serious lack of equipment with which to harvest his crops.

Second, and most important on his list of pursuits, was joining his brother-in-law Bug in the canyons near Bear River City. There they cut corral poles for Martin's Slaughter House and logs to be sawed into lumber at the saw mill.

Finally, the larger truck allowed Iver to collect and haul more scrap metal over to Hank the Jew's place at Smithville. Which, because of the constant rumor of war, brought a much better price than before. Therefore, because of the hear-say factor, he realized more from the junk business than he did from the other two businesses combined.

However, the collection of the would-be Paul Bunyan's equipment for harvesting his allotment of trees was little better than his farming equipment. It consisted of feeble grey mare, that would be forced to snake the logs down the mountain trail, an oil burning truck to haul the logs to the sawmill, two axes and a willing, hard working son, the one called Chad.

Because Chad was sixteen, he, like his father, wondered much about the rumors of war. But Iver always assured him that his friend, F.D.R., would keep the United States out of any war.

"In any case," Chad's dad would regularly prophesy, "the next war we will see won't be between us and the Germans. It will be between the rich and the poor, right here in our own country."

"That," Chad would always remind his dad, "will put you and your best friend on opposite sides." To that warning expressed by his son, Iver never responded.

Now, LeRoy Jensen wasn't rich, but he was also far from the poor house. Yet, regardless of their differing circumstances, they counted each other among their best friends. A friendship that flourished in spite of Iver's gloomy prediction of their eventually coming to blows .

At least once a week Mr. Jensen would guide his Dodge pickup onto the Krough yard while blasting its horn. And Iver would nearly break his neck getting out of the house to greet him.

Irene had only one regret when she heard the familiar sound of the Dodge horn - it always sounded, much to her and the children's dislike, at their meal time.

A stranger viewing the scene might have wondered why a visit from a friend, albeit a good friend, could ignite such heightened excitement. But to Irene it was no mystery.

She knew that her husband had rehearsed, and stored away in his mind, every kernel of inspired reasoning and philosophical thought that he had accumulated since LeRoy's last visit, and that he had every intention of confronting his horse trader friend with every gem of that inspiration during their next vigorous discussion.

Just as with Irene, the subjects of war and peace, politics, and rich versus poor would take up most of their discussion time.

Mr. Krough sincerely believed that the distribution of the country's wealth was clearly out of whack. And he believed this in spite of the fact that he had neither the economic expertise nor the statistical evidence to prove his opinion. As Iver put it, "I just feel it in my bones."

So, with all the sureness of a bearded prophet robed in white bed sheets and standing on a mountain top aiming his privileged gaze into the future, Iver would sometimes yell at LeRoy such statements as, "After Europe has settled its problems, there will be a war in the United States: a war between the rich and poor."

Mr. Jensen knew better than to take his good friend's warnings of such a catastrophe seriously; however, he did enjoy teasing him on the subject just a little bit. So he would jokingly remind his friend of the fact that the rich not only controlled the means of production, but also the means of distribution, not to mention all of the money. "So," as LeRoy put it, "it wouldn't be much of a war." Iver, though, always had a comeback remark of some sort to offer Mr. Jensen.

"LeRoy," he would say, raising his voice to an alto pitch, "the rich may control the production and the money, but the poor control the pitchforks, shovels, axe handles, and butcher knives. And there are a lot of 30-30's and 30-40 krags under a lot of beds to boot. So, for every rich person with a hand-etched fancy rifle, there will be a thousand poor folks after him. And one rich person couldn't blow many heads off before a poor person stuck the pointed end of a pitchfork up the rich person's ass or through his belly."

All through the duration of such a struggle, Iver believed that F.D.R. - patron saint of all poor people - would be their leader.

However, on the last occasion that the pair argued the subject of rich and poor, LeRoy gained the upper hand which, no doubt, was the reason Iver never raised the subject again.

"How," he asked his feisty friend, "would you divide-up the people?"

"What do you mean?" Iver asked.

"Well, on what basis would you decide who is rich and who is poor?" questioned LeRoy.

"Simple," assured Iver, "by how much money and property they own."

"Ok," agreed LeRoy. Then he asked, "how much money do you have right now?"

Thinking that he was a nosey bastard for asking, Iver decided to answer anyway. "Twenty-two fifty in money and eighty-seven cents in postage stamps," he confessed.

"Now," explained LeRoy earnestly, "you have nearly twenty three dollars. Suppose Alfred Allen has a hundred dollars hid under the newspapers in his barn. That would make him rich and you poor - right?"

"That's bullshit!" snapped Iver. "How in God's name do you figure that?"

"Because, Iver, everything is relative. Now, Alfred has a hundred dollars ... right? But suppose Doctor Blodget has a thousand dollars. Now that makes the doctor rich and the preacher poor ... correct?" Iver said nothing, just nodded, so LeRoy continued his assualt. "Now, because everything is relative - including wealth - that creates an interesting evolution of your impending 'rich-poor conflict theory.'"

"Like how?" asked Iver.

"Well, your one big war would become forty million links in a chain of small wars involving three people at a time."

At that statement from his friend, Iver slid his butt to the front edge of the truck seat, sat on his tailbone, pulled his hat over his face - resting its brim on the bridge of his nose - and said nothing.

So LeRoy finished his explanation.

"Now, because of my relativity theory, what has happened is that each person with money is fighting the one ahead of him trying to take some of it away from him while, at the same time, trying to fight off the person behind him who is intent on taking away some of his own money. So, can't you see, Iver, that in a rich-poor war there would be no winners - or losers - just a cloud of dust and a lot of bloody noses."

Then a glimmer of hope registered on Iver's face - that had admitted defeat - hope that he might, at least, have the last word.

Flight of the Kroughs

"I must say, LeRoy, that what you have just said is ninety percent true. But, you lost your ten percent when you said that there were no winners. Because, you see, there would be two persons that would win."

"And who might that be" questioned Mr. Jensen. "Well, obviously, the only two winners would have to be the one at the top of the wealth chain and the person at the bottom of the chain."

"And why?" asked Iver. Then answering his own question, he explained "The one at the top had only the person beneath him to contend with. And that person would be kept busy protecting his own wealth from the one just beneath him. So the one at the top would have little trouble in holding onto his wealth. And so would continue to prosper."

"But what about the poor slob on the bottom?" LeRoy asked.

"Well, because he could concentrate on the guy that was one link ahead of him, who would be busy trying to rob the one ahead of him, the guy at the bottom would have a better than average chance to move up the chain a link or two. Because, if you're at the bottom LeRoy, the only direction open to you is up."

Although LeRoy perched on an elevated level of the social order relative to his pal, and, notwithstanding the fact that he considered Iver worthy company, he took much pleasure from inciting his friend's opinionated nature. And, without exception, he would do it whenever a bare spot appeared in their many conversations.

What LeRoy would do - through sleight of mouth - was throw a question at his friend that was designed to rattle his confidence like, "what do you think of chiropractors, Iver?"

"As quacks, I place them right up there with doctors, but ... right at the top of the list," Iver shot back without as much as a thoughtful pause.

"Lots of people swear by them," offered an amused Mr. Jensen.

"That's because they always agree that there is something wrong with you but never cure anything."

"Hold it just one minute Iver, you had better explain that last statement." After a sympathetic headshake, Iver said, "OK, I'll do that just for you."

"Now, you know as well as I do that it's human nature for most people to leave the doctor's office feeling disappointed or even cheated if their doctor could find no reason for them to be feeling badly. So, is it any wonder that a chiropractor can say to a person that the reason for their headache is an out of joint big toe, and that it will take five treatments - at ten bucks apiece - to correct the problem •.• and get away with it?" he charged.

"Well, then, Mr. Krough, who would you say keeps them in business? Most of the folks I know are, like you, much too smart to be taken in that easily," joked LeRoy.

"Mostly over-the-hill frustrated women is what I believe from what I hear," offered Iver.

"Like who - give me a name," persisted a perkier Mr. Jensen.

"Erma Wilson," Iver quickly answered. "The one whose husband is always off somewhere buying cattle for Martin's Slaughter House. I hear from a person that's in a position to know with airtight certainty that Mrs. Wilson travels to Smithville to visit her glorified masseur every time Mr. Wilson leaves town. And she always goes with the same ache."

"Well, what does that prove Iver?" questioned LeRoy.

"It proves," he half whispered, "That if a person - a female person in particular - has the money, and the right ache, that regardless of the quality of sex life she enjoys with her husband, she can go to the city and have her body stimulated to fulfillment by a pair of clever male hands. And, as far as I can tell, without breaking man's law, or God's law either."

Secretly impressed with his friend's argument, and suffering a quantity of jealous excitement as well, LeRoy asked Iver if he didn't believe there was something a little bit unfair about such a situation.

"Hell, yes" was his quick answer.

"Well, then," Mr. Jensen continued, "how do women get to be so lucky to experience those grand feelings?"

"Must be their sex and their plumbing," Iver giggled. Then he added, "We would both understand better if there existed such a person as a young, pretty lady chiropractor, LeRoy." Iver then joined his friend leaning back hard on the backrest of the seat enjoying a good laugh.

Another time Mr. Jensen asked Mr. Krough how he felt about lawyers. And as always, Iver was ready.

"You see, LeRoy, tacked to the inside of my brain are three lists. Lists of people who make my ass ache. And on one of those lists is written the word doctor along with other professions that claim to possess the magic of healing, one of which we have already discussed.

"On the other list are those who claim the authority to preach - and those who preach just for the hell of it. That list I discuss with Alfred Allen whenever I can't avoid him."

"And included on the third list up there in my head, and to satisfy your curiosity LeRoy, are the words lawyer, the law, and justice."

"To my way of thinking, there are three things necessary to guarantee man's freedom. And as those three things are necessary, there ought not to be price tags attached to them"

Iver waited for his listener to display more than just polite interest before he resumed his lecture. Not that he wouldn't have raved on anyway, but he relished having his ego stroked as regularly as possible. So he sat

Flight of the Kroughs

stone faced, silently vowing not to go on until he received a response from LeRoy, regardless of its intensity.

"Well for God's sake, Iver, what are those three things you hold so sacred?" LeRoy kindly demanded after two minutes of his deliberate silence,

"Well, I knew you would eventually get around to asking, but you being a Republican, it may go over your head," Mr. Krough teased sarcastically.

"Try me," LeRoy shot back in a nearly restrained voice.

"Well, back to front, here they are," Iver said after sucking in a deep breath. "Third among those three things is a man's home. I'm not talking about a farm with chicken coop, pigpen, and a barn ... but a house and a chunk of this earth big enough to hold it. And the government, whether it's in Bear River City or Washington D.C., shouldn't have the power to tax it away from him."

"Second of those three things that shouldn't be based on a person's ability to pay is a man's health. By saying that, I don't intend to lead you to think that I believe doctors should work for nothing. But they should be paid by the government - and they should earn no more than school teachers."

"And first among those conditions necessary to insure a man's freedom, and to deal directly with your question, is justice."

"Honestly, the wacky way in which the law doles out justice is a crying shame, LeRoy" ... Iver began to yell just a little bit.

"But I have a plan that I think would do a lot to set things straight."

"As it goes now, the pile of money that stands the tallest does the talking and gets the slickest lawyer. So, the outcome of a case may not depend so much on the right or wrong of an issue as which lawyer put up the most convincing argument. So, God forbid, if a poor man was to be party to such proceedings, he would have about the same chance a red worm would have swimming back- stroke through a school of piranha fish."

"Now, although what I am about to suggest to you may not be gospel, LeRoy, it's by a damn sight better than the way it's done now."

"To begin with, there ought to be a large, long room, attached to every court house in the country. And in that long room would be a chest high counter which would stretch from one wall of that room to the other. And behind that counter the lawyers would be confined behind a government oak desk. There, disputes would be settled by way of negotiation and not confrontation. Leaving the marble floors and polished wood paneled halls of the court house to the judges for the purpose of dealing justice to thieves, murderers, molesters, and those who would swindle the common folks." After those words, Iver was silent.

D. Raymond Anderson

Secretly relieved that his friend had finally finished ex- pounding what to him were simplistic theories, LeRoy considered in his mind the fact that those ideas expressed so confidently by Iver were especially lofty coming from a guy who never bothered to vote.

Then, as always, the two men ended their encounter by discussing what was happening in Europe. And just as he had on all other subjects put to him by LeRoy, Iver showed shameless confidence in his understanding of the festering situation and its implications.

"Speaking of confrontation, Iver, have you got any ideas about our getting involved in Europe? Seems to me it's inevitable, or that queer looking son-of-a-bitch will do his relentless devil dance all over the continent, south from Russia in the north to Italy. And west from Poland in the east, to the Atlantic shore of England. And while in the process, put a couple and a half hundred million people under his bloody thumb."

Before responding to his friend's question, Iver made sure the places LeRoy had referred to were etched sharply in his mind. So later that evening he could scan his mutilated sixth grade geography book to see precisely where those places his better educated buddy had talked of were located.... then he was ready.

"First Mr. Jensen, I wouldn't call what is going on in Europe confrontation. As I understand it, the word implies that there are two parties willing to oppose each other fiercely. And, except for a few diehard partisan heroes, its been more a matter of abdication so far. But, for God sakes, man, even a paid-up Republican such as you ought to be able to understand that Hitler will eventually fail at his insane try at uniting Europe. And without the loss of one drop of our boys' blood. If, that is, the remaining countries, get smart."

"My hell, Krough, you talk as if you have tripped at the limits of reason and fell over the edge to nowhere. There is no way in heaven or hell, let alone this crazy world, that the old countries can hold out against the Nazi plague without the help of our boys and our factories," Mr. Jensen insisted.

"You, my friend, have been taken in by some of those rich Republican industrialists who view war as a way to get richer," accused Iver.

"You know, Krough, your head is so full of crap that it should be counted as one of the wonders of nature that you can actually reason, let alone talk. But, I never want it said of me that I didn't listen to the other man's point of view. So go ahead, explain to me how and why Adolph will fail in his cruel undertaking."

"All right, know-it-all, I would be pleased to do just that" agreed Iver. So away he went.

Flight of the Kroughs

"For starters, it is obvious that none of the European countries have the resources or will to resist the German army. So, that being the case, the smart thing for them to do is just allow themselves to be occupied."

"Now, if that's not the most ridiculous statement I ever heard," laughed Mr. Jensen.

"Wait just a God-damned minute, will you let me finish?"

"Sorry Iver ... rave on."

"Suppose" continued Mr. Krough "that you, yourself, was put in charge of a group numbering one hundred men, and was provided with the most powerful and up-to-date weapons of the day. And suppose you were then given the order to march against several other lesser equipped, and less inspired groups and subdue them."

"You would probably discover, and much to your satisfaction, that your first encounter was merely a matter of moving onto their territory and assuming authority."

"Then, having secured that group, you would prepare to move on to your next victim."

"But after assembling your troops in preparation for your next conquest, you would suddenly become aware of an unsettling fact. The force of a hundred fighters you started out with was now reduced to ninety. Because see, you had to leave those other ten behind to guard the group you had just conquered."

"And so it would go. Soon your army of one hundred would be consumed by your success - guarding all of those folks you had defeated."

"And before long those enslaved people would realize the fact that the only thing they had to fear was the bluff that the few troops guarding them presented. So they would rise up and set themselves free. And your grand dream of dominating all those people would go unfulfilled ... ruined by your own success."

"Just how in heaven's name would the local citizens pull-off such a trick?" teased LeRoy.

"By taking to the streets and simply absorbing your over- extended army within the population," Iver explained. "Which," he continued, "might result in some of the citizens getting shot by the invaders just to get their attention, true. But even in such a situation as that the invaders would fail. Because very soon after the shooting got started one of those secret guns covered up by three layers of overcoat would become uncovered to blow the invaders son-of-a-bitchen head off. Then all hell would break loose and the invaders would quickly be swallowed up by the crowd and stomped to death."

"Ah-ha" cried LeRoy. "What about the collaborators who believe that their heritage demands that they give me aid and comfort in order to help create that powerful and perfect race? And what about those who would cooperate with my invading army so they can be on the winning side? Wouldn't they make my army stronger?"

"Shit, those kind of people," answered Iver casually, "are like hemorrhoids: a pain in the ass. Besides, for every one of those misguided bigots or those spineless traitors, there are at least ten patriots."

Irene appeared, at least outwardly, patient as she walked the plank-traced linoeleum floor waiting. Her arms were folded across her lower chest, and she hummed a light classical tune taught to her by her mother back when she was being groomed by Mother Coburn to meet, and impress with her beauty and charm, a fine southern gentleman and potential husband who would take Irene, and maybe mother and sister too, out of their grimy world of mines and miners. The Krough kids had long since gathered in two groups at each of the two southern exposure windows. There they pressed their faces against the cool panes of glass. They watched impatiently amid a chorus of hunger pains as the two would-be diplomats sitting in the horse manure scented Dodge argued away two hours.

The children knew from past experience that the world's major problems would need to be discussed before LeRoy would finally leave. And only then could the Krough family sit down to a nearly hot meal.

Irene would, on that day, for reasons she withheld from Iver, until an hour or so later, rush the family through that afternoon meal. Then she, Erma, and Clara cleared away the dishes from the table and quickly washed them. After which, the two girls began to prepare the house for their expected, but their father's unexpected, visitor.

At about four-thirty, and unaware of the wrenching affair that was about to befall him, Iver had leaned himself on the pig pen fence ... deep in though. He didn't wake to his wife's presence in his area until she was standing by his side.

"Iver" she said softly, "I need to ask you a big favor?"

"A favor?" he asked as he cocked his head to the side.

"Yes" she returned.

"What kind of favor?" he questioned.

Irene hesitated, then she went on "Would you please shave?"And while you're at it, put on a clean shirt." Husband guessed right away that it wasn't family coming. Because, she never asked him to shave or change clothes for them - not that he would have in any case. But Irene's manner of speaking, along with her special request, told him that his castle was about to be invaded by God knows who.

"Who's coming?" Iver snapped.

Flight of the Kroughs

"How do you know someone is coming?" answered his wife - who, by way of a subtle strategy, was trying to put off telling him the facts pursuant to her surprising request.

"There's an old saying, dear, that says 'don't ever try to bullshit an old bullshitter'; now, tell me who's coming?"

"Alfred Allen is coming to see us ... The Bishop is sending him," she confessed while bracing herself.

Iver's face turned stern looking.

"What's that skinny twerp up to now?" he said with a suffering moan.

"I don't really know" replied Irene. "All I know is that someone gave a handwritten message to Glen saying the Bishop was sending Mr. Allen to deliver a special message to our family."

Iver turned slowly from the pig pen looked at the ground for a second or two while in though; then he disintegrated a neat, fairly fresh, pile of horse manure with the toe of his boot ... a symbolic gesture he would, if he was honest, admit.

They both started toward their house at the same time. However, he soon lagged behind. By the time he at last poked his disgust-masked face into the kitchen, Irene had already poured hot water into the wash basin and had folded a clean shirt for him over the back of the nearest chair.

Not only did Mr. Krough have clean clothes to put on, but by some unexplainable reason, so did the Krough kids. Not that Irene didn't concern herself with the cleanliness and appearance of her children, but with so many of them, and so few clothes, it was difficult to manage their wardrobes to fit normally occurring situations, let alone unforseen ones.

By the time Iver had raised his appearance to the level of respectability he figured Mr. Allen deserved, a bonny knock vibrated through the front room door.

Eight-year-old Glen was first to respond to the knock, so he was allowed to pull the door open.

When he did, in Mr. Krough's mind anyway, it revealed a comical-looking person standing on the front porch framed by the oblong door hole. It made Iver want to come right out and laugh. But, out of politeness and concern for what his children might think, he restrained himself and only roared inside.

As Mr. Krough sized-up the emissary in that instant, he decided that he looked like a six-foot-high fence post - four inches in diameter - standing inside a four-foot-high piece of stovepipe - six inches in diameter. "Thank God for suspenders," he quietly mumbled. Then, as his surveying gaze moved upward, he added, "and for big ears as well, because without them, old Alfred's specs would rest on his upper lip ... My God, how can a human being have such large ears, and such a small, narrow nose and face?"

Irene nervously waited for her husband to do the courteous thing ... which was to rush over to the door and drag the frail visitor inside with the aid of a good handshake. But, no such luck. Instead, Iver hooked one of the legs of the best chair, which was reserved for their guest, with the toe of his boot, then slid it toward Alfred, and in the same manuever, he beckoned for him to enter.

Watching her husband's performance on that occasion reminded Irene of how one beer-drinking person might greet his buddy at the pool hall. Although she had no first hand knowledge that such was the case.

Mother Irene had pre-arranged her Krough kids in such a way that they would all be in the same general area, surrounding their parents. This would make it simpler for Mr. Allen to issue his message, whatever it was to be.

The visitor at the door tilted his head and offered a thin smile as a gesture of acceptance to Mr. Krough's understated invitation. He then stepped up to and over the threshold into the plain front room and seated himself before the shabby but clean family.

"Well, Brother and Sister Krough, it's been quite a spell since we last talked."

"Not long enough" thought Iver from the back of the group.

"And, gracious, how the children have grown."

"Small talk," whispered Iver. "What the hell does he really have on his mind? If he wants me to go to church, why don't he just say so ... then I can just tell him that I don't have a suit good enough for that purpose."

Then Mr. Allen continued, "The Bishop has received urgent correspondence from the Prophet that concerns all of the inactive members of our church, such as you folks, who the Bishop considers special. And I, too, feel the pair of you are special." Hearing those words, Iver shook his head and rolled his eyes until they nearly rotated out of their sockets and out of sight.

"Because of these troubled times," Mr. Allen went on, "the leaders of the church have determined that every Mormon couple who has not had their marriage solemnized in the temple of the Lord should do so with little delay."

"So, to take care of folks such as you, Iver, and you, Irene, we are going to provide temple-preparation classes. Classes that will help both of you to attain worthiness."

Alfred Allen's last few words brought memories of the smoking Deacon affair to Iver's mind. Causing him to speculate on the title that the regular, active folks might attach to a group such as that he was proposing ... "Alfred's Angels?"

The purveyor of official church policy continued his speech - which interfered with Mr. Krough's thoughts - "Now, Iver," Alfred insisted, "if

Flight of the Kroughs

you and Irene will get on your knees and earnestly pray for it, I'm sure the Lord will forgive your past sinful ways. And seeking forgiveness is really a simple matter; all you need to do is join the active congregation and stand on your feet and publicly confess your sins and beg the Lord and his earthly disciples for their forgiveness."

"Then the way will be clear for you and Irene to, at last, be eligible to enter the temple of the Lord and on the road to attaining everlasting celestial glory. As then, you will have been joined as husband and wife. Think of the possibilities, living in the highest kingdom for time and all eternity - as one, in the sight of the Lord."

"And furthermore," then Alfred looked into the mass of children, "you children have a sacred duty and glorious opportunity as well. For, if you boys attend to your church duties - attain the priesthood - and honor it - and if you girls keep yourselves morally clean, then each of you will be listed on the holy record with your parents. You will all be there together - just one big happy family."

Iver had squirmed on his noisy seat waiting for a chance to speak as long as he could bear it. So he rearranged himself on the squeaky chair and cleared his throat, hoping he could get the messenger to shut-up for just a moment so he could begin a rebuttal speech. Finally, Mr. Allen did stop talking.

"Mr. Allen," Iver said, "may I please ask a question?"

"Why, of course, please, all of you, ask as many questions as is necessary."

Iver was overjoyed at the opportunity. He again shifted his weight, and cleared his throat of any obstacle on which his words might become impaled.

"Now, Alfred," said Iver, trying his best to sound obediently inquisitive, "there are a couple things I would like for you to straighten out for me." "Yes, whinnied Alfred.

"You said that the church leadership counseled that everyone should have a temple wedding in order to enjoy full heavenly privileges ... correct?"

"Yes," Mr. Allen nodded.

"Then what will happen to those who don't have such marriages?" asked Iver. "Well" answered Alfred, while squirming on his own chair, and clearing his throat, "when the husband and wife die and depart this earth and go to their earned reward, they do it without a partner."

"Wait ... a ... minute" yelled Iver, as Irene turned her flushed face away to hide her embarrassment. "Are you trying to tell me that God breaks up families?"

Alfred fished for an answer, but before he landed one, Iver was on him again.

"And what about those who never marry?"

"Well now, that's an interesting situation, one that needs delicate explaining."

But Iver didn't give Alfred Allen the time to devise an explanation.

"And how about those who pass on before they have the opportunity to marry, are they damned as well? And how about those who are born intellectually less fortunate than you and I Alfred, who will speak for them?"

Knowing that he had lost the upper hand and had allowed the discussiion to lose its focus, Mr. Allen decided to lay on Iver the one argument that he could not dispute.

"Iver," he said, "I'm sure you know that there exists among we mortals enough questions to fill this universe and things that we mortals, God knows, should not question. But, rest assured, I know just as sure as I'm setting here with you and your family, that our Heavenly Father has a mechanism already functioning that will achieve a solution to those cases you mentioned." Then he relaxed a bit, as he was reasonably sure that he had his domination over the discussion restored. He was wrong again.

"What about the children?"

"What do you mean, what about the children Iver?"

"Well," he drawled, "if marriages are dissolved divinely upon death, for the unworthy, does that mean the children are damned to wander the heavens unclaimed forever?"

"No, Mr. Krough," suffered Alfred, "the Lord will see to them also."

Seizing a moment of silence, the slender preacher checked his pocket watch, then rose to his feet and took three quick steps to, and opened the front door, where he concluded his message.

"Well, Iver, and you too, Irene, think about what I have told you. It's important. And if Iver will tell the Lord of his questions in sincere prayer, he will no doubt have his doubts washed away."

Alfred pulled the Krough front door shut behind him and stood on the front porch for just a moment.

Looking out the window, Glen was sure that he saw the ex-visitor look toward heaven and shake his head no.

Unknown to Alfred, however, and unknown to his wife as well, Iver did think much about what they had just argued about. He knew that, deep inside, the only real difference between himself and Mr. Allen was that Alfred was content with his blind faith, and he wanted clear and concise answers.

After the following days washed away some of the thoughts of that meeting, more and more Iver thought about the ugliness that was going on at the doorstep of his country of birth in Europe.

Just as it was with his religion, he wanted what wasn't possible to have ... all of the answers.

*****

Finding the treasure is less of a reward than the search, according to something that Irene had read somewhere. So it was no mystery to her why her husband spent as much time as he did with his brother-in-law at the logging camp where the million riddles of life were analyzed and as many futile attempts made to unravel them.

In consideration of accuracy, a description of Uncle Bug's "Logging Camp" is in order. It consisted of any area in Left-hand Canyon that was handy to the trees and large enough to allow parking and the loading of his International truck. There also needed to be a stump or two to sit on while eating, smoking, or arguing, and there had to be a tree with enough of its own space to attach his old bay mare to. But such a place was seldom in the same area two days running.

Glen would long remember his Uncle Bug's logging camp and his Uncle as well, due largely to one visit in particular, in fact, his first visit. It was late June of 1940 and the canyon had at last dried out from the consequences of the previous winter's snow pack.

Then, Iver was more relaxed about taking his truck up Left-hand Canyon. There to join Uncle Bug and his truck in a smaller sub-canyon that branched off, called Big Hollow.

He had relented to Glen's early morning persistent pleading and said yes to his son going along with him and Chad to the mountains. "After all," Chad spoke up in his little brother's behalf, "Glen is eight years old, and he is big enough to carry water and lead the horse up and down the mountain trail."

At seven-thirty a.m. the Krough crew was carried by their Chevy truck off the main canyon road and forded the river. Then they headed up the winding, two-rut lane, into Big Hollow. In the short space of ten minutes, they bumped and swayed into Uncle Bug's campsite. As it was seven-forty five, Bug had just finished his breakfast of fried potatoes, bacon and onions. To Glen, regardless of the fact that an hour earlier he had filled his belly with hot cracked wheat cereal, the area around the campfire smelled delicious.

Having seen his brother-in-law's thirty-two Chevy being negotiated toward him up the mountain trail, the mountain man yanked two more cups from his grub box. Counting his refill, he poured three cups of strong black coffee. They each sat on vestiges of once regal pine trees and enjoyed their hot brew - all, that is, except Glen; he mingled with the environment of the camp and felt twice his age and size.

D. Raymond Anderson

The three grownups said little. They only sat there, letting the black liquid subdue the snapping coolness of the crystal clear mountain air and lubricate their bodies and minds into action.

First on the list of many things that Glen had wanted to do was explore. But Chad, earlier that morning, had briefed the young man concerning the rattlesnake danger, so the eight-year-old quietly crawled atop Uncle Bug's bay mare and stretched out on the gentle animal's warm back. Soon the two older men, who had, just a few years back, reached the summit of the hill and were then heading down the other side, and the sixteen year old, finished their coffee and chucked their cups into Bug's grub box. Brother-in-law grabbed the two-man crosscut saw and Iver picked up two axes. One of the two axes was a double-bladed one. That one belonged to Bug. The other of the two was a single-blade axe; that one belonged to Iver. He hated double edged axes. He couldn't understand why an implement used for chopping needed two blades anyway. After all, one could only chop with one side at a time, and, besides that, they were dangerous. Every time he saw one of the things, he imagined some innocent person standing behind the user of such a tool and receiving a split personality on the back swing. Iver and his brother-in-law had debated fiercely the relative merits of the two designs on more occasions than they could remember.

Chad untied the bay mare's halter rope from its aspen tree anchor and instructed Glen to sit up and straddle the animal properly. Then he ordered his little brother to grab the mare's black mane and hang on.

The logging crew, Iver and Bug in the lead, Chad, the mare and Glen bringing up the rear, slowly moved up the sunny side of the mountain.

They climbed until the two older loggers were out of breath.

Shortness of breath aside, they had reached the snow line, which, offered a less revealing reason for Iver and Bug to halt themselves and their crew.

The experienced pair stood their tools against a rotted, but still trying, pine tree and searched nearby for acceptable victims to bury their blades into. Chad searched also, but, as he was young and hadn't yet blackened his lungs with tobacco smoke, he chose for his challenge the largest tree in sight.

As his son began his swinging assult, Iver looked at Bug, and with a proud wink joked, "Chad's only trying to show us old guys up."

Each of the two older ones whacked off a three-quarter-square-inch piece of chewing tobacco and they watched and waited as young Chad sliced a v shaped wedge out of the base of his tree with his dad's razor sharp single blade axe. Then the older ones each spit on their hands and took hold of the two-man cross cut saw to do their part in the operation.

Flight of the Kroughs

Having the greedy teeth of the six foot by four inch section of metal properly inserted opposite and just above Chad's precise wedge, the salty logging team looked at each other, and smiles invaded their faces simultaneously. On a silent signal that secretly passed between them, the saw began to slowly move lustily back and forth with perfectly coordinated strokes.

As the next few seconds slipped unwasted by, the speed at which the two men pushed and pulled the saw increased, and the spring steel grinding through the silent pine giant had begun its song. Another pine in pain, Bug hummed. Alternately, BB-sized kernels of woody flesh were dragged from the deepening cut at either end of the cross cut saw, and a turpentinic smell permeated the surrounding forest which was, except for the noise broadcast by the chewing of the hungry saw, bathed in silence. Glen had never witnessed the execution and fall of a one hundred foot piece of vegetation before, but Chad had seen many of them come crashing to the earth.

As he leaned on a boulder resting up, he put his arm around his little brother's shoulder and briefed him about the safety rules of that impending occurrence as well.

"First," Chad warned, "you never stand, or sit, on the side of the tree as where I cut the wedge out. Because, that tells the tree to fall in that direct. And you always chop on the uphill side. Also, you saw and stand clear on the downhill side.

"Two things are important to remember, it's easier to run downhill to get away if something goes wrong, and second, when you fall a tree uphill it means that the butt of the log will be pointed downhill, so it will be easier for the mare to snake it down the mountain. And another thing to remember, always stand a greater distance from the tree than its height, and watch out for airborne pieces of scrap tree as it falls."

Seeing that the leading edge of Dad and Bug's saw was approaching the very core of the handsome pine, Chad led his little brother by the hand to safety. About two minutes passed: then a sharp snap split the cool morning air.

Glen's young heart began to pound against his thin chest, and his stomach seemed to turn a flip as he watched the proud, giant tree begin to stubbornly tilt, while fighting to its last grain to remain standing. The young man had the urge to cheer for the tree.

As it tipped to a greater angle, it naturally gathered speed. Then, in what seemed like an instant, it bullied and clawed its way through its lesser surroundings. It climaxed its journey among mangled protective limbs, smashed lifeless against the earth.

Glen's body tingled. Why, he did not understand. Later he asked his older brother just how long it had taken the mountain to grow that tree. "For every foot of tree you can figure about one year," Chad answered.

"One hundred years ... WOW," Glen replied, full of wonder. The young man thought he finally understood what he had felt, and why he felt it, as he had watched his first important tree fall.

Before noon the three loggers had laid six pine trees to rest on the warming side of the mountain and had stripped them clean of limbs, twigs, and needles. The co-bosses decided that they had earned dinner, so they all hiked back down the mountain to camp.

Glen ran with a galvanized bucket to the edge of the frigid transparent creek that slipped over a bed of rock and hid, where possible, under green velvet tongues hanging on a thousand species of bush and trees.

He plunged the two-gallon bucket into the stream with a mighty swoop and pulled it out three-quarters full. Then he struggled through the boulders and stumps, whistling and splashing his way back to camp. They would have potatoes with their jackets on, so Iver had already quartered them, peel and all.

Glen passed his dad the bucket, then only half full of water. He poured it over the potatoes until they were just covered in the pot. Bug stripped the skin from two onions, sliced them, then tossed them into the boiling pot. After that, he seasoned the mixture with salt and pepper. Iver removed a large can of pork and beans and a pound of bacon from the Krough grub box and handed them to Chad. The sixteen-year-old set the can of beans on a stump; then, with the blade of his axe, he made two cuts in the lid of the can - one north and south and ther other east and west. Next, he pried the four corners created by his expert cuts upward and dumped the contents into a black cast iron skillet. Next, he separated the strips of bacon and stirred them into the beans. They ate like nearly starved cannibals. Not because they considered the food to be of gourmet proportions, but because the morning's work had emptied their bellies.

After eating, and a quick clean-up, Iver and Uncle Bug, laid their decaying bodies on the cool earth and their backs leaned against the remnants of two once great trees, each removed their sweat-stained felt hats, and each rolled a bull durham smoke.

Chad knew from much past experience that a vigorous discussion would, as always, take place. As he had already listened to at least a hundred or so of their shouting matches, he didn't, on that occasion, expect to learn anything new. So he yelled Glen out of a shallow sleep. Chad removed the rope from the aspen tree that gave only the appearance of being tied, and gave his little brother a leg up onto the mare's back. He told Glen to grab her mane and urge her up the mountain while he latched onto her tail

Flight of the Kroughs

for some free help. Up the steep slope the reddish brown animal trudged, with one body on her back and one in tow.

Back at the campsite, Uncle Bug was first to speak, "Where's James?"

"Oh, he's off on one of his wild hair trips again ...where, God only knows, but I expect him to return any day now" explained Iver.

"It's a damned shame that he needs to wander like that. He will never get anyplace. Not until he settles down anyway. Hell fire, Iver, you know as well as I that work is hard enough to find, no use making it hard on himself" preached Bug.

"I guess he's searching for something," Iver answered - with more than a little insight.

"He'd better find it fast," warned Uncle Bug.

"Why did you say it that way?" asked Iver.

"Because things don't look at all that stable in Europe, and I hear at the pool hall that Mr. Roosevelt is going to let some of our boys go help them out, and the first to go will be those boys who are out of work," Bug prophesied.

"That's bullshit" Iver shouted. "F.D.R. said he would keep our boys out of war, and I believe him."

"Bullshit my ass," returned Bug. "Can't you see that if we give England and France enough airplanes and boats along with a few out of work men, then the Germans will take a good ass kicking."

"I still think you're full of shit," insisted Iver. "I have heard every one of Mr. Roosevelt's chats, and he never said anything like that. What you are doing is spreading rumors, and there ought to be a law against that, and besides, if your own boys weren't too old to go, you might think differently."

More out of compassion for his friend than concern for the validity of his argument, Uncle Bug finally agreed with his brother- in-law and shut up.

Moments later, as he sat with his stare riveted to the ground, Iver confessed to his good friend that he was, in fact, fearful of losing James to a war that seemed to be creeping closer to, not only his son, but many others just like him.

His sensitivity to the upheaval going on in Europe had abruptly increased when he had learned that on the ninth of April, 1940, King Christian of Denmark, to whom he was yet a subject, had yielded to Hitler's ultimatum of surrender to the German "XXXI Corp" with little or no fight. Iver was heartsick about it because he still had close relatives living there, as did Bug.

Uncle guessed correctly that his brother-in-law was brooding because of it, and he felt as if he was to blame. So he got to his feet saying, "There ain't no use worrying about the old country; they're not our concern - for

D. Raymond Anderson

God sakes, we're Americans now and we're too damned far away from the old country to do anything about their situation even if we could, which we couldn't. So why don't you take your citizenship papers and let old Christian see to his own worries."

In Iver's opinion, everything that the toothless logger had told him was gospel truth. Feeling extremely uncomfortable all of a sudden at being talked down to, Iver followed his partner and rose to his feet, so if there was to be anymore preaching, then at least, it could be face to face. However, just as their father had come to his feet, Chad and Glen, and the bay mare with two logs tied behind, broke clear of the trees and brush. Glen led the animal to within four feet of Uncle's International, and brought her to a halt.

There, Chad removed the chain from the logs and he and little brother headed back up the mountain with the mare to get another load. Iver grabbed the crosscut saw, and with silent thanks to his two sons, he headed for the two logs waiting beside Bug's truck.

Soon the older men were at each end and had the limb-bare tree hacked into three sections each.

By that time Chad and Glen and the horse had snaked the remaining four logs down the mountain. By the time Dad and Uncle had sub- divided them into manageable lengths, there was plenty to fill-up two trucks. So in another hour each outfit sat poised at the campsite with nine logs on each of their backs, ready to take on the mountain trail. After the crew had loaded and chained the ex-trees safely into place, they turned to the task of cleaning up the campsite, and finally, to the job of seeing to the overworked, but willing, and gentle, bay mare. Chad tied the rope securely around the base of her aspen tree; at the other end of the rope was a leather belt which he wrapped around one of the ankles of the animal's front legs. While the young man was doing that, Iver and Bug went to the creek with her water tub, and Glen piled fresh hay in front of her. Then each of them gave the mare a hug so-long.

Iver jumped into his truck and was followed closely by his sons. Brother-in-law Bug did the same act with his truck, and after stomping on the gas pedal six times, his outfit roared to life. Because of his truck's position, Bug had to be first out, he slammed the shifting lever into compound low, and engaged the clutch, but all he accomplished was rubbing the hide of the mountainside raw with the trucks spinning dual tires. Bug gave 'er a little more gas, and the tread dug deeper and slung debris halfway up the mountain, but to no avail. Try as it would, the International could not pull itself out of the depressions caused by the defrosting of the canyon floor and walls. Bug finally gave in to frustration and let fly a blast of profanity such as Glen had never heard before. In fact, some of the words

Flight of the Kroughs

used by his Uncle would never rattle his eardrums again. Until, that is, he was fully grown and out in the world.

Iver leaned on the steering wheel of his truck and watched Bug's performance through his rear view mirror, and he really enjoyed it - every minute of it. After a respectable length of time had passed, Mr. Krough finally removed himself from his own truck and strutted toward his red-faced relative to see if his assistance would be appreciated. "For hell sakes, Bug, shut that damned corn binder down about ten notches. Get some chain, and I will be glad to drag you out of here."

Bug looked at his relative, by marriage to his sister, in cynical disbelief. "So you think that miserable, broken down, tin lizzy of a Chevy will do the job, huh? Why, if you tied a chain to your hat, that truck couldn't pull it off your head ... in fact, it couldn't pull the Goddamned chain." But, all the while he had been blowing those words at Iver, he was also busy hooking the two outfits together with a thirty-foot log chain.

After Bug had finished the unhappy task of attaching the two loaded-down vehicles together, the two men marched quickly in opposite directions, and leaped simultaneously into the cabs of their respective trucks. When settled in his seat, brother-in-law poked his head through the window hole of his outfit and yelled, "Give 'er hell, Iver."

A mischievous look moved across Iver's face like an incoming tide, and settled on his lips as a smile. He floored the gas pedal, rammed the shifting lever into compound low, and popped the clutch. The chain clanked tight with a quiver against the frame of the International with business-like authority. At first Bug's truck only reacted with a snobbish shudder, and for just an instant refused to budge.

But, when the Chevy, along with the cornbinder's spinning back wheels, built enough energy, it gave in and lunged out of its mucky trap in a barrage of rocks, mud and old bark.

Iver was grinning ear to ear, as Chad, and Glen with a teary smile on his frightened face, hung on for dear life. After pulling Uncle Bug, who had started to swear again at Iver, and his truck halfway down the two-rut Big Hollow lane, the truck in front at last came to a stop. Iver casually climbed down from his outfit and just as casually strolled back toward his embarrassed brother-in- law who was already coiling up the tow chain. He jokingly told his logging buddy to be more careful where he parked his truck next time because he may not be there to pull him out.

With no more difficulty, the two trucks made it across the river and onto the main canyon road. There Iver stopped.

"Oh shit," Bug moaned, "what now?"

Iver just looked at the older son, it was the look that Chad was hoping for.

The excited sixteen-year-old ran around the front of the resting truck as Glen stood up so his dad could slide under him to sit by the passenger side door. Like the expert, although unlicensed, driver that he was, Chad took charge of the loaded outfit and drove it to the mouth of Left Hand Canyon. There, the four of them quickly unloaded their hard earned logs at Baldwin's Sawmill, finishing the job just as the sun had finished its trip mountain top to mountain top across the Virtue Valley sky. From the sawmill, the trucks went their separate ways.

When the Krough boys and their dad arrived home, they were dirty as hobos and twice as hungry. But before Iver was allowed to eat, he had to read a note sent to him by his good friend, LeRoy.

Debating with his friend had recently become a thing of the past. Because, on the occasion of the last general election, Mr. Jensen had run for and had been elected to the Bear River City Council. Whereupon the Mayor appointed him to head the Roads and Sidewalk Departments. Which, meant that he was responsible for keeping one man, one tractor grader, and one dump truck busy. The first matter of business that LeRoy took part in concerned his own department ... a beautification project.

However, with the added work also came the authority to hire a man to work on the project... part time.

Irene handed the note, scribbled on official city stationary, to her husband. He read it through twice before telling his wife what it contained - as if she couldn't read and as if she hadn't read it.

"The Mayor wants to give me a job."

"A job! Really" cried Irene. "What kind of job?" as if she didn't already know.

"Do you remember those young trees we saw in the bed of the city dump truck when it was parked behind the barber shop the other day?"

"Yes, I remember," answered Irene.

"Well, they need someone with a pickup to plant them, and, during the summer, haul water to them. So all I will need besides the Ford is two fifty-five-gallon steel drums. And those I can get from Hank the Jew."

Within an hour after supper had been wolfed down, Mr. Krough dispatched Chad with a note to the rookie Councilman agreeing to take the job regardless of the pay or his second-rate equipment with which to do that job. Iver knew, but didn't make an issue of it, that he could compensate for the lack of serviceable equipment with physical labor.

One and a half hours after Chad had left home with the note, he returned to the Krough house bearing another note written on official paper that described Iver's duties and starting date and time. At the bottom of the message was written a P.S. that stated his wages were negotiable. "That's OK," said Iver as he read the P.S. "LeRoy wouldn't cheat me."

Flight of the Kroughs

For four hours each late afternoon during the next three months, as two miles of trees had been planted to dress up Main Street all the way from the cemetery west to the fancy dance hall, Clara, Glen and JC had a ball. And they each earned twenty five cents a day in the process.

Iver would just drive slowly along the edge of the road - first west toward the downtown area, then east toward home, and as he passed each new tree, the three Krough kids would each scoop a bucket of water from the steel drums and heave it over the sideboards of the pickup. Sometimes they hit bullseye, and sometimes they came close.

It was a half-assed job, and Iver knew it, but he also knew that all the city fathers, except LeRoy, were snickering among each other, and behind Mr. Jensen's back, that a half-assed job was better than nothing.

Most of Iver's time during the watering trips was spent leaning on the Ford's steering wheel deep in thought and fraught with worry.

At the top of his list of cercerns was his health. A concern his wife was unaware of. Two of his sisters suffered with goiters, and, based on their symptoms, he knew without a doubt that he was afflicted with the same disease. Yet he wasn't convinced in his own mind that the problem in his neck was the reason he had, for some time, felt run down. In fact, he had become so concerned about his health that he even lost his desire to go to the hills with brother-in-law Bug.

While leaning on the hand-polished steering wheel deep in thought, Iver decided two things: first, he would let Doctor Blodget see to the goitrous gland in his neck, and second, he would take the necessary steps to become a naturalized citizen of the United States. He felt the latter of the two goals to be the most important because of the world situation.

He reasoned that if his oldest sons were to get involved then he himself ought to be at least a certified American. He figured, however, that before he could do either of those things, there was just one more job he would like to take on. A job which, he assured himself, would supply enough money to pay for the operation, and maybe there would be some left over. The job, unfortunately, that he was seriously considering, would require the procurement of a better truck than the one he already had. In honesty, though, any truck that would run would have been a better one than a Chevy with a rod thrusting out of its engine block.

With no research on the subject at all, Iver knew that Irene would have grave doubts about going into debt, especially for another truck. But he also knew that it would be, as it had always been; he would tell his wife of his carefully considered plan, and what glorious benefits the Krough family would enjoy. Irene would then say "Iver, I know all too well, that you do what you want to do, and that, in the past, what I had to say influenced you in no way, shape or form, so you go on as always and make up your own mind."

By creating the imaginary discussion in his mind, he had flushed away any doubts that might have hindered any decision concerning his intended course of action. The very next Sunday he confronted his wife with his idea ... it was no contest, and Iver once again proved himself a prophet. As, Irene caved in to his unique logic and surrendered her blessing on his applying for the job and the loan.

The government's opportunistic answer to rural and wilderness decay, the Civilian Conservation Corps, or "CCC" as it soon became known, was invented to give purpose to young men who were shut out of the work force. President Roosevelt decreed that all such young men languishing on the streets of the cities of the east and midwest felt useless and discouraged: so, by putting them in green wool uniforms and putting them on the payroll at a few bucks a month, he would nip a potential problem in the bud.

While in the Corps, the city boys would acquire valuable skills that would stand them in good stead in later, more pleasant, times. They would learn how to plant trees, lay telephone lines, build roads and bridges, and develop campgrounds.

Iver truly believed that his hero in Washington had been divinely inspired when he had created that agency, and that it was his duty to give him a hand in making it a success.

Monday morning Mr. Krough sat at the kitchen table with his hands cradling a steaming cup. All of a sudden he said, "To hell with it," to no one in particular, and he walked quickly to the water bucket, picking up the wash basin as he went. He splashed some water on his face, combed his hair, then left the house saying it made more sense to get the job before going into debt.

"How sensible," Irene said quietly.

He reported to the shiny new "CCC" Camp that sat at the mouth of Left-hand Canyon full of hope and anticipation. He was halted by an olive-skinned guard at the entrance of the camp and was asked what business he had there. Iver politely asked the young man in the new coarse green uniform where he might find the contracting office. Not knowing, for certain anyway, the curly haired sentry directed the visitor as best he could. So informed, Iver set out to find the office on his own. The way he had it figured, there would be hordes of people there to apply for the job. So, he informed himself, just find the place with the most vehicles parked around it. And his plan worked.

There were several cars and trucks, but most of them were olive green. In fact, his was the only car that belonged to an applicant for the job. On the

Flight of the Kroughs

main door were listed the names of several offices housed in the building. Iver found his three from the bottom.

He wandered the halls of the large administration building with his hands in his pockets playing with two pennies, a quarter, and four matches.

Finally, another uniformed corpsman rescued, and escorted, him to the correct office, which was empty, except for a fat, balding civilian warming an oak executive swivel chair behind an oak executive desk. He waved Iver into his obviously lonely twelve-by- twelve office with the excitement usually reserved for a long lost friend.

After showing his guest to a chair, the half bald, all fat, bureaucrat asked of what assistance he could be to Iver. Iver told the sweaty government official about the job flyer he had run across at the Post Office while scanning the "wanted - dead or alive" posters.

Not wanting to appear to be under-utilized, the heavy official shuffled several sheets of irrelevant papers then said "Yes, I believe that position is still open. We have interviewed several people, but as you are here now, you are very fortunate because we need to hire someone right away. So it seems, the job is yours, that is - if you want it."

Had the large man presented the facts honestly, he would have told Iver something like this, "We have talked to many applicants, but unfortunately, none of them would take the job."

"Well, what was the problem?" Iver would have naturally asked. Then the official would have answered "Most of our young men stationed here are Italians from the eastern part of the country, and they are Catholic."

"Ah, I understand" Mr. Krough would have said in return "the fact that they are Italian and Catholic makes no difference to me. I want the job."

The official didn't say those things though, but Iver did say yes and got the job. His new position safely in hand, he returned home in a hurry to find his wife wandering through the berry patches and vegetable garden waiting for him.

When he had parked his pickup in the dusty front yard, she met him at his truck door.

"I see you were serious about going up the canyon."

"Yes, I was," he said as he cleared his throat.

"Do any good?"

Irene could tell by his actions that Iver had news, and that it she pressed for an answer, then he wouldn't keep her in suspense.

"I got the job, if that's what you mean" he said. Then he waited for his wife to respond. When she did, she said what he wanted to hear ...

"I suppose this means a trip to Smithville tomorrow." Iver nodded "yes."

D. Raymond Anderson

He then finished getting out of his pickup and went directly to the cowshed and pigpen to see if the three younger boys, Glen, Jackson, and Harvey had done their assigned chores ••• they had.

Irene shut herself into her kitchen where she peeled and boiled some potatoes, fried some salt pork, and opened a two quart jar of peaches. Forty five minutes later she issued her first, and last, call to supper.

About halfway through the meal Irene awakened to the realization of an odd fact; she hadn't thought to ask, and Iver hadn't volunteered to tell her, just what the nature of the job was anyway - and why did he need a truck. So, she cleared her throat of food and asked her husband about it.

"Not much of a job really," answered Iver, "all I do is haul the Corpsmen to the movies on Wednesday and Friday, and to the dance on Saturday."

"Then it's not a real fulltime job?" Irene said in a tone of disappointment.

"No, I wouldn't call-it that," said her husband, then added, "bout twenty hours a week, I guess."

Viola, eighteen and a little more, seemed to shiver a little inside when the subject of the young men stationed in Left-hand Canyon came up. Lucky for her, that Wednesday when Iver made his first trip to collect the CCC boys, Chad and Viola were by his side.

Chad wondered just what kind of people those olive-skinned conservationists were. Did they eat regular food, did they speak a language a Krough kid could understand, and were they as loud, large and self-assertive as people said they were? And was it true that they prayed to the Virgin Mary and not God? Some of his questions would be answered that first night. But Viola's thoughts didn't address such concerns. Hers were more sensual in nature. She wondered if the young men they were about to meet were as tall, dark and handsome as some of the girls of her social standing said they were. And would going out with one of them be like dating the devil as Alfred Allen said? "If so, did that make the devil Catholic?" Viola wondered ... she wasn't convinced.

When the guard at the gate caught sight of Iver's shiny new, but used, truck coming up the canyon road toward their camp, he sent a runner to alert each barracks chief.

Within two minutes, and by the time Iver had parked his outfit, he was overrun by fifty shouting Italians waving their four hour passes in the crisp canyon air. Chad sat in the truck over-whelmed by the amount of noise, disguised as strange words, coming out of their mouths. Viola's head was floating in excitement.

After ten minutes of chatter and shoving, the last passenger wedged his body into the mass of wool coat covered bodies that smelled like a crate of

Flight of the Kroughs

mothballs. Iver looked at Chad, and the young man knew his courage was about to be tested. So he opened his door with a mighty shove and ran to the back of the truck like he was running by the cemetery.

He pulled the rear flaps of the canvas canopy that covered the truck together and hooked the chain that tied the opposite side boards together. Chad then made a quick retreat to his side of the truck. He jumped in and looked at his dad through eyes that were, for Chad anyway, very large, and that said, "Well I made it, and without getting killed."

The guard made a quick visual inspection of the loaded truck. Satisfied, he then slapped the driver's door with his hand and waved him out of the camp and down Left-hand Canyon road.

Within twenty minutes Iver parked his truck loaded with human cargo across the street from the Show House; then he turned the peculiar pack loose. Some went to the Pool Halls, some wandered around town enjoying the attention paid them by the local citizens through drawn but slightly shifted shades, and some actually went to the picture show.

Because it was the first night of his new job, and because he wanted to see how things went, Iver decided not to return home during the Corpsmen's four-hour liberty, but remain parked in town.

He dispatched Viola to Allen's Market at the east end of town to buy something to snack on. While returning from the store carrying a bag filled with bologna, bread, and soda pop, Viola met two of those notorious tall, dark, and handsome, boys from back East. They started a one-sided conversation with Viola, and even volunteered their names. The blushing teenager, did likewise.

One of the pair seemed to her to be a real gentleman because he suggested that, as they were all going the same direction, he would carry the grocery bag, which he did.

The three of them walked the two hundred and twenty yards together making small talk as they went. And they went slowly.

Much to Viola's relief, after the nicer one handed her back her groceries, her two new friends bade her goodnight, crossing Main Street to the Show House just before they reached the tail lights of her father's truck.

As she moved along beside the bed of the truck toward its cab, Viola felt blessed at not having to explain being in such company. She tapped lightly on the passenger side door, and Chad pushed it open for her. Absentmindedly, she passed the food to Chad, and he obediently passed the food directly to his dad.

Iver spit his gum bleached wad of chewing tobacco onto the street. From the snacks he made several sandwiches, and told his children to help themselves.

To Chad's delight, Viola refused the food but accepted the soda pop; she had other, more satisfying – although forbidden – things on her mind.

Later that same evening, all of the young men showed-up to fight being forced to stand at the rear of the truck. Chad quickly roped and chained them in.

Later that night, when Iver had rolled into bed next to his half sleeping wife, he was very satisfied within his own mind that the first night on his new job had went well. And had he requested his daughter's opinion, she would have voted very well. That routine was repeated over the next two weeks, and with the same results.

Viola made her usual trips to Allen's Market where she would meet her two friends, talk, then separate just in time.

However, on the Wednesday trip into town on the third week, the routine, as far as Viola was concerned anyway, changed dramatically.

As had become her custom, Chad and his older sister accompanied their father on his twice-times-a-week part-time job on that Wednesday. But on that evening, Viola complained of feeling ill

Her father suggested to her that she should return home ••• straight home. And she agreed.

As she walked swiftly past Allen's Market, her body was jolted with excitement, and a tiny bit of fear. Because, from the shadows of the dark, east side of the store, emerged the polite Italian she had been meeting on the street for the past two weeks.

As usual, Gino greeted Viola politely and warmly, and she returned a greeting equally in the same manner. Because she had just passed her normal terminus, he asked where she was off to.

Viola answered truthfully, that she hadn't felt very well, and that her dad had ordered her home.

Snatching an unexpected opportunity that he hadn't dared hope for, Gino sucked up all of the courage within him and asked Viola if he might be allowed to walk with her to her home.

She thought deep and hard for many seconds ... then, tentatively, she said, "Yes, I guess it would be OK."

He quickly positioned his five-foot-nine, slightly soft body between Viola and the outside edge of the sidewalk, and then the two of them walked arm in arm up the hill and dissolved into the darkness beyond the street lights of downtown River City.

Their pace was slow, and they talked a great deal, he about his home and family back east, and she about her hopes and aspirations for the future. The young lady felt a good helping of joy being escorted home by the curly-topped, tan-skinned young corpsman.

Because none of the "churchie" local boys would have anything to do with Viola, except of course, if she accepted their disgusting propositions to meet secretly in the shadows somewhere, which she refused in embarrassment, that evening seemed even more delightful.

After passing the cemetery, and because they were but a block from her house, Viola became the escort and led Gino to the other side of the street. For the rest of the way, under the cover of darkness and the drooping limbs of a row of boxelder trees, the pair made their way, unnoticed to, and through, the gate, then into the then vacant house where she had once lived with the rest of the Krough family.

The young couple concealed themselves in the front room. They then sat on the bare planks and leaned their backs against the water traced wallpapered walls.

In shafts of moonlight streaming through paneless windows, Viola looked down shyly at their joined hands. She was unaware that she had lost her bit of fear several blocks ago.

Gino raised his right arm to give it a phony and innocent stretch and gave an equally phony but innocent yawn. He did all of that to make it easier to innocently maneuver his arm behind Viola and around her shoulders.

She turned her face to the right and studied for a moment the hand that grasped her shoulder. As she did when Gino had stepped out of the shadows, she felt fear ripple throughout her body. Or, at least, she believed the feeling to be fear.

They talked more. He told Viola of his parents back in Brooklyn, and she told him more about her family across the street, sleeping.

Then, acting as if enough conversation had taken place between them, the young Italian pulled Viola's head up to his and placed an awkward kiss on her lips.

He kissed her more times than she could count, and he got better at it as he went along.

After what had seemed like a few minutes, when in fact it had been two hours of heavy necking, the inexperienced teenaged lady began to worry. Not that any physical harm might befall her, but whether or not she would be able to manage the situation she found herself in.

Viola was suddenly concerned as to whether she would become so aroused that she might be tempted within herself to do things that she didn't ordinarily do. So she began to consider that if, or when, such temptations did occur, how she would deal with them.

She knew that she had good reason to worry. Because, based on what his condition was at the time, any rational behavior would be left to her.

So, the middle part of the night was consumed by the exhibition of a two-way struggle; on the one hand, the struggle was between her and Gino. On the other hand, the other struggle was between her and her conscience.

The struggle was so intense that the fact that her father had returned home with his truck and son went unnoticed by her.

Viola resisted Gino's love-starved sexual assaults time after time. Between each of his unsuccessful advances, Viola suffered the distress of denying herself the satisfaction of her own desires.

By three a.m., and quite unaware that such a late hour had arrived, the young lady resisted for the last time. Gino finally had to admit the crushing truth that conquering Viola's body and will was impossible.

The pair stood on their feet and prepared to issue their final farewell to each other.

Viola's clothes were wrinkled, dusty, and askew in odd positions. But, throughout the passion-filled night, they had remained, although sometimes grudgingly, where they belonged ... on her body.

The young couple walked from the falling-down house together and onto the unlit street. Gino gave Viola a dispassionate kiss, then told her goodnight. Then he quickly marched east toward his camp in the mouth of Left-hand Canyon, worrying about the consequences of missing bed check.

She watched him disappear into the ever chilling early morning, and couldn't help feeling a bit of sadness for him.

Then Viola turned and ran lightly, her feet barely touching the ground, to the Krough house. She carefully turned the front door knob, opened the door just as carefully, and ever so softy entered the front room.

She might just as well have knocked the door off its hinges using a sledge hammer. For, sitting on the edge of her bed waiting for was her mother.

Through the moonlit gloom of the living room, Irene looked hard at her daughter ... and said sternly, "I will see to you in the morning, after the kids have gone to school."

Then Irene pulled her legs and feet onto her bed and under the covers.

Viola stood frozen for just a moment; then she dropped onto her shared mattress to hopefully sleep away what was left of the night.

The following morning, after the other children had left the house for school, Mother Irene made preparations to keep the promise that she had made to her daughter just five hours earlier.

She first went to the irrigation ditch-bank where she snapped a small limb from a willow tree that measured about one half inch at the butt and tapered to nothing in the space of four linear feet.

Irene then returned to the house, stripping leaves and twigs from her weapon as she went.

She picked-up her two babies and called four-year-old Harvey to her side. She placed them in the kitchen, then, with plenty of sugar cookies and milk to keep them occupied she shut the door. She returned to the front room and turned her attention to Viola, who, was on her mattress and under her cover, but not sleeping.

Irene looked down at her daughter and dreaded with every molecule of her being what she was about to do.

She then showed her weapon, and at the same time yanked the cover from Viola's body.

Although awake, Viola was caught by surprise. So she quickly sat up and pulled one corner of her quilt beneath her chin with both her hands.

Then she saw the milky green slender branch stuck in her mother's white-at-the-knuckles right fist. Next Viola looked into her mother's red eyes and pled, "Please mother, nothing happened." She then began to cry.

Irene's eyes watered-up with anger mixed with sorrow, and she yelled at her terror-stricken daughter that she would teach her a lesson that she wouldn't soon forget. "For," she yelled, "staying out all night with one of those wild Italian heathens."

"God only knows what went on," she screamed.

Mother Irene then began to swing wildly at Viola with her disciplinary magic wand. The young lady protected herself the best way that she could.

While in the process of rendering the undeserved punishment upon her daughter, her reason for doing so, somehow, changed. Irene began to recall the shit she had to take from her husband's snotty sisters and his mother too. And she remembered the hardship she had endured between Alabama and Utah ... the wornout clothes cast her way by insensitive neighbors, the poverty and welfare of the depression ... and, most of all, for throwing away the secure future promised her by Mother Rosanna if she would but use her beauty and Southern charm to impress some well-to-do Southern gentleman.

Before many swings had hit their target, the beating was over. Suddenly Irene was in tears and sitting alongside her nearly eighteen-year old daughter who was yet engulfed in tears.

Irene softly massaged her daughter's reprimanded body. She was thankful that it wasn't damaged beyond a few red marks.

She took hold of Viola's trembling hands with one of hers, and with the other she wiped her daughter's face dry with the corner of the bed sheet.

Although it was difficult for her to say the word love and also to convey her innermost feelings, on that occasion, Irene forced herself.

"Viola," she began, "because I love you so very much, I want you to have a life different than the one I have had so far. You are a very beautiful girl, and you possess much artistic talent. You have a fine singing voice, and you are far from lazy. All of those qualities are important to you if you expect to land a husband who can take you out of this mess."

"As important as those qualities are, however, there are three that are more important: one is self respect, another is a pure body, and lastly, but most importantly, a spotless reputation."

After her mother had finished her say, and still suffering the after-effects of sobbing, Viola again repeated, "Mom, nothing happened."

"I believe you," answered Irene.

"I suspose I was too worried about you messing up your life and throwing away your future, and that I was trying to live your life for you. But even worse, and I hope, someday, that you will forgive me for this, I was punishing you, but I was disgusted with myself for giving you so little help while you were growing up, and using you as the scapegoat. That is a terrible thing for any human being to do to another, let alone, a mother to her daughter."

In just an instant after Irene had finished her apologetic speech, the pair was hugging each other, and once more, both were in tears.

Knowing what was going to take place that morning, Iver had retreated to the barnyard where he could lean on the pigpen fence and think.

Beside him, and also deep in thought, leaned Chad. The young man was first to speak: "Do you think that it's all over now. Dad?"

"Well, it's pretty quiet up at the house now."

"Mom was awful mad, wasn't she?"

"That she was," said Iver.

"Do you think Mom hates the CC's now, Dad?"

"Well, I don't know why she should. After all, Viola is old enough to know that she has to suffer the consequences of her actions. And that shouldn't be too hard, because she certainly has been taught right from wrong ... Anyway, I warned your mother, and often, that girls are more difficult to raise than boys."

"Is it true what they are saying in town, Dad?" Chad asked.

"I'm sorry. Son, but unless you tell me what you have heard, I can't give you much of an answer to your question."

"Well, when I visited Allen's Store last evening, I over- heard some of the men saying that Mr. Martin had contacted the senator while he was in his Salt Lake Office and suggested to him that some changes ought to be made at the "CC" Camp."

"Hold it, you don't need to say another word, Son," Iver said as he showed Chad the palm of his hand like a New York traffic cop.

"Back a few years I used to work for that cow-killing son-of- a-bitch. And even as far back as that it was common knowledge that he had our senator safely in his wallet pocket."

Flight of the Kroughs

"Now don't tell me, Chad, because I'll bet that I can guess the rest of what you heard ... they are going to ship the Eastern boys out, right? And did they also say that, they were going to close the camp down for good?"

"You are half right, and half wrong. Dad. They are going to ship the Eastern boys out. But they are going to replace them with some guys from Kansas and Missouri, and they will work the place."

Much to his son's surprise, Iver didn't seem to show much concern about the rumored change at the camp. He had just used the occasion to blow off steam about his former boss. But, the reason he showed little concern for the swap of residents at the camp was because he had decided to cease shuttling the corpsmen to and back from town in any case.

Upon learning that. Chad was beyond surprise; he was shocked.

Because Iver believed that he was forced by circumstances, he felt justified in making the decision to quit.

During the three weeks of hauling the young Italians, they had ripped the bed and canvas cover of his truck nearly to pieces.

So it was either put out money to have the truck repaired, or give up the job. Iver chose the latter.

Just for curiosity sake though, Iver questioned his son about his reason for being concerned about the fate of the "CC's." But he was woefully unprepared for the answer Chad provided him with.

"Because I want to join-up" was the young man's brave reply.

"For God-sakes kid, why would you want to join that outfit only to be shipped off to some forsaken place the other side of the country?"

"That's the neat part about it, Dad. I won't even have to go out of state."

"You see, the corps has this camp that's run by the Forest Service in the mountains, at a place called Huntsville. About thirty miles southeast of here.

In Iver's mind he wanted to throw his arms around his son's shoulders and give him a hug. Because he knew that he was about to lose a dependable helper and, at the same time, lose a young pal.

Later that same evening, right after supper, when the younger children were out of the house playing and the older children were off visiting their friends, Mr. Krough talked his son's stated intentions over with Mrs. Krough.

They reluctantly agreed to extend to Chad their blessing.

When the young man returned home later that evening, his mother was waiting for him. As he came into the kitchen, she rose to her feet and met him face to face.

Like her husband, she wanted to throw her arms around Chad's shoulders and give him a hug. But, unlike her husband, she did. Standing rigid and a little red-faced in his mother's embrace, Chad likewise became a pinch emotional as well.

"I do so hate to see you go, Chad," his mother spoke while nearly choking-up.

"Well, it's a good thing in a way, mom. Because, Dad is without real work. And after I join the "CC's," the government sends part of my pay home. And you are welcome to use that money for the family."

Hearing her son utter those words, Irene was reminded of why she felt the sorrow that she did upon learning of his plan. So she gave Chad another squeeze, then let him go.

The next morning, the young man jumped from his share of the cot very early. Instead of picking up one of his western novels and heading to the outhouse for an hour's worth of serious reading, he went straight to the animal sheds. By the time his mother had made a fire in the kitchen range and had boiled a pot of coffee, Chad had fed the pigs, fed the chickens, milked the cow, and had chopped enough wood for her kitchen range to last at least two days.

"Do you think he's excited?" chuckled Iver as he moved from their bed to the kitchen table for his early morning coffee.

"Are you kidding me? He was up past midnight tossing and turning because he couldn't sleep," said Irene. "So he lit the lantern and sat behind the kitchen stove and read his novels."

Iver was very aware of the fact that his wife was more than a little sad about her son's impending departure. Also he knew her reason as well: she had come to depend on her sixteen-year-old son. Whenever there was a shortage of money in the house, Chad always managed to find some sort of work. When he was paid-off, the money always came straight home to his mother. Irene knew in her own right that she too was about to lose the company of a dependable helper and friend.

At about nine-thirty, with Chad in the middle, the three of them rode the Model "A" onto the main road. Iver was at the wheel, and Irene sat by the passenger side door clutching her son's right arm. They were headed north to the county seat and the post office building.

There, he was sworn-in along with a dozen or so other out-of- work young men.

Upon the conclusion of the swearing ceremony the government ranger circled the room and gave a reassuring handshake to each parent. He then invited the parents to follow their sons outside to the Smithville sidewalk to say their goodbyes. After which they could watch as the new corpsmen boarded their transportation and wave them on their way.

"Isn't October a bit cold for those boys to be riding in the back of an open truck like cattle" asked a concerned Irene.

Flight of the Kroughs

"Aw, they are tough young men" answered Iver. "They will be just fine."

After seeing their son off, the Krough couple got back into their Model "A" pickup and headed back toward Bear River City.

While traveling the seven miles south not a word passed between them. But in secret they both wondered how Chad would fare in the "CC's"; it being his first experience on his own.

Three weeks passed before Iver noticed any change at the camp in Left-hand Canyon. So he, and most others as well, wondered if the rumor mill had manufactured faulty goods.

Then, on the morning of the twenty-fifth of October of forty, a convoy of government olive-drab trucks rumbled past the Krough house headed west.

Immediately Iver recognized the boys loaded on the backs of the trucks as the ones from back East who had nearly destroyed his own outfit. He knew then that what Chad had overheard in its rumor stage was fact, part of it anyway.

Within two hours the other part of the rumor became fact.

Up the road headed east from the train station came the same olive-drab trucks loaded to the tailgate. As they passed by Iver and Irene's house, they could see that the new corpsmen were much different in looks than the ones just shipped out. Sure enough, as they proved when they shouted their answer to Iver's question, they were from Kansas and Missouri.

Viola and her mother watched through the front room window as the convoy paraded by the house.

They told each other that this had to be a better bunch or Mr. Martin would never have agreed to let them in. And saying that, the two women had, just like Iver, given Mr. Martin more power than he deserved. "But we will see," said Irene to her daughter, "the first time they have liberty ..." which, as it turned out, wouldn't befar off.

Two days later, Saturday, a truck, this time a government truck, sped by Mr. and Mrs. Krough's house and stopped between the Show House and the Saturday night dance hall with the floating floor.

Irene turned a little bit sick when she had watched the truck loaded with corpsmen go by. She suspected that the commitment she had made to her daughter a couple of months back might soon be tested. Because, as coincidence would have it, Viola had, herself, planned to attend the dance with her girl friend that same evening.

So when the young woman came into the kitchen with her rich, auburn, full-of-body hair falling on and all around her shoulders and wearing her freshly washed and ironed cotton dancing dress, her mother found herself wobbling on the fence of indecision. And she wasn't sure which way she was going to fall.

Irene took her daughter's hands in her own and, for just a moment, studied her daughter's lovely, but flushed with suspense, face.

"Have a good time," Irene said.

The young lady had sensed a raging battle going on inside her mother. And that it was extremely difficult for her mother to relent and allow her to go. But Viola had already vowed to herself that, if given the chance to prove it, she would not again give her parents cause to distrust her. Just as Irene had vowed to herself not to so control her oldest daughter's life that it might cause her to do things that in later life they both might be sorry for.

Irene made another promise to herself as well: that if Viola, or any of her other children as well, was lucky enough to stumble, or marry, into good fortune, she would be happy for them, and not be envious of them.

Feeling as if a great burden had been lifted from her after that evolved attitude, she broke into quiet song and went happily about the chore of preparing her four youngest children for bed.

At the same time the dolled-up young lady went to the front room and joined the older ones who were in a loose cluster around their dad engaged in conversation, except for two. Clara stood at Iver's right shoulder and was styling his more than adequate supply of silver gray hair. And on the floor Glen sat massaging his father's rheumatic lower legs with alcohol.

Before a half hour had passed, Viola's friend showed up, so she jumped to her feet and took hold of brother James' hand, pulling him off his chair.

"It's time for you to take us downtown" she said in a festive voice.

James stretched his six-foot-two frame, yawned, then snatched up his denim jacket from the back of his chair and said "OK, let's go." Then the three of them headed for the pickup.

The two girls had arrived early, yet the dance hall was already nearly packed to capacity.

For several minutes Viola speculated on the reasons that the place was so packed on that particular Saturday. Then the real reason finally occurred to her; many of the people were there to simply evaluate the new boys from the camp.

After checking their coats, and visiting the powder room, the pair made their way into the dance hall proper. The band was busy setting up, and the city cop (who many of the people called Sherlock instead of his real name, which was Eiroy Hillman) was making diminishing circles around the floor sprinkling dancing dust.

Normally, the dance hall crowd divided itself into two groups long before the conductor struck up his band. The ladies lined themselves up along the east wall - where their powder room was located. And the

Flight of the Kroughs

gentlemen would line themselves up along the west wall - where their restroom was located.

Since the construction of the "CC" camp though, the dance hall crowd consisted of three groups: the females in their customary place, the regular Virtue Valley males in their customary place, and clustered tightly and cautiously near the exit signs at the south end stood the "CC" males.

After Sherlock had concluded his sprinkling act, he would march off the slick floor with red and blue and green lights reflecting in its leather like buffed finish, and strategically position himself between the two male groups. Then, everyone knew, including the leader of the band, that it was time to start the Saturday night dance.

By the time Viola and her friend had at last found a vacant piece of floor on which to stand and wait as the six-piece band was swinging into action ... not being of name band quality, some of its members could swing better than the others.

Six couples served as pioneers and bravely ventured onto the vast, deserted expanse of semi-darkened dance floor. So, when not asked to join-in, Viola and her friend didn't feel the least bit cheated.

When the notes of the third song floated throughout the building, the major share of the crowd was on the floor, and the molecules in the springs beneath it were warming to the occasion also. There were few people standing on the sidelines. Most of whom were the ones standing shyly at the front of the hall.

Only then did Viola begin to feel a bit uncomfortable.

She wasn't surprised when none of the Bear River City boys dropped by to ask her to dance. Because to them she was unworthy ... Why? She didn't know and couldn't care less.

She knew it wasn't just because she was part of a less than affluent family. There were many girls present who endured circumstances equal to, or poorer than, her own. Yet some of them were just as popular as the rich girls. The only thing that most of those popular poorer girls and the richer girls had in common was that they were inferior to Viola both in looks and in talent.

Yet she and her brothers and sisters were treated badly by the fine citizens of Bear River City.

She didn't worry long about such things though. She was there to have fun after two months of self-imposed exile from the River City social scene. And in any case, there were boys at the dance that came from one end of Virtue Valley to the other. So she knew that sooner or later someone would walk by and take a chance on her.

Viola hadn't allowed herself to consider any of the thirty or so "CC's" as candidates for possible dancing partners. When she dared ask herself why, she was without an answer.

In any case, she decided to break the monotony by visiting the ladies room.

Upon her return trip toward her spot on the firm outer floor, she felt an uncertain tap tap-tap on her shoulder from someone behind her. And for just an instant she froze.

Viola spun around to see who had sought her attention, as much out of curiosity as interest. When she did she stood face to face with a dark haired "CC". Before she could stammer or apologize her way out of her predicament, he asked her to dance with him - and he asked very politely.

Her first impulse was to flatly and indignantly refuse. Just having the "CC" speak to her caused the events of a few months earlier flash across her mind.

But that first impulse, and right after that, the unhappy memory, soon melted into her subconscious.

Viola knew that she couldn't say no to his polite request. In fact, she didn't want to say no, because he seemed different.

She collected the rest of her uncertainties and cast them aside. She said, "yes, I would love to dance with you, if, that is, you are willing to risk your beautiful shoe shine."

"I doubt very much that my feet are in any danger," he answered in a smooth confident voice and with a slight but pleasant smile. He was correct. As Viola was an accomplished ballroom dancer. Just another of the lady like characteristics she possessed that would have qualified her to marry into the privileged class.

In addition to her serene grace on the floating floor, she was well known in the city for perceptive finesse in her artwork. As if that were not enough, she was often called upon to vocalize at church and civic functions.

Oh yes!! They did move well together. He was also graceful and very athletic as well.

After the second set of dances, they decided spontaneously that the time had arrived to exchange names: "Viola ... a beautiful name, my name is Greg."

"How he fits his name," she thought to herself. The interested young lady guessed him to be at least six foot one, and he was all of that. His hair was coal black and his skin was a deep natural tan color. Greg had brownish-green eyes surrounded by features that looked to Viola as if they were chiseled from granite.

Flight of the Kroughs

By the time the last dance began, she had so thoroughly studied those features that it seemed to Viola as if she had known Greg for years instead of just one and a half hours.

Exiting the hall after the last dance, Greg took hold of Viola's arm and gently stopped her just as they reached the sidewalk.

"May I walk you home?" he asked.

"Oh, I don't think so." Then she added "It's a long way, and I'm sure that the driver of your truck wouldn't wait for you."

"I suppose you're right," Greg admitted in a tone that suggested a quantity of dejection.

Then Viola herself, announced a suggestion that surprised even her.

"Would you please come to Sunday dinner?"

"Tomorrow?" Greg replied. "Well, I don't know," he went on. "How would I find where you live anyway?"

"That's no problem" said the excited young lady. "When you come out of Lefthand Canyon headed toward River City, our house is the first one on the right - you can't miss it."

"Or, just in case those directions aren't enough, just look for the place with all the scruffy kids surrounding it."

Hearing that description of her place, he laughed, then they both laughed.

It caused Greg to silently asked himself "Is she kidding?" while at the same time, Viola was asking herself what he might say if he found out that she wasn't kidding.

"Well, OK," said the handsome "CC." "Is twelve o'clock all right?"

"Sure," answered Viola.

The government truck's horn blasted the silence of the mid- night air as the young couple parted with smiles and a handshake.

After retrieving her hand from his, Viola looked around for brother James. She knew that it was a waste of time to search for her girl friend. At about eleven o'clock she had caught a glimpse of her back as she left the dance hall with some guy.

As she did not see her brother anywhere, and as she wouldn't lower herself to begging a ride, she decided to walk, but ended up running home.

When she arrived there, Viola was surprised to see that her younger brother Chad was home for the weekend, sleeping in his customary place.

Also sleeping in their customary place, the southeast corner of the front room, were her mother and father.

Wanting to dispel any lingering suspicions that her mother might have, she quietly knelt by her bedside and lightly nudged her shoulder.

Irene immediately rose from her bed to a sitting position, and spoke her daughter's name in a questioning way.

The young lady softly reassured her mother that she just wanted her to know that she was home, in spite of brother James falling asleep and forgetting to pick her up.

Then the urge to relate to her mother the news about Greg overwhelmed Viola. And it seemed appropriate, regardless of the hour pointed out by the hands of the clock. Soon the pair was sitting on one side of the double bed cross-legged, facing one another like Native Americans about to pass the peace pipe. On the other half of the bed, half awake, Iver wished that the two women would quickly finish their after-midnight powwow and go to sleep.

"Mother," Viola began; then after a pause, began again, "I met a terrific guy at the dance tonight."

"CC?" asked Irene.

"Yes," answered Viola honestly, with not one hint of anguish.

At that point, Irene gave a disappointed but not forbidding groan that was aimed over the right shoulder of her daughter.

Upon hearing her mother's response to her news, Viola wasn't real sure if she should tell her the rest of what was on her mind ... the part about Sunday dinner.

"What's this guy called?" Irene asked.

"Greg."

"Good strong name; where's he from?"

"Kansas City" replied Viola.

"Kansas City!!" Irene responded in a perkier tone.

"You know, that is where you were born, Honey."

The younger of the two ladies setting on the bed slapped the side of her face lightly and shouted in a whisper, "Why didn't I think to tell Greg that? A great opportunity unfulfilled," she then added.

"Do you believe that to be a bad sign, Mom?"

"I don't believe in signs child. I believe in what I see in a person's talk ... face to face."

"Well, Mother I do hope you won't be angry with me, but you won't have long to wait before you can make your face-to-face judgement - in fact, tomorrow. Because, I invited Greg to Sunday dinner."

Visibly shaken by Viola's last, and surprising statement, Irene pivoted her body then sat staring into the darkness while sitting on the edge of her bed and scuffing her bare feet on the cold floor.

"Isn't that just a bit sudden?" Mother Krough begged as she imagined events occurring faster than they could be thought about in the light of reason and rational self interest.

"Well, I won't say what's done is done, but it's going to be up to you - and Irma and Clara, if you can get them to help - to clean up the house. It

Flight of the Kroughs

will take all of my time just to rustle up some decent food to feed your guest. Maybe I can talk your father into killing a couple of the older laying hens. From which I will stir-up some chicken pot pie. But for right now, honey, goodnight. Go get some rest so you will look beautiful tomorrow," stated Irene.

Oh, how Viola did rest. In fact she hadn't known such peace and contented happiness since she was a child. The remainder of that night went swiftly by.

Regardless of her "late night before," the day began early for Viola. She had rolled out of bed at six o'clock thinking herself to be the first one up. But she was brought to wide-awake by the stuttering sound of the old Singer sewing machine. She couldn't imagine why it would be in operation so early in the morning.

While rearranging the covers over her two sisters, she decided that one, or both, of her baby sisters had left their mattress and were having some fun with the old machine.

Before whoever was playing with the thing wakened the whole family, Viola decided to leave the yet dark front room and investigate. When she did, she received a startling surprise. For there, at the Old Singer, sat her mother. She had just finished remodeling a hand-me-down once-fashionable dress. Irene had transformed it into an up-to-date fashionable dress.

Irene noticed her daughter enter the room that was a kitchen by day and bedroom by night, and right away she told her to get the dish-doing pan then go outside to the water tap and fill it. Then bring it into the kitchen and place it on the stove to heat.

Viola guessed that her mother intended that she should give the new dress a quick wash and hang it on the line to dry. After which, the dress would get a good ironing.

The young Krough lady had anticipated her mother's wishes correctly, so quickly and without question, she went about getting the job done.

After seeing to her dress, Viola then made another trip to the outside water tap. That time she filled a large, blue enameled sauce pan three quarters full of cold water. Next she returned to the kitchen where she put the container of liquid on the hottest area of the stovetop.

When the water had arrived at a brisk boil, she sprinkled a little salt into it, then dumped about a pound of rolled oats into the water as well.

She let it cook vigorously for about five minutes. Then she slid the off-white mixture to a cooler area of the stovetop.

The clock showed that it was then seven a.m., Viola created as much racket as possible while taking the odd assortment of cereal bowls from their second shelf resting place in the cupboard. She deliberately made an equal amount of noise as she placed them on the red-checked oilcloth covered table.

She then hurried throughout the house, shaking as she went, the occupants of each sleeping place out of their dreams. While doing that, she apologized for the early Sunday morning wake-up.

After a fast breakfast consisting of the oatmeal, fresh milk, wild plum jam on homemade bread toast, with hot coffee for the grown ups, Viola again, as she did all during that forenoon, hurried the family through their assigned tasks.

By eleven-forty-five, she, her parents, her brothers and sisters, and the house, were suitably prepared for the occasion ... the occasion on which, for the first time ever, a young man called by the Krough house to visit one of the five daughters and take dinner with her family.

Viola's last thoughts before her guest was to arrive concerned her family and her guest's reaction upon meeting them.

"I'm sure," she reasoned, "that if Greg runs for his life when he gets here, it won't be due to a dirty house, or scruffy children."

The young lady was right. For, thanks to her, the house, her parents, and her brothers and sisters were spotless. An accomplishment that bordered on miraculous.

Thanks to her mother, Viola's appearance was nothing short of beautiful.

Then an afterthought further reassured her. "After all," she mumbled, "he couldn't have come from much better circumstances, or he wouldn't have enlisted in the "CC's.""

During all of that morning's preparations there was one thought that didn't occur to Viola: that he might not show-up at all. So spending all of that time and effort was a waste.

As it turned out, Greg did, in fact, show up. And his visit was a rare success.

Irene had whipped up a tasty chicken potpie that even a lover of gourmet food would have raved over, if, that is, he had the guts to do so.

After dinner was over and compliments to the chef had been voiced, Greg soon discovered from Iver that the Krough's had spent much time in and around Kansas City. So, they had plenty to reminisce about.

Chad also had a few things in common with the visitor. Major of which was the fact they were both members of the "CC's."

So far, the day had seemed like something out of a fairy tale to Viola. Before the day would end, Irene would know that her daughter's course to her destiny had been set.

Greg said his goodnights at about seven-thirty that evening, and the Krough family was sorry to see him go.

Flight of the Kroughs

As soon as he had caught a ride back to camp and was out of sight, Viola ran to her mother to tell her that she just had to go see her girl friend and tell her of the fantastic day that she had experienced.

Irene understood, and a pleased expression crept across her face, then changed to a smile as she watched her love-stricken daughter rush through the front door, and disappear down the path.

After nearly being steamrolled by the speeding female body as he was returning from a quick visit to the outhouse, Chad re-entered the warm front room.

Everyone was in a pleasant mood - thanks to Viola and her new boyfriend - so Chad decided it was a good time to make a self- serving suggestion.

"Mom, how about me taking Erma and Clara to a movie in Smithville. If, that is, dad will loan me two dollars ... and the pickup."

He acquired his dad's permission, money, and the use of the Ford surprisingly easily. However, there were conditions attached.

The major one being that Chad must use the back road. Because, neither the truck, nor Chad, were licensed. Iver didn't bother with such useless bureaucratic interference gadgets as a license.

So away the three young Krough folks went: down cemetery hill - the back side - through the bottom lands, past the pea viner, past the bean canning plant, then along the railroad tracks, through the north fields, and, finally, through the back door to the county seat. There, four movie houses lay waiting for them to choose from.

The girls, especially Erma, knew that if they happened upon one at which a western shoot 'em up was playing, the choosing would be over.

Chad parked the Ford on the side of a street that was dark enough to hide the absence of current plates; then he unloaded himself. As did his passengers.

They walked the four blocks into the heart and lights of Smithville, and prepared to check out what was playing at the theaters. Just as one might expect, the first show house they came to was featuring a Class C western. So Chad naturally nudged his two younger sisters toward that theater.

To help get them inside, their brother assured them that it would be a good picture as he had read the story in one of his cowboy books.

Regardless of Erma's rotten mood, which was caused by what she considered a trashy choice of a show to see, she relented, and took a seat. However, to Clara, the choice of movie wasn't important, To her, a show was a show. Even if it was, as Erma put it anyway, "Horseshit and gunpowder."

D. Raymond Anderson

After the cowboy program had ended, and a small coke each had been downed at Dick's Cafe, the trio headed through the north fields for home. And, to Irene's reckoning, they arrived there at about ten o'clock.

The three of them climbed from the pickup and headed for the front door. But as they arrived at the front porch, Chad said that he heard a strange noise coming from the barn, and that he was going to see what it was all about.

Erma and Clara went on in, and to bed and thought no more of it.

After checking things out around the barn, Chad decided that the noise he had heard was most likely restless pigs.

As it was warm for a middle December night, the young man decided to go for a walk.

Chad wandered up and down the snow covered dirt lanes and gravel roads near the Krough house for about an hour or so. He then walked up the road towards Left-hand Canyon.

About a half mile from home he came upon the new service station that the Allred's had just built.

He peered through the windows at the dimly lit interior. Then, as he passed his gaze over the merchandise, the candy display caught his eye.

For some reason he had the urge to go around to the rear of the building. As he did so, he walked by the side entrance. Chad indifferently reached out and dragged his hand across the doorknob - and it turned!

The first impulse to invade Chad's inner systems told him to run. But the pinch of larceny hid away in some part of that system took hold and overruled that first impulse. So he crept into the moonlit service station. To aggravate the criminal act, he was hungry.

As he strolled among the crank-operated reservoirs of motor oil, racks of fan belts, water hoses, and candy bars, the last items brought Chad to an abrupt stop.

Without thinking much about it, he clawed at four or five varieties, stuffing his pockets as full as they could get ... then he ran.

He hurried across the moonlit north-south main highway then hopped over the barbed wire fence that impounded a twenty acre alfalfa field. The stubble of that field ended just across the lane from the Krough house.

He then slowed to a very slow pace. He began stripping wrappers from candy bars, devouring them like a pelican eating fish.

By the time Chad had finished devouring four of the sweet chunks of candy, his appetite was absolutely numbed. So he dreamed- up the very best story he could and climbed over the fence, then headed across the lane, to the house.

Flight of the Kroughs

Quietly, he opened the front door and made his way across the front room floor that was littered with mattresses that cushioned from the floor at least, three bodies each.

When he at last arrived at the bed occupied by his mother and father he stopped and sank until his knees were on that floor.

The young man lightly moved his mother's shoulder. She was wide awake in an instant.

Chad reached into his pockets - pulled his treasures out - and displayed them in candle light to his mother.

"I brought these home for you and the kids, Mom."

"Where did you get them?" she naturally asked.

"Oh, I met some guy up on cemetery corner, and he gave them to me."

"Why didn't he want them?"

"He said he had bought them for his kids and found that they were allergic to them."

"My word," Irene snapped, "I have heard better stories than that from one of your brothers or sisters when they were six years old."

"Why don't you wise up. Chad, give them all to me and go to bed." From her son's manner, Irene had a notion that Chad had done something stupid, if not downright illegal. "Go to bed," she ordered again, "You, me and your dad will discuss this matter further in the morning. And talk they did, loud and uncompromising.

The truck that would carry Chad back to his mountain "CC" camp was due to pass through Bear River City at eleven o'clock that same day, allowing Iver and his distressed son plenty of time to go the quater mile to Allred's Service Station.

When they arrived, Iver was thankful to find that only the owner was present. So he decided not to "horse ass around" as he liked to say.

"Mr. Allred," he began "were you missing anything from your shop this morning when you opened up?"

"Well, nothing that I'm aware of," was his tentative response.

"But I can tell you right now that I am damn lucky. Because, like an idiot, I ran off last night and left the side door unlocked."

Chad wanted to kick, gently of course, his dad on the shin and not admit to anything. But no such luck.

"Well," Iver said as he piled the sweet loot on the counter, "I think my boy, Chad, has a confession to make ... right, Son?"

"Yes sir, I do" he said shyly.

"I was walking last night and found your side door open. So I went in and took these candy bars" Chad admitted.

"Wait just a minute now, not so fast."

"Are you trying to tell me that you were in my place - in the middle of the night - with all this expensive equipment, and all you took was candy?" said Mr. Allred in a mild state of shock.

"Well-I'll-be-damned, if that don't beat anything I ever heard." He continued "But it's obvious to me that you wasn't out with the intent to steal. And I must bear some of the responsibility for being so irresponsible as to leave a door unlocked."

"In a way I was lucky it was you, Chad. So let's just say we both learned something. So if Iver will pay for the ones you ate, I will forget the whole affair."

Iver gladly tossed the man a half dollar.

He knew that if that kind of news made its way to Chad's camp, he would be summarily dismissed ... dishonorably.

Feeling much better for their good fortune, the father and his son climbed into the Model "A". Then Iver looked at his son and said, "Now you owe me two-fifty."

As the pair whizzed off the filling station's cement and onto the asphalt highway, Iver shook his head and nearly shouted, "Of all the God -damned things to swipe and bring home to your mother - candy bars."

As Irene had already packed Chad's things into the bed of the Ford before their trip to the service station, they needed only to stop by the house long enough for the young man to say goodbye to his family.

So Iver parked beside the road and waited.

It took Chad but five minutes to say his farewells, and then he was back beside his father sitting quietly, headed to meet the truck that would take him back to camp

Petty larceny notwithstanding, Iver felt a great loss again as he watched his helper and young pal leave River City. But his sorrow was, to some extent, tempered by the knowledge that the holiday season would soon be there, and Chad might be able to take leave again and come home.

Between Greg's first visit in October and Christmas, little of his free time was spent at the "CC" camp.

He was at the Krough home or out with Viola some place every minute of every liberty.

So by the time Christmas Eve had arrived, the couple had just about decided that they were going to marry.

In fact, all that was holding the announcement up was the non- existence of a ring to make it official.

Everyone, the Kroughs included, hoped for a white Christmas. On the holiday of nineteen-forty, they got their wish – and with a vengence.

Not in half-dollar-sized flakes, as was their secondary wish, but in BB-sized frozen projectiles that were carried on a twenty mile an hour east wind.

In spite of the weather, Greg had made it to Viola's house by six-thirty, just in time for a sandwich and milk supper.

Then, as soon as Clara and Erma, under Viola's supervision, had finished the few supper dishes and straightened the kitchen up, Iver and Irene gathered the Krough kids around the tree.

Greg held back just a little.

Back in Missouri his family didn't make that much of Christmas, if the truth was known, he felt just a little bit embarrassed on behalf of his adopted family. For, looking around him, he could see nothing in particular that they had to celebrate.

There were few presents under the nicely decorated tree touching the crazed plaster ceiling.

And he could see no special fixings for Christmas dinner.

But, after a little coaxing and tugging at his arm by Erma, he finally agreed to join in. Before many minutes had passed, he was, in spirit, a full-fledged member of the group.

Iver then did something that shocked the visitor silly. He quietly asked that everyone join hands. When they all had shuffled their bodies into such a position that enabled them to do as he directed he offered a short but heartfelt prayer.

After Mr. Krough had offered his words of thanks and praise to the Almighty, a different feeling descended upon the huddled family, and the guest as well.

He, the guest, wondered again to himself, how such a large family that had so little to do with, could manage such love. Both in general, and for each other.

Erma was the first to break the momentary silence when, as in years past, she stood up and announced that it was time to sing.

Iver always experienced much joy from that part of the celebration. Because that was the time he could display his rich, near enough to perfect, baritone voice. Not to mention his wife having the opportunity to show off her soprano singing skills.

Chad, agreed once every year, to provide the accompaniment with his guitar - the rest of the year it only played to western signing.

James, the oldest, was a natural high tenor. Erma and Clara sang alto. And what was leftover of the group, the five younger ones, joined Viola carrying the melody.

The guest sat back in amazement. What Greg had expected to hear was, at best, twelve people, thirteen if a lipsyncing Roland was counted, but he couldn't carry a tune in a cast iron bucket, singing slightly off key in four different octaves.

But the Krough family sang as he had never heard a family sing before. They all sang in their correct pitch, and their voices blended as smooth as the colors of a rainbow...in spite of Roland. When the group finished their singing, Greg silently begged for more. But Irene and her daughters had other plans.

Knowing the routine, the younger ones gathered at the feet of the older ones, who were still gathered around the tree, and bargained for spots around the Christmas tree where Santa would leave their treasures. While, the oldest ones drank coffee.

In about fifteen minutes the guest was surprised again. For marching from the kitchen came Irene, followed by three of her spruced-up daughters. Each carried a Christmas Eve treat. "Irene must be some sort of a magician" Greg thought to himself.

The mother carried a large clay bowl full of punch made from the juice of wild plums picked from trees that lined the canal banks when it was summer.

Viola carried home fried potato chips, also from the summer garden - but fried in bacon drippings given by one of Iver's former thinking friends at the pigpen.

Clara brought up the rear carrying a jar of homemade tomato sauce for a chip dip.

Greg could tell by looking that none of the food came out of a store. And, oh, how he enjoyed the rare treats.

When the snacks had been wiped out, it was the custom in the Krough family to open the gifts under the tree, gifts that the family had exchanged. They always drew names from a jar which guaranteed that each had a least one present - Greg included.

Each, starting from the youngest and working up, took their turn opening their gift.

When it came Viola's turn, she had two gifts to open. And, naturally, she opened the one from Greg first.

When she did, she nearly fainted ... it was a ring ...and it was strikingly beautiful. She was first surprised; then she was happy beyond words.

Irene cried: Iver's voice cracked while issuing his congratulations to the couple, and a house full of brothers and sisters cheered.

By that time it was close to nine thirty, and the wind had stopped. But, not the snow.

Greg and Viola had the need, but not the place, to be alone, so they settled for a walk in the freshly fallen snow.

Mother Irene began her nightly chore of assigning sleeping places to her tired but excited brood.

When the lovers returned to the house, they found their own corner and curled up together - fully dressed - under Greg's bulky government overcoat. Just before kissing Viola goodnight he turned to her and said, "You know. Honey, it wouldn't matter how cold it got outside, no one in this house could ever die of frost- bite."

"Why?" Viola asked.

"Too much body heat," replied Greg.

Viola laughed - they kissed goodnight, and then they somehow fell asleep.

The three younger boys, Glen, Jackson and Harvey, lay on their mattress in the southwest corner of the front room just opposite the Christmas tree.

Of the three, the two younger ones dropped into sleep right away. But Glen's mind was wide awake and in motion.

He gazed through the tattered window shade at the cobalt, comatose sky. He thought about winter, and wondered why the snow had to be. Then he gave himself an answer.

"For Christmas of course, and good old Santa Claus." "So" the eight-year-old Glen thought, "he can guide his laden sled through the heavens and land it with no trick."

He imagined runners riding smooth and true on frozen moonbeams. And watched as dump trucks, games, and dolls, exited his bottomless bag, which were aimed at each sleeping child, side-by-side with their dreams.

Glen could see in his mind's eye other things. Like old Santa's team of nine. As they used diamond-like stars for stepping stones.

Oh, the older ones at school and church boasted that Santa was no more than a parent and child's imaginary ghost. But, as far as Glen was concerned, he had proof that they were wrong. Although he was young, Glen knew his family was poor, he also knew that his father's health was so destroyed that his body ached at every joint. But all these things didn't matter. Because, early every Christmas morning when they charged to the tree, they always found pile after pile of gifts and toys.

Some of those toys showed signs of being slightly used. But, in spite of that minor problem, the Krough kids were no less gladdened. Iver put their minds to rest when he jokingly said that they were last year's demonstrator models.

With that last thought Glen passed into a deep, satisfied sleep.

Iver and Irene sat at the kitchen table late into the night talking. They were filled with the same spirit that those who were better off, were, at the same time no doubt, feeling.

When they were sure that the children were in a deep, dreaming sleep, they, as always, would pull from their hiding place, two articles for each of the five youngest ones. The items consisted of one toy and one piece of clothing.

Then as usual, at about midnight a truck would coast to a quiet stop in front of the Krough house. From which three men would jump, each carrying a large cardboard box.

They would walk a shadowy route to the front of the Krough house, then quickly depart, leaving the three boxes setting on the front porch.

Although Iver and Irene were aware of what was going on and that the gifts were provided by some Men Only Club in Smithville, they never interfered or risked spoiling their caring fun.

So every year the Krough kids enjoyed a fine Christmas, regardless of where it came from.

The Christmas of nineteen-forty, however, was special.

Granted, the news of Viola's impending marriage to Greg did much to take Irene's mind off the troubles that swirled around her. Unfortunately, though, the knowledge of the widening war in Europe lay waiting to cast gloom on every day.

Hitler and his Germany was on a roll in their war against the world in the spring of nineteen forty-one.

It took just twenty-nine of his divisions three weeks to bring the country of Yugoslavia to its knees. At the same time Nazi tanks entered Athens.

During that period of time rumors of the extermination of what Hitler called "a parastic germ" - the Jews, - began to circulate around Europe and as far west as Virtue Valley, USA.

Also Hitler launched his most ambitious campaign of the war ... when his troops invaded Russia.In the beginning, millions of Russians were ready to greet Hitler's armies as conquering heros.

But the ruthlessness of the elite SS Troops that followed in the wake of the advancing German armies turned every Russian into a bitter enemy.

They rounded up and liquidated Bolshiviks, Jews, Gypsies, "Asiatic inferiors," and "useless eaters," such as the mentally unbalanced and terminally ill.

Unfortunately for them, by the time the German war machine arrived at the gates of Moscow, it was out of gas and frozen stiff. In fact, it was one of those winters that the young would judge all later winters by, but the old would say that it was one nearly as bad as the one back in ought six or ought something.

Because Iver's regard for Stalin was so low, that turn of events, to him, was at best a mixed blessing. In fact he described the German failure in Russia as "getting cancer to cure a cold."

Flight of the Kroughs

The bitter cold wasn't confined just to Russia. In Bear River City as well, it was a winter to remember.

Snow piled up around the Krough house until it was level with the window sills and the perennial east wind pushed the below zero air through every available crack. It took two stoves working most of the night and day to keep the old place within survivable limits.

So, by the time March came around, nearly everything made of wood that wasn't nailed down had gone up in smoke.

Due to the foul late winter weather, much time was spent around the hot stove, talking. And the talk among the young men was about adventure, and that adventure was the possibility of war.

Such was a Saturday afternoon in late March. It was too cold for the Model "A" to crank and too cold for anybody with any sense at all to be walking to the dance. James, therefore, and his two best friends, Jess McBee, a first cousin, and Rod Bostock, met at the Krough house and talked for many hours with their shoes resting on the kitchen range open oven door.

They discussed their future, and what they each intended to do with it.

Then James changed the direction of the discussion.

"Do any of you guys know where Hawaii is?" he asked his two buddies.

"Heard of it" answered Cousin Jess.

"How about you?" James asked Rod.

"Well," Rod said thoughtfully, "ain't it in the Pacific somewhere? Off the coast of California, right?"

"Quite a way off the coast of California to be correct," answered James.

Then Jess grabbed control of the conversation and asked, "What the hell has the location of Hawaii got to do with the price of green beer at the pool hall anyways, James?"

"It's got nothing to do with green beer or the pool hall," returned James. "But that island, or to be precise, group of islands, could have a lot to do with us."

"You've lost me, James, I haven't got a hint of what you are trying to say," moaned Rod.

"Well I'll try to simplify it for you," reassured James. "I read in the newspaper that Uncle Sam is going to send a lot of soldiers to the Pacific, mostly Hawaii, and the army is in desperate need of volunteers."

"Hey!!" Rod yelped, as he jumped to his feet and into the conversation, "ain't that the place where the native women wear skirts made of straw, with nothing at all underneath or nothing above the waist either?"

"God, what I wouldn't give to lay on my back in a stampede of ten thousand of them and find out for sure" cried Jess.

"But what about dough?" Jess went on, "I hear it ain't too good."

"Twenty-one dollars a month and everything you need from a comb to foot powder and everything in between" said James.

Rod yelped again "Hell, you can't mean it, a vacation in paradise, and I would get paid for it. Shit, Man, where do I sign-up?"

At that point the character and tone of the conversation became a bit more serious.

"You know," said Jess, "there is as much rumor of war in the Pacific as there is real war.in Europe. And if we did join up and go to Hawaii, and if something went wrong, then we would be right in the thick of it."

"Bullshit" snapped James.

"Dad says Japan is a country no bigger than California. And it takes all the rice, fish, and deep fat fried grasshoppers they can beg - borrow - or steal just to feed their people. So tell me, how are they gonna make war?"

"Good point," nodded Jess.

"I'll go it James goes," Jess said to Rod. Jess then spoke for all three when he rubbed his palms together, and through a flushed smile said, "That warm weather and all those half-dressed women, shit, I can hardly wait".

And, they didn't wait long.

It was a dreary April first afternoon when James stepped out of the car he had hitched a ride in from Smithville.

He walked into the kitchen where his mother and dad were seated at the kitchen table enjoying a cup of coffee.

"Where you been, big boy?" Irene questioned in a friendly but suspicious way.

"Oh, to Smithville," answered her son. "What's doin' over there?" asked Iver.

"Oh, nothing special," answered James. Then the kitchen suddenly fell silent. So James did some quick thinking.

He decided to lay it on them straight away. "Mom - Dad, he said in a quivering voice, "I went to Smithville to join the army. And I got accepted."

Iver was at a loss for words to fashion a response from.

But Irene did have words to say. "You know, James, if Mr. Roosevelt needed you, he would just send you a notice to report. You really didn't need to volunteer. But being you did, I know you will make a good soldier, and I know the Lord will let no harm come to you - Did Jess and Rod go with you?"

"Yes, they did, Mom."

"God knows what their parents will say. They think the army is someplace they send someone that has done something so rotten that going to jail for punishment isn't bad enough."

Flight of the Kroughs

Then Iver spoke up. "What is army pay worth these day?" he asked, negatively.

"Twenty one bucks a month," replied James.

"For God sakes, son, you can double that working in the hay for LeRoy," spouted his father.

"Well, I know it looks like that on the surface, Dad, but you have to remember that everything I need is free in the army, and, besides, it ain't summer, and I'm tired of hanging around the house."

"Well, go on and do what you want to do, James, but just you remember two things: first, you know you have been a first class wanderer since you were fifteen years old. If you get itchy feet in the army, you won't be able to take off to scratch them. Because if you do, you know damn well where you will end up... In a place where they make pebbles out of thousand-pound boulders using a ten-pound hammer. And, second, you know war is coming just as sure as Alfred Allen is a sanctimonious asshole. So, if you end up in one of those places where shooting is in progress or about to start, and you get hurt, just remember, I didn't twist your arm to go."

All the while her husband was making that speech to his son, Irene was thinking that it was worth it to her son to join the army if only to escape the hopelessness he, and others like him felt in their situation, even if he had to face great risk.

His armor of confidence only dented, James nodded, taking into account his father's warnings. But for Iver, now forty-nine, as far as Irene knew anyway, sicker than anyone knew - and beginning to regret some of the things he had done earlier in life, it was difficult to watch his oldest child leave on a trip from which he might never return.

Unswayed by the potential danger, James, Jess and Rod said their goodbyes to their families and friends, then boarded the train headed for Texas. There, they would learn to be good soldiers.

Their torture, called basic training passed, contrary to their belief that it never would. At the same time the German army was continuing its subjugation of Europe. To make matters worse, the Japanese/American dialogue was becoming increasingly more hostile toward one another.

James wrote home as often as was possible under the circumstances. And his letters were an important event. Because, for the first time in several years, the Krough's received something in the mail other than bills.

On the fifth of July, Iver made his daily jaunt to the post office. Expecting a letter, he was surprised to find a "Too large for box" notice from the postmaster.

So he reported to the window as directed by the card. He handed it through the bars to the attendant and received in return a fat, ten by twelve, envelope. Iver guessed it was from his son - and he was right. But what was inside to make it so bulky?"

Believing it to be important, he hurried for home. So they could open it together.

Irene nervously snipped the brown cord, and ripped off the brown paper wrapper ... and, looking up at her, from an eight-by- ten frame, was the face of her son.

She gasped at the way he looked in the picture. He looked so clean with his professional hair cut. His shave was no doubt achieved with the aid of a new blade. And his uniform, contrary to popular rumor, fit his six-foot-two frame perfectly.

She wanted to say her son was beautiful - but settled for handsome. And for just a moment she actually believed that the grief endured giving birth to and raising eleven children, twelve counting the first one that didn't survive, was worth it all.

Starring at the tinted portrait, Irene found it hard to believe that three short months could arrange such a change in one of her Krough kids.

While her eyes were becoming wet with pride as she studied the glossy portrait of her magnificent son, Iver had begun to read the letter that was also enclosed. As he read, his muted joy turned to quiet concern. "What's the matter?" asked his wife.

"Read it for yourself," replied a shaken Iver. And she did.

"Dear Mom and Dad, and family," the letter began. "Things have gone great for me since I have been here. The food is great and two clean sheets each week is more than I could have imagined before I left home."

"Although Jess and Rod are assigned to different companies than me, we still see a lot of each other, usually at the service club dances. While I'm on the subject, do you know they bring girls in to dance with us... pretty nice girls too."

"In fact we met there just last night, and we compared orders. And, wouldn't you know it, we are going in opposite directions, me east - they west."

"To be more specific. Rod and Jess are going to a place called Bataan. Which is located on an island in the Pacific theater of operation. And the island is called Luzon. It is actually part of the Philippine Islands. According to the map, the island is about the size of Rhode Islands - We went to the library and looked it up."

"But first, the lucky shits get to spend two months in Hawaii for some jungle training."

"I wasn't that lucky. So I guess I won't get to see any grass skirts. But I will get to see some of the old countries - maybe even Denmark."

Flight of the Kroughs

Iver knew that that last line was a ploy to soften what his son knew would be a hard piece of news for him to swallow.

"But before I sail across the big pond to Europe, I am going to receive more training in Georgia."

Iver's disappointment settled into his stomach with a silent thud, and he occupied the nearest seat.

Irene circled her arm around his shoulders and assured him that his son would be just fine.

It seemed to Irene that things which never bothered her husband before, now did.

For days Iver had nagged his wife about getting the paperwork together so he could go to the courthouse at Smithville and file his "Declaration of Intent" to become a certified citizen of the United States of America. Of the papers needed, one was a birth certificate, and another was a current picture.

Iver and Irene decided that they would see to the photograph the following Monday, the tenth of August. That would be the most convenient time because Greg and Viola were getting married that day. So they could all ride together to the county seat.

Irene had been talking to Iver's mother concerning his birth certificate each time they had occasion to meet. But Hanna always had some sort of lame excuse why she couldn't go for it right at the moment, or, as on the last request, she couldn't find it.

After the wedding was over and Iver's picture had been snapped, the four of them headed for Bear River City and home.

Because of the new responsibilities that he would soon be assuming, Greg had resigned from the Corps and taken employment at Martin's Slaughter House.

The newlyweds had also made previous arrangements to rent a small house just four blocks west and one block south of the Krough house.

The young couple was on top of the world on that August tenth when they finally moved in.

But Iver's had a different frame of mind. He was becoming more and more restless. Because, he wanted so to secure his citizenship.

For the first time it dawned on him why his mother was so reluctant to hand over the needed document to his wife. And that realization shot excruciating pain across and down his hard-labor- bent back.

Pain or no pain however, Iver decided that he must take matters into his own hands if he was to acquire the certificate. After a period of building much self encouragement, that is. During the process of fortifying his courage, he also devised a plan to evade Irene's scrutiny of that piece of paper.

He figured that if, when he returned from his mother's house, he waved the document like a flag, the wife would be so overcome by relief that she would grab it from him and stuff it in the box with their other important papers for safekeeping before it became lost. One more time, Iver was a prophet, because that is just what she did.

Feeling as relieved as a crook in the chair when the circuit blew a fuse, Iver went directly to his pigpen, where he fed and talked to the tenants.

Irene though, being a mildly curious creature, and more quick-witted, through experience, decided to find out just what a Danish birth certificate looked like anyway.

So she slid it from its hiding place and began studying it intently.

Although she hadn't the ability to make much out of the foreign words, she could read the numbers. When she arrived at the line showing Iver's date of birth, she was thumped with surprise. Because it had his birth date recorded as 11-28-82, when during all the twenty-one years of marriage, Iver had let her believe it to be 11-28-92. So via some quick mental arithmetic, Irene calculated his age to be fifty-nine - not forty-nine. In an instant, much that was going on physically with her husband began to make more sense.

Not that fifty-nine would be considered exactly elderly in late nineteen forty-one. But it would explain, in a more logical way, some of the ailments he suffered; such as rheumatism, goiter, and a weak heart.

As Irene held the document in her shaking hands, she was again surprised, this time at herself. Of course, she felt no anger - shock? yes, but no anger toward her husband for deceiving her.

She even went so far as to rationalize the shock away with a comical though: "What," she chuckled aloud, "if he were really only forty-nine? I might have ended-up with more kids - who knows."

Meanwhile Iver had returned from his social and domestic duties at the pigpen, feeling extra good in the knowledge that he would go unpunished for deceiving his wife.

He even pitched in and helped Irene put some supper on the table. After the meal, he washed, she dried.

Iver then pulled the ash pan from the front room stove that he used for a spittoon - cut off a chunk of a new bar of chewing tobacco, which he tossed into his mouth - then put his head to the radio and listened to as many news reports as he could find on the dial until nine o'clock.

By nine-fifteen the kids were bedded down, and the two lights in the Krough house were doused.

As he lay staring at the ceiling, courage was building in Irene as she, too, studied the invisible ceiling.

Before as many as ten minutes had elapsed, she rolled over to face the side of his face.

"Why did you lie to me about your age?"

Iver knew without hesitation it was too late to play dumb - his secret was now history.

So he figured that the best tactic to employ was that of telling the truth.

He knew from past experiences with his wife that she wouldn't leave it alone until she got what she knew was the truth.

Giving in to the wisdom of that reality, he said to himself silently, "here goes."

"Well, Irene, to be absolutely truthful, I thought, when we first became friendly, that if you knew my true age, you would have nothing to do with me - and I was probably right - right?"

Her answer was direct, and to the point. And soon after hearing it, Iver wasn't so sure it was the answer he had hoped for.

"Iver," Irene said slowly, then she paused for just a second, then continued "you are one hundred percent correct." And that, as far as she was concerned, was all that needed to be said about the matter.

Again they both lay on their backs and stared toward the ceiling for several minutes.

Irene again rolled on her side and faced the side of her husband's face.

He rotated his eyes in their sockets in the direction of his wife, leaving his head where it was. Then he silently moaned, "Oh shit, here we go again." But, he was wrong.

"Sweetheart," she said softly - as if in a deep philosophical quagmire, "why do you suppose there exists such a horrible event as war?"

At that moment Iver was so pleased at the change in subject, that he would have gladly given all the money he had - if he in fact had any - to help elect a Republican.

"Well, Irene," he finally answered, "it's like a mother-in-law when she has no place else to go, you just have to live with it."

She had meant for her question to be taken seriously. So she propped on her left elbow, then proceeded to remind her husband that when she asked a serious question, she had a right to expect a logical answer.

Iver searched his mind and gave his wife the most logical answer to "Why war" that he could find: "Not being God," he confessed bluntly, "I wouldn't know, and war being an invention man, I'm not at all sure that the man upstairs has the answer either."

"Except for three groups," Iver continued, "few people gain anything out of war."

"Doctors gain knowledge; they learn how to hook a body back together after it has been taken apart by a fist-sized chunk of lead. So it can be returned to the battlefield to dodge more chunks of lead."

"Lords of industry gain something. They learn how to produce new weapons that are more efficient and how to refine old systems so they are twice as deadly as before... meaning kill more people for less money. And it's common knowledge that there exists no better place to try out new ideas than on the battlefield where there is an ample supply of live targets."

"And the makers of war, the generals," Iver went on, "they learn something as well. They learn to not make the same tactical mistakes in the next war and to improve their casualty-success ratio."

Sleep finally came to Mr. and Mrs. Krough.

Morning was on the horizon in the next instant. Iver bounced out of bed and flipped the radio knob to the on position then searched the dial for some world news. But before he found what he was looking for, there was a knock at the door.

Using as evidence its flimsy nature, Iver knew who was standing on the other side.

He opened his front door six inches and no more and peeked into the seven a.m. morning scene. Against which, the attired bean pole of a man was silhouetted.

Alfred while offering an embarrassed smile, extended a cracked good morning.

"I need to talk to you Brother Krough, but if it's too early I can come back later" Alfred Allen whinned.

"Son-of-a-bitchen nosey poker" Iver thought in the safety of his mind.

"Well, ok. Give me ten minutes" he slowly answered.

Thirty minutes, and after a leisurely cup of coffee, Iver opened his front door and reappeared to Mr. Allen and offered him a seat on an upside down, dried clean, pig swill bucket ... which Alfred accepted. The host stretched his body out in the morning sun on a pile of slabs from the sawmill up Left-hand Canyon.

Wanting to conclude their meeting as soon as possible, Iver queried Brother Allen concerning the reason for his early visit.

"Well, Mr. Krough, I have about a half acre of picked-over corn that I need chopped down, and I wondered if two or three of your kids would like the job of doing it for me. They ought to be able to do the job in a couple afternoons - and I will pay them each five cents an hour."

"Bless his cheap heart," Iver thought.

At that point in their conversation, Iver got off his back and told the visitor that he would send Jackson, Glen, and Clara down that same afternoon. He fully expected Alfred to turn and leave. But Alfred didn't

Flight of the Kroughs

leave; he just looked down at the earth and stirred the dust with the toe of his left shoe.

Iver guessed that there were other things on Alfred's narrow mind.

"Things are changing, Iver, and not for the best," moaned Mr. Allen. "I hear that a pair of couples in Smithville got divorced, then exchanged partners and remarried - and they act as if they are happy as four pigs wallering in their own muck ... Can you imagine that, Iver?"

"And since so many of our young men have started volunteering to go into the army, a lot of disgusting things have been going on."

"Like what?" asked Iver.

"Like some of the wilder boys playing on the sympathy of their best girl in order to have their way with them - destroying the purity of their bodies. I have even heard of some of those boys going off and leaving fatherless children in the womb."

"It's that damnable war that's to blame - too much money and nothing to spend it on but picture shows, dances, and booze."

"You know Alfred, I don't find news like what you have just agonized over all that disturbing, especially the bit concerning the partner swapping. After all, maybe they were just being honest."

"How so!" came the words from Alfred's mouth like the crack of a bull whip.

"By admitting to each other that they were party to bad marriages. So, rather than cheat, they did the honorable thing: they swapped" Iver boldly offered.

"No such thing," Alfred Allen whined.

"Oh, I beg to disagree with you," Iver insisted. "If you would quit using those specs of yours just for reading and look around, you would see a lot of Sunday marriages."

"My word, Iver!! You know the Lord doesn't recognize a divorce - except in one or two cases that is; those two cases being unfaithfulness or physical cruelty. So what gives you the right to talk about such a terrible event as divorce so casually."

"I suppose you have an excuse for those young people also."

"Well, maybe not an excuse," offered Iver, "but for sure a little understanding."

"You see, Alfred, those young men going off to war know that their trip may be one way. And they feel as if they have the right to experience all that life has to offer. True ... sometimes things go wrong. But I doubt very much that many of those young men shirk their paternal responsibilities."

"As you well know, from our past discussions, Iver, that I can neither accept what you say, or understand the reasons for you thinking as you do.

But I, for one, wouldn't be surprised to see the Lord come down and burn clean this planet gone silly."

"Well, Alfred, as you truthfully say, you and I have disagreed about God many times before. And as far as I am concerned, this is another case where you fail to give God his just dues."

"Please, tell me in what way," Alfred Allen begged.

"By underestimating his perceptiveness and flexibility," Iver answered.

"Well, then, and so I can better understand your position, give me the best example of a bad marriage you can think of - excluding, of course, the two I have already mentioned."

Iver quickly took up the challenge.

"There are many examples of a bad marriage. But the worst of the lot is one in which it is easier for either of the pair, depending on the situation, to give the other a nice funeral, rather than cut his or her mate loose while still alive and well enough to make a new life."

Alfred looked at his poor adversary and slowly shook his head. Then he stated that he wouldn't be surprised to see the Lord come down from heaven and personally cleanse this planet gone silly... repeating himself.

He looked Mr. Krough in the eyes and sternly ended his side of the argument by saying, "Again you have made your common mistake Iver. You view every situation as if death erases it, and you know that it doesn't. You also know that we believe every marriage should be made eternal."

Iver was glad for the chance to finally shut up on the subject, accomplishing two things at once.

First, he could get rid of his tormentor. And second he would be able to blunt the sting of guilt he had recently been experiencing whenever he argued religious principals with that same tormentor.

It was then halfway through August, of nineteen forty-one. And Hitler's mean and efficient war machine of destruction had romped, unchallenged to a great extent, over most of the well-built stone towns and daisied fields of Europe. But, time had a way of passing, regardless of the colossal tragedies man threw in its way.

The days between middle August and December eighth were no exception.

Irene could remember hearing about trade and the friction that it was causing the United States with Japan over her husband's shoulder as he listened to his radio, and she was confused.

Why, she wondered, was there so much concern about Japan, when the war was in Europe?

But, on December the seventh, she would have her wonder become irrelevant..

Flight of the Kroughs

As it was a clear, warm day, for early December, Irene was at the line hanging out clothes, humming a light classical tune she once knew the words to.

While leaning over to collect the final garment from the basket, she detected a weeping cry coming closer to her. She looked in the direction from which the sound was coming and caught sight of Mrs. Johnstone, running faster than her age should let her, moving down the lane, coming toward her house.

When the hysterical woman was about a hundred feet from the house, Irene was, at last, able to make out what she was screaming.

"We have been bombed - we have been bombed," she repeated over and over again.

Irene's first impulse was to look around to see if there was anything going on in the neighborhood that she had missed. She saw nothing.

Then she realized that something important had happened somewhere, and she sought to find out what it was.

She ran toward Mrs. Johnstone, and the two women met in front of the house.

Mrs. Krough tried to get some information from her neighbor, but all she heard was sobbing through an apron Mrs. Johnstone held to her face with cupped hands.

"They have bombed Hawaii," she finally said; and then she said it again and again.

Iver had also heard Mrs. Johnstone yell that Hawaii had been bombed. He rushed directly to his radio for some official news.

He listened to bulletin after bulletin concerning the facts surrounding the incident.

Every report was the same: that swarms of Japanese air craft had bombed Pearl Harbor, destroying most of the United States Pacific fleet, they had killed scores of American soldiers, sailors, and marines.

By the time Mrs. Johnstone had calmed to a point where she could, at least, talk with a quivering voice, Jess's mother arrived in just about the same condition. Then Rod's mother.

Why they all converged on the Krough place wasn't quite clear. But as Mr. Johnstone was off to the hills tending sheep - the same as Mr. Bostock, and Mr. McBee was up Left-hand Canyon digging in his worthless mine, Iver was the only male in the neighborhood left at home.

Perhaps, Irene thought - without knowing for sure - maybe Iver could put the events in some understandable perspective for the women.

But he was wise enough to know, without trying, that he would not be able to console three mothers whose sons were fodder in the jaws of the Japanese trap.

Mrs. Johnstone had never forgiven James, nor Jess, and Rod for coaxing her son, Boyd, to follow them and also enlist. Which he had refused to do until two weeks after the other three had departed Virtue Valley.

Consequently, she was full of "I told you so's".

By four p.m., the bad news would spread the length and width of Bear River City. Friends, neighbors and enemies would gather in various-sized groups all over town, to talk about what had happened.

Someone, no one knew exactly who, would call a relative in California and be told that unidentified airplanes, most likely Japanese, had been spotted off the coast.

So some of the easy to impress groups would predict, publicly, that mainland USA was next.

All along Main Street one would hear statements like: "We ought to kill every slant-eyed bastard in the world" or "Ain't it just like a dirty Jap? One talks nice to your face while his buddy stabs you in the back with a jeweled sword."

Back up on cemetery hill Irene did the best she could to say the things that would give the three neighbor ladies some peace of mind.

Later, Iver emerged from the house and his radio to offer what support he could.

The initial shock over, and having shared it, the three worry-burdened mothers accompanied each other toward their homes, each departing to her own destination along the way.

That particular December evening was funeral quiet. That, in spite of the ten Krough kids scattered throughout the house chewing on their treat ... Jonathan apples.

Roland and Erma were old enough to understand what historically important event had taken place that day. But the six younger ones knew only that something had happened to make everyone sad.

Iver and Irene did share sadness. As they lay in their bed staring into the gloom of night, she was the first to break the silence.

"You know, Iver, I felt so sorry for those poor mothers today. And I think, although they didn't put it into words, that I know what they really felt ... a feeling of hopelessness."

When our children are at home, and there is trouble - like with Chad - at least we are here to help. Even if there is little we can do. But when children are half a planet away, as James, Jess, Rod and Boyd are, all you can feel when there's trouble, is hopeless, even useless. Seeing those mothers in such distress made me feel almost guilty. Because our James is still safe in Georgia."

Flight of the Kroughs

"You shouldn't feel that way Irene," Iver answered. James joined with every intention of going right along with Rod and Jess to Hawaii. In fact that was the only reason for him signing up."

"I know, Iver, and thank God for James' good fortune, but that doesn't do much to relieve the suffering of those other three mothers."

"I know all that Irene, but even if James was shoulder to shoulder with those three boys, it wouldn't make the odds on their safety any greater. Or make their mothers feel any better, now would it? Because the sad fact is, that the supply of grief is one of those things that doesn't diminish when it's shared."

"You are right, dear. I just wish I knew what to do for them."

"I guess," said Iver "we will all know what to do, or expect what to do, tomorrow. I heard on the radio that Mr. Roosevelt will lay out his plan for the people then when he speaks to us on the radio, and I don't expect it to be pretty."

And it wasn't. The next day Congress quickly declared war on Japan. The voices of reason and diplomacy were lost in the clamor for revenge, without counting the cost.

Within days, the peace Irene had felt for her son, James, who was safe in Georgia, vanished with the stroke of a pen, because a declaration of war was made official between the United States and the German/Italian axis as well. By the first of February, James was on a troopship headed for Europe. From where, before his next Christmas, he would be storming the beach at North Africa.

Not to be outdone by his big brother, big in size that is, Chad quit the CCC's.

Irene thought it odd for her son to be walking the mile from the railhead to his home in the middle of the week. And with a burlap bag slung over.his shoulder as well.

He entered the kitchen - said hello to his mother - then asked where he could find his dad.

"Wait just a minute, not so fast young man. Just what are you doing away from your camp on a Wednesday?" she questioned.

"In a minute, Mom, where is Dad? I need to talk to him," Chad demanded mildly.

"Well if you must know, he is up at the barn trying to get the big truck he couldn't pay for to run," Irene answered disgustedly. Then added, "The finance company will be here tomorrow to pick it up."

Chad tore out of the house and down the footpath that led the barn.

Hearing the quick footsteps, Iver pulled his head from under the hood of his truck. He, too, was surprised to see Chad.

"Are ya in trouble at the camp son?" Iver asked.

"No, Dad," Chad answered in a slightly offended way, "I quit."

Iver heaved the pliers he was holding at the dead engine. "You quit!!" he yelled,

"Now, why in God's name did you go and do such a dumb son-of-a-bitchen thing like that for anyway?"

His dad's violent reaction to his news knocked Chad back a step or two.

Then Iver started up again, "Do you realize it's the middle of February, and the snow is up to Alfred Allen's ass? There ain't no work around here - so what do you intend to do, sit on your ass and read those cheap western novels?"

Chad got the distinct impression that he had caught his dad on a very bad day because, at the very least, he was in a poor mood.

But the young man understood that his dad really didn't mean to be so cranky. So he decided to hang around for a few minutes more to see if his dad's mood was going to change - and it did.

Iver didn't apologize to Chad, but he did ask his son to hand him different tools as he slaved at reviving the big truck. And he asked for the tools in a very nice way.

That was good enough for Chad. So he decided to confront his father with his plans.

"Dad," he began tentatively, "I am going to join the Army, and I would like for you to go with me to Smithville tomorrow to watch when they swear me in."

Iver stopped working - but didn't throw anything. A good sign Chad thought. Then he turned to face his son. For a few seconds Iver found it hard to believe that it was Chad he was looking at. "Wasn't it just a couple weeks ago that a boy named Chad was tagging me around up Left-hand Canyon?" he silently asked.

"Why?" he begged. "You're just barely eighteen. Why don't you stay home until you are done growing up? If they need you, they know where to find you."

"Well, Dad," answered the young man, "it seems to me that if things keep going like they are, I will go regardless if I want to go or not."

Iver knew his son was correct in his logic, so he said no more, but went back to his troubled truck.

Without being asked to, Chad did the chores and chopped a good supply of wood for the stoves.

He then went to the house and asked his mother if there was anything she needed from the store for supper. She told him that the kids were a little sick of salt pork so some hamburger would do a lot to cheer their appetites up.

Flight of the Kroughs

Off he went to Allen's Market. There, he spent every cent he had in his pockets.

He arrived home one hour later carrying hamburger, sweet rolls, all-day suckers for the kids after supper, and, for breakfast, a box of corn flakes to trade off with the customary cracked wheat or rolled oats.

After the special evening meal, neither Iver, nor Chad told Irene of the shocking plan or that Chad had quit the CC's. But as soon as she had her son alone, Irene planned to clear-up that matter.

However, before she could manipulate a situation, the evening was used up, and it was lights out at the Krough house. Seconds after that, Iver and his wife rolled into bed, and she was up on one elbow asking her husband why Chad had quit the corps.

Iver quickly rolled a couple ways in which he could tell his inquisitive wife across his mind. Ways that would make it easier for them both. But he gave that up as hopeless and admitted to himself that telling it like it was made more sense.

"Well, Irene," he finally began, "how do you know he quit?"

"Because I dumped the contents of his duffle bag by the washing machine and everything he owns fell out, including his western novels. That being two, I added to it the other two, it being the middle of the week, and I arrived at quit."

"You are right, but don't be too hard on the boy," Iver cautioned his wife, "because Chad feels that there are more important things for him to attend to - and right away." "Like what?" Irene asked skeptically. "There is no work to be found in the valley. I do hear that the government is hiring at the defense depots across the mountain, but, without dependable transportation, fifty miles is a long way off."

"Well, that's not exactly what I meant when I said more important things." "Well, for hell sakes, Iver, say what you mean and don't talk in circles to me, ok?" demanded Irene. So he did.

"Chad wants to, or is going to, join the army." That bit of information brought Mrs. Krough to a sitting position.

"Why?" she whined. "Isn't one of our boys risking his neck enough? Aren't we doing our fair share?"

"What about all those rich shits?" Irene went on. "Why don't some of them go?"

"Well, dear," Iver offered, "the rich shits are the educated ones and also the ones with the pull, and they are flocking to the Air Corps to fly all those airplanes they're building. The work is just as dangerous, but at least they will keep clean."

"Well, somehow it don't seem fair" lamented Irene. But she knew it was time to shut up or her husband would slip into one of his "political theory as it applied to social injustice" tirades.

And Irene had long since given up trying to understand the way in which the masters of the world carried on business or politics with each other.

she rolled away from her husband and fought her way to sleep, leaving Iver to think alone.

The following morning at about ten-thirty, Chad stood at attention before his mother as she inspected him to make sure he would look presentable to the recruiter.

Outside, Iver waited behind the wheel of his Model "A" pick- up, puffing unconsciously on a homemade cigarette, in deep-deep thought - about what no one would ever know.

Just two days after the induction ceremony, while Chad was waiting for enough recruits to be collected to make up a large enough group to send, a letter arrived in a fancy envelope. Tucked inside the envelope was an invitation to be part of a going-away party.

Iver remembered having read in the Virtue Valley Review that such affairs were about to begin. But he had figured that they would be private affairs for the upper class to send their boys off to pilot school or officer training school, in style, then to be written up in the Review's society pages as social events.

However, on Tuesday, the twenty-fifth of February, nineteen hundred and forty-two, just after the shock of his announcement had worn away, Chad coaxed his dad out of the house to the pickup; within ten minutes, after just three trips down the short incline in front of the house pushing, they had the engine purring like a sucking kitten.

Mother Irene then emerged from the house. Before allowing herself to be seated in the middle, she inspected her two fine- looking escorts, and they passed.

Then out of their yard and down cemetery hill the trio coasted. Iver knew that Sherlock would be otherwise occupied, so he, the unlicensed driver, behind the wheel of his unlicensed pickup, drove down Main Street boldly, as if he had every right to do so.

It was just past seven when they arrived at the fancy hall. And already there were a few people inside watching the telling hands of the clock move toward seven-thirty, the official starting time.

One person, then two, but in groups nearly always counting three, the people slowly entered, and soon the hall was about to over- flow its legal capacity.

Flight of the Kroughs

The dozen fly-branded, forty watt bulbs hanging from the ceiling offered their barely adequate sympathetic glow. As sadly, on that night, thirty of Bear River City's young men would be told their official farewell. At what, at the very most, could be described as a solemn celebration.

The program was set in motion when one of the local religious leaders offered an opening prayer. After which, the master of ceremonies, Mr. Gunderson, himself an old soldier, introduced the many digniteries from the south end of the valley who were in attendance.

Then Mr. Gunderson read the roster of those young men who were being honored. As he mentioned the name of each, as requested, they stood. When the last man was standing, he bid them welcome, then allowed them to sit.

Next, as the high school band played patriotic hymns, half-learned, because it was haying and vacation time, old legion warriors posted the gold-fringed colors.

Alice Anderson was then introduced. She sang "God Bless America", and she was obviously trying to out-do Kate Smith.

Mr. Gunderson introduced the first speaker; the mayor of Bear River City, Mr. Nelson.

He told the audience what a rare pleasure it was for him to be asked to speak to those fine young men, their parents, honored guests, and others who had come to join in farewell.

He continued his talk by saying, "There are but a handful of times when a few of us have the opportunity to stand up and defend something that is good and stand against something that is evil. Now is one of those times," he declared.

"Two evil dragons," he said in a dramatic fashion, "have raised their greedy heads, and they threaten to devour most of the lands of the world. Thereby destroying all that is good as they scratch and claw their mad dog covetous way across the continents."

"However" Mr. Nelson shouted, "we have joined hands with our friends around the world ... friends that share our democratic values. We will soon put a stop to that wave of heathen filth in such a way as to make the world a safer place for democracy."

"We will win this fight," he said, "because we have three things in our favor that cannot be disputed, or defended against."

"First," he went on, "we are right, and those Germans, Japs and Italians are wrong."

"Second, God is on our side. What more do we need?"

Then he proceeded to answer his own question - "What we need is the third element for our arsenal ... those find, strong young men setting out there in the audience."

At that juncture of the speech, the people in attendance broke into spontaneous clapping.

Chad was becoming increasingly restless. He wasn't accustomed to sitting for such an extended period of time on wood benches. The boards were beginning to wear through his layers of meat and fat, that were measurably below average in thickness, to the bone, and it was painful.

Besides, he wanted the talking to stop, so he could storm the buffet table - which was loaded with potluck specials.

At last, the Mayor finished his speech by reminding the young men that, although God was one of the elements in the plan for victory, they would need to do the dirty work. God would provide the inspiration.

Mr. Gunderson shuffled back to the podium and thumbed through his obviously out-of-sequence program. "Here it is," he chucked, "we will now be pleased to hear from Brother Jensen." Mr. Jensen was the president of a group of local Mormon wards, or what some might call parishes.

"My dear Brothers and Sisters," he began. "May I first comment on the quality of this marvelous program. Our good sisters have no doubt put in many hard hours cleaning, polishing and decorating this historic hall. And can anyone fail to hunger for that lavish display of food piled high on the dinner table?"

"I'd rather eat than listen to you and your phony praise," Chad silently commented.

"How wonderful it is," continued the anemic gray-looking church official, "to live in a country where people are so free to display their God given talents, such as our lovely sisters have done tonight - Let's all give them a hand." most in the audience obeyed.

After that show of appreciation came to a halt, the speaker went on with his eloquent remarks, "All I want to say on this important occasion to these choice young men we are honoring to- night is ..."

"I have been called a lot of names by the people of Bear River City before," Chad broke in - in thought, "but never choice ..."Then the young man returned his attention to the speaker and what he was saying. "That when - or if, you find yourself on the battlefield, you will never be alone. Even if your nearest buddy is hundreds of yards away. Because," he went on, "He will be with you. For, and just as our Mayor told you, the Lord is on your side."

To the sound of nearly silent noises coming from empty stomachs, the preacher continued, "There is nothing on this earth or in your mind that you can't talk to God about or ask him. And if you place your unqualified faith in him, then you will be one of the heroes that will march home to a grateful welcome when your job is done."

"Never forget another fact, though, a very important fact - you are Mormon men ... so keep a clean mind, and a clean body, and, although you may be surrounded by the torment of war, I promise, that all of you will be bathed in a pool of blessings."

Mr. Gunderson stumbled back to the podium once more. "We will now be entertained with a duet by the Bailey sisters. They will sing, America The Beautiful."

That time the ancient master of ceremonies just stood aside from his post while the teenage sisters did their number.

When they had finished, he returned to his prop and announced that after the audience and dignitaries joined in singing "Farewell To Thee," Brother Alfred Allen would offer the benediction. "After which, if everyone would kindly help arrange the chairs and benches next to the walls, a buffet supper will be served, then a dance, also in honor of our departing brothers, will be enjoyed by all," the out of breath Mr. Gunderson shouted over the buzz.

When all of the rigmarole had been completed, Iver and Chad charged to the table and were among the first to pick up a plate, thanks to their speed afoot, and being devious of mind. They heaped their plates as if it were their last supper.

Irene, feeling a little embarrassed, followed an appropriate distance from the front of the line and only sampled two or three of the items. She told herself, and it was true, that she wouldn't enjoy the classy food if the children at home weren't allowed to also share the feast.

So fed, praised, challenged and preached at, Chad was ready to hit the road for home. His father and mother quickly agreed. So they wrapped their coats around their bodies and headed out the door of the fancy hall.

Just as Iver was about to pass through the opening, he felt a tug at his shoulder. He spun around, and staring him in the eyes was Sherlock.

"Iver," the lawman said, "drive carefully when you go home, but do me a favor, when you go somewhere please use the back roads. It will make my job a lot easier."

Iver, his heart still pumping at two-hundred-percent capacity, joined his son and wife at the Ford. Before they moved the pick-up down the hill to start it, Iver informed his wife and son that Sherlock was a damn good cop.

So he drove the back way home and felt blessed all the way. When they arrived at their house, they all discovered that they weren't tired.

Irene brewed a pot of coffee for her son and husband - none for her because late coffee kept her awake, and there was plenty to do that already.

When it was finished and poured, they engaged each other in deep, what if, conversation.

"What if you, or James, or both of you get hurt?" questioned Irene of Chad.

"I know you won't lower yourself and pray for your safety, and neither will James," Irene said sarcastically.

"Aw, mom, how can I get hurt? If somebody wants to do me any harm, they will have to outrun me. And so far, I have come up against few who could do that. So just think how fast I could run if I was scared."

"Don't act like a Jack-ass Chad" snapped Irene. "Nobody on earth can outrun a bullet or escape a bomb."

"What if you get hurt, and all you can do is just lay there, with no one to hear your pleading - so you just suffer....then what?"

"Well, Mom," Chad answered in a way not meant to be taken seriously, "there is one thing you haven't thought of ... I am worth more to you and Dad dead than alive ... because of the insurance."

If Chad had calculated that statement to dissolve any of his mother's worry, then he missed his mark badly.

What her son had said was more than she could stomach.

"Shut your damn mouth" she screamed. "You bet your sweet life I haven't thought of such trash. And, what's more, I never will - to me that's like giving up. Hellfire, why don't you just go behind the hay stack and put a bullet in your head. As long as you are under this roof, such as it is, don't ever let me hear you say such a terrible thing again."

Chad got her message. And Iver was thankful that he hadn't said something so foolish.

With the termination of her sudden anger, Irene checked the clock, it showed eleven-thirty. "Let's hit it, Iver," she said in a stern way. Within five minutes the Krough house was dark and nearly quiet.

Irene quickly dropped into shallow sleep, and Iver lay planning the many things he wanted to accomplish that following spring and summer.

In the gristmill of his mind, he had ground out a priority list. And on that list could be found those things that he felt he must accomplish during the spring and summer seasons of forty-two: Number, one become a citizen. Number two ... see doctor about goiter. Number three, rent field across the lane from the city. Plant beans, peas, potatoes and corn.

Number four ... add another room to the house.

He knew that he had loaded himself down with the many things that he had planned to do. But, something within him said that those things had to be done.

So true to item one on his list, he went around collecting all of the necessary documents that would prove that he was, in fact, who he claimed to be.

Flight of the Kroughs

On the first day in May, Iver rose from his bed early and walked to the front porch. There, as the sun grew out of the eastern rim of Virtue Valley, he honed the edge of a well broken-in single- edge razor blade on a piece of old shoe leather. At the same time, his wife was putting a pan of water on the hottest part of the stove to heat.

Just when he had buffed the invisible faults from his blade, beads of heated moisture began to collect on the bottom of the pan.

Within seconds they were floating to the surface. That told Irene that the water was ready for her husband's face. Right away he commenced giving himself a better than average shave.

When he had finished that phase of his personal clean-up project, Irene stood ready with one of his best shirts in one hand and, in the other, an adequate tie. The neckpiece was an article of clothing which she had held back from a box of worn-out neighbor clothes, just before she chucked them into the garbage pit positioned halfway between the house and the barn.

Iver delicately pulled the knotted tie snug around his neck, then slipped a black-pinstripe-on-gray suit coat that he didn't recognize anymore than the tie over his just pressed white shirt.

"I guess I'm as ready as I'll ever be," Mr. Krough bravely reported to his wife. "So I suppose I had best be on my way."

With the expression of that indecisive farewell, Iver left the house feeling, dressed as he was, like he could be going to Smithville to open his professional office for the day's business.

But when his look fell on his beat-up Model "A" pickup, and when he realized that it wasn't a Buick Roadmaster Sedan, his feet touched earth again.

As he climbed into his small truck and slammed its tinny door, he mumbled "I guess you will have to do." Then with a deep inhale of fresh breath and a wave to Irene, Iver headed his Ford north, toward Smithville - going by way of the north fields and unpatrolled gravel roads, of course.

After parking his unlicensed transportation, Mr. Krough quickly walked the six blocks that took him to the center of town. When he arrived at the County Court House, he hurried directly to the room marked "Clerk of the Third District Court."

Iver impatiently waited for the lady working behind the long nearly chest-high oak counter to finally get to him so he could inform her as to the nature of his business with the court.

When he did finally get the lady's attention and proudly announced the consequential character of his business, he waited for her response. The lady, made cynical by years of dealing with foreign-talking people, only looked back blankly at Iver as if, she thought, that he thought, the world was supposed to shake upon his announced intention.

Iver's mood was somewhat and suddenly altered.

"How long have you been in this country Mr. Krough?" she snapped.

"Fifty ... six years," he blushingly replied.

The chunky gray haired lady, attired in basic black, shook her head side to side. Unconsciously, she slapped on her counter top a ten by sixteen official looking sheet of paper filled with ornate headings, fine print, and black lines.

She directed Iver to a hefty, long oak table, sitting in the main marbled hall. There, alone with his memory and his pen, he could fill in the pertinent information on the designated blank.

On the very top of the form, printed boldly in the shape of a rainbow, were the words "United States of America." Under that, arranged horizontally, were the words "Declaration of Intention." Next were some blank lines, for official words to be entered by official people, Iver guessed. So he moved on to item number one:

I <u>Iver Hans Krough</u> aged <u>60</u> years, occupation <u>laborer,</u> do declare on oath that my personal description is: color white, complexion light, height <u>5 feet 8 inches,</u> weight <u>150 pounds,</u> color of hair grey, color of eyes <u>blue.</u> other distinctive marks <u>none.</u>

I was born in <u>Bojorn, Denmark</u> on the <u>28th day</u> of <u>September</u> anno domi <u>1882;</u> I now reside at <u>Bear River City, Utah.</u>I immigrated to the United States of America from <u>Liverpool, England,</u> on the vessel <u>USS Wisconsin;</u> my last foreign residence was <u>Copenhagen, Denmark,</u> it is my bona fide intention to renounce forever all allegiance and fidelity of any foreign prince, potentate, state or sovereignty, and particularly to <u>Christian X, King of Denmark</u> of whom I am now subject. I arrived at the port of <u>New York,</u> on or about the <u>30th day of April, 1884,</u> anno domini; I am not an anarchist: I am not a polygamist nor do I believe in polygamy: and it is my intention in good faith to become a citizen of the United States of Ameriica, and to permanently reside there-in, so help me God.

The chunky lady was pleased to discover that the applicant had done it correctly, without a single trip to her counter for explanations.

The fat, middle-aged, lady swung her saloon-like half door open and invited Iver to come behind the counter. From there the lady clerk of the court led him into the inner chambers. There he was required to swear, in the presence of a judge and with his hand on the Bible, as to the truthfulness and accuracy of the information that he had just entered in the blank spaces on the form.

That part of Iver's Americanization seen to, the woman led him back to his proper side of her counter. She then told him that he could expect, through the mail, some information concerning his petition within the next few days ... and ... that he was excused. Iver broke into a quick walk,

Flight of the Kroughs

feeling higher than the pigeon droppings on the roof of the building he was just leaving.

He hopped into his nearly used-up Ford then headed south through the fields toward home.

In Fact he was in such good spirits that he broke Sherlock's rule and nipped onto the main road about halfway between the county seat and River City. After turning south and filching a mile of travel on the main road, Iver brought his truck to a stop in front of a roadside stand where he purchased a glass of beer.

He sprinkled some salt into his drink, then he quickly poured it down his throat. He turned-tail and headed back to safer traveling offered by the north fields gravel thoroughfare.

Irene couldn't ignore the unnerving chatter created by four wheels loaded with loose components, that her husband called a pick- up, warring its way onto the east side of the house yard. And she knew without giving it a thought or even looking, that Iver had returned.

He bounced through the front room door to a chorus of "Daddy's home. Daddy's home."

His answer was, "Your American daddy's home; your American daddy's home."

"Do you mean to say that you're done with the paper work, and it's official already?" inquired Irene.

"No, not quite yet" answered Iver. "But it's as good as done, and I feel good - damn, if I had had any idea that becoming an American felt this good, I would have done it years ago ... Let's have some dinner on the table."

Mrs. Krough gladly agreed and gathered fourteen-year-old Erma and twelve-year-old Clara around her, and they went to work.

Soon, the table top was loaded down with boiled potatoes, milk gravy, fried bologna, sweet corn, red beet pickles and, for dessert, bottled red raspberries over generous squares of white cake.

Following the cheap, but highly elegant, by Krough standards anyway, meal, Iver traveled to the barnyard. There, he greeted and fed his few animals: two pigs - one to kill in November and one to have babies in October; one Guernsey cow - for three gallons of milk every- day; an old grey gelding - to pull the rusted cultivator between the rows of beans, corn, and potatoes; and a dozen homeless laying hens - that laid their eggs wherever it was convenient for them to do so.

Having seen to his afternoon chores and spending an hour at the pig pen fence sharing his chewing tobacco with the pigs and thinking, gentleman farmer Krough returned to the house.

Having burst into the front room, he did as he always did; he chased the children, compassionately, into the kitchen so he could have the radio to himself until six-thirty. During which time he could listen to all of his favorite news commentators who would keep him abreast of the destruction of democratic institutions in Europe.

But on that particular evening, Iver pulled himself away from his static-squeaking brown box earlier than usual.

"Perhaps," Iver speculated, "the reason I feel like shit is because of the excitement I experienced today."

Since he had admitted to himself, a year or so ago, that his body was aging fast, it had become his custom to analyze any unusual ache, or, for that matter, whenever he felt badly. His first impulse always told Iver that he needed to be alone. So he would go to the barnyard and, with his hands in his pockets, he would wander among his animals.

In his mind, he would carefully reconstruct the events of the past few days; if his back hurt, or if the slight hernia in the lower regions of his body hurt, he would ask himself, "Did I lift too heavy a load?" If his gut ached, "did I eat something that had gone bad?" Or, if his head ached, "Is there too much pollen in the air?"

Before he ever gave up on his unique process, Iver had usually settled on a likely incident that was responsible for his feeling the way he did.

So he turned in early that night, which inspired the rest of the Kroughs to follow his lead and retire early to their own beds as well.

Although Irene had followed her husband into their bed, sleep didn't visit her right away. She waited for several minutes, then asked Iver if he was feeling badly.

"Yes I am, but, I think I can lay the blame on all today's excitement."

"Bull" his wife shot back at him in a forced whisper.

"Irene;" Iver said in a voice that started out in a baritone pitch, but ended up soprano. "Don't talk like that, it sounds like hell. You know very well that good Mormon women don't say words like 'that'."

"Well, that may well be true Iver, but don't forget, I have heard - on several occasions - Bishop Petersen curse his cows as he chased them out of his young alfalfa before they became bloated. And, tell me you, he used words that even Uncle Ben would be proud to know and use."

"Well, I suppose you are correct, Irene," admitted Iver. "But Bishop Petersen was only proving to his cows that he was only human. And that he was capable of doing some inhuman things to them if they didn't behave. So, in my book anyway, he is still a damn good man - let's try and get some sleep."

Flight of the Kroughs

For his wife, morning came swiftly. But to him, every hour seemed like a full day. When eight a.m. rolled around, he felt even worse than he did the night before.

Iver moaned his sympathy-seeking body out of bed, dressed it, then ambled to the kitchen table, looking for some of his black, magic, morning-healing substance, called coffee. After downing two cups and walking the path both ways to the out-house, he retreated to his bed. There, like a flat stone skipping across a body of dead water, Iver was barely in and out of sleep for the next two hours.

At about ten o'clock a.m., Irene showed-up at her husband's sickbed carrying a glass that contained six ounces of water mixed with two tablespoons of baking soda.

After using up about five minutes convincing her husband that drinking the disgusting liquid wouldn't kill him, Irene then sat on the edge of his sick bed and felt his forehead for fever ..she reckoned it to be elevated two or three degrees. Having determined that Iver's temperature was higher than normal, she then went to the kitchen cupboard and removed two asprin from their bottle, which, was hid among the assorted dishes and glasses on the top shelf. Then she scooped a cup of water from the water bucket and delivered it with the medicine to her sick husband.

"Does your belly hurt?" she asked him.

"Yes," he moaned.

"Do you ache all over?"

"Yes ... and why the hell all the questions?"

"A foul mood being another symptom, I can now tell you what's wrong with you big boy" said Irene while ignoring his question.

"You have a case of the flu."

As it so happened on that day, in accordance with instructions contained in his Bishop's manual, Mr. Petersen was in the Krough's neighborhood surveying the needs and general condition of his flock ... both spiritual and temporal.

When he reached Iver and Irene's home, he stopped by just as if they were regular active members.

He knocked and was cordially invited into the living room/sick room combination. And was politely offered the most adequate chair in the house.

Accepting the hospitality of the home, and the chair, the Bishop quickly adjusted his position in order to secure a better view of the flush-faced Iver who, after his cup of coffee, remained in a sitting position on his bed out of respect for the visitor.

Right after a round of vigorous handshakes, the upper-middle- aged religious guide - with heavenly powers nearly equal to Alfred Allen's - then opened the family meeting with a prayer.

He asked, during his earnest petition to the Almighty in behalf of the Krough family, that, among other things, he search his heart and if he could see his way clear and, if Iver was worthy of it, that Iver might be made well.

But, during the course of his visit, Mr. Petersen either received divine inspiration or, on his own, had a better idea occur to him - the latter was most likely true - just in case Iver didn't quality for holy intercedence.

After closing the official get together with another prayer and dismissing the rest of the family from the room, Mr. Petersen eased his chair closer to the scarlet-faced victim of the "bug."

"Look Iver," the Bishop half whispered, "now you know our religion forbids the consumption of alcohol in any of its forms. But I maintain, within the limited space of personal experience authority of course, that it it is used strictly for medical reasons, then it's alright by the Lord."

Iver nodded his weak concurrence of course. "Who am I to disagree with such apparent wisdom?" he privately decided. Further- more, he was desperate to try anything that had a chance of chasing that infernal bug from his body.

Then Mr. Petersen leaned his considerable weight back on the creaking, overmatched chair and shoved his right hand into his trouser pocket, nervously playing with his loose change and car keys.

The patient impatiently waited for the Bishop to say something relative to the betterment of his own sorry condition, and after a delay of two minutes, disguised as two hours, Mr. Petersen finally did.

"Now Iver," Mr. Petersen began again, "what I'm going to suggest to you should in no way be taken as an endorsement of the regular use of hard liquor. But in your condition, as I indicated before, I believe it to be justified."

"Here is what you do; take a bottle of whiskey, it doesn't matter if it's cheap whiskey, open it, then hang your favorite hat on your bedpost. Then have your wife stack all the covers she can muster on top of you. Start drinking the whiskey. When you see two hats stop drinking. If you aren't sleeping by then, you soon will be. And when you waken in two days, I guarantee that your flu will be gone." Now Bishop Petersen knew that Iver couldn't afford a bottle of whiskey. And even if he could afford it, he was in no condition to go to town to get the stuff in any case.

Later that evening someone rapped on the Krough front door. Glen quickly answered the knock and, as earlier in the day, it was Bishop Petersen. The door had hardly opened halfway when the visitor shoved a "not so acceptably disguised" paper bag full of something into the surprised ten-year old's hands, then negotiated a hasty retreat to his still running car.

Irene knew what the bag contained, as she had listened in on most of the Bishop's and Iver's conversation. So she hustled the package straight to her husband's bedside.

Iver grabbed the package and quickly tossed the brown bag aside. Next he ripped the state tax seal from the neck and cap of the bottle and gave it a deep inhaling smell. And he discovered just what he expected - cheap whiskey.

"Ah, what the hell," Iver mumbled through fever dehydrated lips, and in the next breath ordered a quart of water to chase the junk with. And the favorite hat was no problem, because Iver owned only one.

In a way Mr. Petersen's prediction of curing the flu would prove to be correct. But just before the patient implemented the remedy, he realized that nothing had been said about feeling better.

Following those fourteen hours of drug induced sleep, Iver did, in fact, notice a change in how he felt.

For then, as it turned out, the misery he had suffered in his chest, stomach, and bowels had all joined forces and attacked his head. This, therefore, had erased any memory of those previous individual complaints.

The more awake he became, the more he wanted to run to one of the pool halls to get something to re-impose the sleep he had just arrived from.

Mr. Krough had thought of the pool halls because he had heard from some regular drinkers that the best way to get rid of a hangover was to wash it away with more booze. Regardless of his second-rate condition, finding one of the saloons would be no trick. Because, they were separated by four doors.

However, the two pool palaces might better be described as beer gardens that also provided a couple pool tables each. With their fancy, hand carved, oak and mahogany bars and back bars, they displayed far and away the most elegant interiors in Bear River City.

In River City, as it was called by the white, of European extraction, natives - all other natives had been removed about eighty years back - it required little talent to distinguish the good guys from the bad guys.

The good people were the ones who attended church on Sunday, rain or shine with the only exception to the rule being automatic excuses for the gentlemen farmers when it was time to get the money crops to the canning plant for processing.

Describing them as "gentlemen farmers" was due to the fact that most farms in the valley were small. So that being the case, most Virtue Valley farmers held down second jobs to supplement their income.

For them, and others, the war was just the ticket. Because anyone who wanted to, could go over the mountain and work at one of the five defense plants.

On the other hand, the other guys - sometimes called bad by the good ones—slapped each other on the back and used profanity when shouting their greetings. And they were, for the most part, ranchers, cowboys or unemployed grade school dropouts.

The other thing that set those described as "bad" apart from those described as good, was that the bad ones met at the beer joints four or five times a week, instead of once a week at church like the other group.

The pool halls served the town in another way also; thanks to the handy proximity of Wyoming it provided after dark sales to a few of the good guys for their special occasions. That, in spite of covenants they had contracted with a higher authority.

So on the day of Bishop Petersen's visit, it became apparent to Iver that Mr. Petersen was one of those few. "Or how else," Iver reasoned, "could he have given me such a rare, if not effective, remedy. No wonder I like the man," he added.

Because the prayers outnumbered the drinkers ten to one, River City's allotment of two alcoholics were very visible.

The town, no doubt, could boast of having more problem drinkers than those two. After all, the state-owned liquor store did a brisk business. So the others must have hid their habit in closets tucked safely in the walls of their elegant and not so elegant homes; Homes that were defended by mountains that circled their burley arms around Virtue Valley.

What made the River City drunks so special was that they were totally uninhibited. They felt quite at ease pissing in the gutter or on an unlucky telephone pole in full daylight.

During noon hour, the school boys would run all over town. They would slug each other on the shoulder and roll on the ground with laughter when they saw one of the two pitiful persons in the unashamed act of self relief.

But most citizens would pass the "degenerates" by, paying them no mind.

It was as if the non-drunks accepted such deviates. Thinking, Iver assumed, that "Thank God it's them, and not one of our family, or some other person of quality we know."

Iver sat on the edge of his bed, with his head buried in his hands. And as he sat there he wondered if Mr. Petersen had anymore instant healing methods up his sleeve. "If he does," Iver thought, "I hope he keeps them to himself." But, unfortunately, his pain was not over.

Because, somehow, Alfred Allen got wind of Iver's sickness. He decided the very next day that he would try once more to convince Mr.

Flight of the Kroughs

Krough that his cure wouldn't be accomplished with the aid of doctors or drugs, but with faith and prayer.

So the skinny preacher cinched up his suspenders - hooked his glasses to his ears - put on his hat, and marched up the street, past the cemetary and on to the Krough house.

He slapped his fatless knuckles against the door, and a surprised Irene responded.

Surprised because it was but seven o'clock a.m.

"I heard Iver's sick" he said before Irene could speak sensibly.

"How's he doing" he asked dryly.

"Not so good this morning, but better than yesterday" Irene replied.

"May I speak to him?" Mr. Allen asked, almost demanded.

"Well ... I suppose, just one moment."

Irene closed the door on the visitor, then panic stricken, she ran to her husband's bed and told him to get back into it and quick. "Because Alfred is outside waiting to come in, and you're not dressed."

"Are you bullshitting me, Irene? It's only ten past seven - tell him to get the hell out of here."

His negative reply was too late, because Irene was at the door ready to open it. Before she did, she turned to make sure her husband was ready. But that was a wasted worry, because Iver was always ready for Alfred Allen - appearance wise that is.

So, on cue from her husband, Irene pulled the door open wide. And the early morning May sun fell into the room. Then a skinny shadow intruded upon the door-sized cascading shaft of light.

Alfred, looking a bit confused, entered the front room - confused because Irene had come close to slamming the door on his face - and was offered the same chair that Bishop Petersen had sat on just two days earlier. Only when Mr. Allen sat on it, he didn't cause it to make the same squeak and groan.

"What's this I hear about your health going bad, Mr. Krough?"

"Where in the ... world did you hear that trash?" asked Iver.

"Oh, it's not important how, or where, I found out. What matters is, just what you intend to do to make yourself whole again" Alfred preached.

"Now, Mr. Allen" Iver patronized, you don't need to add the condition of my health to your long list of worries. I know you have concern for everyone's well-being, but you don't need to spend your precious time on my behalf."

Having said that, Iver fully expected his visitor to take the hint and leave. And as he left, he might have said something like, "Well, if you need me Iver, you know where to find me." But no such luck.

D. Raymond Anderson

"My time is free to you, Iver, so don't you worry," Mr. Allen said in return. Then he got right down to business.

"I understand Bishop Petersen spent some time with you the other day ... is that true?" he asked.

"Yes, he came by to visit the family for a little while" confessed a curious Iver. He was curious because Alfred Allen had no right, or justification, to be checking up on Bishop Petersen's comings and goings.

"Why do you ask?" Iver inquired sharply

"Oh, just a suspicion I have" answered Alfred.

"Now you don't need to get upset, Iver, but I know all about Mr. Petersen's famous cure."

"But, Iver, there is one thing you ought to consider, and it is this: if you would only read our Mormon literature you would find it written that even the highest official, even in our own church, can deceive you and lead you astray."

"Wait ... a ... minute" howled a little bit upset Iver. "I like Bishop Petersen and believe him to be a good man. And I don't feel right about us talking about the Bishop without him being here to defend himself."

Alfred knew in an instant that he had dropped a clanger. Because, he also knew that most of the people in Iver's neighborhood felt just as Iver did about Mr. Petersen.

In spite of his tactical mistake however, the determined red-faced Mr. Allen continued.

"You are one hundred percent correct, Iver, and it the Bishop were here right now, I would happily apologize. But what I'm trying to get to is the condition of your health. And to make you understand that patent medicine, regardless if it comes through the front door of the drug store, or the back door of the pool hall, won't help you regain it."

Upon Brother Allen's conclusion to his last statement, Irene gathered up her children and herded them into the kitchen just in case the conversation between the two men got out of hand. But no such situation came about.

Mainly, because Iver had already guessed the route of their discussion based on its direction to that point. And it gave him hope that it would end at a particular destination. There was a great deal on the subject that he wanted to get off his chest.

"Well, Brother Allen, what would you have done for me?" Iver asked slyly. "Here I was, too sick to go to the outhouse, and too sick to die."

"If Irene had called for me" Mr. Allen answered piously, "I would have dragged you from your bed and we would have fallen to our knees together and prayed together for the Lord to give you relief."

"Then I would have called a couple Elder friends of mine and we would have laid our hands upon your head and commanded you to be well."

Flight of the Kroughs

Iver felt absolutely fulfilled. Because, just as he had hoped, the conversation had arrived at exactly the point he desired. So he took charge, and began his offensive.

"Well" Mr. Krough drawled, "I guess that makes you and I pretty special doesn't it?"

"Brother, in the eyes of the Lord, everyone is special," Alfred answered with a wide satisfied grin.

"But maybe you misunderstood me," returned Iver. Then he continued, "What I really meant to say, was, that if you and your friends could make me well by laying your hands on my head, then that makes you and me more special than a lot of other folks."

"I don't mind saying, Iver, that you have me just a little bit puzzled."

"Well then, let me clear it up for you, Brother Allen."

"Say, for instance, when Viola has her baby, and it gets to be two or three years old ... then the child becomes deathly ill, so I call you and the other Elders to pray over the infant, will God take pity on the child?"

"Of course he would" boasted Alfred.

"Then does that mean all those babies being killed by flies and hunger in the remote parts of the world, and those bombed to death in Europe and Asia don't matter to God because there is no one to pray for them or lay hands on their heads?"

"And what about our young men dying around the world? Why would God take the trouble to heal me, a worn out, nearly old man, and allow those fine young men to die. To my way of thinking that ain't logical."

"Someday, Iver, and I predict, very soon, our church will be strong in every country on this earth, except of course, Africa, and when that comes about, no one need suffer."

Alfred made that last statement hoping to cause a swing in the momentum of the discussion from Iver to himself. But Mr. Krough simply avoided Alfred's evasive maneuver, stayed right on course, and decided that it was time to confront his adversary with what he knew would be the most devastating declaration of their debate.

"Alfred," Iver said sternly, as he looked him straight in the eyes with his own bluish grey eyes then flashing with intensity, "I cannot accept how you envisage God."

Alfred gasped upon hearing the words that had just exited Iver's mouth.

"Iver;" he implored, "please don't say such things. You know that in the hereafter we will be judged by what is written in the book of life. And you also know that there will be no strikeovers, or erasing in that book. And furthermore I'm sure you are aware that every deed - thought - idea - experience - and every opinion we express is punctiliously recorded."

"God is God, Iver, there is no such thing as a your God - my God" Elder Allen protested.

"I'm sorry if what I have just said offends you Brother Allen. But in your case and my case, I believe there is a wide difference in perception."

"Well then," Alfred said smugly, "why don't you tell me of this 'God' of yours."

"How would your God explain illness?" questioned the pious visitor..

"In the first place," Iver jumped right in and said, "I don't believe that the Almighty creates illness - he simply allows it to exist, because he has no other choice."

Allen snapped his tongue on the roof of his mouth and rolled his head around and back in an exaggerated gesture designed to inform his God that he dismissed as trash everything Iver was saying. But he let the talker continue unchallenged.

"And further more," the piqued orator laid out for the listener's approval - or in that case, disapproval - "I don't believe God dreamed up war, not even for the purpose of population control." Iver instantly thought about being responsible for fourteen children - so far - and wished he had phrased that last comment differently.

"And the same goes for disease and famine" Iver went on. "But God did create man and provided him with the intellectual capacity with which to conquer those things."

"But what is your basic belief? You talk confidently about the bad things that our Heavenly Father didn't create, things that we are told he did create, if only to test our faith. So tell me, what kind of person is God?" Alfred cross-examined.

"Well, for me that's easy. But, too many people make him so complicated that in their minds God disappears behind a veil of contradiction."

"God, the God I worship anyway, is first, and foremost, fair," Iver voiced loudly after taking a deep breath. "And by that I mean he treats everyone the same, even Catholics and Baptists."

"And I am sure that when he created this earth, along with whatever else is floating around out there, he also set into motion the physical and biological rules that will sustain those worlds. So it is up to humans with their superior brains to understand and use the rules to improve the lot of mankind. And not explain them away as powers commanded by the Almighty to turn on and off on a transient whim."

Alfred could only boil with regret as he watched and listened to Iver damning himself with his sacrilege. But he did manage to wedge in another question.

Flight of the Kroughs

"Then who will be the ones that will attain the glory of living in the presence of the Lord?" he asked confidently.

"Well, that is a tough one" Iver drawled ... quieter.

"I don't pretend to have an opinion on that matter," he confessed.

"But I will say that if you and I are lucky enough to make the grade, we will both be surprised by who is also there, and who is missing."

"However, if you had asked me who had the least chance, I would say the acceptors. By that I mean the ones who fool themselves, and others, into believing that they have found God and start building fancy shrines with spires, in his tribute. When the money could be better spent feeding the starving and healing the sick."

Iver could tell that Alfred was getting increasingly nervous. So he decided to offer a conclusion to his argument right soon, or he might be talking to himself.

"Brother Allen," he began again in a slightly apologetic tone, "I think we should all admit that God has feelings just as we do, only compounded to several-million fold. So when he looks down - if it is down - and sees a child suffering to death, he weeps real tears. Or when he watches as a person abuses his free agency by getting drunk with power and unleashing his armies to commit rape on the surrounding lands, he may even doubt his own wisdom. Because, though he is omnipotent, he would never change any rule, least of all his."

Although Brother Allen would never admit it, he was impressed to the point of mild admiration at the depth and honesty of Iver's religious philosophy.

So, with Iver's last comment ringing in his ears, and after telling himself that he had heard enough heathen slurs, Alfred quickly jumped to his feet.

"Well, Iver" he said, "this has been, at best, a rare kind of discussion. But if nothing else, promise me that when you visit the hospital, you will keep the Elders in mind. Because, who knows, you might be wrong, so why not let them pray over you and anoint your head with oil, just in case."

With those words, the well meaning, yet self appointed emissary swiftly, and without ceremony, left the Krough house and headed homeward.

"Now where in the hell did that know-it-all hear about me going to the hospital," Iver wondered aloud.

Then he answered his own question - and the answer was Irene.

Right away he made a mental note to remind himself to take up with his wife the matter of discussing private family business with neighbors. And a week later, as Mr. and Mrs. Krough made the ten-mile trip to Smithville to sign Iver into the county hospital, he obeyed his mental note.

However, he didn't make a real issue of it. He only told his wife that if she were a man, he would tell her to keep things under her hat. And by the time they had parked in the hospital lot, Irene had admitted talking too much, and had vowed never to make the same mistake again.

After killing the engine by unhooking the hot wire that ran from the battery to the key switch - that had long been stuck in the on position - and pushing the shifting lever into reverse position - to act as an emergency brake - Iver leaned on the steering wheel, and stared through the windshield in contemplative silence.

About five minutes into his uninterrupted thin trance, Irene nudged his shoulder. But before she had a chance to make the suggestion, Iver looked at her and said, "Yes, I guess it's time to face it."

Irene grabbed from the seat the brown paper bag that contained a razor, a bar of chewing tobacco, and two sacks of bull durham, and slid from her side of the pickup and waited for her husband to circle from his side of the vehicle. Then, side by side, the pair walked through the doors into a strange world of alcohol fumes and uncertain fear. Although neither of them would admit the fear part. Iver did poke his wife in the ribs with his elbow and asked her, "people die here, don't they?" She didn't answer.

Doctor Blodget had alerted the staff at the hospital that a Mr. Krough from Bear River City was ... supposed ... to check in for treatment on his diseased thyroid glands. So with little paperwork, and a minimum of ceremony, a nurse hustled the new patient from the area, leaving Irene standing conspicuously alone in the middle of the waiting room.

After a fair amount of time had passed, a lady of approximately the same age, but dressed much better than Irene, grudgingly moved from behind her desk and took pity on the lost looking woman. She told Irene that her husband hadn't disappeared forever, and that after he had been fitted for pajamas and slippers, she would be allowed to spend a few minutes with him.

So Irene sat on a chair provided for waiting ... and waited.

She watched the many people coming and going. But she was most intrigued by the pale ladies leaving the place with their stringy hair, carrying beautiful fourteen-day-old babies. "What would it be like," she wondered, "to have a baby here and be pampered for two weeks?"

Thirty minutes after Irene sat down to wait, a frail, anemic- looking nurse - so white in fact, that it was difficult for Irene to distinguish her from the uniform that she wore and the walls that surrounded her - reported to her that it was ok to go to the third floor and visit her husband.

Irene was anxious, but decided to take the stairs, giving the elevators only a suspicious glance as she passed them by on her way to the staircase.

Flight of the Kroughs

Upon reaching the third floor, and only slightly out of breath, she was lucky. Because when she reached the final tread, she found that Iver's room was just across the hall and directly in front of her. Lounging on his adjustable bed in fresh pajamas and robe, was her husband.

He had been thoroughly scrubbed, top to bottom, and his silver grey hair had likewise been washed, then combed to perfection.

He seemed resigned to his situation, but overwhelmed by his sterile surroundings.

The couple forced a conversation of shallow small talk, and avoided discussing what Iver had to endure that afternoon and on the table the next morning.

In an attempt to comply with the nurse's instructions to her, Irene looked at the clock. It said nearly noon.

"Iver, I think Roland is probably in the parking lot with Greg's car now, so I had better leave. And the kids will need their dinner soon."

He agreed, and watched as his wife sank from sight six inches at a time, down the staircase.

As soon as Irene had melted from his sight and mind, lonesome Iver began to run a special inventory of the items on his priority project list through his mind.

He was acutely aware of the fact that, if he intended to start - and finish - the third room on the house, and plant the twenty acres across the lane, he would need to be in, at least, half-way decent physical condition. Which, caused him a concern he hadn't considered before. "What" he worried "if they cut me up so badly that it takes me months to recover?"

As he lay back on his nice clean pillows thinking about that possibility and a couple others even more upsetting, he drifted nearly into sleep.

About five minutes after he had dozed, a nurse silently slipped into Iver's room and shook him at the shoulder, bringing him full awake. In her left hand she clutched several three by five slips of paper.

"It's time for your work-up, Mr. Krough" she ordered.

Iver had no idea what the lady of mercy meant by the term "work-up." But he was convinced by circumstantial evidence that it was something sinister. Because he had learned enough from reading that whenever a person or institution wanted to cover up something painful or distasteful, they would give it a high sounding title.

"Like slicing a man open and ripping out a part of his body that God must have put there for a reason, and calling it an appendectomy."

Regardless of the patient's apprehension, the nurse led him down the hall to the elevator for a trip to the second floor, there she left him in the charge of a young man who looked to Iver as if he should be in the army taking care of his boys. He sat Iver down on a metal stool and told him to remove his robe and pajama top. Iver was feeling worse with each step of the process, sure that any minute something terrible was going to happen to him.

Having the patient in a sufficient state of undress, the young technician yanked a drawer open from a gray metal stand, then pulled a macaroni-sized, two-foot-long, rubber hose from inside it. He stretched the hose and let it snap back, giving Iver a good scare. "Smart alec showoff bastard," Iver thought. But what really worried him was where the young man was going to put the hose. "Raise your arm please," asked the man in white. And Iver did as he was told.

The young man then wrapped the rubber "whatever it was" tightly around the patient's arm between the elbow and the shoulder - but closer to the elbow - and expertly scooped a long needle from that same drawer. Felling like a victim, Iver's eyes grew larger.

"My God, a blood test," Iver whimpered beneath his breath.

To reduce the pain, he turned his face, that was then closer to the color of his hair, away from his tormentor and told himself that it wouldn't hurt ... himself lied.

That over with, Iver speculated that the blood test was surely the most fear inspiring of the tests he was required to undergo.

And he was correct ... in a physical sense, that is.

The lab man then checked Iver's heart. He stared into the medic's young face, searching longingly for a positive expression. But all Iver could detect was a dissatisfied frown. Next the young man read the patient's blood pressure. His reaction was a repeat of the heart performance.

After finishing that phase of the examination, the young man said nothing. Iver knew that was bad. He believed it to be human nature for people to say something encouraging, even if they needed to exaggerate just a little. So the man from Bear River City began to worry just a little bit more.

"Now for the last test," the technician announced. While he spoke those words he handed Iver a bottle that would hold four ounces.

"What's this for?" he asked.

"Urine specimen," answered the medic.

"Well, what do you want me to do with it?"

"Go to the bathroom and fill the thing up."

Iver was devastated. "Do you mean to say that you want me to go take a leak in that bottle? Shit man, the smallest thing I ever aimed at was a toilet hole," he said all of that silently.

In a few seconds the young man in white gave Iver a cold stare.

"I'm very busy Mr. Krough, so please, go to the men's room and see to the urine specimen."

Flight of the Kroughs

Iver walked sheepishly, flapping his slippers, toward the bathroom. But before entering he made damn sure it was empty. It was ... so he dashed into the nearest cubical and fumbled with the string on his pajamas. The string had somehow evolved from a bow, into a knot.

"Why don't they make these son-of-a-bitchen pants with a fly?" the frustrated patient cried - again silently.

Iver finally gave in to the knotted string and wiggled his little butt out of the yet-tied pajama bottoms.

He grabbed at the bottle from the toilet's water tank, but missed the target by two-thirds of an inch. The third that did make contact only succeeded in knocking the bottle over the edge, and onto the stool, then onto the white ceramic tile floor. "Thank God the seat was closed," Iver said, as he crashed to the floor to retrieve his unbroken container.

He felt as if the whole hospital staff had gone on coffee break just so they could watch him.

While standing at the stool forcing the liquid into the little bottle, he suddenly yelled a "son-of-a-bitch," in a hushed voice. Because, it seemed, when the bottle was full he didn't get his tap shut off in time, and so some slopped over.

He quickly pulled some toilet paper from the roll and gave the jar a good wiping down.

He wiggled back into his pants, then cautiously poked his head out the barely open bathroom door to make sure the way was clear. And it was. So he made a dash for the young man in the white outfit, carrying his warm prize like a baton ready to be passed to the next runner.

The technician snapped the jar from Iver with a rubber gloved hand, and dismissed the patient back to his room.

By then it was close to three o'clock. Mr. Krough knew that Dr. Blodget would be by to see him any minute. Therefore, it was back to his bed..

At three forty-five the Doctor peeked into the room through the half open door and yelled "Ya decent, Iver?" "What else could I be in here?" Iver answered. The nurses are too old and ugly to chase, and they dress you like your a certified nut damned for life to a funny farm."

Dr. Blodget, busy entering the room as Iver had gone through his latest fatuous editorial, hadn't paid that much attention, but took a seat by is bed

"Well Mr. Krough, I have had a good look at your tests, the ones that are finished anyway. And although they show you not being in the best of shape, I think we ought to proceed with the treatment of your goiter."

From that point in his briefing, the doctor jumped right into the details of the operation that, to him, were routine, but to Iver, inconceivable.

It seemed to the patient that his operation was more a research matter, and less of a hope of cure. Being consistent, Iver wanted the facts. And those facts needed to tell him that the operation was simple and would be a total success. The physician could give no such a guarantee. Doctor Blodget, at last, completed his pre-surgery briefing of Iver and left the room at about five-thirty.

Iver was emotionally battered. And the seeds of a plan began to germinate, and flourish, in his mind.

Being five-thirty, it was also suppertime - they called it dinner, but he called it supper - but the look of what they delivered him to eat, burdened either description.

He downed the juice with little trouble, and ate the half of a peach. But the rest could rot as far as he was concerned.

Again, after supper, he nodded off. And before he knew it, it was eight o'clock.

It was dark outside, the third floor was saturated with visitors about to leave, and, there was a new shift on duty, perfect conditions for Iver's great escape. Quickly, he rolled out of his bed, and swiftly changed the disgusting pajamas for his favorite bib overalls and long Johns. Next he pulled his shoes on.

He stood silently by the door that was cracked an inch, and no more, and waited.

Not ten seconds had passed before he had skipped into step with a group of visitors that had passed by his door and were headed for the elevator. He looked like a perfectly good visitor when he mingled with the people leaving the hospital.

Safely outside, he stopped long enough to smell the natural air of freedom; then he headed for the parking lot to greet his Ford.

With his pockets loaded with chewing tobacco, bags of smoking tobacco, a razor and blades, and a half dozen bars of individually wrapped soap, that they would never miss, he completed his escape.

Iver kicked the shifting lever into neutral, then with the help of unknowing accomplices, he pushed the escape vehicle into a position that would allow it to coast down the steep hill into downtown Smithville. Then, Home to Bear River City, he would shout. So his unsuspecting help let go of the Ford's rear bumper, and down the hill the little truck shimmied. About half way down Iver discovered why the engine wouldn't run. In his haste to complete his escape, he had neglected to re-attach the hot wire back to the key wire.

He yelled "Oh shit" and wedged his left knee under the steering wheel to maintain the truck's course, while he hooked the two wires together.

The truck traveled another hundred feet, then its engine exploded to life.

Flight of the Kroughs

The escapee arrived home at a quarter after nine. The two rooms - soon to be three were pitch black.

He studied the little house for a few seconds, then told himself, that, although he would still have his aches and pains, at least he would be in good enough condition to start the new room, and plant the twenty acres next door.

That decided, he removed his body from the pickup, and softly shut its door. He walked across the dust of the front yard, and just as softly, he opened the front door. Then he tip-toed across the front room floor, unhooking suspenders and unbuttoning his shirt as he went.

When he reached his side of the bed, all he needed to do was let go, which he did, and his clothes folded to the plank traced linoleum covered floor. Iver had forgotten he had loaded his pockets with the precious items that he had escaped with.

Consequently, when the middle part of his bib overalls met the floor, it was with an insulated thud.

Hearing the noise through her sleep, Irene straightened off her mattress from the waist up like some kind of spring-loaded toy.

For a moment, in the darkness, it was debatable which of the two was the more shocked.

Irene was the first of the paled pair to come to her senses. And she was also the first to speak.

"What in hell's name are you doing here, Iver?"

"Now don't over react, Dear, I just changed my mind, that's all," he offered feebly.

"What do you mean 'I changed my mind'... once you're in the hospital, you can't change your mind. And you can't leave either, unless the doctor tells them to let you go."

"Well, I left," bragged Iver.

"And I will tell you right now, that those God-damned quacks won't lay their hands on me again."

"For God sakes, Irene, all they wanted me for was a guinea pig. Maybe when I get all my work done, in a couple of years I would guess, I will go talk to Alfred ... who knows, he just might have something with his spiritual medicine."

"Tomorrow I'm going to get hold of Bishop Petersen's horses and plow, and get my ass busy across the road. So if you wake up early, make sure you wake me too."

With those words he rolled into his bed and prepared to sleep.

Which, left his wife sitting up in bed searching for words that would express her anger mixed with disappointment.

Defeated, she settled back onto her pillow and faced opposite Iver.

In about five minutes she softly called out her husband's name.

"Iver," she said, "I agree with you. Those doctors must be quacks if they can't tell a guinea pig from a chicken."

*****

Faithful to his word and good intentions, Iver bounced from his bed early. He was replete with ambition and was eager for action. Irene put fire to a pot of coffee while he sauntered across the dusty lane to survey his twenty acres and make a mental plot plan.

As he turned to return to the house, he looked at the lane he was about to cross and silently joked that that strip of earth was all that separated him from his poor house and financial success, a gross misrepresentation of the fact at best. Or worse, unsophisticated expectations.

When he at last sat down to his steaming coffee he didn't say a hell of a lot. But there was plenty on his mind. Standing in the fore-front of his thoughts was an image of a double-crossed Doctor Blodget.

Iver, for a moment anyway, wondered just how badly the Doctor was going to feel when he arrived to do his stuff but his patient failed to show up. "Aw, what the hell," Iver rationalized, "he's got more to do than he can handle anyway, he won't even miss me." There was a good chance that he was correct in that assumption. Because, the Doctor never did bother to summon Iver to get an explanation.

That source of guilt swept from his mind, the anxious farmer finished his now lukewarm drink. He said nothing to his still-brooding wife but headed out the door then down cemetery hill to Bishop Petersen's place.

He explained, in detail, to his respected friend all about his plans for the chunk of ground that Bear River City was saving for a future park. That he was going to plant the twenty acres, and all that was holding his project up was the need for a team of horses, and the equipment with which to prepare the soil.

Soon it would be middle May, and, as he had long since planted his own seeds and, in spite of certain reservations concerning the quality of Iver's latest venture, Mr. Petersen allowed him the use of his animals and implements.

Not wasting another minute, the two men went about harnessing up the horses. That done, the Bishop and Iver loaded the plow and harrows onto the wagon. Then Mr. Petersen backed his team of matched bays in their fancy metal and glass decorated attire into position, and hooked them to the hay wagon. With a handshake, the Bishop parted company with his friend, horses, and equipment.

Iver felt like an ancient Roman nobleman as he commanded the fine set of animals as they pranced toward his home. Had a tractor passed him by,

Flight of the Kroughs

he might be tempted to spit on it, depending, of course, on who was in command of the tractor.

In fact, Iver had two sets of thoughts running concurrently. Because, while he was feeling exhilarated in the company of the snappy dressed horses, and by his twenty acre farming project, he was also feeling a deep emptiness. For, between Bishop Petersen's place, and his own place Iver had wished a dozen or more times that Chad was there to help and give him companionship.

But with the help of Clara, Glen and, sometimes, Roland, the plowing and planting was finished by the beginning of the next month.

Then it was June. In the fields, straddling seemingly endless rows of infant plants of corn were three young Krough boys, aged seven - nine - and ten, with red faces, and red bodies half uncovered.

Within the short space of only a few days, the Virtue Valley sun would change their reddish milky winter skin to terra-cotta tan.

Best of all though, if the boys had any say that is, was the fact that June had closed those erected in nineteen-thirty-four by WPA, kick-corrupted school doors. Which also put a stop to rules and days knowing no end.

When the three finally had a chance for some fun, the pasty earth in the lane had turned to flour like powdered clay.

On that day as they chopped their way up and down the green ribbons of pampered vegetation, the noise that they had become familiar with again began to grow in the western sky.

"Look;" shouted an excited Glen to Harvey and Jackson, or J.C. as he was called.

In unison, all three saluted the sun to shade their eyes, then sent an upward cheer.

The cerulean sky became streaked with gray vapor trails, and the bragging drone of formations of star spangled fortresses sent tingles up the bare backs of the three boys.

True, the aircraft's automatic cannons were as yet in anger uncharged, they looked vicious from the ground sticking outward from their bubble turrets.

"Where are they headed?" little Harvey - seven years old - asked.

"To help our brothers," boasted Glen.

"Where are James and Chad anyway?" questioned J.C

"Oh, across some wide, cold ocean," said Glen

"Why are they there?" J.C. continued.

"To fight history's falsest prophet, Dad says," offered Glen.

"But why our brothers?" asked Harvey.

"Because they were too common to buy deferments, whatever that means," answered eleven year old Glen, again repeating his dad's words.

"But there ain't no war over here, so why did they need to leave?" persisted nine year old J.C.

"Because," preached Glen, "according to Dad, our country is almighty chosen to be free. So now, I guess, our country has a duty to help other countries not as lucky as us."

Their hoeing done for the week, the next day was consumed by the three in the act of playing. There was much for them to play about. To help them, they had their dandy toys, which, they had procured on last Saturday's shopping trip to the city dump.

The three young Krough boys dug and shaped the tan, cool dirt in the lane to a nice smooth hump.

Then with their fingers and palms, they carved out winding roads that left their pile of clay. Through Quaker Box tunnels, the roads traveled to everywhere; some ended at far off play wars.

As always the unlucky enemy was Germans, Japs, or Italians. It was easy for Glen to dream up such wars. Because he learned firsthand while listening to the radio over his dad's slumping shoulders. He watched with wonder as worry lines melted down his father's face.

Other roads the boys engineered snaked through forests of weeds and rust eroded cans. Then returned to where they started, contented, going nowhere.

As Glen, J.C. and Harvey, made their way through their temporary imaginary world, Iver sat at the kitchen window and in secret watched his three young sons for hours.

Because of the subject of their play which, indeed, was all children's subject of play in those days, he felt a little sorry for them.

Although he knew it not to be an original thought, he always told himself that the young can only wonder what might be, but the old can remember what was. As far as he was concerned, his childhood in Bear River City was richer and was free of the pressure of war.

However, the energy with which his three young sons built also rubbed off on Iver.

After some stern negotiating with Roland, the pair went to work constructing the third room.

They worked in the early cool of the morning, and the after sundown cool of the evening.

Within the space of one month and a half, Iver and his son had emptied a hole twelve feet square by seven feet deep right next to their house.

On the sixteenth of July, forty-two, Iver drove Irene to Smithville where they secured a government-backed home improvement loan amounting to five hundred dollars. Using for collateral their home and his signature, and

Flight of the Kroughs

a promise to faithfully repay the loan out of proceeds derived from his crops busy growing-up on the twenty acres across the lane.

However, no surprise to Irene, her husband's projected return from his miniature farm exceeded actual reward. For all their hard labor, they achieved a fifty percent shortfall. A perfect example to illustrate that harsh fact of life was the pea crop. Because, they were the first to mature.

Through unfortunate circumstances, but more accurately, lousy planning, Iver had no machinery with which to harvest the vitamin rich green vegetables.

Now those peas weren't planted in neat rows spaced about a foot apart in a cute little garden out back of the house. This was a five-acre field of plants planted as thick as clover.

On that Sunday afternoon when the field man for the canning company came by and judged Iver's peas ready for harvest ... and within hours: to achieve a product at its prime, there was no way to duck it. It had to be done.

Without necessary equipment, Iver did the only thing he knew to do. He chased every member of the family to the pea patch, including the two little girls, Karia age five, and Lu Ann, age three. Not because those two were expected to work, but because there would be no one at the house to look after them.

Himself, Irene, Roland, Erma, Clara, Glen, J.C., and Harvey, all got on their knees or bent over, and pulled the pea vines by hand and tossed them into the bed of the little Ford pickup.

Farmer Krough knew that it would be useless to ask Bishop Petersen to help, because he was busy in his fields harvesting as well. So, to and from the factory the pickup circled until late into the day. The Krough family worked harder than humans were meant to work, until, at last, Iver called a halt. "To hell with the pea contract" he shouted "let's go to bed."

Early the following morning, Irene and her husband made the rounds and rolled everyone and their aching, sleep-craving bodies from their beds. After a cup of hot cocoa, and some toast each, back across the lane to the field they started.

But, as they filed out of the house feeling like prisoners sentenced to hard labor, their dread turned to celebration, for parked in the lane with his team of matched grays that were hooked to a mowing machine, was Iner Larsen. And he had also brought along a couple pitchforks.

So elated was Iver, that he took hold of Roland and Glen - ordered his wife and the children back to bed - then headed for the half harvested field of peas. Offering a glad hand to his neighbor as he passed, showing him the way.

"Now it's easy," thought Glen. "Especially compared to last night." Because all he and Roland had to do was follow the mower and throw the hacked off vines on to the old, but willing, truck.

By ten a.m. the job was finished.

Before Iver delivered the last load of the diminished in quality money crop to the shelling plant, he first stopped by the house. Soon, the midmorning unusual silence in the Krough house was split by the sound of a relentless horn.

Not knowing, at first, to what signal she had responded to, Irene staggered from her bed toward the front door to investigate. She pulled the door open just enough to see what had caused the clamor.

She was met by the sound of her husband's voice shouting "Hey, Irene, bring the kids, and ride to the factory with us."

She agreed, but only if they went the back way, so they could avoid the amused looks that they would receive when the classier folks of Bear River City caught site of the curious looking outfit with kids poking from every conceivable location ... Iver agreed.

So Irene quickly had the children out of bed and dressed.

While mother was herding the other five young ones to the truck, Iver looked at Roland, and the young man understood. So he acknowledged with a wide grin, and slid behind the wheel.

As Mother Irene crawled into the cab of the half ton, she hesitated just for a second when she saw who would be in charge of the nearly brakeless piece of scrap metal on wheels.

But, after shooting a look of question at her husband, she shimmied her bottom between the exposed seat springs, pulled the two little girls in after her, then she signaled with a wink to her son that it was ok to proceed... as soon as the older ones had attached themselves somewhere on the vehicle.

Clara jumped on one fender and straddled the headlight, Glen did the same on the other side of the truck, and Harvey and Jackson burrowed into the load of delicious cargo weighing heavy on the gallant conveyance.

Down the safe route behind the cemetery and through the north fields they bounced. Then into the yard of the processing plant. There, the strange looking green contraption was steered into a stall, and Roland, with the help of his little brothers, tossed the pea vines into the shelling machine.

Iver waited at the scales where the machine spit the green vegetable BB's into boxes twelve inches wide by six inches deep by eighteen inches long.

After having his produce weighed, graded, recorded and boxed, Iver marshaled his family and led them in an assault on the plant ice cream stand. There they enjoyed a cone full of the best ice cream in the world, according to the Krough kids that is.

No sooner had the pea harvest been suffered, but the pole beans and corn stood waiting for their last hoeing.

When hoeing time rolled around, Roland would disappear. Of course Glen and Clara could never get away with such a trick. So the major share of such stoop labor was left to them, but with some small amount of help from Harvey and J.C.

However, Roland did have an excuse, even though it was a flimsy one.

He was busy helping his dad beg, borrow, and steal, one- inch boards. Boards from which they would construct the forms to pour the concrete into - to make the basement walls - that would support the new room.

It took two full weeks for the father and son team to search enough neighbor backyards and barnyards to find wood enough to do the job.

So it was a happy occasion when Iver and Roland nailed the random-sized planks together to, after the wood was reinforced, hold the glorified mud.

All was in readiness by the middle of August. Forty-five bags of cement had been delivered; a substantial load of sand and gravel had been dumped in the yard; and Roland had hauled several loads of large rocks from the river bed in Lefthand Canyon. Rocks that would make the forty-five bags of cement swell to eleven cubic yards of concrete instead of only nine.

When the alarm clock screamed six-thirty a.m., on the sixteenth of August, Iver had his crew: Roland, Glen, J.C., and little Harvey lined up at the edge of the hole in the ground, and their boss/father gave them their instructions.

Roland would throw ten shovelfuls of gravel into the wheelbarrow; Glen would throw six shovelfuls of sand on top of the gravel; Iver would shovel four scoops of cement into the formula; Roland would dump the water from a previously filled five gallon bucket into the ingredients; then Roland and his dad would each take-up a hoe, and, with one of them standing at each end of the steel barrow, they would commence dragging their mixing tools through the mixture until it was a thick soup.

Then Swede Larsen - who, as Mr. Krough semi-privately complained, wore a size sixteen shoe but wore a size five hat — would hook his massive hairy hands around the rusted steel pipe handles of the wheelbarrow and move it to the edge of the hole and dump the load into the forms.

He would then return his empty implement to the mixing area and hook his hands onto the other wheelbarrow. Swede Larsen gave his labor in exchange for corral poles that Iver had kept two years for a project, that, somehow or other, never was started let alone finished.

In any case, then, as soon as the mud hit bottom, J.C. and Harvey would be responsible for tossing the cantaloupe-sized rocks from the river bed into the forms so they would land strategically spaced in the wet mud ... so things went, just as Mr. Krough had envisioned that they would.

The crew that had been assembled worked hard and with precise coordination. And as Iver worked, much over his head - in terms of physical ability - he did a great deal of thinking. "How ironic," he silently commented. "Here, my younger boys are building for the future. While, over there, my older boys are destroying part of the past." That flash of realization past, another thought occurred to him, "God knows, for the next six months I won't need to wonder where my aches and pains came from ... I hope Irene appreciates what it costs in work to do this project."

"Maybe what I should do is have her go get Brother Allen and have him pray over this hole. And, because he is so religious, maybe a room will just grow out of the earth, all finished. It would no doubt be a nice room because I'm sure that God is a much better carpenter than I."

That day the men and boys of Iver's crew couldn't afford to take a break from the concrete-making phase of the project. Because, as the boss rightly said, "If we stop pouring the concrete for more than just a few minutes, what we have already dumped into the forms will have hardened enough so that when the fresh is poured on top of it, a seam will result, and the basement walls will surely leak."

At last, at nine p.m. - fourteen and a half hours after they had started - Mr. Larsen finally dumped the last load of the mud into the forms, and Iver buried all but the two threaded inches of the last anchor bolts into the soft green mush . Then, the crew finally rested and stood proudly viewing their work. For the first time their noses became the recipients of tantalizing cooking odors floating through the cracks of the house from the kitchen.

"By God, Iver!!" Swede remarked, "Whatever she's cooking does smell good. But the wife expected me home three or four hours ago, so I gotta go."

Mr. Krough brought-up the rear of his crew as they marched into the kitchen in a state of extreme tiredness. In truth, Iver felt dead tired.

They each took a turn at the wash basin, then sat their weary bodies on a chair at the dinner table. It was covered with hamburger meat cakes, boiled potatoes, creamed early peas, hot biscuits, and milk. Irene piled each of the five plates high and the five Kroughs attacked the food lustily. But, starting with the dad, after two, maybe three, mouthfuls, they, except for Mrs. Krough, discovered that what their bodies felt wasn't hunger. Because in reality their pains were from stretched muscles, and working under the hot sun of August for all those hours, hatless.

Not wanting to hurt their mother's feelings, regardless of their dulled appetites, the boys forced food into their stomachs until their plates were slick. Iver did the same.

Then one by one, the Krough boys lay on their mattress. Still dressed in their dusty jeans, without traveling to the outhouse, they all dropped into a deep, well-earned sleep.

For the following three days the new concrete was allowed to harden. Then early on the morning of the fourth day, Roland ripped the knotty wooden hide from the greenish gray cellar walls. This signaled that he and his dad would spend the day doing more cement work: Roland above, mixing and dumping his recipe down the wooden chute to his dad who was on his aching knees toweling it out to make a quite level floor. And much to the delight of both of them, that phase of the add-on project was history. "After only five hours worth of hard labor," Dad thought to himself.

The next morning, but not quite so bright and early, the self-proclaimed builder and his four sons were at at again. When two hours had been used up, floor joist and sub-flooring had begun to cap the freshly concreted hole in the ground.

As for the origins of the framing lumber, it had been sawed from logs cut in left hand Canyon by Chad and Iver a year and a half back. And in the few days just passed, hauled from the saw-mill by Uncle Bug, who cussed - with his usual skill - every board foot as he stacked it neatly as near to the building site as possible.

Bug figured it to be a terrible waste of time to pile the lumber so nice when the Kroughs would be using it up within the next few days.

Irene was excited beyond any description. With her apron flapping in the August eastern breeze, she supervised each step in the construction of her precious new room, even though she knew quite well that her comments and suggestions were bouncing off deaf ears.

"What the hell does she know? She can't tell the difference between a two-by-four and a sixteen penny nail. I just wish she would keep herself and the two little girls out of my way so I can get this miserable job done with."

He mumbled those words as he finished straightening the last dozen of a Quaker Oats box full of nails that Alfred had discovered in his barn and had donated to Iver's cause.

Though he was every bit as exhausted in the morning when he started his work on the room as when he laid his hammer down in the evening, Iver stuck with it ... to prove something, Irene quite rightly guessed. Sure enough, just three days before Thanksgiving, he slapped the last trowel full of plaster to the walls. As far as he was concerned, the job was finished - as were the building funds.

He then went and fetched his wife and led her by the hand into the room that was so new that it smelled of wet plaster.

As he rested his right arm across her back and over her shoulders, he informed her of the fact that, as the money had ran out, paint for the walls would be out of the question until more money could be saved.

Mr. Krough left his wife standing alone in her new room with her dreams and walked outside.

Then he, at last, had the time to sit under the boxelder tree, that shaded the front yard, on a five gallon can and admire his work ... causing his insides to pulsate with pride. Not because of the new room by itself. But because it was the last entry listed on things he had wanted to accomplish on his mental priority list. Although, some might question the check mark in his mind behind the entry titled "see Dr. Blodget about goiter."

Irene, though, had no time to sit and ponder her accomplishments. She, through stern verbal means, soon motivated her several able children. So almost immediately after her husband had left the house, furniture was being shuffled from one room to another.

Mr. and Mrs. Krough's large bed was taken apart and was shifted to the back room. From the back room, the kitchen furniture, such as it was, was relocated in the new room.

Then a second, or maybe third, hand couch that converted quickly to a double bed was placed in the front room. The couch had been resting in the bed of the Ford pickup under a piece of canvas for a week ... "Ten bucks well spent" thought Irene as she viewed it in its new surroundings.

Within the short space of two hours, Mrs. Krough had her home scrubbed top to bottom and the furniture rearranged. Now she had a real kitchen to cook in - a real bedroom to sleep in (though she shared it with her husband and several of her children) - and a real front room to rest and receive visitors in (though at night it turned into another bedroom.)

Sleeping space was becoming more abundant by then. And not just because of increased floor space.

Because age was also, at the same time, continuing to provide an escape for the older Krough kids.

Suddenly, and unknown to Iver and Irene, the number of bodies scattered about their dwelling would decrease by two.

By the middle of December of forty-two, Irma had arrived at the age which allowed, or more accurately, demanded that she be considered a young lady ready to assume responsibility for part of her own subsistence.

For sure, some would argue that describing a girl of seventeen as a young lady prepared to start making her own way in the world was nothing short of foolhardy. Such an opinion was obviously formed out of ignorance.

In the case of the Krough children, it wasn't age that marked the arrival of adulthood, it was mileage ... so to speak.

Flight of the Kroughs

Without the knowledge of her parents, and with a little covert assistance from Viola in the form of transportation, Irma had answered a help wanted ad in the Virtue Valley Review telling of a housekeeping position in Smithville. Not only did the job call for house cleaning talent, but for talent in the care of children as well. For which, in both cases, Irma was uniquely qualified. When the attractive red-headed young lady exited the hand carved front door that belonged to the wealthy attorney, her face was lit up with a smile. And as she stepped into Viola's car, she nearly shouted the news that she had been hired. Then Irma had to ask Viola if she could possibly take her home so she could collect her belongings. Then bring her back again.

Difficult as it was seeing their daughter leave home at such a tender age, Iver and Irene, would, in a day or so, receive a real shock concerning Roland.

It began with but an innocent, restless itch within the mere boy of fifteen and a half. But it took only a few days for the slightly discomforting itch to fester into a full-fledged obsession. Which even he didn't fully understand.

Roland would start out with honest intentions of going to the picture show. But, only halfway there, he would lose interest and retrace his steps toward home, as far as their barn. There, he would hide, think, and smoke.

Irene had a keen understanding of each of her many children, so she knew instantly when something was eating at one of them. So it was with Roland.

Not wanting to risk the sorrow of seeing one of her flock get himself into some kind of trouble, or be drawn into trouble by someone else, she decided to confront the distraught teenager with the fact that she was aware of his damaged emotional state.

The following morning when her husband had gone to visit his pigs, Irene made good her promise to herself.

"Roland," she said, "is there something in particular that's bothering you? Or, just everything in general."

"No," was his quick, and only, reply.

"Now look, you, I'm not stupid, or blind. So why don't you just tell me what's on your mind?" she insisted.

"There ain't nothing wrong ... honest."

Irene decided that she must have been making some headway, because she sensed that she was making Roland feel uncomfortable.

She settled for directing just one more question at him. But she expressed it more so to gain assurance: "Just put my mind at ease, and tell me that you're not in some kind of trouble."

"Well, Mother, you can put your worry to rest, because I can guarantee you that I'm in no kind of trouble."

"I'll make a deal with you then, ok?" bargained Irene, "You go talk to your dad, and I won't question you any further."

"A great deal" Roland figured as he dumped the last of his once hot cocoa down his throat. So out the door he tripped.

Mrs. Krough hadn't intended to be so nosey concerning her son's frame of mind. But thoughts of James, and what some of those CC's had fed him in a cigarette had been the first thing that flashed across her mind when she first noticed Roland's change of mood.

Followed closely by the recollections of a younger, and foolish, Chad risking severe punishment for a few candy bars for his brothers and sisters, and his parents.

For his part, Roland hadn't meant to display such obvious symptoms to his wise mother.

When the young man arrived at the sad excuse of a barnyard, his dad was leaning on the pigpen fence chewing on a three stick wad of gum - a replacement habit acquired in trade for the tobacco habit.

He made the trade as a result of constant nagging by Irma. She used as her weapon pointed oblique remarks, or cute saying like "Hey, Dad, you know ... you used to spit over your chin, but now you spit all over it."

So, in the end he decided that it was keep the habit and move to the barn to escape his daughter's concern - expressed through satiric needling - or drag up all the will that still lived inside his decaying body and give up a habit he had cherished, and at the same time cursed, since the tender age of twelve. It did, without doubt, make Irma happy, not to mention his wife, who had offered her quiet blessing to the red-headed beauty's success.

Wishing he had a stick of gum to present his dad as a prescription for mellowing his mood, Roland proceeded toward the animal confinement area.

He snaked through and around piles of miscellaneous treasure that Iver said he would use someday for something or other and leaned - without an offering or without ceremony beside his dad.

Iver rotated his head just slightly and experienced a feeling of profound satisfaction upon noticing his young helper, the son he could depend on, standing so close to him.

Neither spoke for several minutes. Because, it appeared to Roland, that his father was off on some mental excursion of abysmal proportions.

"Perhaps to a place where everyday cares, such as poverty, war, and illness ... a place such as Alfred always spoke of maybe,.. wasn't allowed to exist."

But Roland hadn't maintained his respectful silence long before his dad came back to life and spoke his son's name.

"Roland," he said, "I don't often see you down here in these parts. Is this a special treat for me, or would you like to tell me what is troubling you?"

The young man sucked up all the courage he could muster before saying a word.

He looked straight into the back wall of the pigpen, then softly, he began his explanation.

"Dad," he said, "I want to join the Navy."

Like his son, Iver fixed his dew-impaired, and shocked, stare on the back wall of the pigpen. And every muscle in his arthritic body became rigid.

Roland wondered for an instant if his dad was fighting the urge to slug him for just mentioning something that, to him, must have sounded like nonsense.

"But Roland," Iver at last pleaded as he tentatively laid a hand on the young man's shoulder, "you are but a boy and shouldn't even be thinking such thoughts. Now don't let me hear you mention the Navy again."

That same evening, as the Krough parents lay in their old bed but in their new room, Iver felt obligated to inform his wife of the conversation that had occurred at the pigpen fence between himself and Roland.

When the difficult task was finished, Irene drifted into a state of confusion.

She tried, but just couldn't comprehend such a thing.

"How can that be?" she asked her husband. But he was fresh out of answers.

"A boy of fifteen going to fight a war, why hell, he can't even grow hair on his face yet."

"Tell me, please, what would make a boy want to get involved in a dirty dangerous war anyway?"

Iver finally arrived at the conclusion that he would, at least, need to fabricate some sort of reasoning to reassure his floundering wife.

"It's simple," he began, "our boys go to war full of the same excuses that their boys go to war with ... because that's what civilized men have always done. In the beginning, it's a matter of adventure, glory, or the thrill of shaking hands with death, and living to boast about it."

"But," Iver theorized to his wife, "the real reason for making war has nothing, even remotely, to do with the reasons for which those who fight the war think they're fighting."

"You see, the higher ups have always interpreted the reasons for waging war for the benefit of the lower downs."

"And one of their most useful devices to accomplish their goal is to use high-sounding catch-all phrases like, 'It's in our national interest' - but what does that mean....?" Irene shook her head to indicate that she hadn't a clue. So Iver continued.

"I will tell you what it means; it means that most wars are fought for one of four reasons, which are, political, economic, self defence, or wars of liberation - which usually means sticking a nose into a civil war of some country to insure a desirable out- come to that war."

"If war is a matter of national political policy, then the young men fight, and die, to save the ass holes of the politicians."

"If the war is for the purpose of defending one's own country, then young men fight and die because the man on the throne, or the gray-bearded man points a finger at them. And tells them that it is their patriotic duty to fight."

"And if the need to make war is for economic purposes, the young men fight and die to save the fortunes of the rich fatcat bankers and crooked industrial tycoons."

"If you add to all that, the propagandizing posters and movies that our young impressionable men are bombarded with - well, what chance has common sense got."

"Naturally, the cruelty of such distortions aren't realized until those fine young men are in mud up to their waists. And trying to keep warm by hugging a dead buddy. Or when they are scared - hungry, and with the business end of a bayonet between their shoulder blades."

"Only then is the romance of war lost."

"And, as the God damned Germans and Japs are going to find, they will at last know that it is easier to start a war than to win one."

"Maybe," Iver went on, "an over-educated person could describe what I have just tried to describe for you better, Irene. And for sure more eloquently, but he wouldn't know it any better than I."

After the shocking news of his son's intentions had filtered deeper into his consciousness, Iver repeated to his son the very things he had told his wife concerning war. But added the fact that no one, even those who survive unscathed, are ever the same afterwards.

But did Roland listen to his dad's words of wisdom? Hell no. So, on the fifth of January of forty-three, Iver signed on the dotted line that certified the fact that his son was old enough to get killed - but, only if necessary.

On that same fifth of January, Irene made the unexpected discovery that the impossible was, indeed, possible. Because when she witnessed her fuzzy-cheeked young son hold up his right arm and swear to defend his country and its constitution against all manner of threats, she believed her spirits to have sunk as low as they possibly could. But she was wrong. For, on that very grey day, Irene at last had to admit to herself that she was pregnant.

All during what was left of that day she kept asking herself, over and over again, "how could such a thing happen? It just can't be true."

"Here I am forty-two, nearly three. And there stands Iver, sixty-one and worn out. Oh Lord, I hope this is just some cruel joke my body is playing on me. Because if I am, the poor baby doesn't stand a chance."

"As hard as I have tried," she told herself, "the only thing positive I can think of is that I'm not superstitious, so the fact that the child will be number thirteen won't, in its own right, matter. Which, is the only thing in my favor I can think of."

Though she felt devious about it, Irene decided to keep her condition her own secret. Not because she was ashamed - it was, and she knew it, too late for shame–but because she just couldn't find the words to explain such an occurrence without evoking, from some, ridicule, disgust, or astonishment. But, most particularly, her concern was for Iver's reaction to the news.

She knew full well that he would explode in her face with male logic of the day.

He would come out with such statements as, "For God sakes woman, how could you let such a thing happen? Haven't you learned anything about the facts of life in the past twenty-four years?

So, as a temporary self defense, the agitated woman purged all thoughts concerning her almost certain pregnancy from her mind. "Because," she reasoned, "I do have the luxury of a few month's grace."

It seemed, life had once again played a cruel prank on Irene; robbing her of the license to concern herself with her own problems, by having to endure such an abundance of trouble among those around her that she loved.

Once more, Irene threw her own troubles aside and focused her concern on her husband and her children.

Following his enlistment day by two weeks, Roland was gathered up with the other new joinees and draftees, so the citizens of Bear River City could honor them with a party at the fancy hall with the floating-action floor.

However, on that occasion, Iver and Irene stayed only for the speeches and musical program. Neither of them could muster an appetite.

But Roland remained; he consumed enough food for the three of them.

Suddenly, it seemed, after but a few weeks of training in northern Idaho, Roland was operating a radar set on a transport ship that was under full steam, headed for Hawaii.

It seemed to Irene as if she and her husband were swept up in a raging flood of events that they had no influence over. And they weren't alone.

Now Irene had to split her worry five ways. But it wasn't the same amount of worry chopped into five pieces; it was worry compounded.

First, she worried about her mate. Then she worried about the children. Chad was in England - headed for God knows where. James was someplace in North Africa, and Roland was floating somewhere on the Pacific. Now, instead of shunning the news reports, Irene absorbed it all, good, bad, and trivial. Plus, now she had to worry about her own secret condition.

Notwithstanding the worry, Irene and Iver did have several sources of much joy ... two beautiful granddaughters in particular, as Viola and Greg had wasted no time in starting a family. Another source of satisfaction, for Iver primarily, was that he had received his official certificate of naturalization. Making him, once and for all, a citizen of the United States. And one more thing that gave Irene some peace of mind was the knowledge that it was already middle forty three, and her three sons were, as of yet, well.

But not so for Viola.

Because of the young mother, Irene's worry would compound once more.

Since her marriage to Greg, she had acquired the habit of picking at a small mole in the area of her left temple. Everyone who cared about Viola warned her about the nervous habit. Greg complained about the ugliness of it. Mother Irene warned her daughter about the likelihood of infection. Iver, choosing to be a hair more blunt, told her that the sore would, if she didn't let it heal, surely make its way to her brain and she could die.

In a vain attempt at getting her daughter to cease harassing the colored spot on her temple, Irene insisted that it was a beauty mark. But in return, Viola told her mother just how much she hated the mark. And that she figured that if she picked at it long enough, it might disappear.

Alas, in spite of repeated warnings, Viola kept up her assault on the mole.

In the fall of forty-three, just as her mother had earlier that year predicted, Viola began to feel less than good. As the result of much persuasion from her husband and coaxing by her parents, the young pregnant wife consented to go check with Doctor Blodget.

Two weeks later Viola sat nervously exercising one leg that was flipped over the other, waiting for the Doctor to finish his preliminary evaluation of her examination.

Approximately twenty minutes later, the door to Doctor Blodget's inner sanctum opened. Viola and also her mother were invited in.

He offered them each an institutional-looking chair; then he circled his desk and sat on his own black leather chair that reclined and swiveled - he

Flight of the Kroughs

reclined and swiveled. Now it was obvious to Irene that their family doctor was stalling.

"Perhaps," she spoke silently, "he is fishing for the words he needs to describe my daughter's condition, and that can only be bad."

When Doctor Blodget had swiveled two trips between two hundred seventy degrees and ninety degrees, he at last summoned the courage to bring his fancy chair to a dead stop, making him face the patient and her mother.

Even after the nearly young physician had come to a halt he waited several seconds before speaking.

Viola and Irene attached their attention to Doctor Blodget's face in an anticipatory trance.

At last, the opening where the sound of speech exits began to move ... slowly. "Viola," he began, "first of all you are pregnant."

Instinctively a burst of guilt mixed with fear rippled inside Mother Irene. Also, she felt a hot flash that she was sure had reddened her face.

"No kidding, Doc," Viola answered in thought. "That news is as new as sin."

"About three months I would guess," he added.

Mother Irene had seen through the Doctor's tactics and waited on the edge of panic for the rest of the story.

"But," Doctor Blodget resumed, "I wish I could tell you that your being in the family way is responsible for you feeling badly."

"I won't be able to get to the bottom of that until the results of your tests have been returned to me, and I have the opportunity to evaluate them."

"All I can tell you right this minute is get plenty of rest. But, most importantly, leave that mole on the side of your head alone so it can heal."

Viola assured her Doctor that she would faithfully follow his instructions; then she led her mother from his office.

As they left the small white stuccoed building, Viola looked at her worried mother and said, "You know what they always say 'No news is good news.'"

The next two weeks passed quickly. With no word from the Doctor, the young woman started to relax and repeated to herself, several times, that old saying.

But on Wednesday, not far beyond the two weeks mentioned, Doctor Blodget sent word to Viola, through her mother, that she should report to his office, with a specimen in a sterilized jar, promptly at nine o'clock the very next day.

So Irene scribbled a note to her daughter and dispatched Clara to deliver it.

The next day, a dreary day, the two women did as they were ordered and reported to their family doctor's office.

Once inside, the pair waited among the doctoring paraphernalia and the odor of disinfectant for a full thirty minutes before the doctor showed his face.

When he did finally show up, he hurried straight to his desk carrying Viola's chart in his right hand. That day there was no stalling. In fact, Irene sensed urgency in his manner. He did, however, begin the session by repeating some useless information.

After a quick, but gentle greeting, he got right down to cases. "Viola," he said, "as I suspected, you are going to have a baby. But that's not what concerns me."

"There is, I suppose, no easy way for me to put this to you, except to say that you have a very serious illness... cancer."

Irene gasped, then grabbed her young daughter's hand.

Viola was shaken. But not knowing how grave the illness he called cancer really was, she fully expected Doctor Blodget to follow his diagnosis with a remedy that would make her well. But no such news was issued.

The young mother became pale as she glanced, first at the solemn-faced Doctor, then her glassy-eyed mother. And only then, did she realize that whatever cancer was, it wasn't too pleasant.

Irene was the first to speak. "Is there anything that can be done?"

"Well, I would like to refer Viola to a specialist in Salt Lake City for radium treatments." The Doctor then looked at the young lady sitting in hushed silence and added, "If you approve of course."

Viola knew then, just as the man across the desk from her did, that she didn't have a choice. Because, she also knew that there were two individuals one didn't disobey ... doctors and God.

So, together, Irene and her ill daughter answered positively.

Then Viola nearly shouted, "When do I have to go? I have the girls to think about."

"Oh, I will get in touch with you as soon as I have made the necessary arrangements," the Doctor answered reassuringly.

She would eventually make four of those trips to Salt Lake City. Sadly, with each trip the stay was longer and was more painful.

His daughter's sickness also caused Iver a great deal of grief. He himself was walking around in a condemned body. His daughter's hopeless condition caused his own condition to decayed even more.

It was a struggle for him to supervise the planting and harvesting of the crops in forty-three.

Flight of the Kroughs

The real difference between the two years was that Glen and his dad had switched places; father rode the horse, guiding it between the rows of corn and spuds, and the son held on to the cultivator.

The most important lesson the gentleman farmer had learned - from the pea incident - was to plant crops which could be easily harvested.

Although his contracts with the canning company brought some money into the house, Mr. Krough had to admit to feeling the pinch of indignity that comes to those who can't provide for their families; actually, not a new concern for Iver

Thanks to his sons, though, there was a fair amount of spendable cash on hand in the Krough household each month. As, freely, and without being persuaded, their boys in uniform each sent part of their meager income, which had increased due to promotion and hazardous pay, home to their parents. However, money alone couldn't cure the Krough family's troubles.

In the summer of forty-three, three months after certain natural biological truths had begun taking place inside her body, Irene was forced to tell her husband of their impending blessed event - at least, she prayed that it would be blessed. And the words she feared and expected from her mate bounced from her face.

When her daughter was feeling poorly and was due to take her second trip to Salt Lake City, Irene, for the very first time, did something behind her husband's back ... she summoned Alfred Allen and his Elder friends to pray over Viola.

Not long after the Elders had anointed the ill mother's head with consecrated olive oil and had begged God for her deliverance from the scourge that had possessed her young body, Alfred asked Viola how she was feeling. "Better," she answered in a quiet, timid voice. That was good enough for Alfred. He left the house feeling sure that he had once more been instrumental in coaxing another miracle from the "powers that be" upstairs.

Then Irene left, with considerably more peace of mind than before the divine ordinance was performed.

When she arrived at her own residence, she discovered Iver stretched out on their bed. She went directly to him and sat on the edge of the bed and felt his forehead for fever. There was none.

"Feeling badly?" she questioned.

"Oh, now that you mention it, I do feel a bit off center."

Then she dared make a suggestion to her husband that shocked even herself.

"Listen, Iver, why don't I call Brother Allen and his friends?"

Her ears were pounded with exactly the response she had expected. But, a million miles away from the response she had hoped for. "God-damn-it, Irene, haven't you learned anything in nineteen years worth of knowing that pious hypocrite? You know that when he speaks it's like listening to a recently-remedied constipated camel. So let's hear no more of such bullshit."

Irene, though having been rudely rebuffed, could contain herself no longer. So she came right out and confessed to her husband the good news about the results Viola had experienced at the hands of Alfred and his friends.

Well, Iver was as if he had been struck by lightning.

"What do you mean Viola was made to feel better with the help of Alfred Allen's gang - who called them in anyway?"

"I did," answered Irene, arrogantly standing her ground.

"You did ... and without consulting me first" Iver retaliated.

"Yes, I did," gloated Irene "and I'm damn glad I did. Besides, you know as well as I do what your answer would have been had I asked you."

"Well, just what in the hell did Alfred do for Viola; did he make her sore disappear?"

"No, her sore didn't disappear," Irene answered honestly, but reluctantly. "But they did make her feel much better," she quickly added.

"And you believe that to be some kind of miracle, don't you?" Iver ridiculed.

"Well, Old Boy, let's look at it this way - if you could feel good right up to the split instant you passed away, wouldn't you consider that, all by itself, some sort of miracle?"

That being strictly a rhetorical question, whether her husband knew it or not, Irene continued.

"Just think, Iver, passing through the invisibly thin veil that separates life and death between breaths, and knowing no pain."

The thought of such a wonderful concept of dying appealed to Mr. Krough, but at the same time it stumped him for an instant reply.

Knowing that, Irene silently savored her small victory.

However, although Iver wasn't quite finished, he did change the direction of the discussion. Because in the next instant, he became cynical.

"You know Irene, there are three major categories of quacks on this earth. And you-me-Viola-and everybody else, for that matter, are under their fat thumb."

"There are political quacks, like Adolph Hitler."

"There are religious quacks, like Alfred Allen."

"And there are doctor quacks, like all doctors. Doctors who would have you believe that they are trying to cure the sick when, in truth, what they are doing is earning a comfortable living, for themselves, from sick people's misery. If they get lucky and learn something in the process, they get their name on an article in the medical journals."

"But, Iver continued in a sure-of-himself style, "they won't get their chance to use their polished sterile tools of exploration on me. Because I fully intend to live right up to the second that my spirit departs this shit-pile of a planet."

"And, if I could, I would even choose the means by which I go ... it would be something quick and painless."

"Hardly original," Irene interrupted silently - then allowed her husband to rave on.

"Like maybe having some unknown enemy soft-shoe up behind me with a gun and blow a tunnel through my head."

Irene shot an unbelieving look and a sound of disgust at her rattling husband. But, there was no stopping him.

"Or maybe," Iver started up again, "something hitting me from behind that I didn't see coming."

"In any case, it isn't the dying that frightens me; it's what a body needs to go through just to do it that concerns me."

Continuing the propaganda exercise, Iver said "some people will bargain with death, using doctors and their medicines for go–betweens."

"Not me, not by a damn site. In fact, if necessary, I will sit on my chair and wish myself into the next world."

Irene waited politely - if not patiently - for her under-the- weather husband to cease talking. When he did, then she would have her say. And she did.

"Maybe you are sincere when you say that you don't fear death Iver. But that, in itself, is no virtue. Because to be virtuous a person would welcome death, yet have the guts to do whatever it takes to live. And if that includes eating lizard brains and drinking tea made from tumbleweed roots or, heaven forbid, seeing a doctor, while desperately seeking a cure, then so be it."

"But, if you're interested Iver, I will tell you what I think you really fear" without waiting for his yea or nay she proceeded.

"I think what you are honestly afraid of, is, having the doctor tell you what you already know about yourself."

"Well, when did you all-of-a-sudden become such a know-it-all damn it," returned Iver in a raised sarcastic voice.

"All I'm trying to do is save you some money. Because I know the doctors can't fix what's wrong with me. And as far as I'm concerned, you can also save money on an undertaker when I kick the bucket; just carry my body into the foothills and dump it among the sage brush and anthills, and let the ants, coyotes, and hawks compete for my business. Then when they are done with me, just leave my bones as my monument."

Irene knew that deep inside him, under his amour of thick cynicism, her husband had a strong desire to live. And that the only reason he said what he did was to honor his belief that to scurry around in a state of panic searching for a miracle was the act of a coward.

So she let the discussion lay where it died of silence, then brewed Iver a fresh pot of coffee. Which she left with him and his thoughts.

Entering the kitchen, she went directly to its south wall and studied the calendar with curled corners. Where, for the previous three months, she had placed a diagonal slash across the dates. Casually, Irene thumbed through the proceeding eight months and did some quick calculating.

"According to the way I have it figured," she whispered to herself "I have four days to go."

As she had gained a wealth of experience in her twenty four years of married life, which consisted mainly of having babies, and waiting for babies to arrive, she would be pretty nearly on the money.

For the next few days she insisted to her husband who was, by that time, feeling physically and emotionally better, that the pickup be parked with its nose pointed down the incline at the east side of the house, and in the tank there must be no less than fifty cents worth of gas.

She wanted the truck parked at the top of the slope because it was fall, and cooler, and the damnable thing didn't start like it did in the heat of the summer. So, if her worst tear was realized, then it would be easy for the kids to give it a push start.

On the fifth day, just one day more than Mother Krough had guessed, the signs within her body told her it was time to go see to it ... and luckily, the old Ford kicked right over. A good omen, Irene thought in the middle of the night.

Seven days later, Irene returned from the hospital carrying a handsome boy baby.

He was perfect, it seemed, in every detail except for his color, which was redder than usual.

Doctor Blodget told Irene that the week-old child would need to be closely watched for a few days. If she noticed even the slightest deterioration in his condition, she should make for the hospital with the boy and have his office called

As it turned out, the doctor's instructions were prophecy.

In just two weeks, the lad's little body turned bluish in color. So Irene and Iver drove, as fast as their delapidated little truck would go, back to the hospital at Smithville with their little son. They registered him at the desk, then asked to have Doctor Blodget called, and soon.

Afterward, in the sterilized quiet of the lobby, in late afternoon, Irene turned to her husband and told him that she was going to call the Elders - with or without, his blessing.

Much to her surprise, Iver agreed. He even went so far as to volunteer to make the arrangements. After Iver had departed on his mission of mercy, Irene realized why he had shown such little reluctance; after all, they were in Smithville, not Bear River City, and Alfred would never find out.

Therefore with the blessing of his grieving wife, Iver didn't call Alfred, he called his respected friend, and Bishop, Mr. Petersen.

Two weeks later, in spite of the prayers offered in his behalf, the little boy died.

To Irene, and also Iver, if he could have let go, that loss was as devastating as their first.

So a tearful mother and a somber, guilt-ridden father returned to the Krough house. Irene told the children that their little brother had left them. "And for a better place," Iver chipped in.

The loss of the little guy, though he was in the home but two weeks, took the edge off the keen anticipation of the winter holidays usually felt by the Krough kids. The loss affected the parents especially. But, regardless of their blunted interest, Thanksgiving came, and was observed, then Christmas was at the door- step.

The children, as always, received from their parents what their parents could afford to buy them. And, as always, the mysterious visit in the middle of the night occurred.

That holiday one of the gifts in that anonymous gift box was a fishing pole and reel, marked for Iver.

It was seven feet in length and was made of steel. The feature which made the pole so fascinating to Glen, J.C., and Harvey was that the three smaller sections of the four-section piece of fishing equipment slid and disappeared into the largest section. Iver turned the pole over and over in his hands, and told the three boys that when it got smaller it was telescoping. But they simply called it neat.

On Christmas day of forty-three Iver sat fooling with his new toy while trying to recall from his youth where the best fishing holes could be found in Left-hand Canyon creek.

Irene spent the day thinking of James, Chad, Roland, Viola, and her fading husband.

Once in a while she would think of the baby boy who, had he lived, would have been called David, and she realized that he would have been three months old.

It would soon be a new year, she wondered, tentatively, about that also.

January howled its way into Virtue Valley riding a tide of nasty weather that excreted a yard of snow as its cutting winds battered the Krough house mercilessly.

Those eastern winds took the white stuff and crafted it into a textured sea of drifts ranging in size from two to five feet high.

Also, little driftlets of the virgin powder sifted their way through the quarter-inch gap between the bottom of the doors and the foot worn tread. They remained there until Irene would brush them gently with her hand into the dustpan, then toss them out of the back door ... like, Glen imagined, throwing a lost infant lamb back to the safety of its own kind and flock.

At six-thirty in the morning, the three rooms were immersed in creaking cold. But, under home-stitched denim and Sunday-suit-scrap wool-batted quilts, bodies kept one-another warm.

Unmindful of the cold, at night the three boys were, with Glen in charge, lucky enough to lie by a window on their overwhelmed steel cot. There, with their chins resting in cupped palms that were propped up by arms bent at the elbows, they would raise their shaggy heads to just above the window sill.

They would spread their gazes across the snowscape and to the tops of the western mountains - a picture that was framed by a window and tattered shade. With their eyes they would explore in detail the glacial winter splendor. In their minds, images were easily fostered.

Glen, J.C., and Harvey, imagined the drifts to be ice crystals that were rippled into dune after dune. Like, they thought, some mythical Arab desert scene.

What the three boys saw seemed frozen in the silence of transparent unspoiled air. And the scene was lit up near to noon light, thanks to a full moon and its generous beams.

Then Glen announced to his two younger brothers, with certainty that gave it validity, that he could see hovering above the tips of those tallest dunes, Father Winter and his friend Cyotee standing guard over their masterful creation.

Finally, their imaginary magic carpet landed, and their spell of fantasy gave way to deep sleep. The last thoughts to grow in their minds were about their absent big brothers. Had they known the true condition of their dad's and their big sister's health, they would have been included in their concern.

Sometime during that January, James was wading ashore at a place called Anzio.

It was a carefully planned military campaign which was designed to surprise the Germans. But, as it turned out, the Americans were the ones who got the surprise.

Flight of the Kroughs

The resistance that James and his buddies encountered was so fierce that they were trapped until the next May. Caught in that trap as well, but a stranger to James, was a dark-haired soldier from Maine, called Al Benson.

He wasn't, it seemed at the time anyway, as lucky as James. Corporal Benson had nearly his whole leg blasted off his body instead of only part of it.

So, he was strapped to a stretcher then put on a boat that was stateside bound.

Al arrived three weeks later at the army hospital that was located at the end of Granite Pass, located on the other side of the mountains that insulated Virtue Valley from the rest of the world.

After three months of treatment for infection and therapy on his wounded leg, he was judged well enough to be allowed liberty. It was during one of those liberties that Al and some of his fellow patients traveled through the mountains, via Grantie Pass, past Bear River City to Smithville. They had heard that there were loads of college girls eager for action. According to rumor, the girl students outnumbered the male students three to one. And the rumor further stated that those male students were either young and clumsy or too old to cut the mustard.

There, on Erma's one Saturday of the month off, she and Al met and quickly became acquainted. That, in spite of the fact, that she was no coed. But if looks had been a criteria, she would, without a doubt, have been overqualified.

A month later they became engaged. And a month after that, they married.

Then, sadly, one week after that, Al would be shipped back to the war in Europe.

Also in January of forty-four, Chad was in Huntingdon, England practicing for the invasion of Nazi occupied Europe and being charmed by the local English beauties.

At about the same time, Roland had just finished dropping a load of marines off at a place in the South Pacific called Tarawa, while dodging Zeros.

Roland's campaign was a lot like older and bigger brother's in Italy.

Because, thanks to the coral, the LST's couldn't get close enough to the beach to land their troops. So the marines were forced to wade through chest-deep sea water.

Needless to say, they were but static objects for Japanese target practice.

When Roland and his ship had deposited their load of human and support cargo at what would eventually be a successful fiasco - discounting the human cost of course - they headed back to home port and loaded up a

D. Raymond Anderson

fresh batch of troops and headed for another place in the Pacific called Kwajalein.

However, of those Krough family members, their friends, and their relatives who had volunteered, two were not so fortunate.

James' best friend Rod, and his first cousin Jess who had, in that cold spring of forty, eagerly raised their arms and answered the oath affirmatively to secure a paid vacation on the Pacific Islands, thanks to the U.S. Army, had found themselves in tragic circumstances three years later.

The Batan death march had begun at sun-up on the scourching day of the tenth of May. Thousands of American, Philippine, and some British prisoners were rounded up. They were herded together at the Bataan Airfield just one day after the Japanese had overrun the outpost. The ones who had food had it taken from them. And every prisoner was searched and stripped of all personal belongings, Jess and Rod included.

The American, Philippine, and British prisoners were bunched into groups of five hundred to a thousand each; then their Japanese guards prodded them with clubs and rifle butts, and the forced march was underway.

The sad trek lasted six days and nights. With but one bowl of soggy rice to sustain their bodies and spirit in that whole time.

Rod and Jess showed their stuff. When the walk into despair was over, five thousand two hundred young American men had died. But not Rod and Jess.

Not surprisingly, to those who perished, it wasn't an easy death, though some of the survivors must have prayed for any kind of death.

Death, however, from starvation, beatings, or drowning in one's defecation, comes hatefully slow, as Jess and Rod would swear to, if they somehow were ever to have the opportunity.

Thinking much about the jeopardy her own sons were in, and also feeling for the parents of Jess and Rod, on one winter night in forty-four, Irene made the offhand statement: that some supreme authority ought to outlaw war from the face of the earth.

"No, by hell," shouted Iver.

Irene was taken aback by her husband's response, and asked "Why not?"

"Well," said Iver, "suppose the rich, using their politician puppets, were able to get complete control of our government. Instead of only controlling part of it as they do now. And suppose, as you wish, any kind of physical resistance was impossible - then what recourse would the poor people have?"

"Then," Irene reasoned, "what you are saying is, that if reason won't work, you can always fight ... right?"

Flight of the Kroughs

"If that is what you gathered from what I said ... then yes," returned Iver.

"But honest rebellion is individual. Because, if you become part of a crowd, then you no longer think ... the crowd thinks for you," he quickly added.

And that was all that was said in what remained of January of forty-four, because the next day it was overlapped by February. And it, in turn, by March.

In April Clara took an unsanctioned journey away from home. Soon after being apprehended, the fourteen-year old learned that she was to be assigned to the State Industrial school. Everyone knew that the real name of the place was reform school. As far as titles are concerned, the latter was most accurate. Because some of the inmates did reform - they went from bad to worse.

One less hand in the field, Iver complained, as he made his grand plan for spring planting.

Irene thought about the situation differently.

She accepted Clara's troubles as just another helping of punishment for some crime she herself had committed.

"However," she daydreamed "a person, or thing, or institution, with such great power as to be able to dispense punishment on such a liberal basis must also have the authority to grant rewards. Like," Irene cogitated, "letting me inherit a million dollars and a truck loaded with spending money." But she quickly shook herself back to earth by saying, "Good hell, I'm getting as bad as Iver."

As she had just hinted, Iver's mind had him somewhere else. Most likely across the lane wandering his twenty acres. Every night since April had arrived, after the five Krough kids then at home had gone to their sleeping places, Iver would get a piece of brown grocery bag paper on which he would draw and figure. First he would start a chart by penciling several horizontal lines on his precious paper. At the extreme left edge of each line, he listed a potential crop.

Then he took his straight edge, about the size of a one-foot ruler, cut from a piece of one-by-six for just that purpose, and struck several vertical lines through the horizontal ones. This automatically created several neat columns, five to be exact, including the one already used to list the crop, and to that column he assigned the number 1.

In column number 2 he entered the cost of seed.

In column number 3 he entered other expenses. Which were few, as his manual labor was free, and everything else he borrowed.

In column number 4 he entered the crop's expected yield. And in the last column, number 5, Iver would compute the approximate profit.

Next, he pulled all the money from his pockets and then raided Irene's secret stashes. He piled his resources together on the kitchen table. He counted it - and recounted it - and recounted it. Finally, as in years past, he would shout, "Bullshit!" then add, "I will just contract with the canning company, and they will just deduct the cost of seed from my check. And the brown paper would start the next fire in the kitchen range.

By the middle days of April all of the contractual red tape had been tied up at the canning plant, and Iver waited for middle May to set his plans in motion.

But by the time two thirds of April had passed, things started to change.

The change began with Iver breaking one of the many resolutions he had so positively expressed to Irene in the October that had just passed; he went to the cemetery and selected a family plot.

When he returned, he had a story concocted to defer his wife from saying something smart like, "Have a change of heart dear?"

He would say to her, "Now David has a place of his own," as he walked through the doorway. Then he would add that he had talked to the city boys, and they had assured him that, as David's was a fresh grave, it would be no problem to move, and they would see to it in the next few days.

As usual that's just the way it went. And that was all that was ever said on the subject of burial plots. Irene kindly let a rare opportunity to poke fun at her husband slide by.

At that time, Iver was forced to admit to a couple truths about himself. The major of which, was, that his body felt ruin that compared well-nigh to the cumulative effect suffered by a scrap yard filled with cars used up in a keystone cop movie.

At eight-thirty a.m. on the 10th of May, he pulled his half-functioning body from his bed. When he had shifted to a sitting position on the edge of the mattress, he decided that he felt just a bit rubbery in the lower regions of his body. He was moved to wonder if his legs would actually support the rest of his body.

Irene couldn't understand why he didn't just remain in bed.

"I'M sure, she thought, that Iver is not only hiding the agony he is feeling from me, but from his old friends and antagonist as well."

"He knows that if Alfred was to come by, he would surely drag him from his bed, slam him on his knees and force a death bed prayer for forgiveness out of him."

"If LeRoy was to happen by, he would no doubt bundle Iver up and deliver him to the 'quack factory'."

"If, god forbid, Uncle Bug came by, he would take a look at Iver then ask if he could 'borrow' his truck."

Flight of the Kroughs

As he ambled toward kitchen, still concerned about the dependability of his legs, Irene went about the chore of setting out two cups of coffee.

They sat together, fighting the gloom of despondency.

He looked, at the very least, conspicuous, setting under his bashed-in hat while trying not to rock the near dead rocker on which he sat.

But, to any of his family, friends, or neighbors, he would have looked quite natural.

However, to some invisible spirit lurking in a dark corner of the room waiting to escort Iver to his just reward, he, no doubt, would have looked conspicuous.

Perhaps though, the most remarkable part of the scene they presented was the stark contrast of their outward appearances: Iver sixty-two-looking eighty-two, Irene forty-four and looking thirty- five.

Gray had not yet dared infiltrate the dark brown, nearly black, hair that fluffed full of body over Irene's head and sent its natural curls cascading over her shoulders.

Her flowered housedress was neat and clean and was under a just-washed, starched, and ironed apron. To the seven Krough kids present, she looked dressed for a special occasion.

After he had given-up on the last third of his cup of coffee, he, with Irene's help, returned to the comfort of his bed.

While he sat there in quiet, somnolent uncertainty, wondering - but not wanting to admit, what he was sure was going on inside his body - a comical thought occurred to him. He imagined, in spite of his slowing mental ability, that there were, inside his body, a half dozen or so diminutive creatures who were closing up shop. And each of those shops was a vital organ. Iver hoped that he wouldn't feel anything until the last little creature pulled the main switch, at which time all of his systems would grind to a halt. "Oh if it were only that simple," he begged.

Though he felt his buttocks settle into the sagging-at-the-middle mattress, Iver was conscious of no feeling as his head made its depression in his pillow. He was off somewhere vaguely familiar to him ... somewhere between Utah, Wyoming, Kansas, or Alabama.

He wasn't walking; he wasn't driving a Model "A" or a Model "T"; he was just there ... half in spirit and half in body.

There were several folks around him that he thought he should know. Indeed, had his brain been clear of fog, he would have recognized them all, if only by their Southern talk.

Soon, two images moved from transparency and assumed form about fifty feet from him. There, in the gloom, they stopped and just stared at him ... leaving him but one option, to stare back.

As he did that, he suddenly recognized each of them.

The one on the right was named Anna; Iver had met her in Kansas.

The other lady, the one on the left, identical to the one on the right in looks and manner, was named Rose. Iver had met her in Wyoming. But just as he recognized the pair standing off in the misty distance from him, another, even stranger phenomenon occurred, right before his unbelieving eyes; the two women suddenly became one in the same body.

There was no thunder, no lightning, and no magical puff of smoke ... just Iver's ashen incredulous expression.

Then the most profound discovery of all dawned on him; that together, the two women equaled mother-in-law, Rosanna.

Without his own brain inciting his limbs to move, Iver moved, without wanting to, toward the waiting woman. When he had moved a distance of forty-seven feet, he stopped, leaving them separated by three feet.

"Well, ain't it amazing who one can meet when one doesn't have a gun," said Rosanna. "It's been a few years since you carried my daughter off to that dried-out place called Utah."

"Where is that beautiful home you promised her?" she said as she looked right and left.

"What about the fine clothes and priceless adornments you promised her? And what became of your promise to her that you would slave until your last breath to provide Irene a life of ease and luxury?"

"I tried," Iver offered feebly, "but I just didn't get the breaks."

"Breaks ... did I hear you correctly? Tell me if I'm wrong, but wasn't it you that once sat in my kitchen boasting that a man had to make his own breaks?"

"What you did Iver, was take a perfectly good, beautiful and talented young lady and lock her in a prison of pregnancy for twenty- four years. Then, when the commotion created by all of those off- spring packed in that cracker box you called a home got to be too much for you, you just took off by yourself looking for greener fields ... like, when you left a good job in Kansas to drag Irene and those two babies clean across the country to Utah."

"Now your time is nearly up, and whether you know it or not, you are getting ready to check out. And when you do, what will my daughter do for that bunch she will be left with?"

As Iver listened to the image that had twice before tempted, then tormented him, guilt welled within him. Then, what Rosanna had said to him about soon "checking out" invaded Iver's mind in equal proportion to his guilt.

He hadn't planned to "check out," as his mother-in-law had just put it. He knew that he was a sick man, but he had decided to live with that fact. However, her statement did make Iver think.

Some mornings, in the recent past he recalled, he had jumped from his bed full of piss and vinegar, ready to tackle any job around his house or rented ground that needed doing, or got in his way. But, by the time he had heaved his legs onto the floor and was sitting on the edge of his bed, something within him would change.

While sitting there, Iver would start adding up all of the many things that he wanted to do. Then the thought of all those other things that he needed to do would muscle their way in and impose their claim on his good intentions. Then, finally, all of those chores that in the past he had just neglected, in hopes that time would dissolve them, would also become fresh in his mind.

Those many jobs that had suddenly loomed before him, soon overwhelmed him. His good intentions were soon mixed with the juices of discouragement and inadequacy, and they would crash with a boiling thud in the pit of his stomach. Which would prompt his brain to consider, "What's the use?" and that would be that.

By the time Iver had finished with that latest series of thoughts, his tormentor had dissolved into the curtain of mist that had surrounded her, and it was deathly quiet.

Again fully awake, Mr. Krough began to think about his dreams, and what they told him.

"How little," he silently lamented, "I have done to equip Irene for, and after, this impending event."

"There she sits, no money, and no real income. And living in a shack converted from a log cabin. Maybe it's a blessing that David died last fall. Because if he hadn't, Irene would have seven and not six to care for."

The number was six because Clara had been released due to good behavior. After thinking those thoughts, Iver once again teetered to his feet.

He staggered to the sea chest in the corner of the room, from it he took his clean set of long Johns.

Grudgingly, he wrestled his ivory colored trunk and limbs into the fresh undergarments; then he fell back into bed, and sleep. By then it was noon

Irene occupied herself around the kitchen until early afternoon. She fixed and refixed, placed and replaced, washed and rewashed, and prayed and reprayed. Her prayers were for strength and guidance.

Then Irene went to her husband's bedside and sat on a chair next to him. The slight noise that she had made when sitting on the flexible chair wakened Iver. He said nothing, but looked into the fractured terrain of the ceiling.

Finally, the need to do something - even if it was wrong - overwhelmed Irene. So she took her husband's weak hand in hers; then she looked deep into his eyes, stalling a few seconds while gaining the courage to suggest calling Alfred Allen.

She drew in a deep breath, then let it go, and said to Iver, "why don't we call for Al ..." and that was as far as she made it with her suggestion.

"Don't even think it dear, let alone say it ... I will not give that hypocrite the satisfaction of making a fool out of me."

Rebuked, but not hurt, she turned her face to his, and gave a sincere, knowing smile.

Knowing, because, Irene was secretly pleased that Iver would take at least one of his resolutions to the grave with him. "Too bad," she murmured, "that it has to be at Alfred's expense." Then, at about two-thirty, her husband fell into sleep again. So she went to the kitchen to check the children.

Irene and her seven children: Clara, because she was home on the basis of good behavior; Erma, because Clara had called her home from her work in Smithville; Glen, J.C., Harvey, Karla, and Lu Ann all moved about the other two rooms in silent lethargy.

The two youngest: Karia, age six, and Lu Ann, age four, had no idea about what was going on.

The next two, in declining age, J.C. and Harvey, knew only that something unusual but sad was about to happen.

The three oldest who were present. Glen, Clara, and Erma, knew full well, though it hadn't been discussed with them, what was occurring inside the master bedroom... that one of life's two most inevitable, and profound, laws was about to be administered to their lives.

At precisely three o'clock p.m., the gargling sound of a weak voice floated into the kitchen from the direction of the bedroom.

"Glen," it said, "hurry-up, go get the doctor and tell him I'm dying."

Because she didn't want to seem cynical to her children concerning their father's condition, she passed on a golden opportunity to acknowledge the breaking of another of her husband's resolutions.

She just urged her son on his way.

Glen roared from his house and down the path to Willard Olsen's house where he received quick permission to use the telephone to call Doctor Blodget.

Those words spoken to young Glen were the last to ever pass through Iver's lips.

When Dr. Blodget arrived, he quickly confirmed what Mr. Krough had told his young son.

After a quick, and simple, examination, the Doctor forced a couple pills down the dying man's throat. Then he escorted Irene out of the house and to the back porch.

Flight of the Kroughs

He whispered something in her ear, gave her hand a squeeze with his own, then grudgingly he left the Krough house wishing he had the power to heal. Much later it would be revealed that what the Doctor had told Irene concerned Iver's substantial medical bills, and that she was not to worry about it ... ever.

The rest of that day the three rooms were silent. No one officially went to bed; they just piled up on a cot here and a mattress there. Except for Irene; she sat in her chair staring at the cracks in the floor.

If any of the Krough children felt like eating, which few of them did, Erma would cut a chunk from a home baked loaf of bread and smear some wild plum jam on it for them. One of them tore off a chunk and broke it into smaller pieces, then dumped it into a bowl of milk. And one of them stooped to plastering both sides of a slice of bread with bacon fat and frying it. But Irene had nothing, save three cups of coffee.

At three a.m. Irene realized that the sound of uneven breathing that had been coming from the bedroom had stopped. So she silently got off her chair and went to her husband's bedside.

His color was milky pink, and his chest wasn't moving. Irene knew that her husband of twenty-five years was dead. Before she could feel any grief or any other emotions, Irene's memory took charge of her, and she found herself a girl of thirteen once again.

She was sitting under an oak tree that stood at the east side of the Coburn house back in Brookside.

She was watching with tears flowing down her cheeks, as Mother Rosanna begged her husband, and father to Irene, to please reject that other woman, and stay with his family. But Mr. Coburn turned his back on his weeping wife, and his children. He went through the front gate and disappeared in the evening mist. He headed for the railroad tracks that would take him into Tennessee.

Irene would never see her father again.

When she came back to the situation at hand, tears were wetting her cheeks. Within a minute or so she regained her composure. She went to the kitchen cot and shook Glen and Clara from their shallow sleep and sent the young pair back to the phone to inform the Doctor of what had taken place. And ask if he could please come quick.

In fifteen minutes Doctor Blodget was at the Krough house. And in even less time than he consumed on his last visit, the Doctor pronounced and certified in writing, that Iver, was, indeed, dead.

Although his death did rob the Krough family of a husband and father, it did provide the neighbors and friends with an opportunity to finally say something good about him, and publicly: "He was a good, if not active, member of the flock," said Bishop Petersen.

"He was honest and straight forward," said Alfred Allen.

"He was a good loyal American," said LeRoy.

The children would have said, had they been asked, that he was a good dad.

In her heart, Irene would have wanted to shout her agreement with her children. But before she could offer her qualified support, she would need to consider it for an instant.

So an appropriate service was held for Iver, and then he was put in the ground - not dumped among the sagebrush as he had cynically suggested.

The city fathers passed a motion, voiced by LeRoy, to refund to Irene the prepaid rent on the twenty acres across the lane.

Finally, when all the commotion was over, Irene had the time to feel alone, insecure, and incapable of shouldering the whole responsibility for raising and providing for the rest of her children not yet fully grown.

"Here I sit," she thought, "six dependent children and with no skill to employ, and with little money to satisfy their needs, let alone their wishes."

For the oldest of the young ones yet at home, the adjustment was filled with difficulty also.

What attention had been paid them in the past usually took the form of whispers, behind their backs.

But now, their neighbors, and non-neighbors as well, openly offered their sympathy and words of concern and encouragement to the fatherless family.

This made the Krough kids feel just a little guilty. Because, they felt undeserving of either.

"As far as the children are concerned," thought Irene, "it's a good thing that this happened at the tail end of the school year. Because that will allow them the summer to adjust."

So the summer of forty-four crept by, with the Krough family feeling lost, but, in familiar surroundings.

Glen, J.C., Harvey, and Clara, had planted nothing, so likewise, there was nothing to hoe during the warm months of June and July.

Irene didn't have the shoulder to steal a peek over as impossible plans were being drafted. And the three sons in uniform didn't have an interested father to come home to. A father who would have been thrilled to climatic heights at the chance to sit and talk with his three young men about their experiences. Those Krough boys serving their country felt as if they had, indeed, been cheated by a certain amount, and for the same reason.

Each one of them increased by the same measure, and more, their concern and material support for their mother and their younger brothers and sisters.

Flight of the Kroughs

The added support from her three sons notwithstanding, the fates allowed Mother Irene little time to rest, let alone adjust.

For, just three months after she had managed a decent burial for her husband in Bear River City Cemetery, Viola's health worsened. Greg quickly carried his sick wife out of the house and placed her in their car. He then sped the four blocks east and picked up his mother-in-law, and the three of them headed for the hospital at Salt Lake City.

There, because the doctors in those days knew nothing else to do, they cut Viola's head open behind the left ear and removed what malignant tissue they could.

A month later Viola returned home not much improved, either mentally or physically.

However, her stay at home would be a short one.

On the first of October, the pain in her head had become un- bearable. And had spread to the rest of her body. And again Greg and Irene rushed her to Salt Lake City.

With the aid of nineteen forty-four technology, the doctors did what they could for the frail young mother of three very young daughters.

Tragically, in spite of their valiant efforts, in middle October Viola fell into a merciful coma, from which she would wake briefly but once.

On the first of November she opened her eyes just long enough to whisper to her mother that her dad was outside her window waiting for her; then she stopped living.

*****

During the ninety-odd mile trip back to Bear River City, Irene thought a great deal about many things and experienced many feelings.

She felt sorrow, a lot of sorrow. And she felt concern for her three sweet granddaughters, like her own children, they had been robbed of a parent.

But there were times in between those thoughts when she went so far as to question God's motives.

"Why me?" she would ask silently. "What have I done to deserve such treatment? Enough is enough."

When Irene walked into her front room that night, all of the children were present, except three of course, and they were informed by the look on their mother's face that their sister's hopeless battle was finished, and that she had lost.

Pausing for just a moment, before proceeding straight to her lonely bed, Irene said but one thing to her family, "it's been a bad year for us, a terrible year."

Again, as it was back in the year of forty-three, the part of the year that parents, but especially young people, look forward to - the Thanksgiving/Christmas holidays - were ruined for the Krough family.

Suddenly, after the holidays, the number of children living in Irene's house increased by two.

Greg had decided, painfully, that as he had to hold two jobs to pay doctor bills and funeral costs, someone would have to see to his three little girls. And Irene gladly accepted t responsibility for the two older ones. So then, in the winter of forty-four forty-five, there were eight children that she needed to care for.

Difficult as it was for her, Irene put her head in the air and took charge. She had to see to it that there was wood and coal for the stoves to cook and heat with. She had to see to the ration books and she had to manage what money was sent to her by her sons - which was far and away too little on which to raise a family of eight.

Realizing that fact, Irene decided to visit the welfare office in Smithville to seek some help.

By the time she had filled in enough forms to paper her three-room house, she was so disgusted at the personal questions that she threw her pencil on the table and repeated the scene with the forms. Then she marched in a huff out the door. Saying to herself as she shoved the door open, "If I weren't such a lady, I would have told that fat-ass nosey shit to stick those papers up a place where a pill won't reach." Then she continued her indignant strut to the streetcar station - Virtue Valley's version of mass transit - and bought a ticket back to Bear River City.

With every passing day, more disabled men who, in the short space of three or four years, had been changed from young and innocent to mature and experienced, were showing up on the streets of Smithville and on the electric train that patrolled the valley looking for passengers.

Whenever Irene accidentally happened upon such a person, she would instantly be reminded of her own three sons. Sons who, by the grace of God, she thought or, most likely, by good luck ... were still unharmed even though it was the early winter of forty-five. However, unknown to his mother, Chad had been put into dreadful circumstances.

Likewise, the German army and the Nazi cause were in dire straits as well.

So the German military brain-trust gathered in a safe place with their wine and women and made a plan.

On December sixteenth a German army made up of the most elite of its young fanatical soldier groups was assembled. They had been toughened in battle. And they were drunk with exaggerated patriotism. It was their do-or-die mission to launch a desperate counter- attack.

The German army bent the American battle line, including Chad and his truck and his buddies, back into Belgium. That notorious event would long

Flight of the Kroughs

be etched in Chad's mind, and would be known by historians as the Battle of the Bulge.

Chad, while sitting under his destroyed truck, became surrounded at a place called Bastogn.

For days he was unable to move his disabled fourteen-wheeler. He ate his ice-cold K-rations; he slept - when his body had finally became so fatigued that it overruled his mind; he dodged debris; and he prayed, under the protection offered by his half- blown-away truck. Though his truck was only half there, it had saved his life when it had taken a direct hit.

He was lost, and alone, with nothing but a light field jacket to wrap around him to provide protection against the bitterly raw December weather. All he knew for sure was that he was someplace in Belgium with but a few cases left of what was once a ten-ton load of K-rations. And, that that place might be the last place he would ever see.

He witnessed with his own two eyes as strong stone-built homes were vaporized in puffs of thundering smoke. And he watched in red- eyed horror as bodies were dissected to death by invisible, yet audible, projectiles that plastered the walls still standing with human flesh. Then he watched as blood oozed from the chunks of prime meat and turned the virgin snow to scarlet.

When his skimpy field jacket would no longer halt the numbing, wind-incited cold, Chad ventured from under his truck and ripped a fragment of canvas from its bed. He crawled back to his safe haven between the tires and wheels of the tandem axles and went to work fixing himself more comfortable quarters.

To accomplish his task, he simply piled the snow up to the bed of his truck on the four sides. When he was finished, he had constructed an igloo that even an Eskimo would have been proud to call home

After four days of such circumstances, however, the cold had penetrated the canvas and his jacket. He was blue with cold and was becoming delirious. But Chad held on bull-headedly - with thanks to the half of him that was still sane. He was at last discovered, lying under his GMC in a state of shock, by reinforcements sent by General Patton.

As he had faced death, any romantic notions concerning the adventure called war were purged from the young man's system forever. And that caused Chad to consider his cousin's situation half a world away.

In February, the prison camps in the Philippine Islands were finally overrun. And the American, the British, and the native prisoners set free. Then the terrible truth about the "Death March" was learned. But when the American prisoners were inventoried, Jess and Rod were not there.

Had Chad been in possession of such news, he would have truly understood.

In April of that year, in the general area of the Philippines, Roland's shipmates were off-loading Marines at Okinawa. At the same time, Roland was scanning the sky with his radar searching For Kamikazes. James, though, had the softest duty of all. When he had reached Paris from the South back in forty-four, he was assigned to a permanent hospital as an ambulance driver. As it turned out, that was quite a stroke of luck for him as that job kept him a great distance from the action.

Spring of forty-five found that Irene had become very astute at following the progress of the climaxing war thanks to an old thumb-worn sixth- grade geography book.

So when her boys in Europe wrote her telling her of their respective locations, she would quickly plot their positions on her map.

In middle April Irene received a V-mail letter from Chad. He told his mother that he was being sent to a hospital in Marseilles, France, where he could rest and recuperate, something he had been unable to do since his ordeal.

Ordinarily she, like the many other mothers, might have panicked upon hearing of such news. But, as it didn't come in one of those dreaded infamous telegrams that no one wanted to open, she accepted the news calmly.

She fully understood that her son was in some kind of stress, "But," she reasoned, "if he is well enough to write, then he must be doing all right."

After she had finished reading Chad's letter for the third time and had carefully folded it she placed it in the top dresser drawer with the other letters from her sons. Suddenly, she snapped up her geography book.

She traced the map of France with her left index finger until she discovered Chad's destination. She left that finger there. With her Right index finger, she found James' location she left her fingers where it rested for several seconds.

In those seconds she calculated in her mind that Chad would be but a short distance from where his older, and bigger, brother was stationed. And an impossible plan began to harden in her mind.

"How wonderful," she wished aloud, "it would be if they could, somehow, meet."

Not stopping to think and worry about logistical obstacles that would hinder - and maybe even prevent - such a get together, Irene sat down that second and penciled a letter to each of her sons. Telling them, of course, of each other's location. In that same letter, she urged the two of them to get together. In her euphoric haste, Mother Irene hadn't taken into account the fact that some time had elapsed since Chad had written her and more time would elapse before her letter would be in his hands. But she simply

Flight of the Kroughs

wouldn't allow any negative thoughts to interfere with her desire to have her two sons meet each other in France.

By the time Chad had received his letter, with its plea disguised as a suggestion written on the first few lines, he was already in France. And he was ecstatic about the prospective meeting with his brother. "Hell, that would be nearly as good as a trip home," he mumbled.

The very next day Chad received another letter. And that letter was from his brother James.

Big brother had made arrangements for time off if Chad could but make it to Paris.

So Chad quickly gathered up his letters, and his hopes, and headed doubletime to the hospital commander's office.

As the commander was an ordinary civilian on temporary loan to the war effort, he didn't clutter his way to making a snap decision by first proclaiming loudly all of the reasons why Chad could not take a few days "convalesant" leave.

He read the letters from Mother Irene. Then read the one from James.

Then he called for Sgt. Krough's medical file. He reviewed the file then slammed it onto his desk ... and Chad's heart sank. Just as swiftly, Chad's spirits were set afire again when the Commander said, "Hells- bells, this visit to your brother is better medicine for you than everything in our whole damn pharmacy."

While saying those things, the makeshift Colonel opened his top right hand desk drawer. He whipped out a form that would authorize Chad ten days' leave on which he scribbled his name.

"Now," he ordered, as best he knew how, "take this out to the clerk and have him type the necessary information in the right blanks. And," he said with a wink, "tell the little bastard not to give you any shit, or I will personally pull his pass and he will have to sleep alone for two weeks."

Interpreting the high officer's last "off-the-record" remarks as merely rhetorical, the young sergeant obeyed his first order by responding with a snappy highball salute. Priceless document in hand, he ran swiftly, before anyone had the chance to reconsider, to his bunk and dragged his master lock- secured footlocker from beneath it.

Quickly, Chad stuffed some spare clothes and his shaving kit into his awol bag. Then he ran back to the hospital reception desk - avoiding the Colonel's office of course. There, with his head swimming in anticipatory joy, Chad signed out for Paris. With field jacket slung over his shoulder with continental flair and billed service cap cocked to one side of his head, Chad marched confidently to the motor pool.

As he was a driver of large trucks and, as he had earned a high reputation among the other drivers while swapping war stories with them, but primarily because he spoke their language, Chad had soon secured a ride in a staff car, half full of officers, that was destined for Paris.

So many hours later that he had lost count, a tired and seat-sore Chad arrived at the hospital on the edge of Paris ••• where, as per orders of his doctor, he signed-in. Then he went in search of his brother.

Because James worked out of the hospital motor pool, all Chad needed to do was sit on the hard benches in the drivers' lounge and wait. Chad's body, however, had sat long enough. So he shyly shuffled his way up to the ambulance dispatcher's desk where, after some stammering, he asked for permission to lie down in one of the many disabled ambulances.

"Sure," agreed the dispatcher.

So the trip-weary sergeant scribbled a note to his brother on the back of a voided trip ticket supplied by the Corporal behind the desk. When he had finished, he asked the dispatcher if he would kindly give it to Sgt. Krough when he returned from his run.

Again, the dispatcher said, "Sure."

As he was leaving the building, he heard the Corporal shout at him. Chad whirled around just in time to catch a blanket and pillow and a wish for a good rest to boot.

The nerve-bare soldier had no way of knowing how long he had slept. But, as he was extremely tired, it seemed but an instant. When someone shook his spit-shined combat-booted foot, he was instantly awake and ready for a fight. So came up swinging.

As he quickly looked around, the small green box he was in confused him even more. For a full five seconds Chad was panic stricken, and tears began to stream between his nose and cheeks. James told himself that he was a first class asshole for sneaking up on his younger brother like that, so he did what he could to calm him.

"Hey, wait a minute, little brother... it's me... James, wake-up."

The fog in Chad's head finally cleared away and he remembered where he was and who that someone was standing tall at the open doors of the defunct ambulance.

He rolled over and sat up in the same motion and then just studied his brother for an instant.

The younger Krough then quickly slid his aching body from its canvas stretcher bed, jumped to the ground, and nearly stumbled into James' long, outstretched arms.

They embraced each other as they had never dared to do as children, boys, or young men, back in Bear River City. Because, as they had assumed - not knowing why - they were conspicuous enough because of their appearance without drawing attention to themsleves through the display of outward physical manifestations of love for one another.

Flight of the Kroughs

Oddly, in a way, they seemed a bit strange to each other. Which, no doubt, was due to their not having seen each other in such a long time. And in such different surroundings.

James pulled Chad by his jacket sleeve into the motor pool office where the dispatcher who had been so considerate of his brother stood ready with James' officially-stamped five-day leave orders.

Then he also ran, with Chad close behind, to his barracks. There, just as his younger brother had done at another place, he slid his footlocker from beneath his bunk. From it he grabbed his laundry bag and proceeded to stuff articles into it; he took spare clothes - his towel - and his shaving kit. Then he led his younger brother out the barracks door and back to the motor pool. There it would be no trick to secure a ride to the city.

By that time it was the eleventh of May of forty-five. And the war in Europe had been officially over for three days. German militarism had been halted - but not in its tracks - by overwhelming, if slow and expensive in human terms, superiority. And people, even his German followers, were asking profusely how it came to pass that such a despot as Hitler could so intoxicate a country and its people with such grand plans of world conquest.

James and Chad, however, weren't in the mood to worry about such matters ... not at the time anyway. Because they knew from past experience that the correspondents would dream up enough questions, and concoct an equal number of answers all by themselves.

The depth and extent of their opinion of Hitler and his gang was that they were a bunch of dirty sons-of-bitches. So the events that had chronicled the war in a personal sense to them were already being pushed into their subconscious . Chad and James were hell-bent on having a good time when they could, at last, join a celebration such as the world had never witnessed before.

The two Krough boys tasted the wine; they ate the food; and they felt the warmth and inner softness of the women that Paris was so famous for. And it wasn't long before each of the boys had collected several pictures to stuff into their wallets to use for bragging material when they were once more home in Bear River City.

Late, after a long day and night of fun and pleasure, Chad and James would both wonder why it couldn't be like this, worlds away, in River City

"How ironic," the older of the two thought as he stared at the random-sized chunks of plaster that yet remained on the rattled ceiling and listened to the ceaseless celebration going on outside his window, "Here I am enjoying all of this because some crazy corporal decided to make war."

"In fact," Chad silently chipped in, "I am doing things, seeing things, and loving things that not even the rich boys who elected to stay at home can boast about."

D. Raymond Anderson

For four days the brothers partied. But empty wallets finally put a stop to it. So, the next morning the two, filled to overflowing with satisfaction and fulfillment gained by four days' worth life's most delicious pleasures, stood by the roadside waiting for a free ride to James post while shouting newly-learned, half- accurate, French phrases to the local folks. Who returned happy nods and friendly waves.

Then, in the silence that surrounded them as they rode in the back of a six-by back to the Paris hospital, the subject of their concurrent thoughts was little brother Roland.

The rumor on his transport ship on August the sixth was that the U.S. had dropped a thing called "an atomic bomb" on Japan. Roland reasoned it to be a weapon so destructive, and so scientifically sophisticated, that a common person could never comprehend how it worked, or the limits of its power to destroy.

The rumor also quickly spread throughout the ship that the dropping of the rumored bomb had most likely convinced the Japenese to give up with no more fighting.

The rumors proved to be pretty much correct. And Roland set sail for Nagasaki Harbor.

When he and his ship arrived to land the two thousand occupation troops, the sight and smell turned their stomachs.

Bodies in several stages of decay floated like grotesque troop carriers loaded with a million maggots each.

That, his next-to-last landing exercise, was made in silence.

In late August, when peace finally broke out, a celebration broke out in Bear River City.

As there was no school to dismiss, children led their parents into the streets,

Irene followed her six children and two grandchildren to town to join the spontaneous celebration.

She moved quietly among the young and old who had joined the no-host party, drunk with the joy of victory and relief from worry, and she just watched.

Oh, she was happy that the other half of the war had ended, for Roland's sake in particular.

Her celebration, however, would have to wait until her three boys climbed down from the streetcar to the safety offered by Bear River City.

Every day in that part of forty-five happy reunions were taking place. But not so for Irene. Not yet anyway.

Her first real happy day in many months, though, was about to dawn.

She had received her letter from Chad not more than six weeks following VJ-Day. It had told her that he was about to board a fancy ocean

Flight of the Kroughs

liner bound for New York. And that he hoped to be home soon after docking there.

She had received that letter in middle October, then for another month, she heard nothing more.

Just seven days before Thanksgiving, though, Irene received a telegram. Not considering the fact that it might be bad news, she ripped the envelope open, and, devoured with her eyes and mind what it had to say.

Dear Mother...stop

Leaving Ft. Reily Kansas 19 Nov ... stop

Arriving Smithville twenty-three Nov ... stop

Love Chad ••• stop

The bus station at Smithville on twenty-three November was, just like all days, alive with families and loved ones waiting for their sons, brothers, lovers or, in rare cases, husbands to arrive. Irene and the three children that she had brought along wandered the sidewalk at the edge of the crowd.

Before long someone caught sight of two buses coming up Main Street, about one half mile away. Instantly, the main body of the crowd surged from in and around the station to the front area and lined themselves up four deep at the edge of the curb.

Still Irene, along with Glen, Clara, and Erma, hung back and refused to join the chaos at the edge of the curb.

The overloaded buses rocked their way through the gutter and onto the bus parking area.

The vehicles groaned to a stop, one behind the other, then each of the drivers jumped from his bus and stood politely beside its open door.

Almost immediately, men in uniforms representing every branch of the service began to file nervously out and melt into the melee on the sidewalk as the crowd surged again and formed a tight semi- circle nearly at the threshold of the vehicles.

To the Kroughs, it seemed as if hundreds of GI's came from each bus. But, as of yet anyway, no Chad.

Then the crowd began to dwindle, and Mother Irene's heart began to sink. But just as she was about to say, "To hell with it, that's it, let's go," a sleepy Chad hopped from the landing of the bus to the asphalt of the parking lot.

Most of the members of the crowd had already whisked their returning heros to waiting cars so the parking area was nearly bare of people. Only a few seconds passed before Chad saw his huddled family waiting for him.

Mother Irene was first to greet Chad. Not with a shriek and a bear hug, but with a heartfelt squeeze of his hands and a soft stroke of his reddened face with her other hand. "Welcome home, Chad," she said. At first he didn't verbally speak, yet his glassy eyes spoke volumes.

Letting their mother have the first crack at him, the brother and sisters followed right behind, greeting their long lost brother in their own restrained way.

After the short but dignified welcome, the five of them walked across Main Street to the depot and waited for the six o'clock streetcar which would deliver them to Bear River City.

They arrived at the depot in their hometown at six-thirty. And when Irene and her brood stepped from the streetcar, there was another gang of people waiting to greet the returning soldiers.

A few of those in the crowd shook Chad's hand and welcomed him home.

Irene, Chad, Erma, Clara, and Glen left the station and walked south two blocks to Main Street. Then they turned east and walked the mile and a half to their home. All the way there the group kept up a constant chatter, except when they passed the cemetery.

After he had said his private hello's to the whole family, mother, four sisters, three brothers and two nieces, finishing touches were put on a special meal. A meal that Irene and her girls had started before leaving for Smithville. When the meal had been consumed and enjoyed, and when the happy conversation was exhausted, the Krough family turned to their beds. However, Irene didn't sleep as soon as her head hit her pillow.

She lay in her bed and wondered what the homecoming would have been like if her husband could have been there to greet his favorite son.

Likewise, sleep also evaded Chad - that, in spite of the fact that he, for the first time ever, in the Krough household at any rate, slept alone.

He had the urge to go someplace and see someone. But there was no one to go see. His friends were not yet home and, in a couple of cases, they were dead.

The war had made Chad very restless and had left him with a bad case of inflamed nerves. So during his first night at home no sound went beneath his hearing. And if a noise did sound the least bit peculiar, he came quickly out of bed looking for his gun and a fight.

Regardless of his poor sleep the night before, he was up early the next morning. And by the time seven-thirty had arrived, ex-GI Krough was standing beside the road that ran in front of his house thumbing for a ride to the employment office at Smithville.

The next of her three sons to make his way back to the states was James. From France, he was posted to Fort Wood, Missouri, not far from where he was born.

While stationed there, he met a young lady from Joplin named Mary. Two months later they were married. Ironic, Irene thought, how her first two offspring had married partners who were born and raised not far from where they themselves were born... but, not raised.

In middle December of forty-five, at about twelve-thirty in the afternoon, Irene stood looking out her front room window wondering why an unfamiliar car had braked to a stop on the road in front of her house.

First, a blue canvas bag tumbled out of the car from the rear seat. Then ... in the amazingly long space of ten seconds ... a young man in a blue navy bell-bottom suit followed the bag from the same place.

Irene gasped. After all, she had been given no warning - no letter, no telegram - no nothing. Then she called for her children, but they were all at school. "How stupid of me," she quickly thought. But, at least, her two granddaughters could help with the greeting. A week earlier there would have been three granddaughters, but, as Greg's folks had also moved to Utah from Kansas, they had taken over the care of the youngest. So Irene grabbed a little girl in either hand and stood proudly on the front porch - right beside the window that displayed a banner with three stars on it - and waited for Roland.

When he reached the front porch and his welcoming committee, he handed his mother a gift, then casually said, "Hi mother - what's for dinner?' He walked, with a slight break in stride by her and the children then into the front room of the house. It was as if he had only been gone on a ten-minute visit to the outhouse ... maybe to him anyway.

His slightly confused - slightly disappointed, in spite of the gift, mother asked Roland if he was serious about wanting food. He said he definitely was. So like the good mother that she was, Irene went right to work at the kitchen range.

After enjoying some good, but plain, home cooking, Roland stoked-up the fire. He loaded two three-gallon galvanized buckets of water onto the stove to heat up for a bath.

When he had finished scrubbing the traveling crud from his body, he twisted it into a crisp, clean tailored uniform. His mother was much impressed with her son when he appeared through the curtain from the bedroom.

He said his goodbyes to her and his nieces; then, as an after thought, he told his mother that he would probably be late when he returned home. Then he hit the road for Smithville.

That same evening Irene was feeling so good that she decided to take a couple of her kids and take in a movie, a rare treat for the children, and rarer for herself.

As it was their turn, she informed J.C. and Clara of her plans for the evening, and, needless to say, they were overjoyed.

As the clock struck six-thirty, one of the trio closed the door behind them, and they were off to their night at the pictures.

Glen, because he was the oldest, was left at home to look after the rest of the children and grandchildren. Right after the front door had closed, he ran to the window and watched jealously until his mother, sister, and brother disappeared down cemetery hill.

Roland, in the mean time, was in Smithville trying desperately to find someone he could relate to. Or, at least find someone that he had once known that he could talk to.

He, however, would discover on that night, that he was in a kind of "no man's land." Which was due to his very young age and at the same time his wealth of experience.

He was eighteen but, unlike ninety-nine percent of those involved in the war, Roland didn't age noticeably. In fact, if anything, he appeared to be younger than he actually was.

He knew that, had be grabbed a pool stick with the intention of joining the salty veterans around the table, they would just have ridiculed him as a peach-fuzz-faced kid who had joined up at the tail end of the war, hoping to steal some glory. And if Roland had, in self defense, bragged about his battle ribbons and citations stored back home in his sea bag, they would have, without a doubt, laughed him right out of the joint ... if, that is, he was lucky because they might even have thrown him out bodily.

Even worse, though, Roland knew that to talk to people his own age, he would need either to go to church or to school - neither of which, in all his life had appealed to him.

Church was out of the question. But, in a pinch, he would have tolerated school had it not been for one thing; although he would have been approximately the same age, in experience he would have been five or six steps ahead of them. So what would they have talked about? Besides, he didn't relish the prospect of sitting around making small talk with them.

All of a sudden, he said to himself, "Piss on it, I'll adapt tomorrow, tonight I'm going to get drunk." Which, was a strange thing to do. Because, in fact he shouldn't have been allowed in the place. In spite of being in the thick of battle for two years, he was still too young to buy or consume alcohol.

By eight-thirty, Roland had accomplished his objective. So he stood loosely up on his feet, and, to the wonderment of the veterans playing pool, he shouted a slurred but loud goodnight, then flipped them an exaggerated salute.

He somehow managed to beg a ride back to Bear River City ••• with whom, he would never know. And when he stumbled from that car, he, if possible, was even drunker than when he left the pool hall in Smithville.

Flight of the Kroughs

In the next few days, he would dig deep into his mind trying to extract the name from his memory of the person who had hauled him home. "He must have known me," he moaned. Then he said, "Shit How embarrassing."

On the night of his brother's homecoming, Glen and the rest of the children lined up at the front-room windows and watched in wide-eyed amazement as Roland left a zig-zag path in the snow while making his way to where his subconscious memory told him the front door was supposed to be located. Glen kindly opened the door for his brother, and he tripped his way in disjointed strides into the front room.

Roland leaned his fluid body against the front wall of the front room for support and began to sing some sort of love song, in two languages. One language Glen vaguely recognized as English. The other language was Greek to him ... maybe Oriental, Glen thought. Before he had finished his love song, he stopped singing and mentioned a woman's name, a very strange sounding name to Glen, he then repeated the Oriental-sounding name. Then, just before he folded to the floor like a puppet with its strings cut, tears began to stream down his cheeks.

Glen didn't know what to do. After all, he had never seen anyone that drunk before - including Bear River City's two official town drunks.

Karla and LuAnn, though only seven and five years old, had the good sense to take their two small nieces and hide them in the basement under the new room. There they stayed, all of them.

That left small Harvey and Glen upstairs to move their big brother.

They more rolled than carried him to a mattress by the front room stove and threw a blanket over his still body.

When Irene returned from the show house with her two children, she noticed straight away that Roland had found his assigned bed. And, as she was accustomed to seeing her boys on certain occasions going to bed with their clothes on, she wasn't surprised.

When, however, she went into the bedroom and saw the two empty beds, she panicked.

She ran over to a corner of the front room and roughly shook Glen, who had fallen asleep beside Harvey on their mattress.

He quickly raised his head and was wide awake. "Where in the world are the girls?" she asked sternly.

"I don't know. The last I saw of them they were running down the basement stairs."

"The basement stairs ... what in the world for?"

"I don't know, ask them."

"Oh for hell sakes, go back to sleep, bottle ass."

She found the four girls curled up on burlap sacks in two corners of the basement fast asleep.

"I suppose I will get the facts in the morning," she said to herself as she made four trips up and down the stairs.

The next morning the young ex-sailor rose from his mattress with WW III raging in his head. And it didn't take long for Irene to guess, just by looking and listening to his groans, what had taken place the night before.

He neatly, almost reverently, folded and stowed away his bell-bottom uniform in his mother's large steamer chest, right beside brother Chad's olive greens.

Then Roland and his mother finally sat at the kitchen table and did the talking that they should have done the day before. While Irene listened soberly and her children were mesmerized, Roland told some of his stories about the war. And while doing so he, with the help of his mother, emptied a pot of coffee.

Then at eight-thirty, the young man was on the highway in front of his house looking for a ride to Smithville. And most of the children were on their way to school.

While in Smithville, Roland would visit the employment office and do his Christmas shopping - thanks to his mustering-out pay.

The holiday season of forty-five was much easier to celebrate than had been the last two or three.

Irene felt truly favored of God - something Iver would have scoffed at - because her three sons had passed through that terrible war and were, physically anyway, unharmed.

It was a good Christmas, in spite of the fact that the mid-night delivery didn't occur any longer. And another reason for that Christmas being special was because Greg had remarried, and his new wife was a fine mother to his children. Also, the family had received a letter from James during the holidays. In it, he had introduced the fact that he would be a father in the early summer.

Also, in that same letter, he requested that Chad travel to Missouri and assist him in driving his family back to Utah where they wanted to live.

Such a suggestion filled Chad's heart with joy.

Although Chad, like Roland, had been unable to secure any kind of work, he, like Roland, had joined the fifty-two-twenty club; twenty bucks a week for fifty-two weeks. It was sort of like un-employment compensation earned while making war. It was enough to enable Chad to save up for a bus ticket. "And I can use one week's check to eat on," he told himself. Although it wasn't much, twenty dollars a week for fifty-two weeks was a real life saver to many of the returning men. It would buy a little gas to move the car around Virtue Valley while hunting work. For those who smoked, it bought their cigarettes and helped those that lived with their parents to chip in a few groceries. So, in the larger sense, the program blunted the effects of demobilization, which had released men into a shrinking job market like flashflood down a mountainside gully.

As an alternative to looking for work that didn't exist, many of the Bear River City boys who had high school diplomas went to school at the agricultural college on the bench that overlooked Smithville.

Others obtained Daddy's co-signature on loans that would put them into business - most of which failed - and some bought farms. In a lot of cases, this was merely a transfer of title from father to son, with a fat GI loan carrying low interest as gravy. So it wasn't long before Virtue Valley experienced a tractor - service station - hamburger joint boom.

Well, Chad wasn't prepared, diploma-wise, to go to school. Nor was Roland. And neither of the Krough boys had a daddy to sign on the dotted line with them. But did they worry about that, or hold it against the ones who were luckier than they? No one really knows, all that Irene knew was that her boys didn't waste time feeling sorry for themselves.

Neither Chad nor Roland knew anything about the farming game anyway, so they happily joined the club.

By the fifteenth of June of forty-six, Chad was still out of work. But, as he had planned, he had saved enough money to buy a bus ticket. So, on Thursday afternoon, right after he had collected, then cashed, his check and given half of it to his mother, he was dropped at the bus station by Roland. Within twenty minutes Roland watched his brother head south to Salt Lake City, from where he would travel east.

Virtue Valley was a bad place to be out of work right after WW II because its industrial strength was almost a laugh.

At the north end of the valley sat a sugar factory. But the only time jobs changed hands there was when one of the hands died.

In the middle of the valley could be found the cheese factory. And at the south end of the valley was a trout farm. Totally, at their peak of production, those plants might employ three hundred people at most.

To add to the frustration of those out of work was the fact that all other jobs that became available throughout the valley's service and government economy were passed through the underground employment system to friends and relatives of those already working. So, naturally, what jobs that did become vacant never made it to the classified section of the newspaper, let alone the employment office, or unemployment office as most called it.

However, the college was booming.

Trailer parks and small square rentals were spreading like a grass fire on a windy August day. But, as far as that school went, as stated before, the three Krough boys suffered the same disqualifiers.

During the pre-war depression years in the Bear River City School, those with no financial or material status, were, it seemed, programmed to fail. When just the opposite was true for the more affluent.

When a Krough kid entered school, he or she was expected to fail. Both by themselves, and by the teachers. So it was no big deal when one of them quit or just coasted.

Naturally then, when nearly every GI was taking advantage of some government-underwritten financial-aid package, the Krough boys held back.

It caused Irene to recall the many occasions on which Iver had advised his boys not to depend on the government for help because the only ones that could qualify were the ones who didn't need it. James had run up against the same difficulties in Missouri as those encountered by his brothers in Utah. Only he had a wife and, as of the first of June, a baby to care for. That was the chief reason he wanted to return to Utah.

Chad arrived in Joplin, Missouri three days after he had departed Virtue Valley, Utah. And James was at the bus station to meet him. Thirty-six hours later, the four of them - James, Mary, the baby, and Chad - were on the road retracing Iver and Irene's tracks to Utah. But James' like-new nineteen-forty maroon Ford Sedan made their trip a lot easier to endure.

Five days later they drove through Granite Pass into Virtue Valley, then on to Bear River City. At last Irene's postwar reunion with her boys was, at last, complete. Now, however, there were three out of work. And, once again, the Krough house was more like a barracks. It was about one week after Chad and James returned from Missouri that an old friend of the family called by.

Irene hadn't seen LeRoy since Iver's funeral. So she was naturally surprised to see him park his Dodge pickup in her yard. Debating in her mind about what he was doing there, she watched as he left his truck and headed for her front door. He was allowed to knock twice before Irene went to the door to greet her dead husband's old friend and political adversary and invite him in.

He, right away, inquired of Irene how she was doing; then he sat on the chair he was offered. She told him she was just fine. LeRoy then asked about her boys.

He wanted to know if they had found work. Irene told him that the best they had done, so far, was odd farm jobs.

"Does that include Chad?" asked LeRoy. "Yes, it does," she answered.

"You know, Mrs. Krough, Iver always spoke highly, and fondly, of Chad. Oh, I'm sure Iver loved all his boys the same, but speaking of Chad always seemed to put a sparkle in his eyes."

"I suppose you are right," agreed Irene. "In a family as large as ours, I guess it would be hard not to indentify with at least one of his children more

Flight of the Kroughs

than the rest of them. But," she continued, "Iver always did his very best to treat them all the same. And if I were perfectly honest, I guess I would have to say that I had my favorite also."

"We are all the same in that respect," admitted LeRoy laughing; then he grew serious.

Irene could tell by his manner that LeRoy wasn't there just to discuss her favorite offsrping. So she wondered how long she would need to wait before Mr. Jensen brought the real reason for his visit into their conversation - then he did.

"Where is Chad now?" questioned the visitor.

"Up Lefthand Canyon getting a load of firewood," she answered .

"Well, tell him I am very anxious to speak to him - tonight if possible, Irene. Tell Chad that I would like to talk over some business with him."

She assured him that she would pass his message on, then shook his hand goodbye, and LeRoy left the Krough house and headed west toward his home.

Irene's curiousity was in full bloom. So for the next few hours she alternately stood at the range and at the front room's east window watching for her son to exit Lefthand Canyon. At three-thirty that afternoon, she finally caught sight of Bishop Petersen's team of matched bays with Chad at the reins, prancing west toward home.

In fifteen minutes the young man had his borrowed rig whoa'd to a stop and had parked beside the nearly flat woodpile.

Before Chad could climb back on the wagon after tying the horses to a cedar fencepost, his mother came running from the house yelling for his attention.

Chad responded by leaning cross-armed and cross-legged against the loaded wagon and waited for his mother to come closer to him. But, to his mild surprise, she didn't stop until she was leaning on the wagon, to catch her breath.

"I have your supper hot on the table," she half shouted, "I laid out a clean shirt by the wash basin, and the water's warm." It was plain to Chad that his mother was excited about something, "But what?" he asked himself. Then he asked his mother a question, "What about the load of wood?"

It was a wasted question, because even as Chad asked it, Irene was pulling the maple and aspen trunks off the wagon.

So, caught up in the spirit of whatever was going on, Chad ran to the house and gulped his food down, then he washed up. Next, he slipped into his clean shirt as he hurried out the door and back to the replenished woodpile.

D. Raymond Anderson

Not stopping, and with her son's help in throwing the last few chunks of wood onto the pile, Irene began her explanation; "Now, take Mr. Petersen's horses and wagon back, but before you do I have something to tell you."

"This is it," thought Chad. "I hope what she has to say is good."

"I had a visit from an old and good friend of your dad's today" began Irene.

"Oh yea ... who?"

"LeRoy Jensen," she answered quietly.

Then she waited for her son to show some sign of interest in her news flash. But all the time Irene spent waiting for Chad to respond, he was waiting for her to tell him what the big deal was. Finally he said "So ... LeRoy was here, somehow I don't find that information to be all that earthshaking." Then Chad moved to the cedar post to undo the horses.

"Well, do you want to hear what he wanted or don't you?" Irene asked, in a way that showed she was a bit let down.

At last Chad sensed that his mother had important information.

"And, it must concern me," he figured. So he pulled the leather straps tight around the post again and turned to his mother and asked, in an inquizitive way, "Tell me what LeRoy wanted."

"He wants to talk to you this evening. I don't know for sure why, only that he acted as though it was important," Irene responded.

Mrs. Krough was keeping secret her hope, and suspicion, that the real reason for LeRoy's summons to her son was because he had heard of a job for him somewhere. And, with his influence, it just could be so.

She might just as well have let her secret guess out. Because, Chad was thinking, even hoping, the same thing.

"Thanks for the news. Mom," said Chad. Then he quickly removed the leather straps from the post and hopped aboard the unloaded and spotlessly swept wagon. Then he urged the rested animals north down the east side of cemetery hill toward their home.

After Chad had unhooked the horses, he led them to the barn where he removed their harness and gave them a good drink. Finally, he turned them loose in their pasture. For a pilfered second, he watched the animals run, back and forth, across the grassy field celebrating their freedom.

About that time Mr. Petersen showed up.

He asked Chad it he had finished the wood hauling. Then he told Chad that if he hadn't, he was welcome to use the outfit again the next day.

"I think I hauled enough wood to do mother until fall, so I won't be needing it, but thank you very much for letting me use it." Chad quickly shook the Bishop's hand and walked, until he was out of Mr. Petersen's sight, then ran back home.

Flight of the Kroughs

He stopped there long enough to get a drink of water, then continued his walk/run west into town, to Mr. Jensen's house.

As Chad was an outstanding mover, he made the trip in twelve minutes.

LeRoy's wife cordially invited the young Krough man into her front room. Right away the odor of roasting beef tortured Chad's nose; Sunday cooking at our house he thought.

She led the timid visitor to an easy chair and asked him to sit, which he gladly did.

Then LeRoy made his entrance. The sleeves of his plaid flannel shirt were rolled to his elbows, and the shirt was open from the neck to his middle chest. His graying hair was a lifeless mat due to sweating all day under a western hat. And his face was flushed from a just finished good, cold washing.

It was plain to Chad that Mr. Jensen had been to his farm doing some hard work.

Of course, Mr. Jensen was first to speak.

"Well, how's life been treating you since coming home from the war Chad?"

"Can't complain," Chad offered shyly.

"Anything beats Army food from what I hear, right?" LeRoy said jokingly.

Chad wanted so to agree, and say, "You bet." But, as he was the honest sort, he hesitated.

If LeRoy had questioned quality of preparation Chad would have gladly agreed. But, to be truthful, the young man had enjoyed a much richer and varied diet while in the army than he did at home. Mostly, because he loved meat.

Therefore, Chad responded to LeRoy's remark with the non-concrete statement: "It was really something, your right."

Then Mr. Jensen got down to real business.

"Young man," he started out as he leaned closer to Chad, "I might as well tell you that I know for a fact that you, and your brothers as well, have had a tough time of it since the war. And I would like to see at least one of you get a decent break. So I would like to propose a deal to you that, if you accept and work hard, might in a few years make life a lot easier for you."

Chad's ears were throbbing with anticipation. "What on earth in the way of deal could he possibly offer me?" he wondered silently.

"Are you interested in hearing more?" LeRoy asked.

"A rather stupid question," Chad said in respectful silence.

"Yes sir," he squeaked through a dry throat and mouth.

"All right, then, let me tell you what I have in mind ... You know I have a one-hundred-and-fifty acre farm west of town."

"Yes, I remember Dad taking me there before the war," Chad butted in.

"Well," drawled Mr. Jensen, "I am going into horse breeding and horse selling business - Palominos ... which means that I am going to move to the other side of the mountain. To Salt Lake, to be precise... more people to sell to there." With that remark LeRoy gave a selfish chuckle.

Inside of Chad's chest his heart was ticking like a time bomb. And he had this thought, "If LeRoy sells horses like he gets to the point, he will go broke in a hurry"

"So now I no longer have a need for that farm west of town," Mr. Jensen said.

"It occurred to me the other day, that that farm could be your ticket to success."

If Chad had not been sitting safely in Mrs. Jensen's easy chair, then the Jensen's would have been picking him up from their floor. But, just as suddenly as the shock of being offered the ownership of a farm had raised his spirits to the sky, they fell back to earth again.

As he stared into the Jensen wall, Chad became glassy eyed.

"How can I buy a farm with not a dime of my own?" he thought.

But, Mr. Jensen had a ready answer for Chad's unspoken expression of concern.

"I'm sure your discharge from the Army was honorable... correct?"

In spite of his nervous condition at the time, Chad was just a little miffed at such a question. And answered in a loud, positive voice, "Of course."

"I'm sorry, and must apologize, I phrased my last question very poorly. But what I was trying to say was that to get a GI farm loan, an honorable discharge is just about all one needs to qualify"

"Wait just a minute, Mr. Jensen" Chad spoke up, "Let me see if I heard you correctly. You are offering to sell me your farm, and you tell me that there will be no trouble getting a loan, even with no money down?"

"Well ....," then Mr. Jensen cleared his throat, "I have figured out a plan to take care of the down payment also. You see. Chad, what we will do is tell the government boys that the price of the farm is twenty-five grand, but the real price to you is twenty-two five. So what I will do is write you a check for two thousand five hundred. Then you take it to the bank and open an account, along with ten bucks of your own. Then when we go over the Federal Building to make the deal with the government, you write a check for the two thousand five hundred and give it to me in their presence. That will impress them and insure that you get the loan. But we will keep the matter of the down payment our secret."

As Chad was new at the game of business and high finance, he saw nothing wrong with the deal and shook his head so to LeRoy.

Flight of the Kroughs

"And to make it a better deal tor you Chad, I will throw in all the pigs at the farm."

Chad could hardly contain himself. He felt as if he had just been handed a one-way ticket out of the poorhouse and the keys to prosperity. So he stood on his rubbery legs and, in the most business-like way he knew, he shoved out his hand for Mr. Jensen to shake as a signal of his grateful acceptance of the offer.

He remembered how impressed he was when Mr. Jensen said he was throwing in the animals in the deal at no charge. But he also remembered how disappointed he was upon learning where they were located. So, as it turned out, LeRoy giving Chad the pigs was like a hobo cleaning out his traveling bag and donating its contents to the Salvation Army thrift store. The pigs had been let run free for three years. And they were scattered along the river all the way from the farm up to River City dam.

All that was left of the pens were some twisted one by tens and a few twisted cedar posts that once supported them.

The new owner had no way of knowing just how many pigs there were, only that they seemed to be running everywhere.

So Chad devised a plan. He would recruit Glenn, J.C., and Harvey, and have a pig roundup.

"But first," he reasoned, "I will need a place to put them."

He walked every square foot of the farm's lower section and finally came up with most of the dismantled pigpen. Feeling like everything was going his way, he nailed the pig corral back together and had it done by Thursday.

The big roundup was scheduled for the following Saturday.

Bright and early that morning Chad rolled out of the bunk in his covered wagon and waited, sipping a cup of coffee, for his three younger brothers to show up. He had only to wait a few minutes before he saw them walking toward him across the east section of the farm, just below Bear RiverCity High School.

The brand new farmer gathered his hog wranglers around him and laid out his plan for them.

"We will walk together to the bottom of the valley, then turn east and walk to the spillway of the dam."

"Then Harvey and I will walk west on the south side of the valley and Glen and J.C. can walk west on the north side of the valley. That will force what pigs are scattered through the trees into the bottom along the river. When we get to the lane leading back to the farm, Harvey and I will go a little higher on the south side of the valley and circle around to block them from going west of the lane, that should encourage the animals to turn up the lane to the farm… You guys got that?"

The three boys shook their heads yes, and off down the hill the four of them marched.

They reached the bottom of the valley, turned east according to plan, and snaked their way through a jungle of cottonwood and willow trees. The trees had provided the freedom-loving hogs an environment not unlike their southern wild cousins.

Young Mr. Krough and his crew continued on through the heavy growth until they reached the spillway of the River City dam.

Chad then positioned his troops in a line, across the narrow valley, that stretched about two hundred yards in width.

The oldest Krough whistled his signal, and they all moved west together. It wasn't long before the assault on the pigs began to showresults. Animals of various sizes began squirting from several directions. By the time the pig drive had reached the lane that led to the farm, there was quite a herd in front of the "pigboys."

As the four brothers urged the moody and squatty herd into their recently renovated homes, Chad made a quick inventory. He counted twenty-five head ... "Not a bad harvest" he thought.

All of the pigs, except one, accepted their confinement and fresh water with a measure of civility.

But, no sooner had the big boar been locked in, than he began to take the fence around him down again.

The four boys, who were sitting on the ground enjoying pork and beans out of the can, heard the commotion and ran full speed to the pigpens just as the boar was humping his nasty body over the middle board.

Because the other four legged inmates were squealing their delighted encouragement to their leader, the racket was terrible. And the old boar was as mean looking as the situation sounded. He was a gigantic creature, standing for sure four feet high at the middle of his back, and weighing in at six hundred pounds.

His years of reigning over his jungle-like kingdom had left his body rubbed raw on the outside, but hard as nails on the inside - both physically and mentally.

His long snout was textured with scar on scar. And yellowish fangs hung like tusks over his lower jaw.

Small Harvey, and J.C., made half-hearted charges at the scrambling beast, using clods of dirt as weapons. But he paid them no mind.

Then the animal made it over the fence.

For a moment Chad was out of solutions. Then he quickly scooped up a six-foot two-by-four and knocked the legs from under the seedy animal. In desperation, he used a tool he had learned from his Uncle Bug ... he swore; "You son-of-a-bitchen cock sucker," he screamed.

Flight of the Kroughs

The younger boys were shocked dizzy. They had never heard their brother talk like that before. And they were glad that their mother wasn't there to hear such words.

Red faced, because of the worldly language he had just spit out in the presence of his younger brothers, Chad continued to beat on his four-legged adversary until it finally retreated through the battered fence. But Chad kept after him. And when twenty minutes worth of dust and hell-raising time had passed, Chad had backed the burley pig with impressive testicles into the far corner of the vacant chicken coop.

Because of the grief experienced after the big pig round up, the new farmer made his first momentous decision; he would get out of the pig business as soon as possible. That same Saturday evening, Chad sat in the solitude of his covered wagon home making a crude attempt at figuring just what the disgusting animals might be worth according to the prices quoted on the early morning radio farm program. And, for the first time, he wished that he had paid attention to Mr. Blackly - the principal at Bear River City Grade School.

True, none of the Krough children did well in school. That in spite of each having something to offer in the way of artistic or athletic talent:

James - accomplished vocalist, played guitar ... But he loved to wander.

Viola - art, much of it shown after her death.

Chad - athletics, vocalist, played guitar ... But kept his talent to himself.

Erma - art, vocalist. But, to her, work was more important.

Clara - vocalist ... But wouldn't stay home and develop he skill.

Glen – athletics, vocalist ... But quit when he proved he could compete.

Karla - art, vocalist, dance. But thought meeting boys was her mission in life.

Lu Ann - art, vocalist, dance… Ditto

But what the children of Iver and Irene needed wasn't taught in school. What they needed was confidence. So back to Mr. Blackly.

If, by some miracle, Chad believed, God the Almighty and Principal Blackly were to appear on the stage at the same time, it would be a tossup between them who would be paid the most homage.

Each morning before the first bell, the students were scattered over the school grounds playing various games.

Precisely the same instant, every day, Principal Blackly marched diagonally across the schoolyard toward the main entrance to "his" building.

The gay laughter and bickering always lowered to a murmur, and the army of students separated like the parting of the sea, when the near perfect, if not perfect, specimen of humankind moved across the green carpet like royalty.

Chad always noticed that a subtle sweet-perfumed smell lingered in his wake. He was impressed by the odor and the perfection of the head master's crisp clean appearance as well.

However, Mr. Blackly, unbelievable as it may seem, was one of the contributing factors to Chad's, as well as the rest of the Krough kids, failure in school.

Chad looked at the magnificent principal; then he looked at his starched-stiff, clean, subordinate teachers and was overwhelmed by their appearance and seemingly limitless knowledge. He told himself, just like his brothers and sisters before and after him, that what those teachers were, and what they professed, was not for such low folks as he, and so he turned a deaf ear.

Chad would sit in the back of the room and know that he was sinking in the quicksand of illiteracy but didn't seem to have the will to pull himself out. So had it not been for his natural intelligence and talent, he might have drowned.

He wondered about it and tried to satisfy in his own mind why, when he knew that he could do something worthwhile in school, why he wouldn't do it. There was but one person who had the answer, and she was too proud to talk about it until the curtain was coming down on her own life.

When Iver had first brought his young bride to Virtue Valley, she had become part of one of the smallest minorities ever to exist; Irene was a non-Mormon among recently converted Scandinavian Mormons ... the staunchest kind.

Actually, she was more a stranger to the land than they.

She not only talked funny, but she was by far more attractive than most of the Mormon wives.

That, coupled with the fact that her husband had created for himself a sour reputation, insured that she would never be fully accepted in the community.

Compounding the problem was Iver's habit of leaving her alone in Bear River City while he went miles away to work... for weeks at a stretch. So, during those times, Irene would gather her children around her and hide from her neighbors and fellow citizens of Bear River City to escape their abusive remarks and snobbish attitudes. After several years of such treatment, Irene, indeed, began to believe that she was inferior and, from her, it rubbed off onto her children.

So Irene paid very little attention to her children's success or non-success in school. She believed that they each had the raw material to make it, one way or another,

But none of those excuses, or his mother's confidence, would help Chad then. All he knew was that he had a bunch of low grade pigs on his hands; he wanted to get rid of them, and soon.

Flight of the Kroughs

Not knowing exactly what to do, he did what he could. Monday morning he borrowed Uncle Bug's truck and sideboards. He loaded the beasts up and hauled them to Martin's Slaughter House. There, he got what he could for them. Which was little. Mr. Martin's buyer started with the market price then adjusted it downward. He did, however, leave the stinking place with three-hundred dollars in his pocket.

Rid of the pigs, Chad's list of fixed assets had withered to two pieces of haying equipment, two horses, a covered wagon, a thirty-nine Chevy truck and five cows that ranged in color all the way from tan to all black.

Although he never said so, Chad had always had the impression somewhere in the back of his mind, that, once a person went into the farming business the money would roll in. He soon found out that, as far as he was concerned, the money was rolling the wrong way.

Chad's next disappointment was provided by the first crop of hay.

He had rolled out of bed early and harnessed his team of horses on the June day he had chosen to begin his hay harvest. He whistled to the animals as he attached the layered-leather straps to the singletrees of the mower, giving each horse a patronizing slap on the butt as he finished hooking it up. Then he hopped aboard the mower, picked up the leather reins, and urged his team forward ... the wheels moved but didn't turn, so he yelled, "shit". Because he knew, even with his limited farming knowledge, what was wrong ... the gears were frozen tight from too much wear and too much rust. He heaved a deep sigh and hired one of the successful Nelson farmers to cut the twenty acres of hay using his new tractor- mounted mower.

Sadly, even after having the hay cut, Chad's problems with the crop did not end ... the only thing that ended was his money supply. Regardless of that fact, as he rolled into bed three days later, he hoped aloud that he would have better luck with the dump rake.

Chad hooked his team to the machine the next morning, wondering all the while if that ancient implement was going to work. He hesitated for a second or two, then leaped to the steel seat.

Without being asked, the team of bays, one tall - one short, took off and headed toward the field ... "So far so good," Chad thought.

After crossing the irrigation canal that sliced his farm into two unequal parts, he lined the team up and guided them down the straight, broad rows of fallen alfalfa. Each time he pulled the dumping lever, the ten feet of curved and pointed rods came up and released their load of hay.

By ten o'clock, when the three young boys. Glen, J.C., and Harvey, had arrived, Chad and his outfit had created several long drifts of hay stretching half way across the field.

He pulled his horses to a stop and motioned to Glen. Not knowing what his big brother wanted, the fourteen-year-old walked across the stubbled alfalfa and stopped at the side of the haying outfit. Chad hopped off and told Glen to get on. The young Krough boy obeyed, and off he and his subordinate work plugs went. Although he misjudged the end of the lines the first few times when he released the raked-up hay, Glen did a fair job.

At dinner time, Chad, Harvey, and J.C. moved across the field, stepping over the two-foot-high drifts of hay. Then the older brother ordered Glen to pull the team to a stop. Chad told Glen to dismount from the machine because he had promised small, blonde - to the point of nearly white – haired Harvey that he could drive the team and rake across the canal to the covered wagon. The two boys traded places and down the gentle hill the outfit went, with Chad, Glen, and J.C. following further and further behind.

Then something very chilling occurred to the eldest Krough - he had neglected to warn his littlest brother of the fact that the tallest bay horse had an unusual fear of barbed wire.

He shouted as loud as was possible. But Harvey's joy at being put in charge of the outfit, and the noise it created, erased the sound of Chad's voice from the dinnertime air.

The young farmer knew that he had good reason to worry. Because, where Cotton Top, as Harvey was called, would guide the horses through the axle-deep water, a barbed wire fence also crossed. And the fence was in the same sad shape as the farm.

After years of fighting debris riding the current of the stream, two strands of the rusted wire had surrendered and were pushed down- stream - nearly to the crossing place.

Harvey continued on his confident way. When he reached the canal, he aimed his team of horses at the crossing place. As the water was unusually high that day, young Harvey decided to keep the rig high in case the force of the stream pushed the horses to the left. "If it does," he told himself, "then I will come out in the right place on the other side."

When Harvey started across the stream the tall spooky horse noticed the barbed wire whipping loosely in the swift current. Fear hammered its way throughout the animal like an explosion. Instantly, the horse bolted to the left, dragging his confused smaller mate with him. The team spun around in the boiling muddy water and charged back up the hill, leaving a hail of dirt clods in their wake. Harvey pulled on the reins with all of the strength his small body could muster.

Chad, Glen, and J.C. raced across the mowed field in an effort to stop the runaway pair. But such a plan was hopeless. By that time Harvey was pulling so hard on the leather straps that he was standing upright on his out-of-control chariot-like implement.

Flight of the Kroughs

Chad had never felt so helpless. He knew that he couldn't catch them, but he followed his little brother with his blond hair floating in the wind, as fast as he could run.

As the crazed team left the hay field and entered the weed infested pasture, they jumped a ditch that was about two feet wide and a foot deep. When the hay rake's wheels hit the ditch it caused the ancient machine to bounce four feet into the air. When it landed, it jarred the trip lever with such force that the ten feet of curved steel tines, spaced four inches apart, dropped to the earth.

Chad led Glen and J.C. across the fields on a dead run, tears began to run down his cheeks, and for the first time since he lay under his truck in Belguim, he silently prayed. All he could see of little Harvey was his white hair floating above a cloud of dust. Then, all of a sudden, Harvey's hair disappeared. Because, just five seconds after the raking part of the machine had dropped, Harvey's strength expired, and he fell in front of the giant curved comb that was scraping the surface of the crusted pasture.

Chad refused to believe what his eyes were showing him. And he wished as hard as he knew how, that he could, somehow, live the last ten minutes over again. But in spite of his wishes, his small brother could not be seen.

Harvey was rolled along the ground and through the weeds for about a hundred feet. Then, lucky for him, the rake bounced over another ditch and released him, a lifeless lump tumbling in the dust.

When the machine had landed, it also caused the wood tongue - a shaft of wood four by four inches square and twelve feet long, attached to the front of the machine, that rode between the horses and connected to their harness collar, with which the animals guided the implement - to be ripped loose.

The dust had settled around Harvey's shocked body by the time Chad was fifty feet away. From that distance the boy looked dead. But by the time the ex-GI farmer reached the spot, small Harvey was struggling to his feet.

His face and shirt were both bloody, and his skin had been drained of color.

Chad didn't waste time giving his brother an examination in the field, he scooped the battered young man up in his arms and headed for the campsite and his thirty-nine Chevy truck, hoping all the while he ran, that the truck wouldn't fail him when he tried to start it... it didn't.

When Doctor Blodget had finished exploring Harvey's frail body, he discovered four holes: one in his forehead, one in his neck, and two in his chest. "But none of them, thank God," whispered Chad as he carried his small brother back to the truck, "went deep enough to cause serious damage." However, young Mr. Krough knew that it was too early to breathe easy. For, in the next five minutes, he would need to face his mother.

It was a leisurely drive from downtown Bear River City to the windswept bench where the Krough house sat.

As Chad pulled tentatively into the yard, his mother watched from her front room window and wondered why, when there was so much work to do, the four boys weren't at the farm,

Chad stepped from the truck and sheepishly looked around the immediate area. Then he circled the truck and opened the passenger side door.

Glen and J.C. jumped out, then stood aside. Then Chad reached inside the cab and pulled Harvey out and headed with him in his arms toward the house.

Before he had taken three steps, Mother Irene was charging from the house with one hand covering her mouth. Chad stopped and allowed Harvey to stand on his own as a way of showing his mother that her youngest son wasn't as bad off as he looked.

Irene hurried to the pair then dropped to her knees and gave Harvey an inspection. When she had satisfied herself that Harvey was in one piece, she then turned her attention to Chad.

"What in the hell did this to Harvey?" she shouted. Chad quickly surveyed his vocabulary, mentally, in search of words that he could use to explain what had happened in such a way as to satisfy his mother and not inspire a lot of accusing questions ... he failed miserably. Because before he had completed his search, Irene was on him, demanding a full explanation.

"Hold on, Mother, he's not hurt as bad as it looks," Chad offered.

"What do you mean he's not hurt as bad as it looks? Anyone of these holes could have killed him if they were an inch deeper. Now tell me what happened!!" demanded Irene.

Chad knew that he would need to relate to his mother the whole gory mess, so he asked if she could make a pot of coffee.

Harvey lay on his mother's bed and listened carefully as Chad told of a small boy's perilous trip across the field. And Cotton top was glad to hear what he had just gone through, because his own memory of the incident was locked up in his subconscious. Before the two adult Kroughs left their cups and the table, Chad had given his mother a solemn promise to forbid the three young boys to have anything more to do with the horses. Then Chad collected Glen and J.C. and headed back to the farm.

In the excitement of taking little brother to the Doctor, the young farmer had completely forgotten about the horses. So driving back, Chad wondered where, and if, he would find them. He led his two brothers across the canal

Flight of the Kroughs

and followed the trail left by the crazed team . They walked far beyond where they had found their little brother laying. Then, stuck in a ditch bank, they found the tongue of the hay rake buried about a foot.

It didn't take long for Chad to figure out that the four by four wood shaft had come loose from the horses and had dropped to the ground. And when the horses had jumped the bank running flat out, the tongue, which was sliding along the ground, met that bank with tremendous force. And when it did, the rake stopped but the horses tore loose from the implement and kept running.

Not far beyond the disabled hay rake, Chad and his brothers discovered the animals grazing in saintly innocence. But they were still harnessed and ready for action. So Chad took hold of the team and led them to the hay rake. The three boys worked some kind of magic with the piece of damaged equipment and within ten minutes had it free of the bank and re-attached to the horses.

The human and animal crew worked hard during the following week and managed to finish harvesting the thirty percent crop.

The five cows milked, fed, and watered, Chad sat on the edge of his bunk in the covered wagon and thought about his situation. And the first fact that dawned on him was that, aside from milking his second rate cows, he had nothing to do for the next month or so except irrigate and wait for the next crop of hay to mature.

More important than that, was the fact that, aside from the milk check that averaged eighty dollars a month, the farm produced no income. And at that moment, doubt began to replace his fragile confidence.

More and more he stayed away from his farm. The milking was left to Glen and J.C. who had to walk three mile and a half twice a day to do the job. That arrangement lasted but one month. Then Irene put her foot down. So beginning with the first day of the next month, Chad did the morning milking, and Glen and J.C. did the evening milking.

It was about three weeks after the institution of that new arrangement when Chad's excursion into the world of farming met its final obstacle.

By then he had sold his horses and hauled his equipment to the junk dealer where he received one half cent a pound for it. He figured that he would keep milking the cows until the hay stack was gone; then he would sell them as well.

So the young boys wouldn't need to face the long walk from the Krough house to the farm each day, Irene had given Glen permission to stay with his big brother in the covered wagon.

At about seven thirty on a middle July morning the pair had finished the milking and had loaded the milk in brother James' neat maroon Ford.

D. Raymond Anderson

Chad jumped behind the wheel, and Glen jumped in the shiny, like-new Ford, on the passenger side. And off they went toward the milk depot.

As they moved up the hill on the gravel lane that crossed the tracks then met the highway, Chad broke into song - a western song at that.

Just as the car topped the hill, however, and the would-be western singer topped the musical scale with words like Montana or bandana, or silver horse, Glen would never remember exactly which, Chad yelled "Son-of-a-bitch." His little brother looked at him in embarrassment due to his language then he, as well, caught sight of the two-car electric commuter train coming their way. Although it was but a second or two before the metal monsters would slam into the overmatched Ford and its passengers, in Glen's mind everything began to take place in slow motion.

He looked at the train, then turned his head straight ahead.

He experienced no fear and would experience no pain.

The next sound to reach Glen's left ear was that of Chad saying to his younger brother, "This is it." Glen wasn't sure what he meant.

Chad, being swift of mind, as well as foot, managed to stop the Ford. Then tried to ram the shifting lever into reverse. Reverse because, he knew that if the streetcars hit their Ford anywhere around the middle, it would simply roll it down the tracks taking it apart as it went.

So although he was unable to move the car back off the tracks to safety, he had stopped it with only the front third of it in mortal danger.

The train blasted the air with its powerful horn, and a split second later crashed into the maroon Ford where the hood and Chad's door met.

The force of the blow spun the car around on the spot. A half second after the first blow, a second one hit the rear of the Ford. That blow picked the vehicle up and threw it, without effort, twenty-five feet into a barrow pit, leaving the front third of the battered piece of junk in the deep swift canal.

Inside the protective body of the Ford on its unscheduled trip, things were going on that Glen neither felt nor observed.

The sudden collision tripped some cryptic switch in Chad's head and set in motion a visual recording of what had happened to him a year and a half back.

What he had first seen coming toward him was a train, but by the time it had hit the Ford, it was a German tank, and the car was no longer a car; it was an Army truck.

The armored vehicle coming at him and at nearly point blank range unleashed a seventy-five MM projectile that tore the front of his truck cleanly from the rest of the vehicle.

The force of the blow left Chad dazed with fright. And later as he sat under his truck, he was relieved to have a friendly uniformed officer take hold of his arm to comfort him.

Flight of the Kroughs

But as the mist cleared from his head, Chad noticed that the color of the man's uniform wasn't olive drab, but was shiny deep blue. And the officer didn't have his helmet on either. He was wearing a squared-at-the-crown billed cap that sort of resembled hats worn by the police he had seen when he had met his brother James in Paris.

Chad finally realized that he wasn't sitting in the cold Belgium winter snow; he was sitting in brother James' stirred-up Ford which was wet from a blizzard of foamy milk and a hail of milking paraphernalia. And the man shaking him was the smartly-dressed train conductor.

When the streetcar operator had received the signal from the conductor that both Krough boys were in good shape, he ran to the nearest house and called the police.

Glen shoved his door open and quickly shut it. Because, had he jumped out, it would have been into the swift current of the main canal. So he crawled through the mess into the back seat and exited through the backseat side window.

He calmly viewed the damage to the once neat Ford, then became more interested in what had hit them. So the drenched boy of fourteen walked the three hundred feet to where the two rail cars that were coupled together and made some exciting discoveries.

First, although the train was much larger than their Ford, it had suffered some major damage. The cattle guard had been ripped nearly loose from the commuter train and had plowed a three inch deep furrow through three hundred feet of ties. Also dangling in an odd position was the fancy side light.

Observing the damage, Glen felt just a tint of pride. "Kinda like a challenger knocking down the champion just before being beat senseless himself," the boy thought.

And second, Glen was able to tour the empty and unsupervised train. Even the cubby hole where the operator pulled the handles and blew the horn.

The first thing Chad did after crawling from the wreckage was, just like Glen had done, survey the damage. But, unlike his younger brother, he did it in detail.

He first noticed that the Ford's hood was missing as well as its battery. He next saw that the inner portion of all four wheels had been ripped loose from their rims. And that the battered body of the once proud Ford was bent in a gentle "U" shape. And it had been shortened by about two feet, thanks to the kick it had received in the rear from the train. And finally, the polished maroon finish had disappeared under a coat of dust mixed with oil.

By the time Chad had finished his sad inspection, a large crowd had gathered and mingled with the half dozen passengers from the disabled streetcar.

The inexperienced farmer had just told his story to the policeman when George Nelson's thirty-six Ford slid into the scene. The passenger side door flew open and James leaped out. He moved quickly through the crowd, and when he received his first unobstructed view of the devastation, his legs turned to wet spaghetti, and the color drained from his face.

Fortunately for James, George was at his side and helped him to a soft landing on the gravel road.

With some bystander's help, the policeman revived the oldest Krough boy and helped him to his feet.

James went no further, but turned around and returned to his friend's car.

James never said which had caused his spell: the sight of the wreckage of his once beautiful car or the realization of what might have happened to his two brothers.

As the thirty-six Ford carrying James left the accident scene, a large wrecker truck entered.

The operator took his outfit off the lane and backed rear bumper to rear bumper with the mutilated sedan. While the truck driver attached the chain from the boom to the car's bumper, several people, including Chad, scouted the surrounding area looking for missing parts of the Ford.

In a field of sugar beets across the canal, about a hundred feet from the Ford, they found the hood. And just a few feet from that someone discovered the battery. The front and rear bumpers were found pushed into the earth under the car. And a missing milk strainer was found wedged under the rear axle.

After the loose components, had been placed on the bed of a two-and-a-half-ton truck, the crowd dispersed, and the train, with its cattle guard tied up using barbed wire, went on with its rounds. Then, like a funeral procession, a caravan consisting of four vehicles moved slowly eastward.

Leading the caravan was the wrecker; then came the truck bearing the twisted metal remains. Next in line was a forty-two Chevy pick-up with three people inside, two of whom were Chad and Glen. And finally, a green thirty-five Dodge sedan with Chad's girl friend at the wheel.

In a small, naturally dull, town like Bear River City, a serious accident caused much interest. So when the string of vehicles passed through the downtown area, it emptied most of the homes and all of the business establishments.

The people standing on the sidewalks gawking at them reminded Glen of the Fourth of July parade.

Flight of the Kroughs

James had forewarned his mother about the accident but had kept the details of the accident to himself. But just the mention of trouble at the farm sent shocks of anxiety throughout her body which at several minute intervals caused Irene to suffer painful back muscle spasms.

She first saw the caravan as it passed the cemetery. And as she stood on the lane shading her eyes from the sun, Irene began to see just how serious the accident had been. Consequently, by the time the large truck had stopped in front of the Krough house, and Chad and Glen had been dropped by the stranger who had taxied them, and Marion, Chad's girl friend had pulled into the yard ... Irene had gathered up her apron in both hands and buried her sobbing face into it.

She staggered to her front porch and sat down. There she finished her cry while her family gathered around trying reassure to her.

After Irene regained her composure, she looked up at Chad, and quietly, yet forcefully, said, "Son get rid of that worthless piece of dirt you and LeRoy call a farm. It has brought us nothing but trouble."

Chad said nothing in return. But underneath he was relieved. Because he had been in the process of doing just that for sometime but had lacked the courage to confess as much to her.

What remained of that day for Chad and James was spent going to Smithville with their dead Ford to see what they could get for it as junk.

Glen stayed home with his mother and was never out of her sight. At four-thirty in the afternoon he reminded his mother that it was milking time. And, as Chad had not yet returned from Smithville, he ought to go get the job done.

Reluctantly, she agreed. Within minutes the fourteen-year-old was on his way past the cemetery headed west walking toward the farm.

Glen started his milking at five-thirty and was finished by six-thirty. He then fed the animals their meager daily ration of hay and carried them a fresh supply of water.

It was nearly seven o'clock p.m., and the emotional and physical labor he had gone through on that day had suddenly caught up with him.

As he walked toward the covered wagon behind a six-foot shadow cast by the lowering evening sun, he was gladdened by the sight of brother Chad crossing the railroad tracks headed down the lane in his girl friend's thirty-five Dodge. Glen ran to open the gate and greet him.

Chad parked the car by the covered wagon, and as he got out of it, asked his younger brother if he was feeling ok. Glen answered yes, as his brother hopped up into the wagon and prepared to fix a supper of pork and beans and bread and milk.

When the meal had been endured and the tin dishes washed up, Glen watched his brother's every move, praying beneath his breath that Chad would stay at the camp that night and not go out with his girl friend, as was usual.

But his prayers went unanswered. Because at eight o'clock Chad took a shave and stand-up sponge bath. And by eight-thirty he had left.

At about nine o'clock, p.m., Glen had a notion to walk the nearly two miles back to the house. But as darkness was falling quickly, he decided against it.

He undressed to the waist and lay on the camp bed. He dozed right away. But soon his brain began to work, against his will. Then his eyes were open and he was wide awake. He began thinking about the things he had experienced that day. At last, Glen realized just how close to death he had come. Only then had his young mind cleared sufficiently enough to let what might have happened, and how, occur to him.

"What," he wondered, "if I had opened my door and jumped?" In a split instant the answer came to him. "I would have been smashed flat as a pancake - that's what."

"And," he went on, "what if my door had flew open when the train hit us?" Again he answered is own question, "Then I would have ended up on the tracks under the car and the train."

"What if my big brother had tried to jump to safety ... he would have been caught between the speeding train and the Ford."

Then the most devastating fact occurred to him; not one full year before their accident, a family of five had been destroyed by that same train just four hundred yards east of where they were hit.

At that moment Glen's resistance finally melted and he broke into uncontrolled sobbing.

The night was dark because there was but a sliver of a moon. As he was alone, the distraught fourteen year old Krough boy had no one to comfort him.

He lay there for two hours, then decided to go find Chad. In his young mind he pictured his brother parked on some side road not far away being consoled by his girl friend. So he took off, not knowing where, to find that side road.

Glen walked the dark roads and lanes for three hours in numbing fear, then gave up.

He returned to the camp and buried himself deep into the bed and pulled the covers over his head. Wanting to or not, his tired brain relented and allowed sleep to take over his young aching body.

When Chad returned to the camp at two-thirty, a.m., he saw his little brother in the middle of the bed in a deep sleep, and decided not to disturb him. He softly took one of the blankets and retired on top of the small remaining hay-stack.

Flight of the Kroughs

There- he too, spent a restless night wondering what might have been and thanking God, as he studied the stars, that it wasn't. The next day Chad took Glen aside and gave him a good talking to.

"Glen," he said, "do me one favor - please, stay in school, try to profit from my mistakes and you will make it."

*****

Chad gave in to the reality of his situation and moved off the farm, letting it become the property of the government. Glen spent the summer not doing much of anything except swimming in Bear River Lake and, with the help of J.C. and Harvey, looking after Mother Irene's vegetable garden and berry patch.

On rare occasions, Glen thought about the advice given him by his big brother concerning school.

Actually, he should have been one grade ahead of where he was. But back a few year's worth of semesters - second grade in fact - his teacher, based on his poor but passing grades and substandard dress, decided that it would be best if Glen was held back ... Glen would wonder much about who it was better for. He, like most of his brothers and sisters, would never recover from such an embarrassment. Irene was upset too, but felt it would be useless to argue with Principal Blackey.

So after that, regardless of the fact that the young man was capable of achieving passing grades in some subjects and excelling in the rest, he just floated with the tide. And he became an anonymous body slouching in the back row of the classroom.

But Glen did have some interesting experiences during his brief attempt at high school.

The odor produced by freshly varnished doors and woodwork, the odor of freshly oiled but still squeaky, oak floors and the odor from fresh coats of sea foam green paint on the walls and ceiling all mingled with the odor of four hundred or so young bodies in outfits from Sears or J.C. Penney to create a uniquely first-day of school smell.

But the smell that immersed his body wasn't what occupied his thoughts. Glen wanted to know who was going to try to teach him what on that first day of his first attempt at high school... in the autumn of forty-seven.

The freshman student knew that, except for the library which was located on the top floor of the three story building, all of his classes would be found on the second floor.

When Glen first began to finger the list on the last door, he slapped his forehead so hard with his right hand that the sound echoed throughout the high ceilinged hall. Then he groaned. And let the word "shit" slip out of his mouth.

"Mr. Nuedecker, first hour, for language," Glen mumbled. Then added "What a lousy way to start the day."

His first impulse told him to just leave the building. From there he could go to the edge of town and lie on his back on the loading dock of the closed canning plant in the warm sun of late summer and watch as the freight trains lazily dropped off and picked up boxcars. And all the while dream of the better things in life, things like the uncharted hills and valleys of Ellie Thurstin's body.

Then Glen thought of Chad. He knew painfully for certain that if he did sluff, and big brother found out, he would no doubt receive the promised "good ass kicking."

So, grudgingly, Glen moved his stubborn body into the room and took his customary back row seat behind fellow learners; many of whom he had gathered with for the past eight years. And for those past years theline-up had changed little.

Usually, if on one of those first days, a new face appeared in the crowd, he or she was straight away popular. If that new person was suitably dressed and nicely groomed, then that person was first befriended by those people residing in the top layer of the social strata - people like Ellie Thurston.

However, and alas, if that person didn't fit at that level he, or she, simply settled toward the bottom and stopped where the fit was comfortable.

Few remained at the top with Ellie and her friends. But even fewer lit on the bottom with Glen Krough and his like.

Mr. Nuedecker's room - just like all the other classrooms -arranged itself something like this: in the forward couple of rows sat the brains of the class. They believed in the no nonsense intellectual pursuit of knowledge and were about as socially acceptable as the likes of Glen. The next two rows were the athletically proficient students: they were much favored by the teachers... People like Zip Green.

Taking up the largest number of the desks - three rows - were the fun-loving average students. Then in the next to last row were the have-not girls. And finally in the back row slumped the have-not boys.

In actual fact, in terms of athletic ability, the boys sitting in the back row of seats were every bit as proficient as the boys sitting in the middle of the room. The only difference being their equipment: the have-nots didn't own good ball gloves or Converse tennis shoes.

The fact that he didn't own a good pair of athletic shoes failed to interfere with Glen's joining in when games were played - he played in his stocking feet. And on certain occasions, usually when playing football, Glen was able to use his stocking feet to get even with Larry Allen, Alfred's nephew. He would gain his revenge by running directly at Larry so he

Flight of the Kroughs

would either need to tackle him, or get run over. And when the pair untangled, Glen would maneuver one of his smelly sock-covered feet into Larry's face.

However, on that first day of school, as Glen slouched at his corner desk at the back, the room became filled with chatter among his fellow students. Chatter that concerned, for the most part, tales of summer adventures. As he listened, he determined quickly that, compared to his own latest experiences, theirs were second rate.

Glen listened while staring jealously at the boys in the middle of the crowd. Suddenly, a wave of silence moved up the rows of desks, back to front - Mr. Nuedecker had made his pompous entrance.

Without acknowledgement of the fact that there were thirty-five freshmen in the room, he went directly to the supply closet from which he pulled a six-foot pole, about the thickness of a broom handle, with a hook on one end. Mr. Nuedecker then moved with perfect posture to the south side of the classroom. He raised the pole with its hooked end into the air like a magic staff. The brand new students fully expected shafts of lightning and claps of thunder to fall from the ceiling. But, no such thing occurred. Mr. Nuedecker simply inserted the hooked end of the pole into a slot at the top of each window and with one crisp downward motion, jerked it open, which, in the process, created a squeal that disturbed the uneasiness that had settled upon the occupants of the room. And somehow, awakened an awareness between Mr. Nuedecker and his students of each other's presence.

That chore successfully completed, the fabled teacher circled the room, stopping behind his hallowed, but deeply scarred, golden oak desk.

To Glen, Mr. Nuedecker looked as if he had just stepped out of God's perfect machine. His body was wrapped in meticulously clean attire; his black shoes were spit polished, his much used gray suit was clean and the trousers were creased razor sharp and fit his slender body to perfection. His brown tie was winsored into a small hard knot and was looped around the collar of a perfectly ironed starched, green-stripe-on-gray, shirt. And the tie was bowed outward just right before it disappeared into his gold watch chained vest. To top it off, his hair was sheared clean, high above his glossy ears.

The cleaner than life teacher never bothered giving an opening day speech to his new students. He just looked at them sternly with his eyes so dark that they were tinted purple, making the young learners feel transparent, and instructed them to pick up the brand new, sharpened just right pencil that rested on their desk. And on the lined paper before them write, not using less than four paragraphs, a composition based on their summer experiences.

D. Raymond Anderson

Glen figured the assignment to be a snap, and he could do it in a hurry. Because he had but two instances to tell of:

"The day was going good so far. But my little brother kept begging my big brother that he wanted to help. So my big brother finally said yes and let him take the horses and hay rake to the barn. When they crossed the creek one of the horses got tangled in barbed wire and got scared and started running wildly. My little brother fell down off the rake and was drug for a long ways then had to see Doctor Blodget. Another day me and my same big brother got done milking and headed home with the milk. We couldn't see the train coming because the hill was too steep. Lucky we didn't get hurt but the car was smashed to pieces and the milk was all wasted.

Thirty-five minutes after issuing his orders to Glen and his classmates, Mr. Nuedecker called the compositions in ... finished or not.

The students in the front rows leaped to their feet and shoved their assignments toward Mr. Nuedeckers frowning face. The next couple rows - that were filled with the popular boys - talked among themselves about what they had just written as they passed their papers to Zip Green so he could hand them in.

The average and fun loving young men and ladies in the next few rows waited to have their work picked up - some even having the courage to beg for more time.

The bogus freshmen in the back row surrendered their writing assignments over in varying degrees of completeness and physical condition; by the time Glen's paper reached the front of the room, it bore the creased outline of a paper airplane. After waiting until all of the papers had made it to his desk, and he had stacked them neatly Mr. Nuedecker scooped them up with his right hand and held them in the air. The room became deathly quiet. The students could sense that something profound was about to happen...they weren't disappointed. After holding the documents suspended in the air for a full ten seonds, he nonchanlantly tossed them in his sparkling clean wastebasket.

"Students, I want each of you to understand my rule about pencils; as far as I know there is no such thing as a pen with an eraser attached. So, therefore, it will force all of you to be careful to do it right the first time."

Just as Mr. Nuedecker finished his explanation, the bell sounded. But before the back row dwellers escaped through the door- way, he raised his hand in a way that clearly said stop; "Don't forget, tomorrow you must bring a pen ... I will accept no excuses for your failing to do so."

Glen, and his mates: Max Sorenson and Jason Borg, left the room shaking their heads and confessing to each other that what they had heard about Mr. Nuedecker was certainly true. So the next class, which was library, would be a welcomed period in which to unwind. There, after

Flight of the Kroughs

"accidently" dropping their pencils on the floor, they could have the pleasure of, when they leaned beneath their table to pick them up, viewing Carrie Miller's underthings. But after Glen and his friends had each taken a turn at that, they began to ask each other where they were going to find a fountain pen.

Glen arrived home from school filled with worry. He talked about Mr. Nuedecker's order concerning a pen with his mother.

She searched their three rooms high and low. But all she could find was an old Shaeffer that had been long since ruined by J.C. and Harvey when they pretended the pen to be a bomb dropped from an invisible airplane. After which it would end up standing upright in a puddle of blue in the kitchen floor.

She explained to her son the sorrow she felt for not having a suitable fountain pen tor him. But quickly added that as soon as she could rake up the money she would see to it that he would have one.

From the start it was obvious that his mother was more concerned about the order than was Glen; "Aw, don't worry about it, Mother," said Glen. "I can use one of those at school anyway who cares about story writing? For sure not me. Because to tell you the truth Mother, I just don't have that much to say."

"Are you sure you're being honest with yourself. Glen?"

"I don't understand what you mean. Mother."

"Well, are you positive you have nothing to say ... or is it a matter of no confidence in your ability? Or even worse - is it pure damn laziness?" Glen sensed a rebirth of interest in school by his mother.

With Irene's last question Glen became visibly uncomfortable. And he hoped that her lecture was over. But she had one more thing to say, "You know Glen it's one thing to watch while weeds take over the garden before you lift a hoe to take them out, but to let your brain go to mush because you are too lazy to write on paper what it's telling you, is something worse. Your older brothers - and your father, too, if he were alive - could shout reasons at you for hours why you should work hard and do well in school."

To get his mother off his back on the subject of school, Glen agreed to try harder. In return, she said - in an unimpressed way - "Fine, you do that. Then maybe you won't need to chase muskrats around the marshlands or dig through other people's discarded trash at the dumps looking for something to sell for money to buy their stinking cigarettes with, like your big brothers are forced to do." With those words Irene disappeared into the bedroom that she shared with Karia and Lu Ann.

At the same time, Glen began to worry about Mr. Nuedecker's reaction to his being penless.

The next morning the freshmen filed quietly into the language room, and the notorious instructor was waiting for them.

He quickly called the roll, then issued his assignment to the class: "I want each of you to go to the windows – one row at a time, very quietly please, and study what you see as you look at, and beyond, the school yard. Then I want you to return to your desks, take a clean sheet of paper, and with your pen you are to write for me three paragraphs. When writing I want you to pretend that you are strangers to this area, so describe in those three paragraphs what you have seen and what impression it left with you ... Now, would the first row please go to the windows, leave everything on your desks. But before you do that, I want to issue a warning. I do not tolerate any nonsense, so a word to the wise, don't test me."

Not knowing exactly what to do about his dire situation. Glen lagged behind but followed his classmates as they made their round trips to the windows.

As he sat at his desk, he noticed that he wasn't the only one not writing. But a shuffling sound at the front of the room shifted his attention and sent anguish spasms down his back ... Mr. Nuedecker was beginning to stroll slowly between the ranks of desks.

The slender teacher moved the distance needed to screw two desks to the floor; then he made an abrupt stop.

He studied Zip Green's writing instrument closely for a full twenty seconds. He then instructed Zip to take a clean sheet of paper from the shelf just under the desktop and place it before him. Mr. Nuedecker cleanly whisked his own pen from its vest breast pocket home. He leaned gently over and signed his name at the top of the clean paper. His signature was a work of art with its fancy curlicues and character.

"Now Mr. Green," Mr. Nuedecker softly, but precisely, said, "with your pen, I want you to write your own name directly beneath mine."

With fingers and hand shaking, Zip took up his writing instrument and scribbled - as best he could, considering the pressure he felt - his name. And as he did so, the teacher shook his own head slowly.

After Zip had done as instructed, he softly lay his pen in its groove at the top of the desk. But it didn't rest there long. Mr. Nuedecker picked it up and ceremoniously strutted to the south side of the room where he stopped and raised a window. After glancing at his class, he tossed Zip's pen out.

The smart kids in the front rows grinned smugly, Zip Green's friends and equals sympathized with him, the popular kids snickered softly, but Glen and his have-not equals in the back row laughed, unashamed, out loud. That is, until an icy stare from Mr. Nuedecker shut them up.

Before that hour was finished, many pens joined Zip's stretched out on the grass beneath the second floor language room. And many of the freshman class joined young Mr. Green and young Mr. Krough writing their story using those school supplied pens that needed to be dipped into the ink well that was impounded in a hole in the upper right hand corner of their desks. Needless to say most of those who had lost their pen through the window, or who had failed to heed Mr. Nuedecker's order, made sure that they were better equipped the next day.

Although Glen was satisfied using the black enameled piece of wood with a steel point held in one end as a writing instrument, Irene was not.

So before that September of forty-seven was history, she walked two miles to Bear River City High School, pausing on the way just long enough at Allen's Market to purchase a fine green fountain pen. She waited outside the main doors of the school for Glen to crash through on his way to a clump of bushes and a few trees on the downhill side of the campus to eat his sack lunch. As he bolted through the door, Irene reached out and snatched his shirt at the shoulder. Surprised at the grasp put on his shoulder by some unknown person - or thing - Glen came to a sudden stop. Then he became even more surprised, and a little red-faced when it registered in his brain who had stopped him.

Mother Irene handed her young son the small brown paper bag that contained his new pen, and at the same instant instructed him to take it to his locker so he wouldn't lose the thing. Then she quickly turned and made her way - obviously embarrassed about her poor, but neat, attire - through gangs of boys and girls engaged in various forms of entertainment, to the safety of Main Street.

Glen went in the opposite direction and stopped at his customary place for eating his lunch.

There he met his friend, and equal, Elwood Anderson. They each unsacked two peanut butter sandwiches and quickly transfered them into empty bellies. Then the pair crawled into a decorative patch of shrubbery and traveled on their hands and knees until they reached the uphill edge. With lots of open space between their two pair of eyes, they spyed between the limp branches of a bridal-wreath bush at the schoolhouse.

By that time most of the young ladies who had finished their hot lunches in the basement of the school had taken their places on the lawn, and had stretched their bodies out to absorb as much sun and gossip as possible. So it was no accident that Glen and Elwood had chosen an observation bush by the area taken up by Ellie Thurston and two of her equals. Because, the two boys decided, if they were going to take the priviledge of seeing female underthings, they might as well be worn by the best.

One thing always puzzled Glen, though. Were, he wondered, all those sophisticated wiggles and twists made by Ellie and her mates that sometimes showed more than their pure white, lace-edged, under- things, necessary for their own comfort, or were they deliberately staged for his and Elwood's pleasure ... and, hopefully, maybe their pleasure too.

In any case, Glen soon learned that in high school he could discover much more about life than Mother Irene would tell him and, for sure, volumes more than he could learn in the classroom by simply wandering the halls and the campus.

The teachers didn't much give a damn whether or not Glen was in class. Just so he didn't cause trouble. After all, they reasoned, no Krough kid had ever made it to freshman status yet - let alone to graduation. So they were quite positive that very soon Glen would join his older brothers and sisters as students turned dropouts. So when young Mr. Krough failed to show up for class, it caused little concern.

Glen didn't waste his time altogether. He had discovered during his travels throughout the red brick building and its surrounding field of grass, bushes, and trees most, if not all, of the secret places where important senior girls and boy athletes met to exchange physical stimulation.

Glen also had stumbled onto the trapdoor to the roof while rummaging through janitor Ray Ellis' top floor cubbyhole. Having learned much about the habits of the popular seniors, and having a daring plan in mind, Glen arranged to meet Elwood in the upstairs boys' room after lunch, during sixth hour, and they would have a little fun.

The pair waited until the stampede between fifth and sixth hour had finished before carefully cracking the door a couple of inches to survey the hall ... it was empty.

Glen quickly led his friend to the door of the upstairs cubbyhole. He just as quickly jerked a flat piece of metal about half the size of a dollar bill from his hip pocket. Then he slipped the metal between the door and the striker plate and pushed gently, soon a satisfying click occurred an instant before the door opened. The two freshmen then charged inside. Glen, excited about what they were about to witness, and Elwood, also excited, but concerned as to their destination.

The Krough kid grabbed a stepladder and placed it directly under the trap door. He turned to his friend and silently motioned for him to follow; then he danced up the ladder and pushed the trapdoor open wide. He scrambled onto the roof of Bear River City High.

By that time Elwood's head had broken above the plain of the black tarred roof. Glen was crawling on his elbows, knees, and belly toward the east edge of the building. Still not knowing quite why, Elwood obediently followed.

Flight of the Kroughs

On signal from Glen the pair stopped just shy of the building's edge and waited. Elwood was still puzzled about why they had went to so much trouble only to lie on the hot soft tar.

Finally, he asked in a whisper, what the hell they were doing. Glen whispered back, "Trust me."

Within seconds the sound of feet trying their best to walk on a silent cushion of air floated up to the two freshmen, accompanied by the sound of muffled whispers. Only then did Glen lead Elwood to the brink of their secret observation post.

As they cautiously pushed their heads over the edge to get a good and pleasant view, Hal Green's arms were moving up the back of Clairese's body hand over hand, carrying her skirt along as they went.

Glen and Elwood watched in silent ecstasy as Hal moved her underthings and got down to business.

When the sounds from below told the observers that Hal and Clairese were about to reach the point of no return just short of going all the way and enter a climactic joyous trauma, Glen quietly and confidently rolled toward the building's square brick chimney. And from its hidden side he raked four red balloons that were about eight inches in diameter and were filled to nearly bursting with cold water.

Glen pushed half of the bombs to his friend and told him to prepare to fire.

They each took up a balloon and cradled it with both their hands. Then Glen started to mumble something that Elwood didn't quite hear; "This is to pay you back for all those filthy remarks you made to me about me screwing my sister, you son-of-a-bitchen super jock." Then as the last whispered word left his lips, Glen let go. And in the next instant Elwood followed suit. When the missiles hit the wall just above the lovers' shoulders, they froze in a state of shock, because, due to their diminished awareness, except for their own bodies involvement with the other, they didn't know what had hit them, or from where it had arrived.

Quickly Glen picked up his other weapon and took aim at the confused pair below him trying to regain their senses. And again Glen mumbled some words that Elwood didn't understand. "This one is to pay you back for all those times you and your buddies hid in dark places and made dirty suggestions to my sister Clara, you rich ass- hole." Then he let his second balloon go. And as before, Elwood followed his lead.

One of the missiles, the boys on the roof weren't sure who's, hit with a fleshy splat just below the chin of Clairese. Needless to say, it exploded on impact. The cold water cascaded between her bare breasts that hung below her sweater and bra that Hal had pushed up during his fit of passion. Then the water made its way down, over her stomach - between her legs - then collected reverently in a puddle around her feet.

The scream she let out was heard in every corner of the campus, and every corner of the home economics room as well.

Mrs. Jordan, with her instructor's apron tailing in the breeze, burst out of the side door of the classroom. She rounded the corner of the building on the heels of Myra Lang, who seemed to know exactly where she was going. And why not? After all, she was one of those girls that most of the boys figured would, and the rest of the boys knew as a fact that she did.

The two women reached the formerly secret six by six space - that had been mistakenly created when a new section had been added to the building - just as Hal and Clairese had collected their wits and were about to restore their clothing to acceptable standards. When Mrs. Jordan saw the undone pair, she gasped, and then she turned her head up and away. And much to their disadvantage, gained an unobstructed view of Glen and Elwood.

The matter was quickly reported to the head coach and then to Principal Sheldon Jones.

The coach managed to convince the Principal of the fact that Hal was the most valuable asset to the school's fragile athletic reputation. Not to mention the fact tht Zip Green, Hal's younger brother, was about to come into athletic prominence. So official public recognition of the incident might blight the Green family name and stunt Zip's effectiveness in carrying on the family's athletic tradition ... "Anyway," said the coach with a knowing wink as he looked Principal Jones in the eyes, "boys will be boys."

Therefore, the affair never passed the gossip stage. Primarily, Because Mrs. Jordan was told to keep it quiet. And who would believe Myra with her rusted reputation.

However, one week after the incident, both Glen and Elwood were expelled from school.

Irene had taken her son's expulsion hard.

She wondered what Glen was doing loafing around the empty pig pens and cow barn at eleven a.m.

"Why aren't you in school?" she shouted at him. Glen said nothing in return. So Irene shouted to him once more. "Get yourself up here to the house and get yourself here fast," as her shout turned to a scream.

Glen grudgingly obeyed.

He shuffled into the kitchen and took a chair on the east side of the room, opposite his mother, and as far removed from her as possible.

"Now I want the truth, and I want it now Glen ... why aren't you at school?"

Knowing that he was trapped, the young Krough kid stiffened his body and stood erect. Then, on legs that felt stuck in concrete, he moved across

Flight of the Kroughs

the room to Irene. With arms that resisted, he reached down and around to his right rear pocket and pulled out a crazy creased piece of official school paper and surrendered it to his mom.

When Irene held the note in her hand and saw the fancy letter heading at its top, she knew something serious had happened. She didn't want to, but she read it anyway;

"Dear Mrs. Krough, we regret to inform you that, for disciplinary reasons, the Bear River City Citizen's School Board has found it necessary to deny your son, Glen, the privilege of attending our school."

We realize that this matter will cause you great disappointment. So if you would like to discuss the details further, please feel free to call at the office."

Her face had reddened as Irene read the note. Then she suddenly clapped it between the palms of her hand and ground it into dry pulp.

Next she moved closer to her trembling son who knew that he was about to be the object of his mother's boiling wrath. But before Irene was close enough to do Glen any physical damage, she made a sudden right turn and left the house. And Glen relaxed a bit.

But his feeling of relief was short lived. Because within minutes Mother Irene returned to the kitchen with her eyes showing even more rage and her right hand showing a limb from the apricot tree. And again she moved toward her son, stopping a mere two feet from his bended weak knees.

"You miserable little shit ass," hissed Mother Irene. "All I want is for just one of my children to make something of themselves. Why can't you understand that, Glen? You know I can't do it for you. Don't you realize that having one of my children make a success of their life would be all the reward I would seek out of this wretched life. God in heaven knows I have earned that much."

By then Irene was nearly screaming. And Glen was in tears and fearing for his very safety as his mother raved on: "Do you understand what I am saying young man?" With those clearly spoken words, Irene raised the apricot limb above her head as Glen pivoted on his chair while raising his left leg to protect his body and raising his left arm to protect his head.

"Damn you!! Damn you!!" cried Mother Irene, and she began to bring the wooden rod down upon her trembling son - all ninety-eight pounds of him.

But in her disappointment disguised as anger, her mind flashed back to those very early forties when she stood over her daughter Viola's mattress. And in her hand was a weapon from the another tree.

She and Glen were standing eye to eye on the same spot.

In the next instant, Glen's hasty prayers were answered. Because all of a sudden tears began to cascade down his mother's inflamed cheeks. Then she turned and quickly retreated to her bed where she buried her bead in her pillow as much out of shame as disappointment.

Glen left the house and returned to the cowshed where he lay on the dusty hay. He was emotionally bankrupt, so went directly into a deep but comfortless sleep.

In a short time a firm nudge moved his shoulder, and he awakened to see his mother looking down at him.

"Supper's ready ... it's your favorite, meat cakes, cream gravy, baked potatoes. Corn, and for dessert, bread pudding."

Glen didn't respond verbally but rolled off of his vegetation bed and accompanied his mother out of the cowshed and up the path to the house, feeling guilty about the comfort he felt from the arm which circled his back and hung limply over his left shoulder. Just before entering the kitchen door, Irene stopped herself and her son. She turned to him and, with some feeling of self-consciousness on her own part, she informed Glen that she planned to march right down to that school and fight to have him re-admitted.

Although he wasn't crazy about the prospect of his mother barging into the school administration office and making a scene, Glen didn't have the will or the inclination to fight it.

"After all," he thought, "they went to a lot of trouble to kick me out, and I just as soon stay kicked out."

The young Krough kid's secret desires notwithstanding, however, Irene was true to her promise and did, on the very next day, walk the two miles to the high school. There she met with Principal Jones and, as Glen thought later, worked some kind of magic. Because not only was his academic privileges reinstated, but he was also given a job as a janitor's helper. A job that allowed him to work three hours a day, five days a week at a dollar per hour.

Glen was very excited when he returned to school after his one- day layoff. And he could hardly wait to pick up a broom and get to it.

His impatience was rewarded, and after the final bell on that day, Ray Ellis, the head janitor, waited for his junior partner harboring a rude surprise.

"Here kid, here is your broom, dusting brush and dust pan. Now go over to the Industrial Arts building and clean the wood, metal, and auto shops. I want no horse assing around, and when you're done I want those shops to sparkle - got it?"

Glen stammered out a feeble "Yes sir" and trotted out of the main building then into to the lesser building that housed the shops.

Flight of the Kroughs

The job went reasonably well for about a month, and Glen performed his tasks fairly good. In fact, good enough to keep from getting fired, but not good enough to be complimented. And Mr. Ellis gradually became more friendly. After another two weeks passed, he even shared with Glen the distasteful duty of cleaning the shops. Sometimes the young and old partners actually sat together in the cubbyhole. Which they were doing on one of the darkest days ever to descend on Bear River City High School.

As far as Mr. Ellis and Glen knew the building was empty. So when they heard footsteps creaking across the main level floor they decided to investigate.

Ray ordered Glen to stay behind as they stepped softly down the darkened hallway.

As he passed the main office, he noticed light showing under the door. So, as it was past six o'clock p.m., the dedicated janitor felt a closer investigation was called for.

Ray's gumsoled shoes made almost no sound as he moved to within twelve inches of the most important door in the school building. As he arrived at that point, he stopped. He flexed his ears, trying to hear anything that might offer a clue as to who was in there, and what whoever might be doing.

However, what faint muffled sounds he could detect puzzled him. In fact, to Ray, it sounded as if someone might be engaged in strenuous exercise of some sort.

He moved his gray-topped head silently to a whisper's distance from the dark stained hardwood door that cased a frosted glass window, and he dared not breathe.

He then dropped his right arm to belt height and squeezed his sweaty palm and fingers around the slightly loose brass knob. The uneasy janitor sucked in a deep, but silent breath - counted in his head to three - then turned the knob and pushed the heavy door inward in the same move.

What his eyes took in caused all, then some more, of the air he had just seconds earlier sucked into his lungs to be just as completely forced back out.

Ray stood with his legs slightly spread and with his arms hanging at his side, also slightly spread, ready for anything. Ready for anything, that is, but for what he discovered. A discovery that caused him to become ridgid in the doorway framed pale against the darkness of the hallway behind him.

Mrs Ford lay nestled among the paraphernalia of her secretarial profession in unashamed brilliance. Her body just fit her mahogany desk. Her arms rested softly at her side. One deep, naturally tan leg extended straight to show the perfectly contoured lines of her body. The other magnificent tan leg was folded upward at the knee and was tilted generously outward to reveal her black, velvet adorned recently coveted nest. And just below Mrs. Ford's big brown eyes... that broadcast extreme delectation, her moist, pillowy red lips said nothing but, her expression showed volumes.

Thrusting upward proud and substantial, spread her soft breasts.

Mr. Ellis first felt shock - then shame - then guilt. Guilt that made him feel that he certainly would, and deservedly so, be turned to stone for disturbing such a divine environment.

But in that instant during which time Mrs. Ford's body was exhibited before him in all its splendor and perfection, Mr. Ellis had observed more beauty and known more desire than even his most outrageous fantasies had allowed him to imagine.

The time that had been consumed by Ray taking in the delicious sight of Mrs Ford and had experiencing those opposite emotions was in truth very short. For, shortly after he had opened the door, the rustling sounds had quickly turned to outright panic.

Mr. Ellis spun on his heels and made a frantic retreat from the room and, as he did, came near to trampling his young helper, who had also become rigid, into the oak floor.

It took nearly five minutes after retreating to his hall closet before the janitor could erase the image of Mrs Ford's sleek form from his mind and think of the Principal's awkward plight.

Only then did his memory of Mr. Jones hopping from the secretary's office into his own office overwhelm Ray's sense of humor.

When Principal Jones realized that his carrying on with his secretary had been discovered, his slight, but jogging conditioned body reacted almost instinctively.

As he had groped for what of his clothes that were handy to him, his face turned ashen gray.

Eventually Mr. Jones stumbled to the seclusion of his office with one leg secured in his trousers while desperately trying to negotiate his other naked leg into the empty trouser leg.

Mr. Ellis was, after several tries, finally able to control his laughter. Until, that is, he came to the part of the comical skit that had Principal Jones staggering from his secretary's office to his own with his half limp component waving to her goodbye.

Finally capturing his composure, the senior janitor called his junior partner into the cubbyhole saying he had something important to say to him.

"Now, young man, I want what you have just observed going on in the main office to remain our secret ... ok?"

"Yes sir," answered an embarrassed if amused Glen.

"Why don't you knock off early and go home right now ... I think I can handle what little that remains to be done."

Flight of the Kroughs

"Yes sir;" answered a grateful Glen. So he ran from the school, then the two miles home.

He honored his promise about keeping the incident quiet. While, on that same evening Mr. Ellis ran straight to his Bishop.

The fact that Mr. Ellis was a mere janitor between the hours of 3-8 p.m., in no way restricted his importance in the community. This was true because, like most male adults, he also held a position of high standing in the local ruling church. And as the incident was a clear cut act of brazen seduction on the part of Mrs. Ford and an indication of a moral handicap that afflicted Mr. Jones, Mr. Ellis deemed it his duty to report the sensational details to his church superiors.

They, in turn, passed the facts up the church bureaucracy chain of command with bits of damning information being vented to some of the church faithful at each stop.

At the highest echelon of church authority - short of Salt Lake City - it was decided that local norms of social and professional behavior had indeed been violated, so steps needed to be taken, and taken swiftly, to protect the community. And, as the religious rulers were lay folks, many of those same people were also on the school board. Others, folks such as Alfred Allen, were of special status so, therefore, influenced the board. In any case, Principal Jones was made ex-Principal Jones. And was excommunicated from the church.

And Mrs. Ford? She was fired and demoted to a common housewife. And was also excommunicated.

When gossip of the affair reached Irene's ears she just shook her head back and forth. Although unfair, what little respect she had for the institution called Bear River City High School, and those who ran it, evaporated.

She no longer insisted that Glen, or any of his younger brothers or sisters, graduate. Although she did suggest that if they did go, it would probably do them some good.

By the time nineteen forty-nine had rolled around, all but the two youngest, Lu Ann and Karla, had tried but given up on attaining a formal education ... for the moment anyway. But few years passed before most of the Kroughs recognized the error of their ways, and they acquired an adequate education - one way or another.

But Glen's other education, the one gained while traveling the halls and rooftops of Bear River City High School and climaxed by the show he had witnessed at the door of the school office was a great success. And the vision in his mind of the beautiful secretary lounging on her desk would long occupy and excite his thoughts.

*****

The year of forty-nine was also a year during which many journeys both near and far took place among the members of the Krough family.

James grew weary of digging various species of scrap metal from the dumps that were scattered liberally throughout Virtue Valley. Mainly, because unlike during the war, there was little demand for scrap. Consequently, Harry the Jew paid next to nothing for the stuff.

So he loaded his wife and two small girls into his thirty- seven Chevy and headed for Oregon. Why Oregon? He didn't know ... he just figured that there had to be greater opportunity in that part of the country.

As he drove northwest across Idaho, he did much planning. And with a sly grin, he decided to use a technique told to him by his dad, Iver: if a job was available, any job, no matter its make or model, he would boast about his past experience in that line of work; if he had touched it, he had done it.

Three days after saying their goodbyes in Bear River City, James and his family arrived at a small town in Oregon called McMinnville.

As it was way past the reasonable time of day for searching out lodgings, James and his wife settled on sleeping the night away in their car.

James took charge and arranged their sleeping quarters this way: the two little girls on the back seat - one at each end, his wife on the front seat; then he stretched his legs and bottom on the hood of the car and laid his back and head against the windshield. And there they slept, off and on, under the stars.

The next morning James began a systematic assault on the streets of McMinnville, one after another, and bottom to top. As he walked the sidewalk of Main Street, a sign in the exhaust-stained window of an automobile repair shop stopped him dead in his tracks ... "Help wanted" it said. James said softly "Hot damn;"

Determined, but faking confidence, James pushed the door open and stepped inside.

"Looks like a repair shop," he murmured softly as he surveyed the half dozen or so outfits in various stages of repair, or, in a case or two, terminal disrepair.

Seeing no one obviously in charge, he began to stroll casually across the layers of grease that cushioned the hard concrete floor beneath it. Thinking, as he went, "Smells like a repair shop."Then he moved toward a smoke-spewing thirty-six Plymouth being listened to by a dark, stocky, grease-smeared mechanic. At least, three of the car's six pistons were slapping the walls of their cylinder prisons trying desperately to escape.

James tapped the dreary looking auto repair expert on his left shoulder. The man stopped shaking his head at the clattering engine and turned to face him.

"Where's the boss?" asked the intruder.

Flight of the Kroughs

Going in the general direction of the arm and pointed finger offered by the mechanic, young Mr. Krough discovered the office in a far dark corner of the forty-by-one-hundred-foot shop; it was well camoflaged.

James would never learn for sure if it was by chance or by design that the office was hidden behind that tall stack of flat crankshafts, blocks with piston rods sticking out of one or both sides, cracked heads, leaky radiators, and twisted drive shafts - some with rear end and wheels still attached - but whatever the reason, the disguise was effective.

He found the office, then shyly tapped on the door. When two seconds had passed, a raspy voice from the other side invited James to enter.

The young man did as he was asked and found a man, older looking than he really was, sitting behind a coming-apart oak desk piled to capacity with miscellaneous parts and grease-stained invoices. As a backdrop, on the wall behind the worn-out mechanic, hung calendars - showing girls in skimpy clothes - that dated back to nineteen thirty-five.

"Nothing like what I saw in France," thought James automatically.

"What's on your mind?" the boss asked.

"I saw the sign in your window about needing help, and thought I would check it out" answered James.

"Got any experience?" the owner asked.

"Been around cars all my life" said James.

"Now you know as well as I that being around a car don't make you no mechanic. Hells bells, you can stand in horse shit up to your ass for a hundred years but that don't make you no cowboy ... now does it?"

"No, you're right, it doesn't," James had to admit.

"But, I worked from the time I was twelve. And it was to do with cars in one way or another."

"Be specific ... give me something that will let me know what you know or don't know" begged the boss.

Those words helped to restore some of James lost hope, so he quickly explained "Back in the thirties my dad was in the business of wrecking-out cars ... turning them into scrap metal. Whenever he spied a parked-for-dead car, Dad always dickered with its owner on the basis of it being junk. If he was successful, and he usually was, I would guide the thing home in tow behind Dad's pickup. But before he put the torch or sledgehammer to it, he turned the just-purchased car over to me to see if I could make it run. If I was able to do so, he would sell it. And in the deal, make a handsome profit. So sometimes I had to take curburetors apart to clean them, make gaskets out of cardboard or rubber innertube, rebuild fuel pumps, exchange a bent drive shaft for a straight one, and even on occasions replace a bearing or two."

D. Raymond Anderson

The owner rotated his chair and studied the back, calendar adorned, wall. He then reached into the corner of his small office and picked a yardstick from its leaning place. He then rotated his chair back toward the uneasy job applicant, but he didn't stop there. He kept turning until he faced the south wall. He raised his stick and pointed to an eight by ten glossy portrait of a young man in a uniform.

"Good looking kid ... eh?"

"Yes sir" answered James, as he waited for more discussion on the subject. But the boss slowly turned back and faced his visitor.

"Was you in the war young man?" asked the man behind the desk.

"Yes sir, I was" James answered proudly.

"Get hurt?"

"No sir."

"How tall are you?"

"Six foot two."

"How much you weigh?"

"Hundred and ninety."

"Good eyes?"

"Yes sir" answered James, and feeling much better.

"Got any tools?"

"A few."

"Well no matter, I got a set you can use. You better check what's there though. They ain't been used in eight years. Just tell me what ain't there and I will order them for you and take a little out of your pay ... When can you start?"

James sat straight backed and teary eyed, feeling nearly at the edge of emotional explosion.

"I can start in the morning - right now - but I gotta go get my tools."

Then he realized that he was babbling just a little, and shut up.

"Why don't you just get your tools and yourself together and be here at eight in the morning," suggested the boss. And James gratefully agreed.

When young Mr. Krough left the garage and headed toward his car and family, he found himself on the verge of running. Because all that he wanted to do at that moment was to tell his wife the good news.

But, back in Virtue Valley, USA, times were not as happy, for Irene in particular.

Like their older brother, Chad and Roland had likewise grown tired of picking up bits and pieces of work around the valley, so they made an unscheduled and unannounced trip to Smithville. And when they returned, they were the property of the United States Army.

Flight of the Kroughs

"Well-I'll-be-damned" cried Mother Irene. "Why in the hell did you do such a thing? Didn't you have enough the first time around? Are you trying to get yourselves killed?"

Both young men quickly jumped to their own defense. They straight away reminded their grieving mother that, at the moment at any rate, there was no war in progress in which their country was involved ... as far as they knew anyway. But war or no war, the two Krough boys were promptly dispatched to Texas.

Having listened through the post-World War Two propaganda however, Irene, by the summer of forty-nine had become wiser to the ways of the world. So she wasn't surprised when Uncle Sam gladly welcomed the pair.

She had read much in the newspaper and heard much on the radio about a cold war going on between the United States, some European countries on one side, and Russia on the other side.

Although watching her three sons go back out into the world made her sad, there were things that Irene wouldn't miss.

Not having much else to do, James, Chad and Roland had met at he Krough house three or four evenings a week to play pinochle. And without fail, every game had ended in a violent argument over rules or score. Sadly when they weren't arguing the game, James - who favored classical and light classical music - and Chad who favored country and western music, would argue about which station the radio should be tuned to.

Irene wasn't all that concerned about the arguing. Although there were times when she had to step in and defuse the situation. But, still, she understood. She knew that what they were really feeling was the frustration of their personal situations in regard to their unemployment. So Irene was confident that the card games and music had been a means of venting that frustration. So Mrs. Krough felt that the mixed feelings she experienced when the boys left were, to a small extent, justified. But the fear she endured for their safety by far overshadowed the relief.

Like most people of the valley, Irene had been conditioned by those who wrote the newspapers, and those who read the news over the radio, and politicians who made the news, to expect outright war at anytime.

She had heard, and memorized, all of the excuses for war in the recent past: self defense - which, to her, meant get them before they get you; economic necessity - which meant steal from your neighbor in the name of some self-serving claim of divine right of survival; or wars of political liberation - which in Russia's case meant imposing a mean political and social system, such as their own, on a country they pretend to free. And for the American's part, such wars were to protect American companies doing business in another country. That last explanation was one that she had heard from men making small talk while riding the bus to or from Smithville.

By the time the Fourth of July had arrived, Clara, then nineteen, had run off to Smithville and married an alcoholic, much older than herself. "But at least," she defensively explained to her mother, "he has a good job, and he treats me good."Irene couldn't argue with that. But regardless of his good manners and gentle ways, she couldn't overlook his drinking habit.

However, after being married to the man for two years of a four year marriage, during which time two girls and one boy were produced, Clara would learn the reason for his drinking. And she would learn that reason on a bright Sunday morning when an unexpected knock sounded on the door.

She opened it and discovered two uniformed policemen of some kind. The uniformed visitors inquired into the whereabouts of a certain person with the same last name as her husband, but with a different first name.

Clara's husband, listening to the conversation from a safe place in the kitchen, knew that his time had come, and there was no use running any longer. So he entered the front room and confessed that he was their man.

Poor Clara was thunder stricken. And before she could learn any of the why and what for's, the officers had her husband in handcuffs and were hustling him out of the house.

When they had him safely secured in the back seat of their car, one of the officers returned to the house and explained to Clara, that, if she cared to do so, she could follow them to the Sheriff's office and after he had been processed, she would be permitted to see and talk to her husband. At that time, if he was so inclined, her husband could tell her the details of his arrest.

Two hours later Clara sat facing her husband through a heavy chicken-wire barrier. With his head drooping and his eyes pinned to his shaking hands, he quietly confessed to his wife that he had hid-out from the army rather than face fighting and the risk of being killed.

Clara sobbed uncontrollably as she left the Smithville county court house and nearly collapsed on the surrounding lawn. One of the lawmen who had arrested her husband came from the court house and helped the confused young lady to her rattletrap of a car where she sat for the better part of an hour, dreading all the while the fact that in a few minutes she would have to face Mother Irene.

But when the two met and Clara had explained, all that followed for the next minute was silence. When Irene did finally speak, she didn't scold - she softly consoled. And she didn't say "I told you so" - she told her daughter that she knew all along that for a person to drink as much as he did, he must have had a good reason.

Flight of the Kroughs

Because the government was in a mood to leave the war to the history books, Clara's husband was soon released. But try as he did, he couldn't live down the shame he had brought down upon the families:his and Clara's.

Soon, everything they owned was tied up in cheap wine. By the end of fifty-three Clara would petition for, and be granted, a divorce.

After Clara's marriage in forty-nine, Irene had decided that it was time to take some drastic measures.

Although she had taken the job at the most elegant restaurant in Smithville of making salads, Mrs. Krough took other employment on weekends ... cleaning the church house. For this she received some coal and food.

She then enrolled Glen in a guitar class and the two youngest - Karia and Lu Ann - in dancing classes.

The girls succeeded in their dancing efforts and were much in demand in and around Bear River City.

They were also successful in driving the three boys - Glen, J.C., and Harvey - nearly out of their minds with their hours of practice.

It was also about same time that the town discovered the young Krough girls' abundant talent in art. It wasn't long before their posters advertising civic, social, and religious functions began to appear throughout Virtue Valley.

Glen didn't fare as well with his guitar lessons. About the extent of what he learned were four chords with which to strum for singing. So by the fourth week of lessons, Irene could have found him in the gazebo on the city park drinking Pepsi and eating chocolate bars, while strumming his chords to the few songs he could sing, when, he should have been in a room in the city court house learning about the finer points of classical guitaring.

By Christmas time, Glen's interest in music had finally died, following a long illness. As he was nearing his eighteenth birthday, it didn't seem to Irene, or Glen himself, for that matter, that he had much of a future.

He had recently decided that marriage was out of the question because no female in Virtue Valley would have him. Maybe someone outside the valley would have. "But," he figured, "I have no way or no reason to leave." Glen believed his reasoning to be sound. After all, James wife was from Missouri - Viola's husband was from Kansas - Erma's husband was from Maine - and Clara's husband was from Chicago. "So, what chance have I got?" he thought. "All of those marriages came about thanks to Uncle Sam. And now there is no war or CCC's."

Glen had the same gloomy outlook when it came time for him to consider his employment future. Not a day passed that he didn't waste a good part of it in a fit of depression, which was brought on by the regret he felt for disregarding all of the good advice about school given him by Chad and his mother. However, in a few days Chad would again jump squarely on his younger brother's case. Only that time, more vehemently.

It was unusual, even downright frightening when, on the fifteenth of December, at ten thirty p.m., the front door of the Krough house squeeked open. It brought Irene up and out of her bed in an instant.

She stood between her bed and the cot that contained Lu Ann and Karla, trying to decide whether to attack or just yell for some nonexistent person to grab the nonexistent shot gun. But before she could make any decision, a familiar and welcomed voice called out for his mother ... it was Chad.

His voice seemed to have penetrated the aura of sleep that blanketed the children. Within seconds they were pouring into the front room, already decorated for the season. But after hugs and kisses, and fondling of gifts that were to be put under the tree, the younger ones were sternly ordered back to bed. Irene made a pot of coffee, unusual because coffee at night robbed her of sleep.

She and Chad sat at the front room table and talked until the early hours of the morning. Then she too returned to her bed, and Chad unrolled a sleeping bag on the front room floor.

The following morning, after breakfast, and after the two young Krough girls had left for school, Chad left the kitchen and walked to the skeleton of the barn where he knew he would find Glen chasing rats with his five dollar twenty-two.

"Any luck this morning?" asked Chad.

"Scared a couple nearly to death," answered Glen.

"Learners only count in horseshoe," chuckled Chad.

"You're eighteen now, or close to it."

"Thought you said learners only counted in horseshoe," answered Glen with a smile.

"Learner or not, little brother, it's time you thought about being on your own."

That statement was a real shocker to Glen. Because being on his own had never occurred to him. Certainly Mother Irene had never mentioned such a prospect.

"I don't understand Chad. I ain't got nowhere to go."

"Well, Glen, maybe you have and maybe you haven't," answered Chad slyly.

Then the older of the two reached into his military field jacket pocket and pulled from it a paper bag and shoved it into his younger brother right hand.

"What's this?" he asked.

"Look inside and find out, Glen."

The young man did as he was asked and instantly turned red in the face.

Flight of the Kroughs

"Don't be embarrassed," laughed Chad. "Sooner or later every male person reaches this stage in life. And judging by the crop of peach fuzz being overrun by real whiskers on your face, in your case, it should have been sooner. Now take your new razor up to the house and use it."

That, in consideration of Glen's distressed mood, was a cruel order. In fact it was equal in inconceivability to having Alfred Allen ask him to give the opening prayer in church. So Glen replied in the only way he could think of, "I'll do it later."

"To hell with later ... now!"

"I will do it later, I promise."

"O.K., I'm going to Smithville to play pool with some buddies, and when I get back you better look as clean and smell as good as the first rose of summer ... got it?"

Lucky for Glen, since his mother was at work, he was in charge of his two younger brothers. So as soon as Chad had hitched a ride to the county seat, he ordered the two outside to play. And, in the seclusion of the bedroom, he gave himself his very first shave. The rest of the day saw him in front of the mirror a hundred times. In the space of two hours, Glen had changed from an overgrown boy into a legitimate young man.

When Irene returned home from Smithville, she too was impressed.

That evening after good meal and some conversation, mostly between Chad and his younger brothers and sisters, Irene gave them her "go to bed" order. They each obeyed and went their separate ways to beds scattered throughout the house.

Before Glen made it from the front room to his one-third share of the cot in the kitchen, Chad stopped him. As he did, he asked his mother if it was all right for the young man to stay and sit at the table with them. She said that that would be just fine.

At first, not a lot was said. Chad obviously had something on his mind that he was finding difficult to talk about. Irene knew that something was bothering her older son, and Glen sat in silence wondering what he himself was doing there.

Finally, Chad broke the uneasy silence.

"I talked to the Army recruiter today, Mom....they have lots of good jobs available."

Sensing something brewing in Chad's brain that she wouldn't like, she answered. "For whom?"

"For guys like Glen" was Chad's surprising answer.

"Not by a damn sight!!" shot back Irene.

"Now just wait one minute, don't jump on your high horse until you have heard me out."

"No, I won't wait a minute, just because you and your brother got a wild hair, don't think you can come back here and drag Glen off with you, insisted Irene.

"Who said anything about dragging anybody off?" Chad asked.

Glen sat in silence watching the conversation ricocheting between his mother and older brother, still wondering, "What on earth am I doing here?"

"Mom," Chad explained, "Let's face it. Glen is loafing his life away here."

Having said those blunt words, Chad quickly assured his little brother that he didn't mean to suggest that he was lazy or use the word loafing to be unkind, but only to illustrate his hopeless situation.

"Something will turn up for Glen, I know it will," said Irene.

"I think you're wrong, Mom" returned Chad.

"How do you know so damn much?" cried a somewhat irritated mother.

"Because I remember going through the same situation a few years ago," answered big brother in a likewise irritated manner. "These good folks in Bear River City are full of, 'How are you Sister or Brother Krough?' but they never wait for an answer because they don't want to be bothered with your troubles, especially if the problem is an out-of work son or little brother."

The next afternoon Glen returned from Smithville showing more excitement than his mother could remember him ever showing in the past. And he came straight to the kitchen table and sat on a backless chair beside her.

"Mom," he said in a nervous voice, "I feel very good about what I learned about myself today."

"Oh, and what did you find out about yourself ....? That you can count to ten, and you can read Dick and Jane - and all that makes you fit for the Army," lamented Irene sarcastically.

"No, Mom," replied her undiscouraged son. "I found out that I scored in the top ten percentile on the I.Q. test. And if you don't know what that means I'll tell you - it means that I am smarter than ninety percent of the people in the Army."

If Glen was trying to make his mother feel better with that last bit of information, he failed miserably.

"So you come back from Smithville, full of piss and vinegar, and all pumped up with pride because of a test that told you the same thing that I have been telling you for ten years ... so what. Doesn't that make you feel just a little ashamed, Glen? Because no matter who you are, or how people treat you, it's no excuse for not trying."

"You are one hundred percent correct, mom. And from now on I am going to try ... and hard. But the test result wasn't the only good thing that happened to me today ... because of my high scores, the recruiter suggested, and I agreed, that I enlist in the Air Force where there is greater opportunity for advancement. So that's what I did. I go to Salt Lake City to catch a train for Texas on the fifteenth of January.

"Fine with me," said Mother Irene. "Who am I to argue."But argue she would, just one year and two months later. However, that time, there was no big brother around to serve as the instigator.

J. C. had, shortly after his sixteenth birthday, become quite a wanderer. His mother never knew when to expect him back whenever he went somewhere. But on those nights when he didn't come home, Irene was sure that he was safely tucked in at a relative's house in Smithville, usually Uncle Bug's place.

But in the spring of fifty-one he began to bellyache to his mother about joining his brothers in the service. Just as she had tried to do in the past, she resisted. But after a while Irene admitted that she had lost another one.

Therefore, when J.C. brought the DD 1966, parental consent form home from the recruiter's office and placed it on the kitchen table before his mother, she grabbed it up and slapped it back down on the same table saying, "Get me a pen. I'll sign the damn thing."

J.C. had expected Irene to at least read the document so she would know what she was signing. But he needn't have worried, because she knew exactly what she was signing ... she had already signed two such documents in the past ten years.

As Irene waved goodbye to her next to last son as he departed the Greyhound Station at Smithville, the uneasiness she had felt as she shipped the other three out, returned to her. But that time the feeling was more intense. And within two months events gave substance to her fears.

It had started in June of fifty. As the commentator's put it, "an army of North Koreans who are indoctrinated with Marxist idealogy and Chinese puppeteering has charged across the thirty-eighth parallel into South Korea" a place Irene scarcely knew existed.

Within hours President Truman committed American troops to the disposal of the South Koreans, whose government claimed to be democratic.

Within weeks Irene began to get mail postmarked APO, San Francisco. But marked "Somewhere in Korea" inside the letter. First she received such postmarked letters from Chad, then Roland. Then in August, Glen came home on leave on his way to Alaska. It was then that Irene consulted her map and discovered just how close that part of the United States was to Russia.

When she got to the task of placing the Korean war in its proper category, according to her own criteria anyway, it gave her little trouble. Because, as Irene came to believe, the primary reason for North Korea to attack the South was to unite the whole country under communist rule. "In other words," she thought sarcastically, "Misery loves company."

According to the letters that she was getting from Chad and Roland, the war was going great. And by Christmas time they ought to be somewhere near home.

But Christmas of fifty-one came and went. And Irene's hopes crashed in a heap.

Then Christmas of fifty-two arrived and departed with its promise unfulfilled. And Irene began to question the practice of using Christmas as a "quasi official" deadline, or target date.

Not long after the uncelebrated New Year holiday of fifty-two, Irene received a strange letter. It was from the United States Army.

It concerned J.C.

"Dear Mrs. Krough," it began. "We are writing you in reference to your son, PFC Jackson C. Krough.

On 2 January 1952, your son filed with this office an application for transfer to a war zone.

While processing his request, it was discovered that two of PFC Krough's older brothers are already serving with the United Nation's forces in Korea. And, another older brother in currently serving in Alaska with the Air Force.

Although those facts are not sufficient grounds for denial of his request, there are certain qualifications which PFC Krough must meet: As you are a widow, Mrs. Krough, first, we must receive notarized permission from you, as his next of kin, before his application can be approved. And second, letters must received letters from the law enforcement department of Bear River City and one religious leader verifying the fact that there resides at home at least one son."

Irene read the letter over and over again. And at first she vowed to just ignore it. "That will fix J.C." she bluffed silently.

But she pictured J.C. sitting on his bunk impatiently waiting for her to reply and her resolve faded into capitulation.

So the next morning she bundled up warm and waded, through a fresh batch of snow, the two miles to the city offices.

Sherlock gladly granted Irene's unusual request and had the city clerk type out a short, but to the point, statement which he quickly scribbled his signature to.

As the aging policeman handed the official letter to Mrs. Krough, he also congratulated her for her and her son's patriotism. "Thanks a lot," Irene answered dryly and left the building.

Flight of the Kroughs

Her next stop was at the house of Brother Allen. Notwithstanding the fact that she did catch a glimpse of Alfred now and again, Irene hadn't talked officially with him since Iver's funeral.

When she stepped off the walkway onto his front porch, she felt like a stranger.

The widow tapped on his door, and, within seconds, Alishia, Alfred's, so far husbandless, daughter, about forty years old, opened it.

As Mrs. Krough was in the soprano section of the choir and Alishia was piano/organist, they were reasonably cordial to one another.

"Why, Irene, do come in," whined Miss Allen in a nasal monotone voice.

"Thank you, but no," she answered.

"Why don't you come in, it's all right," begged Alishia

"I'd rather not ... would you please get Brother Allen tor me?"

Miss Alien finally, and politely, obliged. And two minutes later produced her father.

"Good morning. Sister Krough" he said in a weak voice.

"My God," thought Irene, "how he has aged."

"What's on your mind, Mrs. Krough?" "I need a favor from you. Brother Allen" responded Irene.

"Oh, and just what might that be?" asked Alfred inquisitively.

"I need you to write a letter to the Army for me concerning J.C."

"Do you mean to tell me that young J.C. is in the Army? Why, he's just a child."

"Honestly, Irene, if I live to be two hundred years old, I will never understand your boys. Why can't they just stay here in Zion - get it right with the Lord - and go to church. And keep their noses out of other people's problems?"

Beside the fact that Irene was becoming a bit chilly, she was also beginning to feel a bit indignant. And decided to put up some defense on her sons' behalf.

"Well, Brother Allen, I believe we are all born with a different mission to accomplish."

Alfred just stared over the top of his gold, metal-rimmed, round glasses at Irene standing straight and tall in six inches of snow on his front porch, and shook his head slowly.

"Well what is it you want me to say?" he asked, and Irene quickly told him. He agreed to do as asked.

After acquiring all of the necessary documents, Irene returned to the downtown area and deposited her fat envelope in the out-of-town slot in the post office wall.

She heard no more from the Army, but by June of fifty-two she was receiving letters from J.C. marked APO, San Francisco.

That late spring, J.C.'s company had been ordered on a mission near the very edge of hostile territory to build a flood control diversion dam and bridge. It was a project that provided benefits to the local farmers and the war effort simultaneously; for the Korean farmers, it eliminated the yearly flooding of their farms. And for the military it guaranteed a more direct route to the north.

J.C. and his outfit were camped on the east side of the swamps and ponds working west. And Chad and his outfit, though unknown to J.C. was camped on the west side working their way east. And in the hills a little to the north of them both, Roland patrolled in his tank.

Uninformed of the other's proximity, for two months the three Bear River City boys worked on the project. Then both combat engineer groups and the armored group headed back to their own areas.

On the first night back, after in-processing nine new recruits who were promptly assigned to the cushie task of guarding the river because they were new and needed to be broken-in, all hell broke loose.

It was gray, cloudy, cold and wet at 0:200 hours. All of a sudden the tanks in the hills surrounding the base started banging away. One of the green troops, it seems, panicked and screamed that the camp was under fire from the enemy. Soon J.C. and his fellow engineers came crashing out of their tents robed in nothing more than their shorts and, in a case or two, less than that but with their helmets, ammo belts, and carbines. Then they commenced to return the fire. Needless to say, their tents were shot to hell. Because the guards, in their state of panic, were firing in the wrong direction.

J.C. and his young friends suffered bellies in the mud, misery, and fear of death before morning finally consented to arrive and rescue them.

They were nothing but a bunch of glorifed Boy Scouts under fire for the first time.

J.C. was scared. And he prayed that, if he was to die, he could be with his dad. But if there was one thing he feared more than death, it was causing his mother to worry.

As daybreak flooded the area with sunlight, the truth of the incident became apparent; the friendly tanks were ordered to practice night firing and, because of half-assed communications, no one except them knew of it.

Two weeks later, J.C. was guarding the river along with seventy new troops. Corporal Krough was in charge of a fifty-caliber machine gun, and the seventy were on walking posts.

Being new, and blessed with hyper-hearing ability, the new boys would naturally react to the minutest of sounds ... they did.

J.C. was just in the act of taking an illegal doze when those heart stopping words shattered the tense silence and thumped against waiting eardrums; it started with the sound of bare feet settling through the carpet of twigs and leaves. Then ... crunch-crunch ... "Halt Who goes there?" ... crunch-crunch, then once more "Halt;;Who goes there?" Then the shuffling of many feet.

The automatic and semi-automatic weapons sounded their stuttering frustrated message that siad, "If you won't talk, then I will get you before you get me."

Before long three companies armed with machine guns, rifles and mortars, opened up on the invisible enemy. And for the second time, J.C. was ready to meet his maker.

The next morning when the junior officers surveyed the area, they counted two dead oxen, one dead dog, and one hundred angry farmers, supported by their wives, and children.

That afternoon the Colonels got together and decided that for two days the troops and their equipment would be at the farmers' disposal. And that's when J.C. learned about honey buckets.

Jackson's company had only just lost the odor from their bodies when they were ordered north to repair a strategically located bridge.

Actually the damaged structure was located in a pleasant valley ringed by mountains that, to him., made it resemble Virtue Valley.Later, about ten thirty p.m., Corporal Krough and his fellow soldiers were marched enroute step back to their temporary camp. Because they were sleepy, tired and subdued, their senses to some degree were dulled to what was going on about them.

As they walked along the darkened, soft and damp road, they made as little noise as possible.

To the north and east, weird noises of all sorts, especially frightening, came rolling down the side of a thickly-wooded hill that rose four hundred feet above them. Each one of the young group had the same thoughful wish: that, like the other two incidents, this was another case of mistaken identity. So onward the platoon marched toward home ... If only they had known what they were in for, they would have broke into a dead run. For, within ten minutes, J.C. and his friends were made part of a full blown war. And that one was real because bullets were going both ways.

After burrowing into the thick vegetation, J.C. called out for his number one buddy, Andy Berrago. And when J.C. received no answer, he parted the limbs and weeds. In the moonlight he could see his best friend lying at the near edge of the road ... a victim of the many hiss-and-thuds that echoed in J.C.'s ears. After that, young Krough lost his fear.

He was, at last, thinking clearly. He realized that safety was most likely waiting behind the river bank. And, so far, the Korean enemy was unaware of J.C.'s outfit. When they opened fire, J.C. also began to pray, "Please God, please make Mother understand better than I do what we are fighting for ... I believe we are fighting for the freedom of all mankind." only then did he join the war ... body, mind and spirit.For three days the small force of Americans battled the Chinese and North Koreans. After the first eighteen hours had passed, J.C. didn't much care who won; all he wanted to do was live.

On the fourth day, a company of the 7th cavalry division and a company of Marines made their way into the valley from opposite sides and escorted J.C.'s battered engineer company out of danger. Then the rescuers watched while the combat engineers prepared to finish their repairs to the bridge. But, before work on the bridge was resumed, the loose ends that come with winning a battle had to be neatly tied up.

His first detail was that of herding, then cataloging, the Chinese prisoners into a forty-by-forty net wire fenced area with a tent placed exactly in the middle.

The night before, J.C. had known a great deal of fear of the Chinese. But, after the battle, which he and his buddies had won, the fear was replaced by measured respect. And he was surprised to learn that, although the prisoners spoke no English, they did manage to mouth those two universal words of war: cigarette and candy bar.

When the battle weary troops had seen to the security, first aid and administrative requirements of their prisoners, they were served a hot breakfast.

J.C. was so tired, and his nerves so tangled, and he was feeling so alone without Berrago, that he only sat, stirring at his re-hydrated eggs, while sitting on a cardboard box full of mangled Aisian bodies, and staring at the mountains that encircled the Virtue- like Valley.

Chad, who was but a short distance away, as was Roland, could have told J.C. much that would have helped him through his trauma. But neither of the three knew of the others' location. And had J.C. been at home with Mother Irene and his brother and sisters, he would no doubt have taken Harvey by the collar and offered him some not-so-brotherly advice.

On a pleasant day in July, Irene returned from her work in Smithville and found Harvey waiting for her. In his hand he carried the dreaded DD 1966 consent form.

Playing it coy, she asked Harvey what the form was and what it was for. "I want to join the Army," was his reply.

"You? ... join the Army" Why you cotton-topped little bottle ass, you don't weight a hundred twenty pounds soaking wet."Then, before she

Flight of the Kroughs

crossed over the line that separated being merely upset from downright disgusted, she stopped ... and realized that her concern was uncalled for. After all, she knew that Harvey would fall flat on his face with his plan to enlist. Because Irene had suddenly remembered J.C.'s situation. And that the letter stated that there had to be at least one son at home.

So, in a revised state of being, Mother Irene calmly removed the piece of paper with all of the fine print on it from her blonde haired son's hand and signed it. It indeed made Harvey very happy.

The next morning Mrs. Krough sat by her youngest son on the bus to Smithville. When they arrived, she smiled at him and wished him good luck. Then she turned and headed toward her work, secure in the knowledge that when Harvey was processed, it would come out that he had four brothers already serving, so would be summarily rejected for military service.

That same evening Irene returned from the county seat extremely tired after turning six cases of leafy lettuce into green salad. She stepped up into the kitchen and went directly to a chair, by which, she dropped her bag and wilted into that chair at the same time.

The two girls were outside under the boxelder tree practicing their routines, and on the table before her lay their art paraphernalia

Irene had just about summoned enough energy to get herself up to make a cup of tea when she heard Harvey whistling and moving about in the back room.

"Strange," she thought, "I would think he would be stung silent with disappointment. Oh well, maybe the frustration of his hopes didn't bother him like I thought it would."

Feeling revived, thanks to Harvey's frame of mind, Mother Krough raised her body and walked in her stocking feet to the cupboard. She removed a cup - the sugar bowl - the condensed milk - a tea bag - and from the drawer she took a spoon. Then she went to the water bucket that always rested on the counter space of the cupboard; it was empty ... she was glad that it was. Because, that would give her a perfectly good excuse to talk to her youngest son.

"Harvey," she softly called out as she pushed the curtain aside that hung in the doorway between the kitchen and the only bedroom. "Would you come on in here and do me a big favor?"

"Sure, Mother;" was his unexpectedly willing response.

"Hell - Almighty, what has hit him?" she wondered. "He probably wants money for the picture show - he knows today was payday."

Harvey marched into the room with a face full of smile and a right hand full of government papers covered with fine print. Irene noticed the papers straight away and experienced palpitation in several parts of her body.

Not having the courage to inquire directly into the subject of the papers, Mrs. Krough attacked the subject in an oblique style by asking her son how his day went.

Harvey rushed to his mother's side - took her by the hand - and told her that his day had been just great."They accepted me, Mother."

"But I thought ... because of me being a widow, and because you are the last son at home, that they wouldn't take you."

"Well that's not exactly the way the regulation reads mother. What that letter you received from the Army about J.C. really meant was, that, as I was the only son at home, I couldn't be sent to a war zone. But at least, Mother, I can still do my part. And I scored very high on my tests. They are sending me to communication electronic school in Arizona when I get out of basic training."

The words about her misunderstanding the letter concerning J.C. were the last that Irene remembered hearing. Because, she had somehow, slipped into a deaf daze.

When she regained her senses and looked up from the chair she had sometime or other during the conversation sat on, Irene asked her soon departing and last at home son to send Lu Ann and Karla in the house to her when he went out to get the bucket of water.

When the three Krough kids entered the kitchen, they found their mother sitting at the table with her purse on her lap. In her hand was a five dollar bill.

"Girls," she said softly, "today in a special day for Harvey, so I want all of you to go to the show together and have a good time. I know he doesn't leave for a week, but I may not have the money then. So go get cleaned up. And by the time you're ready, I will have some supper on the table."

Her feelings of defeat not overcome, but camouflaged, Mother Irene was true to her word. Within forty-five minutes, a steaming supper of hamburger meat cakes, mashed potatoes, corn on the cob, baking powder biscuits, and cherry kool aid sat waiting on the table.

After the three young people had left for town and she had washed the dishes, Irene sat alone for half an hour at her clean kitchen table. As she sat in the silence that surrounded her, a chilling fact suddenly occurred to her ... the realization that she would soon have five sons serving their country at the same time. And as an afterthought she also realized that never, during either of the two wars, did they need to be asked to join. After thinking of her sons and fearing for their safety, Irene's thoughts shifted backward and ended up in Alabama. There was no particular reason for those thoughts, except to wonder whatever happened to her childhood home after Mother Rosanna died and sister Viola had married and moved away.

Flight of the Kroughs

Then she decided to go for a walk. It was late evening, and the sun was fast falling behind the mountains that encircled Virtue Valley.

She walked the block that separated the Krough house from the Krough cemetery plot. Irene walked to each of the three graves, tidying up as she went.

She wasn't the type to stop and talk to people she knew couldn't hear her and who wouldn't talk back. But she did stop at Iver's grave and have some private thoughts.

During her youngest son's last week at home, before he caught the bus to Smithville, Irene was forced to think about things that would be different. Who would chop the wood, who would go to town to get a sack of groceries two or three times a week, and who would see to irrigating the garden and orchard - especially when Irene's turn at using the water came in the middle of the night. And she was forced to come to the obvious conclusion - she would have to do it.

Mother Krough waved goodbye to her son as the bus took him away and, as with all her other son's departures, waited until she was alone to shed any tears.

In September of fifty-two Glen had returned from Alaska. That was the first happy occasion around the Krough house in years. He couldn't stay though because he was just on leave. "But at least," Irene boasted to herself, "he is inside the real United States."

In July of fifty-three the quarrel between the two Koreas had been shoved to the back burner, so the three Krough boys were on separate airplanes headed stateside.

It was a grand reunion when they arrived at their home in Bear River City. Glen took leave from his base in Mississippi - Harvey took leave from his base in Arizona - James brought his wife and kids from Oregon - Erma came, with her kids, from Maine - and Clara, who had remarried and lived but a few miles away, was naturally in attendance.

By the time July of fifty-four had come around, all of the Krough boys - except for Glen - were out of the service, and the majority of them had found success in southern Idaho, Colarado orOregon.

And all except for Lu Ann, were married.

After months of coaxing, and just six months after knowing the convenience of indoor plumbing, Mother Irene gave in to her children.

She packed her furniture and other things and moved out of her modified cabin. She relocated nearer to her children also Southern Idaho.In spite of the fact that she had given life to thirteen children and, at the time, claimed fourteen grandchildren, Mrs. Krough was yet an attractive woman with a head full of grayless dark hair. But that was only her outward appearance. On the inside, wars, worry, deprivation and poverty had taken their toll. At the age of sixteen Lu Ann married, leaving Irene alone.

Contrary to what effect such an event might have had on her in years past, she was very pleased. Because she had lived to see all of her children married.

Thanksgiving of 71 was going to be exceptional for Irene. Special arrangements had been made: James and his family was coming from Oregon - Roland and his family was coming from Colorado - Erma and her children was coming from Maine - Clara and her family was coming from Virtue Valley, Utah - and the others: Glen, because he had left the service, Harvey, J.C., Chad, Lu Ann and Karla were handily living near their mother so would naturally be there.

The Saturday evening before the Thursday Thanksgiving celebration was used up with a get together at Harvey's house where plans were made, times were set, and the menu was decided on. Then at about ten p.m. the party ended.

Sunday morning, at about ten thirty. Glen and Mary, his wife, decided that it would be nice if Mother Irene could have Sunday dinner with them. So Glen called to make the invitation ... but there was no answer.

"Dammit," cussed Glen, "someone has beat us to the punch. Most likely Chad, I suspect."

Irene had risen from her bed early that Sunday morning. After a couple of cups of coffee and a long telephone conversation with Lu Ann, she cleaned herself, then put on her clean up - not dress up - outfit, and she tidied up her house, making it spotless.

Sitting on her couch resting after her burst of ambition, she experienced nervous anticipation. "Will Thursday never get here?" she asked herself.

Before she could answer her own question, Irene suddenly felt tired, and soon she was sleeping.

In the past, Mrs. Krough had often asked herself, "If given the chance, would I make the same choice that I made back in nineteen eighteen?" But she had found the question too difficult to answer. And the reason she couldn't answer was because she had learned one of life's universal truths; that things are never as good, or as bad, as they seem.

As Irene slept, she dreamed of many things; she was back in Brookside, and she was seventeen again.

Mother Rosanna had her and sister Viola sitting on the couch in the front room lecturing them. "Girls, we have a new boarder coming to live with us. He is young and very handsome ... and he is unmarried. Irene, he could be your knight in shining armor, so be on your best behavior. And do try to make a favorable impression." Irene stood up and gave her mother a polite curtsy - just to prove that she understood.

Flight of the Kroughs

Young Miss Coburn spent the rest of the day peering out of the coal-dust stained upstairs window watching for the handsome stranger to swagger up the path to the Coburn house.

At about three in the afternoon, the waiting ended. The man marched confidently up the steps, across the porch, and knocked on the front door.

"Well, don't just stand there like you're struck dumb, Irene, answer the door."

Irene moved quickly and gracefully to the door and opened it wide.

"Good afternoon, young lady. My name is Iver Krough."

"My land, he is handsome," decided Irene. And, had she been awake, her question would have at last been answered.

After that dream was over, another one quickly started up. Suddenly, she was sitting on the longest, widest, and greenest lawn she had ever seen. And Iver was by her side.

As far as her eyes could see, couples either sat, or strolled about, hand in hand. And everyone seemed to have the uncanny ability to call everyone else by first names.

Although it seemed to Irene that there were couples numbering in the billions, there was solitude for any who desired it.

There were no doctors, no lawyers, no preachers and Adolph had shaved his mustache clean off. He painted, while Eva tended her roses.

Uncle Bug had had his mouth washed free of profanity, and LeRoy was no longer worried about trading horses or arguing politics, the same as Iver had.

Those who feared perfection had learned to live with it, and those whohad aspired to it had found it.

There was work for all to do. That work consisted of processing the millions of new arrivals that flooded the reception center every day.

Only two stations existed on the processing trail.

First, all new arrivals had to admit to their transgressions, no matter how trivial.

Which, meant that everyone needed to seek every person that he or she had wronged while on earth and secure their forgivness.

Second, all those who had been born to their worldly homes less than perfect were made whole. And given the opportunity to find a mate. As were those who perished prematurely...like Ruth and David.

There existed no such thing as old age, obesity, ugliness, middle age or young age.

There existed no sickness, pestilence or famine.

And, there existed no jealousy nor greed.

Sex, as Irene had known it with Iver, and sometimes dreaded, was not practiced. But the utter ecstasy of the act was enjoyed at will with every glance or touch from either partner, but with no outward manifestation.

Irene dreamed and dreamed, until there was no need for her to dream any more.

To her children, Irene left a great deal.

Uncle Bug left a shack by the river in left hand canyon.

LeRoy donated one of his daughters to a polygamist cult in Arizona.

Alfred Allen left a worshipful forty-odd year old spinster daughter.

Irene left her children thirty-six years of genuine love and affection. And from the sale of her property in Bear River City, and from her secret hiding places, she left each child one-thousand dollars.

THE END

About the Author

Born into a large family in Hyrum, Utah, D. Raymond Anderson joined the United States Air Force at the tender age of seventeen and served the air arm of our armed forces for twenty-one years. Enlisting with only six grades of schooling, the author educated himself informally while serving his country. After his retirement from the Air Force, he went on to college to earn a bachelor's degree in science.

A man of varied experiences, Mr. Anderson has worked as a janitor at a truck stop, as a retail store manager, a carpenter, a farm hand, a sheepherder, a substitute school teacher, and has even shoveled irrigation ditches. Now retired and a member of the AARP, the author at one time was an instructor in ceramics art for classes held for senior citizens.

With his wife of forty-eight years, Mary, the author makes his home in Cedar City, Utah.

This is the author's first published work.